FAKE IT 'TIL YOU MAKE IT

LAURA CARTER

B

Boldwood

First published in Great Britain in 2024 by Boldwood Books Ltd.

Copyright © Laura Carter, 2024

Cover Design by Rachel Lawston

Cover Illustration by Rachel Lawston

The moral right of Laura Carter to be identified as the author of this work has been asserted in accordance with the Copyright, Designs and Patents Act 1988.

All rights reserved. No part of this book may be reproduced in any form or by any electronic or mechanical means, including information storage and retrieval systems, without written permission from the author, except for the use of brief quotations in a book review.

This book is a work of fiction and, except in the case of historical fact, any resemblance to actual persons, living or dead, is purely coincidental.

Every effort has been made to obtain the necessary permissions with reference to copyright material, both illustrative and quoted. We apologise for any omissions in this respect and will be pleased to make the appropriate acknowledgements in any future edition.

A CIP catalogue record for this book is available from the British Library.

Paperback ISBN 978-1-78513-570-5

Large Print ISBN 978-1-78513-569-9

Hardback ISBN 978-1-78513-568-2

Ebook ISBN 978-1-78513-571-2

Kindle ISBN 978-1-78513-572-9

Audio CD ISBN 978-1-78513-563-7

MP3 CD ISBN 978-1-78513-564-4

Digital audio download ISBN 978-1-78513-565-1

Boldwood Books Ltd
23 Bowerdean Street
London SW6 3TN
www.boldwoodbooks.com

For every person who thought they had to be someone else to be loved

1

ABBEY

It's my first day back in New York after spending six weeks in Texas auditing one of my firm's largest clients.

I hate working away. I'm a huge home bird. I much prefer going home to the one-bedroom apartment my boyfriend Andrew and I share than a hotel, making whatever meal is designated to that particular night of the week, putting on my loungewear and watching one of our favorite shows.

We're habitual but whoever made that sound like a bad thing was wrong. Andrew and I love routine and he absolutely hates surprises. Which is why *I* was surprised to receive his message at work this morning, telling me:

I've made us a reservation at Tia's. 8.30 p.m. We need to catch up.

I love Tia's. It's a Mexican restaurant near where we live in Brooklyn. Not at all fancy and relatively inexpensive but it was the first place Andrew took me when I arrived in New York four years ago from a small town in Alberta, Canada, where we both grew up.

These days, we go to Tia's at 8.30 p.m. every time we have something to celebrate, be it a birthday or an anniversary.

But tonight isn't either of those things.

We need to catch up, though. He said as much in his message. And it sort of is a special occasion – he's welcoming me home from Texas after six weeks of no IRL contact and playing back and forth with missed FaceTime calls. The dominant, rational side of my brain is trying to remember this.

The thing is, when I dragged my best friend, Shernette, to the water coolers earlier and told her about the impromptu date night, she squealed and yelled for half the office to hear, 'OMG. That's it! Tonight is the night! He's going to pop the question. Put a ring on it. Get down on one knee. Andrew's going to propose!'

There's been zero sign that he will. If anything, we've spoken less in the last six weeks than we have in our entire relationship. I really think tonight is just about us getting back on track. But I can't deny that since Shernette's outburst, there's been a giddy sensation, like bouncing space hoppers in my tummy.

Still, it doesn't fit. Andrew is the least spontaneous person I know, and given I have not one spontaneous bone in my body, I should recognize such a person.

Yet, something in my head is screaming, *Oh. My. Gosh. Tia's at 8.30 p.m. He's going to propose!*

I'm going to be engaged to Andrew. Paper perfect partner, tick. Career with a stable income and prospects, tick. Married by the time I'm thirty, tick. Hopefully, maybe, a baby by the time I'm thirty-two, tick.

Uncharacteristically, but more than reasonable in the circumstances, I left the office by six. Now, it's seven forty-five and I'm making my way to the restaurant wearing one of my smarter skater girl dresses – navy with a tied neck – and flats.

The restaurant is small, only twelve tables. The walls are

decorated with traditional Mexican items, like a sombrero and cactus plants. On one wall, there's a large mural of a matador waving his red cape at a bull.

Despite being early, I'm seated at a table for two. There's a small LED candle in the middle of the table, next to a tiny cactus in a pot. I know from experience that prickly little sucker is real.

A waiter comes over and asks if I would like to order a drink or wait for my date. *Date.* It sounds so basic and out of kilter with the man I expect to soon become my husband.

I order a margarita and a glass of water, in a bid to calm my jumpy nerves, which I think are excitement more than anxiety, but right now, it's hard to tell.

Why would I be feeling anxious? This is Andrew. Andrew and me. It's so right, it couldn't be wrong.

It must be excitement.

I also need to remember that this evening might just be a catch-up dinner. The proposal is nothing more than an idea dreamt up by Shernette. It won't become a reality unless and until Andrew gets down on one knee.

I glance out of the window and up to an apartment block opposite. It isn't the most fantastic apartment block in Brooklyn Heights, but it is suggestive of a solid career with a good income. The views from the upper levels across East River and to Lower Manhattan must be beautiful. I can only imagine.

Andrew and I have sat at this very window table on our special occasions and ruminated about who lives in there, what they must have achieved in life to afford it.

This is where we want to live, Andrew and I, when we have enough money in the bank. It won't be long. Andrew is already making strides in his career, and whilst I'm a junior auditor, my trajectory at the firm is all mapped out for me.

I'm still gazing wistfully at the apartment block when Andrew walks into my field of vision. He looks somber. *Nervous?* The thought makes my stomach flip.

I wave, holding up a hand and wiggling my fingertips. I don't know if I manage to smile through my apprehension, but I do try. Andrew holds up one firm hand, then unbuttons the jacket of his black suit as he pushes open the door to the restaurant.

Andrew is a suit kind of guy. He's tall and skinny and a suit makes him look intelligent with it. His hair is slicked to one side with a heavy application of wax. I prefer his hair in the mornings, when it's ruffled from his pillow, but I understand why he likes the more put-together approach. The wax holds his hair in place for long days in the office and that's important to him. He always looks the part of a man in finance.

I stand to greet him. In my excitement, I guess, I don't know whether to hug him or kiss him, and it seems he's uncertain too. The whole greeting ends up being an awkward, tense moment, which isn't like us.

Andrew hates public displays of affection. Me too. But we usually know how to greet each other romantically. Something is most definitely going on.

OMG. This is really going to happen.

I sit and take a large drink of the margarita that has been served to the table, then place my hands together in my lap, as if I'm in a job interview. It all feels very... strange.

The waiter returns and I order a second margarita. Andrew shakes his head at the waiter but does take a sip of water from my glass on the table.

He exhales. Slowly, heavily, whilst his eyes pierce mine across the table and cause me to hold my breath. Waiting.

Is he going to ask now? Will he do it after dinner? How long are we going to be held in this awkward suspense? Should I say something?

Andrew clears his throat. Oh crap, here goes. 'I've thought

about how to say this for so long, Abbey, and I have concluded that there isn't one way better than another. So, I'll just get on with it.' He's so tense, I actually feel sorry for him. The poor guy must have been chewing himself up over this.

I want to tell him it's okay, it's just us, he can ask however he wants and I'll say yes. I don't need verse and chapter about our relationship as a precursor to the big question. *Will you marry me?* is all he has to ask.

'Andrew—'

He holds up a hand, silencing me, which is really quite offensive but I'll put it down to stress. He reaches for my margarita and drains the glass.

He's a mess.

Planting the glass back down on the table, he draws in a breath. This is it; this is the moment.

'Abbey, I've met someone else.'

Huh?

'I didn't mean for this to happen and I don't want to hurt you, but this is over.' He motions between us, pointing a finger. 'You and me, I mean. We're over.'

Come again?

The waiter returns to our table and I reach for my drink from his tray. It's the first time I have ever downed a drink in one. The waiter is still standing at the side of our table, now gawping at me. I raise the empty glass and he takes the signal, returning to the bar to get me another.

'Wh— when? Wh— what? Why? When? How? What exactly do you mean by "I've met someone else"?'

He shrugs. He *fecking* shrugs. Four and a half years and he *shrugs*?

'Her name is—'

It's my turn to hold up a hand. 'I don't need to know her

name, Andrew. Have you slept with her?'

He doesn't need to answer because the way he looks at me is answer enough.

'How long?' I ask.

'We met a few months ago. She's in broadcasting. She was interviewing my boss for *Good Morning America*.'

'Months?'

'Yes, but we only exchanged numbers then. We didn't sleep together until you went to Texas, I assure you.'

'How gentlemanly of you.' I grind the words out quietly, hoping we aren't drawing the attention of other diners.

'Don't be like this, Abbey. It's not you. Brittany is just... She's not like you. She's different. New. Exciting.'

My eyes start to burn. *No, not here, not in public, not in front of Andrew.* 'Do you mean to say she's everything I'm not?' I ask as calmly as I can, but I hear a tremor in my words.

'Yes. No. Yes, but not that you aren't great, just that she's really something, you know?'

The waiter returns with another margarita. I don't think I give active messaging to my legs, but I stand from my seat, take the drink, finish it, and hand the glass back to the waiter.

'Did you sleep with her in my bed?'

Andrew looks like Bambi facing an oncoming truck.

What I want to say is: *Fuck you, you dirty, lying, cheating, no-good Neanderthal!*

What I actually do is: collect my purse from the floor and quietly walk out of the restaurant, glancing up to Blake House apartments as I leave. Realizing how utterly ridiculous I look, all dressed up to become a bride-to-be and winding up a dumpee, I tuck myself down an alleyway, which is empty but for two green dumpsters. Pressing my back to the wall right next to the stinking trash, I let myself cry.

2

ABBEY

The sound of Shernette blending a breakfast smoothie in her kitchen wakes me. I'm on her sofa, which is where I spent the night, and I'm still wearing the dress I chose for the night my long-term boyfriend was supposed to propose to me.

I bring myself up to sit, my eyes stinging and puffy, possibly from tears, maybe from sleeping in my daily contact lenses, perhaps because I drank the most alcohol I have ever consumed in one night.

'How are you feeling?' Shernette asks, handing me a large glass of green juice. 'Detox juice.'

I take the glass and stare at its contents like it's cyanide.

'A movie night and some carbs might have fixed you if you'd stopped at the restaurant cocktails, but the bottle of red wine you near finished when you got here has shifted you into the Emergency Detox category.'

'I suppose it can't make me feel any worse,' I say, registering the pain in my head, the fur lining my tongue and teeth, and the ache in my neck from Shernette's hard sofa. 'And to answer your question, I feel somewhere between numb, stupid, and completely discombobulated.'

Shernette brings herself to sit on the sofa next to me, our thighs touching, both holding our smoothies in two hands, like peas in a tightly packed pod.

'I want to cut off his dick and feed it to cockroaches,' she says, needing to give no explanation as to who she's talking about. Then she sobers and adds, 'I am sorry, Abbey. I'm sorry this happened to you. I'm also sorry for getting so excited yesterday and putting the idea of a proposal in your mind. Truth be told, I didn't love Andrew before all of this but I was happy for you.'

'This isn't on you, Shernette. You've got nothing to apologize for. I was naïve and too trusting. It backfired.' We both stare at the view of a brick apartment block through her lounge window. I suppose I'd better get used to this view for a while because I'm currently homeless.

'This really happened, didn't it?'

'What are you going to do?' Shernette asks.

Still staring out of the window, I tell her honestly, 'I have no idea. I can't really get my head around it. Truthfully, I don't even know if I'm still drunk, hungover, or both.' I put my smoothie on the coffee table in front of us, press my hands to my knees and come up to stand. 'So, I am going to go and vomit in your bathroom. Then, I'm going to borrow the least bright clothes you have that will fit me and I'm just going to get through today with my head down. After that, I'm going to beg you for a spot on your sofa until I can find a new place to live.'

'Well, you can tick clothes and a bed off your list. Stay as long as you want.'

Ah, checklists. A great idea when they're going to plan.

At least I have work. As painful as it's going to be getting through today, nothing brings me comfort like numbers and structure.

* * *

I was definitely still drunk this morning in Shernette's apartment. I know this because now, in the office, my hangover has landed with vengeance. My head feels like trash metal getting squeezed at a junkyard.

I'm nursing the super-strength, triple-shot latte in my little compartment desk, my head buried in emails, praying that my boss doesn't speak to me today. I'd like nothing more than to lose myself in the monotony of a spreadsheet to take my mind off Andrew.

Naturally, because today is today, I have no such luck. I feel a shadow hovering over me and raise my tired eyes to see Cassandra.

My boss is just as impressive for being in command of her skyscraper stilettos – and never secretly taking them off under her desk the way I do my significantly shorter heels – as she is for being a partner in the firm. Towering over me, she grips the divider that separates my desk from others in the pool. Despite being relentlessly busy, she always manages to have immaculate red nails and a smooth blow-dry.

'My office, now, and bring Greg with you.'

Cassandra is standing in front of the window of her office, which has a killer view of Lower Manhattan, but the thunderous look on her face is less than appreciative right now.

Greg and I close the door behind us and sheepishly make our way toward her desk, braced for some kind of tongue lashing with no idea of the reason, which scares me more than if I did know.

Greg reaches to pull out one of two seats facing Cassandra's empty and swanky leather desk chair. I think better of it and when she snaps around to face him and says, 'Don't bother taking a seat,' I internally gloat. Greg is senior to me and gosh does he flaunt it.

Now though, he shuffles back like a withering flower to stand next to me, seeming as anxious as I am for what we are about to receive.

'I sent the final audit report to the client in Texas last night,' Cassandra begins. 'He sent the report directly on to his major stockholders. Thanks to you jokers being late, I didn't have time to review the entire report, so I skimmed the narratives and expected that two professionals like yourselves would have the basic figures correct.'

What? I checked those figures, over and over, relentlessly. I asked Greg to check my calculations and he made no changes.

I have a sinking feeling in my gut. I was so concerned with getting the report back from Greg and to Cassandra quickly that I must've taken it from him before he had even had a chance to finish his review.

Not for the first time today, I want to vomit.

'So, which one of you got the figures wrong?'

If there's one thing I'm not, it's a liar. I hated liars before last night, and now I hate them even more. 'Cassandra, they were my figures. I don't understand how they could be wrong, but Greg made no changes to the report. This is on me.'

It's not like I'm a big fan of Greg, I barely tolerate him, but I won't let somebody pay the price for my mistakes.

Give him his due, he starts to protest, but I shut him down. 'No Greg, it's okay. You were doing me a favor reviewing the work.'

'You can go,' Cassandra snaps in his direction. He eyes me apologetically, but his relief is evident.

Once the door is closed behind him, the only thing I'm grateful for is that my peers can't hear what my boss is about to say.

'The client fired us last night. Fired us, Abbey. One of my biggest clients. So now I have to grovel to get him back on side, or if I can't, I'll have to explain to the other partners why we've lost such lucrative business.'

'I'm sorry, Cassandra. I don't know how—'

'Save it, Abbey. You've been needing to step up for a while now. I'm pissed and disappointed, a toxic combination.'

I know what's coming. The job I love, the only job I've known, the only thing I'm good at, it turns out, I'm not good at. With quick realization, I beat Cassandra to the inevitable and tell her, 'You'll have my resignation letter on your desk within the hour.'

Then I run from the office toward the restroom, unsure of the primary reason I'm going to throw-up – excessive alcohol consumption, betrayal, incompetence, or fear of not having a clue what I'm going to do next.

In the space of twenty-four hours, it feels like my entire existence has been obliterated. My checklist-perfect life is a gigantic hot mess.

3
ABBEY

Three weeks later

'Dee, please tell me this isn't a huge mistake.'

I'm standing next to my younger sister on the sidewalk outside my new home, apartment 7B in Blake House, Brooklyn Heights. A brown box full of clothes is starting to feel heavy in my arms, but I pause, staring at the glass front door I used to dream of walking through.

'This isn't a huge mistake,' my sister replies.

Her smile is as bright as the sunshine-yellow dress she's wearing but I know that behind her shades, her eyes will be mocking me.

'Only say it if it's true. Is this the worst idea I've ever had, honestly?'

'This isn't the worst idea you've ever had, Abbey Mitchell. It can't be, since it was my idea.'

She's teasing me again. I'm no stranger to my sister trying to wind me up; she's done it since the day she was born. But today, I really need encouragement and reassurance, instead of the sarcasm and wit I'm receiving.

I realize I'm chewing my lip, like I do when I get stressed. 'Mom and Dad are going to kill me, aren't they?'

'All you've done is blow your life savings on six months' rent; it's not like you've shattered Mom's hopes of you marrying a model man, who happens to be the second son she always wanted, and ticking off everything on her checklist of things you must do before you're thirty. Oh, wait—'

'Dee! You're not helping here. Mom still isn't really speaking to me since the break-up. Not without an undertone of disappointment, anyway.'

'Maybe that's because you didn't tell them the reason you and Andrew broke up. That cheating, lying bas—'

If I wasn't holding a box, I'd press my fingers to her crude mouth. 'I've got it, thank you. There's no point giving everyone the sordid details and dwelling on things. What's done is done.'

Dee lowers her shades and gives me a school ma'am look, eyebrows raised. 'Right, sure. It's all the faff. That's why you'd rather have our parents off side.'

The problem with siblings, especially the kind who follow you hundreds of miles from home in Alberta, Canada to New York City, and spend far too many nights sleeping on your sofa, is that they know you much better than you'd care to admit.

I'm not going to get back with Andrew. Of course I'm not. No chance.

He's with someone else.

Regardless, I have a modicum of self-respect.

But what would be the point of my parents hating him? Moreover, why would I admit that I couldn't hold on to him?

'Plus' – Dee drapes her arm around my shoulders – 'when I

tell Mom and Dad that I'm knocked up to a fellow actor and we aren't even dating, I'm going to need to deflect.'

'Ah, the truth. This isn't a good idea. It's a terrible idea that you hope will make Mom and Dad more irate than your illegitimate child? You remember they're practicing Catholics, right?'

Dee shrugs. 'My upbringing is precisely the reason Brett and I weren't using protection.'

Despite the importance of the situation, I laugh. 'I still can't believe you're going to be a mom.'

'I know. Crazy, right?'

I don't think, I *hope*, that Dee's flippancy is just because the enormity of the pregnancy hasn't sunk in yet. Otherwise, it's terrifying.

'Have you told Nate yet?' I ask.

Our brother, Nate, successful architect, married with two kids, all by thirty-two years old. Our parents adore him. Their only gripe with him is that they don't see him enough.

But perfect Nate is sooooooo busy.

Dee is four years my junior, one year out of acting school, wild and most often penniless. Yet, whilst she's been making babies, I have been unravelling every life goal I've strived toward since I was a teenager.

'Nope,' she says, with zero concern. 'I'm going to try it out on him first, before the parents. Will you come to dinner with us? Nate will pay.'

I scowl at her, though I feel no menace. 'If you stop showering me in sarcasm, I'll think about it.'

'Thank you.' She gives me a chaste kiss on my cheek then starts walking, empty handed, away from my car load of belongings and toward the entrance of my new, swanky apartment block. She calls back across her shoulder, 'It's not like you have anything better to do now that you're single and unemployed.'

She has a point.

I follow Dee to the main entrance, where she's holding the door open for me, until her phone rings and she takes it from the pocket of her dress.

'Hi, you,' she says, letting the door close behind her.

'Dee!' I call, lugging my box. This is so typical of my sister. I love her but she definitely puts herself before anyone else.

Grunting, I lean back against the glass pane on one side of the double doors, balancing my box on one knee whilst trying to open the adjacent door with my spare hand.

I try to navigate my way through with my butt, but as I do, I lose balance. It's my face or the box; one of us is going down.

The box falls, some of the contents spilling out.

'Argh.' I stomp my foot in frustration. It's that or cry. Today is quickly becoming overwhelming. 'What the hell am I doing here?' I mutter, my voice breaking.

This is way out of my comfort zone. I'm not impulsive. I am not showy. And despite taking Dee's advice, I'm just not the kind of woman who fakes it until she makes it.

I blow a raspberry with my lips, staring at my box and its spilled contents, then I shake my head and shuffle my shoulders. I need to be that woman, otherwise what is the point in all of this? What was the point of blowing my dream wedding fund on a fancy apartment I can barely afford?

'I've got you,' a male voice says.

I glance from my big panties – the large, stretchy, comfy panties I wear for bed when it's that time of the month – which are lying in a heap on the ground, to the dark-blond hair on top of the man's head, who has bent down to help collect my things. My big panties!

'Oh God, you don't have to—'

He picks up the underwear, a nude pair of all colors, and looks up at me from behind a pair of aviators.

The sun is shining right on him, allowing me to see wide eyes behind his lenses. His chiseled face has an almost surreal look – too good to be true – yet it has a softness in the cheeks, the skin, the character lines around the sides of his mouth, that makes him appear... nice? His hair doesn't look like it has been styled; it's messy, a little rugged, yet it complements the rest of his features.

Only now do I remember that this aesthetically pleasing guy is holding my worst offering of underwear in his hands.

I snatch back my nude panties, shoving them into the box.

'They're my bedwear.' I try to explain why anyone other than pregnant women and the elderly would wear these garments, but my words are slurred and blended by mortification.

No one is supposed to see them, *ever*! Especially not hot guys who are...

Whoa!

He rises to full height, towering above me. He's tall but not lanky. He's burly. Manly. The sleeves of his white T-shirt are tight around his biceps but more Chris Hemsworth than Dwayne Johnson.

Nothing like my ex, who was slimline, almost weedy. I like weedy.

But I still don't want Mr Big and Burly to be holding my period panties.

In this moment, I have to concede that Dee has a point about blowing some of my savings on a new wardrobe. If I'm going to commit to this idea of acting the part until I'm legitimately playing the part of someone successful and chic, I need a wardrobe to match my new apartment. The woman who rents apartment 7B in Blake House does *not* wear panties that come up to her neck.

I struggle to heave the box from the ground.

'Let me,' the man says, reaching down to help me.

'No,' I snap. 'I've got it.'

Please never look at me again.

'Okay, let me get the door, then.'

I nod, my cheeks aflame. 'Thanks.'

Please tell me he doesn't live here.

I should be so lucky. As I step into the building, Mr Big and Burly follows.

If I weren't holding a box, I would run directly to my apartment, stopping only to murder my sister for leaving me in this predicament.

But I am holding a box, so I make for the elevator. As I struggle to finger the button to call the ride, the guy is back.

'I've got it,' he says. He's taken off his shades and now I see he has gentle blue eyes, sketched at the edges with the finest of lines.

Muttering my appreciation, my eyes squeezed shut, I step inside the elevator. Before the doors close, I tentatively open one eye, only to find the guy is now unabashedly dangling my large panties from his finger.

'You forgot these.'

Kill. Me.

Kill. Me. Now.

Horrified, I drop the box, snatch the underwear and repeatedly hammer the close button, until finally, the doors comply.

The man isn't smirking or sniggering at my underwear; he's just getting on with the next thing – unlocking the mailbox for apartment 8B – seemingly oblivious to my embarrassment.

When I make it to my new home, Dee is in the lounge, standing at the Juliet balcony with the French doors open.

She turns my way when I set my box on the floor with an exaggerated grunt, fanning myself with my T-shirt, an absolute sweaty mess. 'Would you get a load of this view?' she says, looking back across East River to the city skyline.

Momentarily, my worries abandon me and I remember why I have pined after this apartment block for so long. The view is incredible. Even from where I'm standing at the back of the lounge, I can see the sun's rays dancing on the water. I see small motorboats cruising the river and a larger sightseeing boat.

There isn't a cloud in the sky, and it makes me feel like this place might just hold possibilities, that maybe my luck isn't entirely doomed.

It isn't just the view. The apartment is everything I want it to be. From the cream walls and immaculate hardwood floors to the blush-pink soft furnishings on the cream leather sofa and the glass top of the oak trunk table in the dining area. From the black granite countertops and gleaming white kitchen units to the fancy tap that offers me cold water, boiling water, water with gas and water without.

Along the hallway are the abstract oil and watercolor paintings I remember from my viewing. In the master bedroom is a brand-new, fancy queen-sized bed, and I tell myself that getting to sleep like a starfish will be a wonderful, liberating experience, as opposed to an unwanted and lonely one.

Through the bedroom, there's an ensuite of the size that someone in my unemployed position, who was only allowed to lease on the proviso I paid the entire six months' rent upfront, shouldn't be able to afford. I try not to focus on the 'his' part of the 'his and hers' basins. Instead, I imagine where I will place my toiletries – my toothbrush, in its own area, where no man will be able to put his dirty, soggy one next to mine. There's a bath – *a bath!* – as well as a shower.

Buoyed with excitement, I take myself off to the enormous walk-in wardrobe with a sofabed that could be big enough for a second bedroom, but not for me because I am man and child free. No ties. No obligations. No one to please but myself.

* * *

It's seven thirty in the evening. My sister left around 3 p.m. without having helped me at all to move in. I wouldn't expect a pregnant lady to do heavy lifting, but the reality is, pregnant or not, Dee wouldn't have lifted a finger anyway. I love her for what she is, and in spite of what she isn't.

I've hung up my clothes in the walk-in wardrobe, which seem pathetically few in the large space. My shoes are neatly lined along the purpose-built shoe rack, also looking like a truly meagre offering, more *Big Bang Theory* than *Sex and the City*.

Now alone and pooped by my efforts, I'm streaming a NASA moon-landing documentary on my laptop, I've ordered a chicken pesto pizza and a tub of peanut butter ice cream, and am enjoying my queen bed, just me. The irony is, I'm squished onto one side, on one set of pillows, as if waiting for someone to join me. And those joyous thoughts of my new single life, the hot girl summer I imagined, have abandoned me.

I've paid an extortionate sum of money to pretend that I'm some sassy city girl, living her best life, yet I'm sitting in my bed in paisley cotton sheets, an old T-shirt and shorts, much like the girl who left Alberta four years ago.

Is Andrew alone right now? Is he still seeing the woman he was sleeping with behind my back? The woman Dee found after extensive social media searching on my behalf?

My cell phone is lying next to me on the bed covers. I could call him. Be casual.

Why? Why would I do that?

He *cheated* on me.

It's just... our story doesn't feel complete.

Everyone liked Andrew. He was perfect for me. Until he wasn't.

Everyone *still* likes Andrew because I haven't shared the truth of what happened with anyone – except Dee and Shernette.

In everyone else's minds, he is *still* perfect for me.

Staring at the screen on my laptop, I try to think positive thoughts, like my sister and Shernette have told me I have to do. Finally, a positive thought comes to me, but even as I think it, I know it's not enough: at least I'm not an astronaut stuck on the moon with no sustenance or comms.

Sighing, I close down my laptop, slide it under the bed, double check that my bear spray is where I left it (you can take the girl out of Canada...) and lie back, exhausted.

When there's nothing better to do, sleep. That's what my dad has always said. So I'll sleep and tomorrow will be a new day. A much better day because I won't have to lug heavy boxes from my car to my new, extortionately priced apartment.

I can feel myself sliding toward slumber when... *boom, boom, boom.*

What the fudge?

There's a rhythmic banging, as if someone is repeatedly hitting something full throttle against a wall above me.

Boom. Boom. Boom.

4

TED

With a handful of junk mail and a couple of other envelopes that look like they could be fan mail, I let myself into apartment 8B. After setting down the mail on the sideboard, I turn on the air-conditioning – a necessity given the apartment is one of two penthouses in the building and it doesn't have reflective glass windows.

I kick off my sneakers and move into the spacious lounge area, slipping down onto my brother's extremely comfy but needlessly large sofa. It's Monday morning and for the millionth time in the last forty-eight hours since I arrived here from San Francisco, I ask the empty room, 'What am I doing here?'

Resting my head back against the soft leather cushions, I drag my hands through my hair, staring at the spotlights in the roof.

Should I have fought harder? Or was it always a losing battle trying to keep my own fiancée?

Three days ago, I thought I had it all. A beautiful wife-to-be, a partnership that is making serious tracks in Silicon Valley, and a best friend who I could also rely on as my greatest business ally.

I was wrong on all counts.

My cell phone vibrates in my pocket, and then the noise of its ringtone is surrounding me through every wall speaker in the apartment. I take the phone from my pocket and swipe the screen.

'T bird!' My brother's voice echoes in the vast square footage.

I boot my troubles out of my head and my voice as I respond. 'Hey, you're on extreme surround sound.'

I hear the humor in his voice. 'Yeah, it's handy when you want to be hands-free. So how's it all going over there? Are you still hiding from the world or are you ready to share your woes?'

I sit forward, leaning across my knees, resting on my elbows, my face in my palms. 'The former. You haven't mentioned what's going on to anyone, right?'

'It's not my story to tell, kid, but I think it's a matter of time before word spreads.'

'Yeah, well, a little bit longer to get my head around it all would be nice.'

'No one will hear a thing from me. I just wanted to check in and make sure you're not eating your weight in jelly sandwiches.'

I look across to the kitchen counter, where there's a loaf of white bread and a kilo of strawberry jelly. 'I'm not five years old, Mike,' I reply, instead of outright lying.

'If you say so. Just to let you know, the cleaners will be there today at four. Hide your sticky socks from under the bed.'

I shake my head, though I am, miraculously, amused. 'It's only been three days; I'm not that desperate, yet.'

Mike is still laughing when the *beep beep beep* of the dead call tone comes through the speakers and I have to think about what to do with myself.

It's the start of a new day, which means I can sit on the sofa with a strawberry jelly sandwich or choose a new signed baseball from my brother's wall shelf collection and bounce it off the wall repeatedly until my mind is completely numb.

Rising from the sofa, I select a ball that has been signed by Barry Bond, infamous former left fielder for the San Francisco Giants. I know this because my brother has had small plaques made to sit in front of each ball. Most of his collection has come from ball trades at the end of his games, but some, like his signed Babe Ruth ball, he acquired from auction.

My brother is a catcher for the San Francisco Giants. He's spent the last three years as a starter but recently picked up a shoulder injury that's seen him out of the game for four months, with the physios predicting another two to recover after a number of setbacks.

He earns good money, the kind that means he can afford a second home in New York – which has now become my hideaway.

Mike and I look like dead-ringers for each other. We've even been asked if we're twins a heap of times. In fact, I've wondered whether that means he looks younger than his thirty-six years or I look older.

He's four years my senior, and I've spent a lot of my childhood in his shadow, unable to live up to his dizzy heights of athleticism. I wasn't a bad ball player, but I wouldn't have made a major league team like Mike. When I finally stepped out from his shirt tails, I realized I had a bent for and enjoyed science, analytics and tech.

See, though we look alike, personality wise, Mike and I are polar opposites. He's a devout athlete and sports fanatic and I'm a self-confessed tech nerd. Specifically, I develop forward-thinking, innovative, analytical software.

And, until seventy-two hours ago, I was flying in my field.

Now, I'm just a guy who hasn't got the faintest clue how to get through each day.

Intermittently taking bites out of my zero-goodness sandwich, I decide to grant myself 250 tosses of the ball against the wall, plus an extra one for any missed catches. This is more than double my allowance of one hundred throws I allowed myself as an insomnia cure last night but when I reach 250, I promise I'll check my emails.

Thud. Catch. Thud. Catch. Thud. Dropped catch. *Thud. Thud. Thud.*

I lose count around 170 but I'm sufficiently pacified by the tedium of the activity, and my sandwich has filled a hole.

Reluctantly, I open up my inbox through my cell phone and see the number of unread emails taunting me in bold. That's a count of more than 300 since I walked into my partner's office out of hours and found him screwing my fiancée.

I don't know what irritates me more, the number of emails or the fact that Roman, my ex best friend, is going about our business as if nothing has happened.

Absolute shitbag.

We've been programming together since college. Inseparable for a decade. Seemingly those years of friendship have meant nothing to him. Certainly not more than sex.

I walk to the shelf, pick up another of Mike's signed baseballs – Buster Posey – and throw it as hard as I can at the wall on the opposite side of the lounge.

Brilliant. Now I have a freaking hole in a wall to fix on top of everything else.

The holding responses I've sent to a couple of urgent emails have obviously triggered my assistant's attention because her ringtone, designated specifically so that I know to take her calls, comes over the ridiculous home theatre speakers.

'Mel, hi.' I don't say anything else because I don't know what to say and I don't know whether the rumor mill has yet started at the office. I'm a private person, a relatively quiet person, but I'm the brother of an MLB player, a partner of one of the fastest growing tech companies on the west coast, and my girlfriend is a model with a strong social media following. So, yeah, Mike is right, it's only a matter of time until word gets out.

'Ted, finally. I've been trying to reach you for two days; you've been completely off the grid. Where are you?'

'Connectivity problem with my cell phone, sorry.' Yep, the kind you have when you turn off your phone for two days. 'So... what's up?'

I'm pacing the floor of the lounge, speaking into the open space, waiting for her to cut to the chase and tell me everyone is talking about what happened, some shocked, some ridiculing me.

'What's up?' I can hear confusion in her voice. I guess I've never just disappeared in all the time she's been my assistant. In fact, I've never really taken a break from work since the inception of Vanguard RED Technologies. 'Nobody knew where you were, Ted. Roman has had to step into your shoes for three of the meetings you had in your calendar.'

'Yeah, well, Roman is very good at stepping into my shoes.'

'I'm sure he is, but the people you were supposed to be meeting were disappointed with your absence, and we kind of need to know where you are.'

She isn't wrong. Going AWOL is not only unlike me, it's highly unprofessional, but, silly me, where was my head when I should've been thinking about my business and business partner? Oh, that's right, it was replaying images of my business partner getting it on with my fiancée.

'I know, and I'm going to be out for a few more days. But I'm back online now, so you can tell Roman...' His name feels like dirt on my tongue. 'There's no need for him to take over my role anymore.'

Mel is quiet for long seconds, until she asks, 'Have you and Rome fallen out? Is this like that time he took the biggest office in the new building without asking you first?'

She doesn't know. Ironically, Roman stealing something that was supposed to be mine is precisely what has happened, though on this occasion, it's something less trivial than office space.

'No, it's not like that. Is there a specific reason you called?' I need to spend some time working out responses to questions until I'm ready for my private life to become public news.

'You have an interview with *GQ* tomorrow; their writer is supposed to be coming to our offices. Will you be here? Are you even in the state?'

Crap. GQ magazine. I forgot about that.

'Can we postpone?'

'You've already postponed twice and it's for the next edition.'

Double crap. It's bad enough that the press seem to get any insight into my private life, without me having to give over the details myself. But this is an important interview for Vanguard, and until I know what I want from my business relationship with Roman going forward, I need to keep up appearances. Not least because, if it comes to it and we sell out, we need the business to be mentioned in publications as widespread as *GQ*.

'Wait, *GQ* has an office in New York, right?' I ask.

I hear Mel typing in the background, then she says, 'Yes, they do.'

'Great. Can you call them and tell them I can take the interview in New York? They can email me directly for the address.'

'In New York? You're in New York?'

'Mel, could you do this for me without questions, please?'

'Sure thing, boss.'

'Thanks. And Mel, the fact I'm in New York is strictly confidential. By that I mean between you and me. I don't want anyone to know. Not Fleur, not Roman, okay?'

There's silence on the line and I sense she's switching from business associate mode to friend mode. 'My lips are sealed.'

We say goodbye but before either of us hangs up, she asks, 'Ted, are you okay?'

Am I okay? I feel like I'm hurtling into outer space without gravity or thrusters with no clue how to get back to the world as I knew it just days ago.

'I'm good.'

Ending the call and back in the silence of the apartment, I wince at the mess I've made of Mike's plastered wall. I feel exactly the way that wall looks: like there's a big hole missing from it. Now, to add insult to injury, I need to prepare for my interview with *GQ*. I need to do the last thing on earth I like to do. I need to go shopping for something other than shorts, T-shirts and sneakers.

5
ABBEY

I'd rather walk anywhere in the city than take the subway but Brooklyn Heights to Bloomingdale's, where I am meeting Dee and Shernette this morning, is a trek. I've compromised, taking transport from Court Street station to Union Square, and I'm walking the rest of the way.

The fresh air and takeout coffee en route have been beneficial. When I woke this morning, after listening to the relentless banging from upstairs into the early hours, again, I felt grouchy as heck.

To top that off, I was playing the radio as I got dressed and what came on? Only Jack Johnson's 'Better Together'. It's as if the universe is trying to keep Andrew front and center of my thoughts all the damn time.

'Better Together' was one of *our* songs. Not that we had a *song* expressly but it always reminded me of drives we took back home around Banff National Park, even road trips to British Columbia. I would have preferred to hike together but Andrew was always happier in a gym than outdoors, so we would take scenic drives instead. I'd take climbing the Rockies over a claustrophobic, sweat-filled gym any day.

I replace the lid on my now empty coffee mug and pop it into my satchel. Just as I hold my hand across a ginormous yawn, I see Dee and Shernette waving at me from the entrance to Bloomingdale's.

Dee cups her hands either side of her mouth, making a human foghorn, and calls, 'Are you ready for shoppiiiiiiiiiing?'

Horrified, I glance around me. Unbelievably, every passerby is just going about their business, heading to work, shopping, drinking caffeine on the move. Good old Manhattan – I could have been struck by lightning right here in the middle of the sidewalk and no one would notice. Back home, getting dumped by your long-term boyfriend is the business of everyone from your mother to the distant cousin of the owner of the local store whom you see semi-annually.

I make my way over to my sister and best friend.

'I'm ready if you promise never to do that again.'

Dee scrutinizes my baggy dungarees and foot-fitting sandals. 'I'm glad to see you came dressed for the occasion.'

Scowling at my sister, I hug Shernette. 'Thank *you* for taking a Monday off work. The thought of shopping on the weekends is enough to give me hives.'

'I wouldn't have missed it. The chance to help makeover my bestie and blow copious amounts of cash? Hell yes, I'm in.'

I smile at Shernette, then point at my sister. 'You don't get a hug.' Then I gently stroke her tummy and say sweetly, 'You do, my gorgeous little nephew.'

'We don't know what the sex is, yet.'

'Given girls are born in times of stress and there isn't a stressed bone in your horizontal body, it has to be a boy.'

Dee's eyes visibly brighten. She places her hands on her non-existent bump and glances down. 'A boy, huh?'

Shernette gives me a look that says: *your parents are going to flip.*

She's dead right.

'And on that note, shall we get this torture started?' I ask.

We head inside the store. As I hold open the door for Dee, she tells me, 'Speaking of chilled out people, we have dinner plans with the very antithesis of chilled out on Thursday evening. Meredith is going to book somewhere and send the details.'

Meredith, Nate's wife. It means dinner will be somewhere flashy but since Big Brother will be paying, who cares?

Due to the constant stream of tourists, Bloomingdale's is still busier than I'd like but given it's a work day, it isn't heaving. As we step onto the renowned black and white check tiled floor, I inhale the scent of fresh leather from the wealth of designer handbags, mixed with the hundreds of expensive eaux de parfum.

'Where do we start?' I ask, looking at my makeover tutors. Personally, I'd like to start at Magnolia Bakery but something tells me that won't be the answer.

Dee and Shernette look at each other, then at me. 'Casual wear,' they say in unison.

I follow behind them – Shernette in a bright, floral shift dress, Dee wearing a Bohemian-style romper – feeling sad for my comfy dungarees.

As we ride the escalator, Dee tells me, 'We're booked for facials and make-up in two hours, so we need to get a move on.'

Two hours? Urgh.

New me. New me. New me. Must channel new me.

I will be glamorous, desirable and someone with a fabulous job; in fact, any job would be an improvement currently. A woman befitting of Blake House.

Deciding to see our climbing the escalator as a metaphor for rising to the new, aspirational me, I thrust my shoulders back and step off the moving steps into a Ralph Lauren concession.

After baulking at the price tags of the first three items I pick up, I realize I'm going to have to be led by the clothes and not the price tag if I'm going to make any headway.

I have two pairs of smart pants hanging over my left arm and with my right, I am holding up a blue tailored shirt, when Shernette appears over my shoulder.

'Too safe, too safe and too safe.' She takes the items from me and hangs them on the rail in front of us. 'These are just fancier versions of the things you've always worn to work.'

She waggles a mini tweed skirt and jacket combo at me – pink and lime green! '*This* is your new work wardrobe.'

'Riiiight, for that unemployment line.' I finger the outfit. The material does feel expensive, I'll give her that.

Leaning her head to one side, she smiles. 'For the fabulous job you're going to get, when you decide whatever it is that you're passionate about.'

'Oddly, I was, I *am* passionate about numbers, analytics tools, innovative forensic software, the business world. But clearly, I'm not very good at those things, evidenced by the fact I no longer have a job in the field.'

'You need to start seeing being fired as being liberated,' Shernette says. 'The world is your oyster. Your checklist will be fulfilled in no time. Or at least within six months, otherwise you'll be unemployed, homeless and single. And this little number is going to help you shuck the shell. Go try it on!'

She holds out the hangers until I take them from her and make for the nearest fitting rooms.

'Technically, I quit,' I call back. But maybe she's right. I need to view this forced break as an opportunity to make a change. I'm just not sure to what.

* * *

'Abs, it's me,' Dee says over the stable-style door. Inside the cubicle, I'm still admiring myself in the tweed two-piece. I don't think I've ever worn anything so fancy. 'What exactly is our budget today?'

'Absolute max, I have eight hundred dollars for my entire Blake House wardrobe.' Prior to trying on the pink and green suit, I would have said $500. Shernette's first pick has softened me a smidge.

After splurging on six months' rent, I divided the rest of my savings between socializing (which I do little of) and bills, leaving some leftover for clothes shopping. Essentially, the splurge on a new wardrobe is the difference between me needing to find work soon and yesterday.

Dee dangles a pair of Capri pants in royal blue over the dressing room door. I take the bait, then she hands me a silk, ivory-colored vest, which I also take.

'Have you heard of a capsule wardrobe?' she asks.

* * *

By the time we leave Bloomingdale's, almost my entire shopping balance has been depleted and I have the core ingredients of what Dee describes to me as a capsule wardrobe – a small collection of clothes that I can mix and match to make a heap of different outfits, something to suit every occasion.

'I can't believe I let you guys convince me to spend so much money on clothes,' I say as we head down Fifth Avenue, making our way idly in the direction of Macy's on 35th Street. I stifle a yawn, again.

'And color!' Shernette says. 'Hello World, this is Abbey Mitchell, bold, bright and about to embark on the best years of her life!'

I'm loathe to admit that I do feel taller, cheerier somehow, wearing the shorts and blazer combo the girls encouraged me to leave the store in once I had settled my insanely large check.

'Plus, you can't always wear T-shirts and jeans from Gap,' Dee adds.

Shaking off the insult, I see a café up ahead. I tell the girls I need coffee.

'I agree,' Shernette says. 'You've been yawning all morning. At first, I thought it was sheer boredom, but I'm starting to think it's not that. I saw you checking yourself out in that outfit – rightly so, since you look a million dollars in it.'

'Why are you so tired? You told me your new bed is the comfiest thing you've ever slept in,' Dee says.

I hold the café door open for them and the smell of our savior hits my nose. 'Rich, dark, intense, exactly how I like my coffee.'

'That's exactly how I like my men,' Shernette replies, heading to the counter.

When we're seated on stools in the window of the café, looking out to the traffic and bustle of Fifth Avenue, I finally reply to Dee's question.

'I'm tired because of the freaking guy in the apartment above me. I don't know what he's doing but there's a rhythmic banging like he's going to bounce a shot put right through my ceiling every night. I've half a mind to go up there and tell him to quit it, but you know me, I hate conflict.'

Shernette, now holding her hand to her head as if she has

brain freeze from zealously sucking her iced smoothie, says, 'Sex. He's obviously romping the night away.'

'No, I don't think so. It's been both nights. For *hours*. I appreciate I only have a wanker to compare him to but does any man have that kind of stamina?'

My sister and best friend look to each other, their jaws metaphorically hitting the floor. Then they gush, 'We are sooooo proud of you.'

'Huh?'

'That's the first time you actually called Andrew out on being a complete, total and utter dick-fest,' Dee says, before slurping her decaffeinated Frappuccino through a straw.

I feel a slight turn of my lips. 'It did feel good. Unlike me but kind of cathartic.'

Shernette nudges into my shoulder. 'New apartment, new wardrobe, new woman.'

'I'm not sure about that but I am at least starting to feel like a work in progress.'

'You'll be faking your entire pre-thirty checklist in no time,' Dee tells me. 'Now tell us more about the sex pest in the penthouse. Is he a filthy rich old man or a hot younger model?'

I shrug. 'Objectively, you could say he's young and attractive.'

'Objectively? That's Abbey code for mega hot but she's been denying herself for years, repressing her libido for the sake of Mr Wrong.' Dee rolls her eyes teasingly.

'Well, there's nothing to report. He's a nuisance and, even if he weren't, he's seen my period panties, so it's safe to say he will not be romping the night away with me.'

'Yet!' Dee winks.

I'm still laughing at her, a little buzzed on caffeine and shopping endorphins – the latter very unexpected. And I suppose that's why, when she stops outside the entrance of Saks Fifth Avenue, I agree to look inside.

'I cannot buy anything in here, though. I'm looking with my eyes only.'

As I say this, I'm following behind Dee and Shernette, who are making strides for footwear.

'The shoe department in here is so big, it has its own zipcode,' Dee says. 'We can at least acknowledge the greatness by trying on a few pairs.'

It's an activity I would usually consider pointless but today, I'm willing to step into someone else's shoes. Someone truly glamorous. If only for one day.

As I'm perusing the Dior shelf, picking up some heels to admire, horrified by the deathly height of them, one of the store assistants approaches me. I sheepishly replace the white, pointed-toe stiletto I'm holding. I'm sure one look at me has satisfied her that I'm just not the kind of girl who buys Dior.

'It's a beautiful shoe,' she says. The badge on her lapel tells me her name is Kiara.

Kiara takes the shoe from the shelf and holds it between us, as if I belong here, like I might one day wear a shoe as pretty as this.

'It's called the Aureli 85,' she tells me, turning the shoe to display its various angles. There's a pearl strap across the middle. Delicate. Pretty. Something my mom would adore. 'They're real pearls,' she adds.

I feel compelled to reach out and touch them.

Mom loves shoes. Loves clothes. Loves being the focus of attention, entertaining, and being, as she calls herself, 'front of house' of our family.

She's originally from New York. She was apparently quite the socialite, even forty years ago, when she met Dad. He'd been visiting the States on a business trip from Vancouver, where he lived at the time.

Dad has always been an esteemed businessman. He inherited multiple small to medium tourist businesses from Gramps and has grown them into the unicorn leisure and tourism operation that he runs today.

Whilst I'm lost in thought, Kiara has managed to navigate me to a plush velour sofa and has slipped my feet into the Aureli 85 shoes.

As she helps me stand, now six inches taller than just moments ago, Dee and Shernette reappear from where they've been adrift on clouds of fancy shoes.

Shernette takes out her camera phone. 'Work it, girl!'

With the power of the shoes surging through me, I lean back on my wrists and flick my legs into the air. *Snap*.

I cross one leg over the other and pout. *Snap*.

Pulling my knees up and caressing the shoes, I laugh uncontrollably at what an utter fool I am making of myself. *Snap*.

That dopamine is strong stuff.

Precisely as Shernette takes one last picture of me laughing and pointing to the exquisite shoes, I see the reflection of the broad-shouldered man from apartment 8B in the mirror in front of me.

He seems to slow his walk past the Dior section – in reality, not just my imagination. He has two large Saks Fifth Avenue bags slung across his shoulder and he's holding a blue shoe from one of the women's collections.

Buying for a girlfriend, fiancée, wife, perhaps?

His eyes meet mine in the mirror, searching. I realize I'm staring at him because his face is really quite beautiful and his burly seems less burly today than it did on Saturday.

But why is he staring at me?

As soon as the question comes into my mind, I know the answer. He's thinking: *is that the girl with the enormous panties?*

'That's him,' I whisper to Dee and Shernette who are watching me ogle.

A store assistant approaches 8B and his attention is diverted as he, presumably, asks for the other shoe to match the one he's holding.

'That's who?' Dee says, not whispering at all. I flick her arm with my fingers and shush her, muttering the identity of the man she's now scrutinizing.

Shernette appears between Dee and me, until we are all, ludicrously, gawping at the tall, handsome man.

'The banging is definitely sex, babes. I would happily bang on your ceiling with that man allllll night long,' Shernette says.

Precisely as the store assistant leaves his side, the three of us burst out laughing and Chief Shagger from 8B glances our way again.

'I think it's time for the spa,' I say, now very willing to splurge on more indulgence, if it gets me out of this store and puts out the flames burning my cheeks.

6

TED

It takes me a beat to work out where I've seen her before.

Her laughter drew my attention. Maybe I'm sensitive to it because it seems entirely at odds with how I've felt these last few days and how I am feeling right now, being forced to buy an Armani suit.

And wearing a glamorous outfit, trying on the kind of shoes my ex would flaunt, she is a complete contradiction to the kind of girl whose laugh is as gentle and pretty as hers is.

Wholly unexpected for someone with underwear as large as the pair she dropped in front of me two days ago.

What's more bizarre than that is the fact that when I first met her, I overlooked altogether how attractive she is.

'Can I help you, sir?'

My focus is pulled away by a store assistant, who gestures to the Jimmy Choo shoe I'm holding.

For the first time, I'm thinking of shoes as a platonic gift. Mel has managed to rearrange my entire calendar in order for me to stay in New York for the next week. She's organized a full food shop to be delivered to my brother's apartment, she made an appointment with a stylist here at Saks because she knows one of my worst nightmares would be trudging around a department store shopping for myself. She's even booked a slot with a handyman to repair the hole I made in my brother's apartment wall.

The woman deserves a new pair of fancy shoes. And if I'm honest with myself, I'm buying her silence – I need to keep my specific whereabouts quiet for as long as possible. And in order to do that, I need to have someone onside to help me navigate through the clusterfuck that is my current life status.

'Can I take these in a size eight?' I ask, my eyes flicking back to Lady Big Panties.

The way her cheeks flush as she glances up to me, diverting her gaze when I look back, tells me she's talking about me with her friends.

I scoff. She may have a pretty laugh and a beautiful face, but she's clearly just another It girl, throwing her cash around on designer labels with her friends. Exactly the kind of woman I will never get mixed up with again.

* * *

I'm walking back to Mike's place with my New York wardrobe split into six bags. In part, I'm regretting the decision to walk with the heavy load but after what I've been feeling since Thursday morning, the pain of the strung handles digging into my skin and threatening to cut off my circulation is surprisingly easy to bear.

Usually, I'm a walker. Back home in San Francisco, I'm always outdoors for a hike, bouldering, getting out on the water. I'd take the outdoors over any kind of workout.

I don't like to feel like I'm working out. Getting fit should be a by-product of enjoying physical activity. It's an escape from the sedentary activity of software development: building, testing, protecting and selling our products. Though it's Roman who does the big sell. I'm the behind-the-scenes guy – except for tomorrow.

The thought makes me look to my right hand, where my new suit is causing the tips of my fingers to turn a shade of blue-ish purple.

My stomach grumbles as I'm heading east on Bowery. I'm familiar enough with Manhattan to know I'm somewhere near China Town, making my way toward Manhattan Bridge and, ultimately, Brooklyn.

Flicking my wrist, I ask Siri via my watch, 'Where will I find the best steamed dumplings in China Town, Manhattan?'

I'm happily a few blocks away from Siri's recommendation on Grand Street. Even better, Siri, as if aware the woman I thought I was going to spend the rest of my life with has been screwing my best friend, informs me the café is great for people eating solo.

I've never felt more seen.

I order a selection of veggie, fish and seafood dim sum and dump my bags on a rickety plastic chair and wonky table, at which I swear my limbs and extremities breathe a sigh of relief.

Curiosity or stupidity gets the better of me and as I take a seat and wait for my food, I switch my phone out of airplane mode.

The device proverbially blows up with notifications. Skimming what's important, ignoring anything from Roman and deciding to call Mel as soon as I'm back, I come to land on a WhatsApp notification.

Fleur – Voice Message

I hate that my stomach flutters at the sight of her name, as if her message is a first date.

I stick my AirPods in my ears, and my thumb seems to hover without my brain's instruction over the Play arrow.

I could kick myself for wanting to hear her voice. For missing her. Us.

But I don't want to know what she has to say. What could she possibly say to fix this? Us?

Pulling up my big boy briefs, I hit the ominous triangle.

'Teddy.'

She sighs.

'Where are you?'

Her tone is a bit snippy for my liking, giving she's firmly in the doghouse right now.

'You can't hide from this forever.'

No, I can't. But I don't know how to face it yet, either.

'Ted.'

Her voice is softer now, calmer. Tender?

'Roman and I... We never meant for you to find out the way you did.'

Huh? Roman and I? They never meant for me to find out.

But they didn't mean to not do it? She isn't sorry? Regretful? Disgusted with herself?

'We love each other, Ted.'

My order number is called and a server behind the counter holds out a box for me. I rise from my seat to collect it, unsteady on my legs, as if they're made of sand.

'Chopsticks and soy sauce are on the side,' the server tells me.

Not wanting to seem rude, I wait until I'm outside the café before I throw the dumplings into a trash can. My appetite is obliterated.

Love?

They're in love?

Roman doesn't even do *love*.

Roman has a bang 'em and leave 'em approach to women.

To the long list of recent derogatory terms I have collated about myself in respect of my ex wife-to-be, I can now add fool.

* * *

My appetite came back somewhere along Manhattan Bridge, when I realized Fleur and Roman can't hurt me any more than they already have. Yes, I miss her. I feel like one of my limbs has been cut out from under me. But monogamy is a hard line for me.

Things don't make much sense at the moment. My best friend is now nothing more than a business partner and I have no idea how or if we can move forward in that relationship.

But I know, deep in my bones, that Fleur and I were done the moment she transgressed. No matter whether it was with Roman or a random guy.

Trust and loyalty are important to me. Perhaps above all else.

Her thinking that she and Rome are in love just puts the final nail in the coffin. It stops the need for any attempts at getting back together. Trying for the sake of what we had. For those honeymoon days in our whirlwind romance that, with hindsight, was altogether unlike me.

Fleur and I are done. Caput.

Unravelling our life together won't be fun.

But, ironically, my life is more entwined with Roman's than Fleur's.

With this realization, I stop to add a takeout pizza to the mass of things I'm carrying back to Blake House.

I'm ravenous and crabby as hell as I wrestle my way into the apartment block.

One of my bags gets caught between the entrance doors and as I tug it free, I drop my precariously balanced pizza box.

'Goddamnit,' I gripe, retrieving and rearranging everything I'm holding and making a move toward the wall of mailboxes.

As I do, I see Lady Big Panties, still dressed in the clothes she was wearing in Saks but now sporting a salon blow-dry and holding a fancy pair of sandals in her hand. She's barefoot as she reads her mail.

She's so engrossed in the contents of the card she's holding that she doesn't seem to notice me.

Then she sinks to her haunches and the arm in which she holds her mail flops to the ground. What looks like an invitation falls to the floor.

I see the words *Vow Renewal* on the gold embossed card.

Oh dear, she'll need a new outfit, how truly devastating.

Okay, that's unfair – a reflection of my foul mood. I don't know this girl.

She finally clocks my presence as I navigate around her in the direction of my brother's mailbox.

She looks up to me through lashes that are clearly not her own. I've seen Fleur wearing fake eyelashes enough times to recognize them.

As this woman meets my eyes, my first thought is sympathy for the sadness she seems to carry.

But my second thought, as I take in her immaculate curled hair, red painted lips, and the overdone color on her cheeks – what Fleur would call *contouring* – is that the woman on the floor is exactly that: another Fleur. Another outstandingly pretty but fake person. The kind of person a man can't trust. No matter how much the depths of her eyes draw me in and make me want to believe a different story.

Ignoring her and her doubtless superficial plight, I set down some bags and open Mike's mailbox. It looks like a couriered package and otherwise junk but I can't sort through it one-handed, so I set it all on top of my pizza box and move toward the elevator.

I hear Big Panties sniff and despite myself, I turn to make sure she's okay. But she looks to the ceiling, shakes her head and comes to stand, somewhat unsteadily.

Day drinking on a Monday. So, likely a trust-fund offspring who's never put in a day of hard work in her life, or someone like Fleur: a model who can keep whatever hours she likes.

She picks up her letters from the floor.

'You dropped one,' she says, glancing down at an envelope in her hand as she steps into the elevator with me. 'Michael.'

'It's Mike,' I say, taking the letter from her. No one calls my brother Michael, not in real life.

She presses the button for floor seven, then turns her back to me, facing the doors. 'Thank you wouldn't hurt,' she mutters.

Was that aimed at me?

Stuck up *and* crabby. Yep, most definitely not my kind of person. Anymore.

'I wouldn't have dropped it if I hadn't had to navigate around you and all your stuff.'

She turns her head sharply, as if her griping at me is acceptable, but I can't retort. Her glaring gives me a second to notice her big eyes are hazel brown, with flecks of gold. Unusual. Exquisitely so.

When the elevator signals we're at the seventh floor, she steps out.

'Enjoy your pizza. I really hope you didn't ruin it when you dropped it, Mike.'

She's as catty as a kindergarten kid who wants the toy I'm playing with. And she thinks I'm called Mike.

'Enjoy the vow renewal!' I shout back.

The doors are closing and she makes me jump when she sticks her shoes between them, forcing them to reopen.

'Are you always this ill-tempered?'

Actually, I'm not. Horizontal. Amiable. Discreet. Respectful. These are all words that have been used to describe me. But today...

'Yes, always. Now, can you take your fancy shoes out of the doorway so I can go?'

She's scowling at me. She clearly wants to say more, get something off her chest.

But she removes her shoes and I watch her stagger ever so slightly into the corridor.

The doors close as I'm rolling my eyes.

Throw me an olive branch here, Universe.

7
TED

It's Tuesday. Circa 144 hours post-apocalypse.

GQ interview day.

It turns out the journalist who was going to come to my home in San Francisco was happy to fly to New York to interview me here, as opposed to sending someone from the local *GQ* Headquarters.

I respect that. She's a lead in business and tech related features and apparently was eager to meet me.

In my head, I'm still the person who spent every night coding until I came up with the idea for forensic accounting software. I've been shaped by humble parents, who taught my brother and I the kind of work ethic that's made us both successful in our chosen careers.

But sometimes things, like the effort this journalist is making, remind me that Roman and I have been one of the Silicon Valley success stories.

Pacing Mike's immaculately clean and tidy lounge, in preparation for the interview, I scoff as I look at my watch. I pick up a baseball from the shelf and start tossing and catching it against the lounge wall, now repaired.

Roman has been on at me for months to convert our partnership to a company and take Vanguard public, raising finance through the sale of stock. I've wanted to keep control. I've wanted us – Roman and me – to be a team going forward.

But now… God only knows where my head is at. Can I continue to work with Roman at all after what's passed between us? Maybe an IPO would be better – dilute the ownership.

Hell, maybe a full sale of the business is the only way forward.

But can I give up everything I've built, designed, created, because I can no longer stand to even utter my ex-best friend's name aloud?

Three minutes late by my watch, the building concierge calls the apartment. *GQ* are here. I stop tossing the ball, answer the intercom, and tell the concierge I'll come down to the foyer to meet the *GQ* bunch.

Glancing in the mirror one more time, I correct a misplaced strand of my unusually combed, tamed and styled hair, and wiggle my shoulders to adjust the position of the shoulder pads in my new suit.

I don't look like me. Messy hair, casual clothes, sneakers. That's me. The guy in the mirror looks more like Roman, or even my brother on one of his red-carpet appearances, though he'd usually have an unnaturally attractive blonde on his arm, too.

But this is a gentleman's quarterly magazine and the interview is about the world of business.

My palms are clammy as I head downstairs in the elevator and I feel jittery, like I've overdosed on caffeine. It's no wonder I ordinarily leave these things to Roman.

I close my eyes for a moment of calm and the elevator halts. Bracing myself with a smile, I open my eyes. But instead of the elevator doors opening to the team from *GQ*, they open on the seventh floor of the building, and who is standing there but Lady Big Panties, her face murderous, her hands on her hips.

She's pouting and the first thing I think is, her lips look soft, natural in size and color. I don't mean to draw a comparison to Fleur's lips, but yes, a thousand times more natural and elegant than lips with fillers.

Big Panties' hair is wet, the make-up and fake lashes from last night are gone, and she's wearing a white string vest with a pair of tiny bed shorts. She's like the girl next door that every guy whoever read a Spiderman comic wanted to date as a kid (and big kid!).

She glares at me and seems to want to speak. Then she blinks and, I think, checks out my new suit. Her mouth opens and closes silently, like a goldfish.

'Are you getting in?' I ask, reaching out a hand to stop the doors from closing.

She steps inside.

'The foyer?'

She clears her throat. 'Yes. Well, no, actually. I was on my way to see you.'

Confusion knits my brows. 'Why?'

'Because...' Her eyes shift to the left as if she's thinking of a response.

'Because?' I don't mean to sound patronizing but I'd expect a little forethought before some random woman came to knock on my door, wearing hardly any clothes.

'Well, I thought you were— Were you alone? In your apartment?'

This girl is all kinds of weird. Thankfully, the elevator reaches the foyer and this time, the doors *do* open to the journalist and production team from *GQ*.

Big Panties' eyes shoot open, like a near-nude deer caught in the lights of a camera crew. She looks to the crew, then up to me. Then she thrusts one arm across her chest and presses her knees together. She isn't naked but she sure feels like she's exposed in her little outfit.

This is brilliant.

I lean down to her ear and tell her, 'This is *GQ* magazine and the only thing that could have made this better is if you were wearing those big panties of yours.'

When she glowers at me, I do something wholly uncharacteristic. I wink at her. And the thunder that comes back to her expression is worth good money to see. Her cantankerous nature just met with karma.

She pushes me out of the elevator and starts furiously thumping the button for the doors to close. The last thing she must see is my beaming smile. Somehow, the woman whose name I don't even know has made me laugh properly, for the first time in ages.

I turn to the *GQ* bunch, who all seem to hold a bemused expression, except Kirsten Stirling, the journalist, who I can tell wants to know which semi-naked girl I just rode downstairs with.

I'm about to clarify that I don't know the woman and that she is certainly not a conquest, if that's the insinuation behind Kirsten's expression, when she holds out a hand and says, 'Theodore? Nice to meet you.'

'It's just Ted.'

'Ted.' She gives one stern nod and I wonder whether she's always so curt or if she's put two and two together and has decided that I've been cheating on my fiancée.

How wrong a person can be.

Out of sheer stubbornness, I choose not to correct her.

Kirsten is young, at best guess about my age, which means

she's done well for herself to be a staple features editor at *GQ* already. I respect her for her work ethic. And I know she's made her own way because no one who has been handed their position on a silver platter would be wearing All Star converse with a tailored suit.

Even I splurged on a pair of shoes that are killing my feet just to make sure they match the suit for this interview. How Roman wears these fancy shoes all day long is beyond me. I'm counting down the minutes until I can get back into a pair of shorts and some sneakers.

The camera crew – two guys and a girl – busy themselves setting up lights and reflective screens and set the scene for Kirsten and me to have an 'informal chat' on the lounge sofa and chair. I offer drinks and I'm thrilled when they only want water because I'm better with Mike's multi-option water tap than his complex coffee machine – something that would be more at home in a chain coffee store.

We come to sit – me in the armchair, Kirsten on the sofa, both posed informally so that we neither face toward nor away from each other.

Kirsten explains what she's hoping to achieve from the interview, the crux of which, I understand, is to highlight some kind of difference between Roman – front man – and me – tech nerd – and no doubt to intrude on my relatively private life.

She seems to have moved on from the air of animosity I witnessed downstairs. Now, she's full of smiles as she rights a few strands that have snuck out from her hair tie and crosses one leg over the other, placing her hands on the notebook that rests on her lap.

I'm nervous. This is not my forte. I much prefer sitting in a quiet room, coding, reimagining, and inventing than giving the company, or worse, myself, the big sell.

'I am going to record the interview, just so I don't have to make so many handwritten notes,' Kirsten says. She isn't asking my permission, since she's already placing her phone down on the coffee table between us and I can see she's already recording.

'No problem.'

I clear my throat, which feels dry, then take a sip of cold water. It's not that I can't easily converse with people. I'm not entirely socially inept. But I am uncomfortable. Even more so than usual, which I suspect is because I know at some point questions will arise about my private life, and how on earth am I supposed to answer them when I don't even have *my* head around it yet?

Kirsten's next words are spoken with what I would describe as a telephone voice, and I know we're now on the record. 'First, thank you for giving us your time today, Ted.'

I nod. 'Thanks for coming East last minute. I appreciate the effort.'

'All part of the job,' she says, eying me closely. 'Why are you in New York?'

Heat builds in my palms. I interlock my fingers, hoping the slight tremor I feel won't show. She has no idea how complex the answer to her seemingly innocuous question really is.

'Business. Always business.' I offer a smile. Faux airy.

It must work because she moves on. 'Let's start at the beginning. How did you go from college student to being a co-founder of what is predicted to soon be a billion-dollar tech business?'

'Can I tell you anything that Mark Zuckerberg hasn't already come out with?'

She laughs with me, and I think, *Screw you, Roman, I can be personable.*

'Honestly, I think everyone in my family wanted me to be a pro ball player, like my brother, but I wasn't good enough, and the only other thing I really enjoyed was computer science, so that's where it started. I was just a failed athlete who happened to find coding the most natural thing in the world, ironically, given there's nothing natural about a tech verse.'

'I'd love to explore that further. Do you think failure made you who you are?'

'I suppose in a way it did.' My mind wanders from baseball to my failed engagement. My failed friendship. Maybe I should start seeing the biggest relationship breakdowns of my life as an opportunity. 'I guess there's always something to be learned from failure.'

I wonder what exactly I'm supposed to be learning from my fiancée doing the business with my best friend.

For the next twenty minutes or so, Kirsten covers most of the questions I've heard before (albeit by telephone or through email, my preferred interview method). She covers business start-up, business growth and goals, what Silicon Valley is really like, and if it is still the Silicon Valley it was in the days of teenage Zuckerberg. I can respond to these things on autopilot, having been asked similar iterations of every question over the last decade.

She doesn't grab my attention until she asks, 'What is it like to be working so closely with your best friend? Can friendships really survive business?'

I wonder if she knows. Whether the word is getting out on the grapevine. I don't think so. I don't think Fleur or Roman would have disclosed it. It hardly portrays them in a good light. It's not exactly Instagrammable. And I'm sure my brother wouldn't have said a thing. I trust Mike with my life, let alone my secrets.

But evidentially, I can't trust Roman.

'Not in every case,' I reply. 'Though in ours, it has been successful. Roman and I are exact opposites. Our skillsets complement each other.'

Kirsten smiles, much softer now than in the foyer. 'I guess it's true what they say, sometimes opposites attract.'

Sometimes, I think. Roman and I are opposites. Fleur and I are opposites. She uses her beauty, her self-confidence, her effervescent presence in company, to be adored by many, not least her hundreds of thousands of social media followers.

Yet, Fleur and Roman aren't opposites; they're alike in many ways. They're both chameleons, for a start. I guess I just haven't been on the receiving end of their changing colors until now.

'Have you and Roman ever had crossed words?' Kirsten asks.

She has no idea how hilarious her question is.

'Crossed words,' I repeat.

'Business disagreements? *Life* disagreements?'

She emphasizes the word *life*, and again, I'm left considering whether my life has become gossip. I hope not. I'm not ready and this interview has proved it.

'No. Not disagreements. We hone and temper each other's ideas sometimes, but disagreements? Not really.'

As I speak, I stare across to the cityscape. The tall, protruding buildings against the calm, cloudless sky. Huge banks, massive companies, reside in those buildings.

Roman and I have disagreed of late, even in a business context. We agree that we may have reached our potential with our current growth structure and it's time for a new wave of financing.

He says it's time for us to take a back seat, enjoy what we've built, claw back some time for ourselves in our lives.

I've told him that it would take something catastrophic for me to want to take a backseat.

Catastrophic, like the breakdown of our relationship. An untenable working partnership. A complete and irrevocable lack of trust.

I come to stand and move to the window, lost in my thoughts.

He hasn't, surely? He couldn't. Wouldn't.

I'm aware Kirsten has asked me something.

'Sorry, I missed that. Could you repeat the question?' I ask, turning to face her.

She asks again but my mind is too busy with its own questions.

What would be worse? If Roman were to tell me he is in love with Fleur? Or if the whole reason behind all of this, him stealing the woman who I should have spent the rest of my life with, was just to force me into agreeing to an IPO?

'You seem like a reserved, private man, and I was just wondering how you came to be engaged to Fleur Dumont, who seems to live her life very much in the public eye?'

I stare at her, almost laughing at my idiocy...

'We met at my brother's birthday bash. Roman introduced us.' It occurs to me how much more likely a relationship between Roman and Fleur had been right from the start. Shrugging, I tell her, 'Like you say, sometimes opposites attract.'

But most of the time, like-minded people screw like-minded people.

At the end of the interview, I show the *GQ* team back down to the foyer and Kirsten tells me that once she has combined Roman's interview with mine, she'll send the feature to her editor in chief. I make polite noises but I couldn't care less. What I just told her isn't real, it isn't truth. It's all publishable crap.

The camera guys head out to the street, where they've temporarily parked their van, and start packing up. Kirsten shakes my hand and tells me, 'If you don't mind me saying so, Ted, you're not a typical rich guy.'

I raise one brow questioningly – *what exactly did you expect from me?*

'You're very... considered. Most of the tech millionaires I meet are eccentric at best and otherwise full of themselves.'

I smirk. 'Like Rome?'

She releases my hand and smiles mischievously.

As I watch her leave the building and climb into the van, all I can think is that being more like a typical millionaire, more like Roman, is exactly how I should behave. Then, maybe I wouldn't feel like someone has ripped out my soul every single day from the moment I wake up until I eventually fall asleep.

8
ABBEY

As is typical of Nate's wife, Meredith has booked a restaurant as far away as she could get. Dee and I are riding the subway. Tonight is the night that she's going to tell Nate she's pregnant. First stop, Nate. Second stop, Mom and Dad.

'How's the morning sickness?' I ask when she stops Whats-App-ing with Brett.

'Real. But the fatigue is worse. I feel like I've been clubbing and having wild sex all night for days in a row.'

'Well, I guess you'd know. Isn't wild sex precisely the reason you have nausea?'

Dee grins at me, despite her tiredness. 'Brett and I were friends with benefits for a while; you know this. But disappointingly, I think the deed that sewed the seed was actually an unmemorable hangover quickie.'

I snort. 'I probably wouldn't lead with those details when you're telling Nate.'

Our brother is the kind of man who *always* colors inside the lines. There's black and white and no grey area when it comes to his 'good person' code.

'Ha, imagine.' Her laughter turns to an actress version of a groan – theatrical, eyes to the ceiling, as if the world is about to end. 'Grrrr, tell me why we have to trek to the Upper East Side.'

'Because Nate is paying and you and I otherwise can't afford to eat fine-dining.'

'Solid reasoning.'

We get off the subway on 77th street and walk on to a restaurant on 78th. I realize I've subconsciously become even more protective of my sister since finding out she's carrying my niece or nephew. I'm making myself stand taller, broader, filling a bigger space and walking so close to her through busy areas that no one can knock her. When she climbs steps, I brace myself for her to trip or slip.

By the time we arrive outside the restaurant, Dee is folded over laughing at the story of how I got caught in my bedwear by *GQ* magazine when I tried to chase after Mike to give him what for about his noise nuisance.

When tears of humor are rolling down her cheeks, I start to see the funny side, a little.

'Imagine if I end up on the cover of *GQ*! I definitely won't be laughing then.'

She rubs her knuckles under her eyes and I confirm that she doesn't have smudged mascara.

'Anyway, we have a name for the man in apartment 8B now. Mike?'

I nod. 'Michael Thomas. Not that it matters.'

'Of course it matters. Not only do you have an actual name to vent at or swoon over but we can also find out how he's famous. *GQ* don't interview just anyone.'

I've been so concerned with being exposed in hardly any clothes and the relentless banging from upstairs at ungodly hours of the morning (and sometimes during the day) that I haven't bothered to think about who the man living above me might be.

Dee is already typing his name into a search engine and I hold open the heavy glass door to the restaurant, relieved when a member of staff from the eatery takes over and welcomes us.

'He's a Major League Baseball player!' Dee announces, turning to smile at the suited man holding open the door. 'That's settles it, the banging in the penthouse is definitely sex.'

'A baseball player?' I think of his broad shoulders and height – I guess that fits, not that I have the first clue about baseball. 'I still think the sound is too rhythmic.'

As the suited man waits for me to take off the short tweed jacket I have teamed with a plain black dress and my new white Dior shoes, Dee places her hands on my shoulders in the manor of a kindergarten teacher reasoning with a toddler. 'He's a pro-athlete, who's apparently recovering from injury, which is code for has nothing better to do, and just look at all these images of him. He's with a different woman in every one.'

Reluctantly, I glance at the phone Dee is now holding up for me to see. I can feel myself squinting as I look at the man in the images. He's quite often wearing shades. Most often in full baseball kit. Frequently mid-action on a baseball field. So I guess that's why he doesn't always look immediately like the guy I've met, but the resemblance is definitely there. It's him alright.

'You should totally get in on that action. That'll cure you of your heartache.'

The front of house guy tells us to follow him to our table.

'Thanks, but he's not my type.'

She looks at her screen and wiggles it close to my face as we walk. 'He's *everyone's* type. Those are the kind of arms and shoulders that can strip you bare on a hot day and make you sweaty even on a cold day.'

She raises her eyebrows – once, twice. I snort. Actually snort.

'I like tall and weedy, not tall and muscly.'

'Nooooo, you liked Andrew and since you've always been destined for him by our families, you've never thought to explore what else might be on offer. Like... hello! This guy!'

I shake my head, bemused. 'What would a guy like that want with an unemployed auditor, who, thanks to six months' advance rent and a new wardrobe, is basically broke?'

Dee rolls her eyes. 'You are a woman living in her dream apartment block, with a completely stunning new look.' She twizzles the ends of my new long bob. 'Who is just waiting to find a career she's passionate about and a man to use for wild sex.'

A guffaw breaks from deep inside of me. 'You were earning top sibling marks until that last comment.'

We're walking side by side, given the restaurant is spacious. This place is one of the best eateries in Manhattan, according to its website, and evidenced by the fact they don't pack the tables together and oversubscribe.

'Ladies!' Meredith stands from a round table, where she's sitting with Nate, and gives us a cheery wave. 'Wow, Abbey, you look...' She holds her arms out in front of her as she looks me up and down. I step into her hold to end the uncomfortable inspection.

'You look lovely, as always, Meredith. Thanks for making the reservation.'

She gives me an airy wave, as if to say *it's nothing*. We both know she loves to organize dinners and dinner parties. It's part of her role as Nate's wife, as she sees it.

'Abbey,' Nate says, like an architect might greet a client. Then he gives me a glancing kiss on the cheek. Ever the affectionate big brother.

I quickly scan the round table, counting the places on its

immaculate white linen cloth, and wonder aloud as I clock the six Louis XVI upholstered chairs. 'Are there others joining us?'

Meredith winces, then her lips rebound up again, as Nate says, 'Drew is joining us.'

'Andrew?' I repeat in disbelief. Nate is one of few people who call him Drew.

'You two are still friends?' Meredith asks, like a person who has never been dumped before, let alone cheated on.

But, of course, to them I've simply parted ways with Nate's childhood friend amicably.

They probably think I'd love to get back with him. In fact, they're probably trying to set us back up – that's the kind of thing Mom would put them up to.

And it's not true. I don't still want to be with him. I couldn't. But I can't deny my stomach is currently tying itself in a bow at the thought of seeing my ex.

Oh God, this is going to be a long dinner.

'Are you okay?' Dee whispers, firing daggers at Nate.

'I'm fine. Surprised but fine. I guess I can't avoid him forever, right? He'll be invited to Mom and Dad's vow renewal in a few weeks.'

'I was hoping he wouldn't have the audacity to—'

I cut her short because, as I take my seat, I remember there are two extra spaces at the table. 'Who else is coming?' I ask to anyone who'll answer because I'm too busy staring at the two spare place settings, suddenly feeling disoriented.

Before I receive an answer, Dee slaps a hand to my arm. 'You. Have. Got. To. Be. Shitting. Me.'

I know it's bad before I even turn to follow her gaze.

Sure enough, when I do, it isn't the opulent interiors of the restaurant that draw my attention but Andrew, who's speaking to the guy on the welcome desk. Andrew, drawing a short white jacket from the arms of an extremely well put together, long and flawless red-haired woman.

Not only did he show up, he showed up with another woman.

Everything seems to have failed me – words, breath, sensibility. All I can do is stand from my seat and gawp at the couple heading our way.

When I think I can't be any more shocked than I am in this moment, my brother does something he never does. He leans in to my ear and whispers, 'I'm sorry, Abbey. I didn't know he was bringing anyone until an hour ago and I didn't know how best to forewarn you.'

'So you just *didn't*?' Dee snarls.

I don't know if I'm mad at my brother. I can't process that right now. But I do know that I'm angry with myself. My naivety. That fleeting moment when my tummy danced.

I'm irate with Andrew. His brazenness. His lack of any semblance of compassion. The absence of any love or even respect for me whatsoever.

This isn't even the woman he cheated on me with.

This is another woman.

He didn't even plan to stay with the woman he cheated on me with.

He wanted her enough to leave me and not enough to stay with her. What does that say about our relationship?

Dee rises from her seat and I can tell she's about to explode. Here. In this restaurant full of people. In front of my brother and sister-in-law and their perfect marriage.

I don't know where I find it from but a wave of strength comes back into my jelly legs, then my backbone and eventually, my hand reaches out to Dee's arm.

'It's embarrassing enough, Dee; please don't make a scene.'

I'm flabbergasted. Dumbfounded. Blown away that he would

do this to me. But the overwhelming sense I feel is mortification. I am the woman who couldn't keep the guy.

I watch the introductions and greetings take place around the table, silent, still.

Then, incredibly, audaciously, Andrew leans in to kiss my cheek.

'This isn't awkward, is it?' he asks in my ear.

What I want to say is: *You have got to be kidding me. It's awkward as hell and you are the biggest asswipe walking this planet.*

What I actually say is:

Nothing. Words have failed me. I'm speechless.

And what angers me more than my inability to respond appropriately is that, when he takes me into his embrace, his familiar scent is warming, comforting.

He is the sole reason that my brain and heart are completely fried. Yet, he's the person who can help make it feel better. I close my eyes as I inhale the scent of nostalgia. Peace. A version of me I'm significantly more familiar with than the current me.

Once everyone is seated and a waiter has taken our drinks order, I excuse myself to the ladies' room and do what every woman experiencing an existential crisis does – I stare at my reflection in the sink mirror.

I'm better than this, I tell myself. *I don't need to hide in bathrooms. I can do this.*

It was going to happen *some*time. Andrew is a family friend. He's been in our lives since my earliest memories – despite the fact I actually didn't like him as a child.

I continue to stare at my face, which is full of more make up than the old me would have ever worn; I stare at my, admittedly rather gorgeous and figure-hugging, little black dress. I might feel like the old me on the inside but I'm not. Just look at me. I am actually the woman I intend to become.

New Me does not shy away from a waste of air like Andrew. She doesn't pine after his cologne. She's courageous and she's about to walk back into that fine dining room and show Andrew and his new girlfriend that she has moved on.

I give my reflected self one curt nod. *You've got this.* I've got this. Then I apply the overpriced lipstick I was lured into buying at my beauty makeover and proverbially brush myself off.

Walking back through the restaurant, I hold my chin high – more metaphorically than physically – and twist my lips up just like I twisted my new lipstick.

I. Am. So. Ready. For. This. Dinner.

'So, how did you and Sasha meet?' Meredith asks, finishing her question with a sip of Viognier and beaming in the direction of Andrew, seemingly lacking any emotional intelligence whatsoever.

Thank God for the vast à la carte menu I choose to get lost in.

I. Am. So. Over. This. Dinner.

The whole point of this disastrous experience was for Dee to share her baby news with Nate. From the way her knuckles are gripping her leather-bound menu so hard I can practically see bone, I know she won't bring it up now.

I make an immediate decision to order no starter, a salad main and skip dessert. Free or not, no meal is worth this. The sooner I can leave and spare my ears the current fairy tale of Andrew and Sasha both gunning for the same yellow cab, the better.

They couldn't be any more cliché.

Stuff waiting for a member of staff. I reach into the wine bucket where the wine Nate chose is chilling. I pour my glass to full beyond etiquette.

9

ABBEY

The best thing about dinner with Nate is that it's over.

It was awful. Beyond awful. The stuff of nightmares.

I was first to leave, making a lame excuse about a work interview tomorrow, before the others had received the desserts and coffees they'd ordered. Dee wanted to leave with me in solidarity but I told her to stay – I know how she loves desserts and she's eating for two now.

I blubbered my way to the subway, thankful to have held it together for more than an hour. Now, I'm heading into a pizza place between Clark Street station and my apartment block.

'I'll take a chocolate calzone, please,' I tell the server, and I cry some more whilst I wait on a bench in the window, passersby staring at this ostensibly neurotic woman.

By the time I get the food back to my apartment block, the smell is killing me. I would happily bury my face in the contents of the box and grunt-gobble it up like a pig from a trough. It may not be fitting of my new capsule wardrobe and these stupid heels I'm wearing – I finally understand what people mean when they say *killer* heels – but it would be fitting of my current mood.

At the entrance to Blake House, I hold my fob to the door lock and back my butt into the main doors.

As I connect with the heavy glass door and start to push it open, a cab pulls up curbside.

For the second time tonight, I am left thinking, *Come. Off. It!*

The long legs of Andrew's new woman are first to step out of the cab. Then, sure enough, Andrew gets out of the far-side of the cab and walks around to offer a hand to his date.

Meanwhile, my butt and I are rooted to the spot, holding open the entrance door.

Andrew looks up. Our eyes connect, both of us wearing expressions of confusion, and I really hope it's not blatant that I've been crying.

'Did you follow me?' I ask.

'Did you follow *me*?' he replies.

'How funny,' his date says. 'Do you live here?'

'Ah, yeah, I do.'

They're approaching me. Andrew relieves me of the weight of the door and I back inside the building.

'Do you live here?' I ask.

'Sasha does,' Andrew says, gesturing to her with a lean of his head.

'You are actually dating someone who lives in Blake House?' I'm incredulous. This is too much of a coincidence but then, we love this apartment block. This was *our* dream. If we lived here, it meant we'd accomplished our goals.

Except he – *we* – haven't. 'Did you actually seek out someone who lives here?'

'Not in so many— No! We were both leaving Tia's one night after awful Tinder dates and—'

'Tia's? *Our* favorite restaurant?'

My voice is raised. I sound hysterical, even to my own ears.

'Abbey, I know you're still upset about the break-up. It's understandable.'

Understandable? Oh my God, he thinks I still want to be with him? Do I? No! I can't stand him. Right now and always.

'Sasha and I are a recent thing, like we said at dinner. Don't take out your feelings on her.'

'My feelings? Don't *you* have feelings? Jesus, Andrew, we were together for four years and you *cheated* on me just three weeks ago.'

'Actually, more like four, when I told you,' he corrects.

I shake my head in utter disbelief. He thinks this is fine. He thinks what he did was nothing. That he can go to *our* restaurant and pick up a woman who lives in *our* aspirational apartment block and bring her to dinner with *my* brother and sister, then come to stay over with her in *my* home.

What I want to say is: *You have some audacity!*

What I actually say is: 'You... you...'

'Should I go up?' Sasha says meekly. Despite myself, I actually feel sorry for her being caught up in this.

'No, I'm coming,' Andrew says. Then he holds up his palms to me. *Hold up...* 'Why are *you* here?'

Oh God, why *am* I here? Why did I blow my life savings on rent in this stupid apartment block – was it actually for me? I really hope so. I really hope I wasn't trying to prove something to an unworthy ex.

'Well, I—'

'Babe, you're back.'

Huh? I feel a heavy arm come to rest on my shoulder and I recognize the cologne of the man it belongs to. Big. Burly. Obnoxious, but in an entirely different way to the sleazebag standing in front of me.

I turn to the rest of his body and sure enough, I see Michael Thomas. Mike from apartment 8B.

I meet his eyes, which are almost dancing with humor, right before he presses his lips to my temple. I'm no longer babbling. For the second time tonight, I'm speechless.

Michael lifts the lid on the box I'm still clutching like my life depends on it. 'Is this for me?' He tears a wedge off the end of my comfort calzone and puts it in his mouth.

Through a disgusting amount of half masticated chocolate pudding, he asks, 'Who's this?' Nodding in Andrew's direction.

'My ex,' I say, suddenly finding my words.

Clearer now, with less food in his mouth, Mike asks, 'The jackass who cheated on you?'

He overheard us, which is embarrassing, yet I smile because Andrew really is a jackass and it sounds even better in what I'm now determining is Mike's west-coast accent.

In fact, his hooded jumper with board shorts and flip-flops and the way his hair is messed up, as if he's just stepped out of the sea holding a surfboard, all suggests to me that he's from the west coast.

I like it. I prefer his relaxed look to the suit he was wearing on Tuesday. Though he did look head-turningly handsome, I've seen plenty of men in suits. The men at work all wore suits. Nate always wears suits. My dad always wears suits. *Andrew* is wearing a suit.

Besides the point. Why *is* this guy helping me out? We can't stand each other.

And he just stole another piece of my calzone!

Mike scowls at Andrew. 'Your idiocy is my gain.' Then he turns to me. 'Come on, babes, let's go to bed.'

He finishes with a cocksure wink. It's vulgar. He is so far from my type.

But right now, he's the lesser of evils, and so I allow him to take the box of *my* chocolate dessert and I follow him into the elevator.

'Why did you do that?' I ask when we are alone and rising.

He presses the button for the eighth floor, then steps back so that we're in line with each other, me holding the now partial calzone and him with his hands in his pockets. He side eyes me. 'Isn't it obvious?'

I look up to him. 'Is it?'

Reaching over, he lifts the lid on my pizza box and tears off another strip of the contents. 'Sweet tooth.'

My eyes narrow on him. 'Well, thank you. I've had one of the worst nights imaginable and without your help, it could have been worse.'

The doors open to the eighth floor. Mike gestures for me to step out ahead of him.

'Don't mention it,' he says, blasé. Entirely opposite to his actions downstairs, yet entirely in keeping with the version of him I have met on every previous occasion. 'After you.'

'After me? I'm on the seventh floor.'

'Not if you want to keep up the pretense of me being your boyfriend, *babes*.' He's enjoying this, the ratbag. 'Your ex and the replacement you are waiting for this elevator, which means we need to get out on the same floor. And why not really rub it in his face by going to the penthouse?'

The second last thing on earth I want to do is hang out with an arrogant guy in his swanky penthouse apartment, giving up my comfort food, but the *worst* thing on earth I can think to do right now is to still be in the foyer with Andrew and Sasha. So like it or not, the jock is right; we need to get out on the same floor, and I want my dessert, even if I am now sharing it.

'You're enjoying this, aren't you?' I ask begrudgingly, stomping past him.

'Sure am,' he says, and I know he's grinning as he walks behind me to the door of his apartment.

I'm happy to report that the eighth floor looks much like the seventh – vanilla walls with a few oil paintings (mostly abstract smatterings of colorful paint), a couple of stone-colored side tables with fancy fresh flowers on top of them.

Mike holds his fob against the door lock and pushes it open for me.

Before I step inside, I set something straight: 'don't ever call me babe or baby or any other massively misogynistic term.' Facing him, I take one backward step into his apartment. 'And for your information, your breed is well on its way to becoming extinct.'

I turn on my painful heels and into the expanse of an absolutely vast penthouse apartment.

The place really is enormous. Not even in the same league as my little 7B. The view I'm familiar with seems much bolder and brighter thanks to the entire wall of windows. The sky is dark now, as dark as it gets in Brooklyn, and against the nothingness of the sky, the everythingness of Manhattan is twinkling.

The downstairs is fully open plan – a lounge with a large L-shaped sofa and a couple of swish chairs, dining area with a twelve-seat table, massive black unit kitchen with a six-stool island. I step further inside, turning on the spot, my head leaning back, and see a mezzanine glass balcony overhanging the lounge to one side of the sizeable turning staircase. To the other side is a hallway and, I suspect, the bedrooms.

The thought of the sleeping space brings the relentless banging every night to the forefront of my mind and I feel the skin of my neck heat, then I sense Mike close to me, right before I feel his arm reach around me from behind.

He grabs the pizza box from my hands and takes it to the kitchen.

'Hey!'

He opens the box on the kitchen island and takes two plates down from a rack shelf. He cuts the pizza in what would have been the original middle, before he started eating it downstairs, then places the unscathed half on one plate and hands it to me, taking the other piece for himself.

'Drink?' he asks, already opening the double-door refrigerator to reveal more bottles of beer than a bar might stock.

After the night I've had...

'Sure, thanks.' I give in and take a seat on a stool.

'Beer or beer?'

I shrug. 'Beer?'

'Right answer.'

Whilst he searches through drawers, eventually coming up with a bottle opener, I consider the space. A very definite sports fanatic pad. Signed baseballs decorate an area of the white walls. Signed jerseys are hanging in frames.

There are massive prints of baseball players in black and white, five in total. All signed. I've no idea who they are, though I'm kind of thinking one is Babe Ruth – based on my reluctant participation in a recent pub quiz.

And one is...

'Tell me you don't have a life-size print of yourself on display in your home.' I flick off the heels that have been crippling my toes and hop down from the stool, moving in for a closer inspection. 'And that you've signed it!'

In the picture, he's wearing a baseball cap that partially shades his face, but it's Mike alright.

If it wasn't for the snigger that comes along with it, I could forget myself for a second and think that slight quirk of his lips, an almost smile, is kind of... sexy?

My capsule wardrobe is going to my head.

'Greatness should be celebrated, babe.'

Oh my God, this guy is such a jerk. Then again, I've demonstrated of late that I'm not as good a judge of character as I thought I was. But I am close to certain that he's a jerk.

I'd physically and metaphorically run for the hills if it wasn't for: one, I haven't finished my calzone, and two, the thought of putting my feet in those shoes again is more terrifying than being called babe.

I remove the first blockade with an elephant-sized bite of pizza and decide that the elephant feet probably won't fit back into the slinky shoes tonight in any event, so I'll carry them instead. The perk of being rescued by an ape in shining armor who lives in the same building as you.

'On that note...' I wash down my food with a mouthful of beer. 'This *babe* is heading to bed.'

'There's a bed upstairs,' Mike says. I could swear he covers a wince with his beer bottle, as if the words left his mouth before his brain clicked into gear. *Quelle* surprise. A typical sports type.

'Just to clarify, was that a genuine pick-up line or a joke? Because FYI, no way, no how, not ever.' I slip down from the stool, pick up my shoes and rise to standing. 'If it wasn't for the fact I need to find a date to my parents' vow renewal in three weeks' time, I'd be sworn off men entirely, forever, irrevocably.'

Why did I even offer that insight? This isn't a girls' sleepover and that's hardly in keeping with the *new* me, who intends to fill that mental checklist, at least within the next three years. I start walking to the door.

'Sorry, I meant to just think that last part but at least you have some context. I'll see myself out.'

His brow is furrowed, his lips are drawn into a smirk. He's mocking me. He raises his now empty beer bottle from where he's still standing by the kitchen island.

'You got it, *babe*. And let me know if you need that date to be super fly and hot as hell. I could bump you up my waiting list.'

Urgh. I'm standing by the open door, holding it with one hand, my fancy purse and murderous shoes in the other.

'If you're such a misogynistic beast, why *did* you help me out earlier? I know it wasn't just for hazelnut chocolate spread.'

He creaks his neck, leaning his head to one side, then the other. 'If you must know, I can't stand cheats. It's cowardly. It's demeaning. It's disrespectful.'

'What do you know – we have something in common.'

I'm smiling, because finally I recognize this guy for who he is: the alpha male with mommy and daddy issues.

I've got your number, 8B.

10

TED

'Sweet dreams, babe,' I call as Abbey closes the door behind her.

'Goodnight, my knight in chauvinist armor,' she calls back.

Then the door is closed and laughter escapes me. Believe it or not, I'm laughing, again. So, I'll admit, behaving like this self-assured Michael Thomas character makes the real me cringe at times. *There's a bed upstairs. Super fly. I'll bump you up my waiting list* – what was I thinking? That didn't sound like a slick alpha male but a horny creep, the worst combination.

But I don't think the real me would have shown up for a woman the way I did tonight. Maybe that's the point. Guys like my brother and Rome can be arrogant but they *always* get the girl. They keep the girl. Guys like the old me don't get a look in.

Tonight is case in point. I was horrible in places, yet Abbey stuck around.

Honestly, I can't figure that woman out. Sometimes I look at her, remembering those ginormous panties, and I think she looks like a really hot girl next door. Other times, I look at her and I see exactly the kind of woman I'm not going to get mixed up with again. Like Fleur. Fancy clothes and salon-styled hair. And then she has this kind of sassy sensibility about her, which doesn't fit with her ex having pulled the wool over her eyes.

I sit on the sofa and stare at the selection of baseballs on the wall. You don't have to be stupid to get the wool pulled over your eyes; I'm stereotyping and it's not right. I'm a smart guy – I have pieces of paper and a bank balance that say so – yet my fiancée still managed to do the dirty on me.

Therein lies the reason I helped out Abbey tonight. Her ex seemed like a complete idiot, and right now, whilst I'm avoiding both Fleur and Roman, I can't imagine what it must have felt like for Abbey being forced to come face-to-face with her ex. For all intents and purposes, they're living in the same apartment block. I genuinely hope for her sake that his relationship with a new woman is fleeting.

Here's something, though, as I stare at the baseballs on the wall, I realize: this is the first night since I arrived in New York, almost a week ago, that I haven't wanted to pick up one of those balls and bang it off the wall, over and over until monotony replaces anger and eventually has me ready to drop off to sleep.

The very last thing I need in my life right now is another designer-wearing woman, but Abbey was company tonight, however briefly. Whilst I was talking with her, I wasn't mourning a life I had just a week ago, or at least a life I thought I had.

The fact is, store assistants aside, Abbey is the only person I know in New York. I'm going to need someone to talk to, someone in whom I have zero interest romantically and whom I can tolerate to be with for some sanity-preserving conversation.

So, I guess Abbey is staying.

Abbey and her sore feet.

I do my ablutions and head to bed, knowing that tonight, I'm finally going to be able to sleep – because my constant rage of the last days isn't present.

As I lie back on the bed, blackout blinds drawn for the morning's early sunrise, the final thought that enters my head is that Fleur would have never gone barefoot in public, no matter how badly her impractical shoes were rubbing her feet.

* * *

It's Friday and the great thing about Fridays is that my assistant blocks out my calendar so that I can have a full day of R&D. I'm working on a new A.I. project, which I think has the potential to be the biggest product Vanguard has offered to date. Let's face it, the hottest thing in the world right now is artificial intelligence.

In a random twist, I woke up with a modicum of energy, so at 5.30 a.m. I went into my brother's small home gym. I used his rowing machine, his treadmill, and his free weights, and have miraculously been left with even more energy. I'm now sitting at my new home office desk with a breakfast bundle from the local bakery Four, which has become my go-to place when I'm not using Uber Eats.

I've been sketching pages of an app by hand, in such a way that the pages map out a storyboard. This is why I love Fridays. I can get lost in a project and forget the noise of the business world, and more importantly today, real life.

As she does every Friday morning at nine-thirty, Mel video calls me and I answer with, 'Hey, Mel.' Her face has appeared on my large computer screen.

I hear it in her voice, the moment she says, 'Hi Ted.' I've known her long enough to pick up on the subtle undertone.

She has my full attention. 'What's up?'

Her smile isn't as bright as usual. It's forced. 'Just the usual check in to see if there's anything specific you want me to action today or if I should just plod on doing my thing.' There's always a hint of feisty, kind of quirky city gal about Mel. Not today.

I interlock my fingers and bring my elbows to the desk, resting my chin on my hands.

'There are a few things but first, what's wrong?' I'm near certain I know what this is about. Still, I ask, 'Are you okay?'

'Me?' She shakes her head, as if exasperated. 'Christ, Ted. *I'm* fine.'

It suddenly strikes me that she's sitting in my desk chair, in my office. She wants privacy. And the way she says *I'm* is the final convincing I need. 'Level with me.'

'People are talking in the office. Playing guessing games as to why you've done a runner.'

I sit back in my chair, putting some distance between us, uncomfortable. 'What's the best guess?'

'That Fleur has been fu— having an affair with Roman.'

She's right. And as far as I'm aware, I was the first person to know as much. Yet Mel's words are like someone unplugged the power supply to my system. As if my body shut down and can no longer perform basic functions, like breathing. Like my heart beating.

'It's true, isn't it? I can tell from your silence. I can see it on your face. That's why you're in New York.' She whispers the location, leaning in to her screen, even though I know she'll be alone in my office. I trust her unreservedly – though my judgment in that department is clearly way off the mark.

'How many tongues are wagging? Give it to me in numbers.'

'Word is spreading fast. Pain and scandal make for the best gossip, Ted. It's not intended to be cruel; it's mindless.'

'Are we in single figures or double?' I don't know why I'm so fixated on a number. Numbers are logical, I suppose. They help make sense of things that can otherwise seem out of control. For instance, *all* of our 176 employees knowing would seem impossible to contain. But 10 or even 20 percent I could live with.

'I don't think you want me to sugar coat it, so I'll say the 50 percent who don't bury their heads in code and analytics all day long.'

I slump back against my seat. 'Where did it come from?'

'Best guess? Kimberley.'

Roman's assistant. No doubt out of jealousy. She's a fairly forgetful assistant, yet Roman keeps her around, mostly for an ego boost. The flirting is mutually enjoyed, I've always thought. So long as it doesn't interfere with business, I don't need to step in.

I mentally chastise myself. *How* have I trusted Roman with *any* woman for so long?

I guess I didn't. I trusted him to be a good friend. I trusted him with me.

'What's Roman saying about it?'

Mel sighs. 'Ted, I— Does it matter? What about *you*? I only care what you've got to say about it.'

'Is he saying anything?'

She looks at me through her camera like I'm a vulnerable, naïve boy to be pitied. I've seen the look before. Whenever I was compared to my brother and found lacking as a kid. Except with hindsight, I know now that I just wasn't the star player in team sports; I hadn't found my thing then. When I found my perfect match in tech, I showed all those people who pitied me. Look at the business I've built.

But I didn't build it alone. Tech may have been my perfect match but my choices in close relationships have been demonstrably appalling.

'I— He doesn't seem to be denying it or trying to stop the chatter,' Mel says.

I knew that would be the case. I wouldn't be surprised if he told Kimberley the truth, knowing he would set a domino train in motion.

He wants out, to cash in. He's trying to force my hand. I shouldn't, I know, she doesn't deserve it, but I feel protective of Fleur. Roman has used her to get to me. He's not behaving like a friend who fucked up; he's behaving like the Green Goblin to my Spiderman.

Closing my eyes, I rub my temples. 'Mel, there is something specific I'd like you to do. Please have Hugh Atkins call me today.'

'Your personal lawyer?'

'Yes. Please.'

Mel types a note on her laptop. 'Will do. Anything else?'

Not that my mind can process. 'Not at the moment, thanks.'

'Okay, boss.'

We each stare into our screens. I'd like to see her. Who knows if I really can trust anyone anymore but if I can, Mel has to be one of the goods ones. I can't face going back there. Not right now. I don't know when. Half the office is talking about me. Soon the whole office will be talking about me. And eventually, the rumor mill will hit Fleur's social media profiles and the wider business world.

'Ted,' she says eventually. 'I'm just... sorry. So sorry. I don't even know what to say. I can't believe they've done—'

I force my lips up. 'Hey, there are plenty more fish in the sea, right?'

I don't believe that. Of course I don't believe that. But it's time to save face, to retain a modicum of integrity. And that's the kind of thing my big brother would say.

It's not like I was going to marry Fleur and vow to spend the rest of my life with her. It's not like Fleur is a model and influencer and has hundreds of thousands of followers on Instagram alone.

Oh, wait...

'Yeah, right. If you need anything...'

I nod, give a swift thanks and end the call. Now I'm going to spend today considering my options with my lawyer, so Fleur and Roman can add to the list of shitty things they've done: ruining Coding Fridays.

11

ABBEY

'The dating cavalry has arrived!' Dee announces when I open my apartment door.

Shernette holds up a large brown paper bag. 'And we come bearing both alcoholic and non-alcoholic prosecco and chips.'

'A fine pairing,' I say, laughing as the girls step inside.

Tonight, we are enjoying this apartment and simultaneously commencing Operation: Find Abbey a Date for the Vow Renewal.

We head into the kitchen, where Dee does a stellar job of locating glass flutes in the first cupboard she tries. I put this down less to her knowing her way around a food preparation area and more to her familiarity with a girls' night in.

Whilst Dee pours drinks, Shernette empties two large packets of chips into bowls and for balance, I take a crudité platter and dips (peanut satay included) that I prepared earlier from the refrigerator.

'You can nudge the coffee table in my direction,' Dee says as we bring the food and drinks to sit in my lounge area, which the owners furnished with a U-shaped leather sofa, meaning no matter where you sit, you can enjoy the view.

Having lived in New York since I was in post-grad college, I've seen the skyline more times than I can count, but there's something special about seeing it from the comfort of my own front lounge. 120 Wall Street. 40 Wall Street. One World Trade Center. The Woolworth Building.

'Despite yet another failed day of job hunting today, I have faith that I'll find something to pay my rent here before my six months is up. Because as long as I'm in New York, I don't want to give up this view,' I tell the girls, before dunking a carrot into hummus and sitting back onto the sofa.

'See, I knew you would eventually come round. This is going to be a great exercise for you,' Dee says, pulling the coffee table closer to her side of the U and taking a huge handful of chips from the bowl nearest to her. 'No judgment, please, this is the first hour I've not felt like I'm going to hurl my guts up all day.'

'The nausea isn't letting up, huh?' I ask.

'Apparently most women improve after the first trimester. But I googled this condition called hyperemesis gravidarum and I'm sure I have it. I feel so ill and tired, like, all the time. And that condition might last for the entire pregnancy.'

Shernette and I exchange a quizzical look.

Dee points at me with one hand as she shoves more chips in her mouth with the other. After a round of crunching, she tells me, 'You don't know how awful this is, okay? I'm certain I've got it.' Shernette rolls her eyes and Dee adds, in her direction, 'You too, girlfriend.'

Once her laughter has subsided, Shernette turns to me. 'So no luck with the job hunting?'

I shake my head. 'There's nothing obvious out there. But I've polished my resume, which is equivalent to polishing a turd when you've quit because you screwed up so badly you were about to be fired.'

'But you weren't fired,' Shernette says. 'In fact, I wouldn't have been so certain that it wasn't Greg who messed up those figures. It wouldn't have been the first time. I speak from experience.'

'Honestly, sis, if I quit a job every time I screwed up, I'd have never filmed an episode of anything.'

Though grateful for their support, I did mess up. Fundamentally. I almost cost the firm a client. I can't simply do a TAKE TWO. And if someone was going to be fired, it should have been me. Greg didn't even look at my report, I don't think.

'I'm at the point of thinking I need to email people and ask for coffees, make unsolicited enquiries,' I say, moving the conversation along. 'Of course, if I could decide what I might be suited to for a job, that would be a lot easier.'

Dee grabs another large handful of chips. 'You're not going to work with numbers anymore? You *love* numbers. Totally weird but numbers are your *thing*.'

'Evidently not. I don't know. I always wanted to be a business analyst but I never felt like I'd have the confidence to give guidance to some big business tycoon.'

'But the new you...' Shernette says.

'Is faking it,' I tell her. 'Plus, it would still involve numbers. Urgh, maybe I need a wholescale career change.'

'One that matches your new wardrobe,' Dee adds. 'Cute pants, by the way; who picked those out for you?'

'Oh, maybe someone with an eye for fashion and the flamboyant?'

She's referring to my satin lounge pants that are completely unlike the real me. They're bright and bold jungle print but I have teamed them with a plain black tee to tone them down. 'Anyway, let's get started on the other crisis area in my life, shall we?'

'Yes!' Shernette says, reaching into the large purse by her feet and slipping out her pink laptop. 'Sorry, not yes to the crisis bit but to the fact I am *finally* getting you on a dating site.'

'Pass me the prosecco; I'm going to need it.'

As I top off my glass, Shernette pulls her legs up onto the sofa and crosses them beneath her, opening the laptop. She's getting comfy. This could be a long night.

'Okay.' She creaks her neck, then interlaces and stretches out her fingers in front of her, like she's warming up for an exercise class. 'We have a number of options. There's eHarmony. For a small fee—'

'Nope. I'm not paying for this. I'm expecting my online dating life to be an absolute disaster and I won't pay for the non-privilege.'

The others share a look of playful irritation. I know there's a sense of real exasperation in their expressions but truly, I'm not expecting to be good at dating.

'I don't even *want* to date,' I say defensively. 'I'm a walking anti-relationship advertisement right now. If it wasn't for the fact Andrew will be at the vows and now we know he'll be bold enough to bring a date...'

I take a large mouthful of prosecco and gulp the bubbles.

'We are where we are,' Shernette tells me, as if I'm a client in a financials meeting she's hosting. 'If you're not paying, that rules out The League, Elite Singles and Zoosk. Though I will say, the fee makes you less likely to find a total waster who's looking for just sex.'

'I don't want a total waster and I'm definitely not looking for a hook-up, but I really do need an *okay* date. Someone normal. Someone I can introduce to family and friends, turn up to this party with, then be done with it.'

'Well, we have Bumble, Hinge and of course Tinder. Hinge is

kind of like the anti-Tinder, though. More of a serious relationship option.'

I inhale deeply. 'Bumble and Tinder it is, then.'

'They are the most likely hook-up sites,' Dee says, dipping her hand in the bowl again – atta girl. 'But, on the contrary to your views, I think a good shag might lighten you up.'

Despite myself, I laugh and bury my face in my hands. 'What am I doing?'

'Moving on, big sis, moving on,' Dee says, giving me the weather, rather than the news, as chewed chips fly from her mouth when she speaks.

'You're gross, Dee.'

'We're blood, so you're stuck with me.'

In less than an hour, Dee and Shernette have extended my fake persona so that my online profile reads: Abbey Mitchell, actress between roles (on account of Dee telling me it's legitimate to be unemployed when you're in the arts), with a swish Brooklyn apartment.

My likes are hiking (true), shopping (I didn't *hate* getting my new wardrobe), movies and theatre (on account of the new profession but also genuinely true) and prosecco (which I hope doesn't make me sound like a goodtime girl).

My dislikes are cats (on account of cat-loving-men freaking me out), poor cleanliness (just leave the bathroom how you would like to find it, that's all I'm asking) and sports fanatics (they don't have to have *zero* interest but some conversation during the football has to be acceptable).

During the hour, I've learned the terms bread crumbing, catch and release, haunting, orbiting and zombie-ing.

My. Head. Is. About. To. Explode. It's going to take me three weeks and one day to learn the language of online dating, let alone find a suitable date for my parents' bash.

In fact, my head is pounding, banging, rhythmically, like the continual beating of a drum and exactly like the noise pollution that has just started from upstairs, again.

I spring up from the sofa, courtesy of three glasses of prosecco.

'This!' I declare, pointing to the ceiling. 'This is the constant banging I'm talking about. What the hell is he doing up there?'

'Oh yeah,' Dee says, as if it's hard to hear the absolute BOOM of each sound. 'I'm not convinced that *is* 8B having sex.'

'Wow, that really is loud,' Shernette adds.

We're all staring at the ceiling. Listening. Considering what the heck the noise could be, when my alcohol-induced low inhibitions-cum-confidence comes over me.

'Right, that's it, I'm going up there. I didn't move into this apartment block to have an ex and his new bit blindsiding me. And I certainly didn't move in expecting to have a nuisance neighbor practically coming through the roof on a Friday night.' I locate my furry slipper boots and start pulling them on, so angry my foot misses the hole one time, two times, then on the third attempt, I slam my foot into the slipper. 'Enough is enough.' I storm toward the front door. 'This is supposed to be my dream fecking apartment!'

'Wait for us!' Dee shouts.

Shernette hurries behind her. 'We aren't missing a showdown with hot stuff. Not for the world!'

With my girls hot on my heels, I stomp my fluffy boots to the elevator.

12

TED

Having started the morning well, my call with Mel obliterated my Friday plans. I can't create an AI persona whilst feeling devoid of any personality myself.

I feel as if I've raced through almost every stage of grief today, then rinsed and repeated, over and over. I've felt shock, denial, anger, bargaining and waves of sadness.

Shock. Unbelievably, I've felt shock. I thought I was all shocked out after walking in on Fleur and Roman mid-act. But somehow, finding out the inevitable, that tongues have started wagging, took me by surprise. I'm not sure how long I thought I could keep the whole sordid thing under wraps for, but I thought I'd at least have more control over the release of the information.

Denial. From believing the entire thing must be some kind of mistake, to disbelieving that Roman would help spread the rumors. From believing Fleur still loves me, that she's been lured into a false sense of love by Roman's charm and cunning, to finding it completely unfathomable that Roman might have concocted this whole thing as a way of forcing me to IPO our business.

Anger. I'm really fucking angry. I throw the baseball in my hand against the lounge wall, again. I've been sitting on the sofa for lack of anything better to do, tossing a baseball over and over.

Bargaining. Telling myself that if I could be more confident, more charming, a little less Ted and a lot more Roman and Michael, that Fleur might still love me, or that maybe I could wake up and everything would be back to where it was just over a week ago.

Is that enough of a backward travel? One week? When did the affair start? How long has it been going on? Did I notice changes between Fleur and me? When did they start? Between my work and her modelling career, we spend so much time apart, I just don't remember when we were last in a really great place. Not that we weren't; I just can't place us together, laughing, smiling, making love.

I pound the ball at the wall and bend forward to retrieve it from the floor where it lands, not bouncing back far enough for me to catch it.

Stupid ball. Stupid throw. Stupid fucking everything.

Thud. Thud. Thud.

Either my head is throbbing or someone is hammering on the door to the apartment.

'Answer this door right now, Mike!'

Thud. Thud.

Abbey from downstairs?

Taking the ball with me, I peel my ass off the sofa and pad barefoot to the door.

Sure enough…

'Abbey.'

Her hair is tied messily into a ponytail. She isn't wearing make-up. Her lounge bottoms are outrageously vivacious but they hug her hips in a way that's subtly sexy. Her black tee fits everywhere it touches her top half. For a moment, my mind blanks. I see nothing but the relaxed yet crazily alluring woman in front of me.

Then I see her big fluffy boot slippers. My mouth betrays my grumpy mood as I feel myself smirk.

'Mike.' Her scowl is melodramatic and she plants her hands on her hips, really overplaying the part of a madwoman.

I'm not sure why but I find myself leaning into the door frame, a move which shifts my position such that I see Abbey has brought a girl gang with her. I hold up a hand, aloof, as I say, 'Ladies.'

Ha, the Mike Thomas version of me is pretty cool.

The other women both smile. One of them twinkles her fingers at me.

The move, or the exchange, has the result of angering Abbey, who is already irate for some reason. This woman is certifiably, off the charts, nuts. One minute she's sobbing into a hazelnut chocolate spread calzone; the next she's chasing me down in our apartment block, again.

In a move I've seen on my brother, a move that has made me even more pissed with him when he's done it to me mid-argument, I casually toss the baseball I'm holding and catch it one-handed.

That would have been horribly embarrassing if I'd dropped it. Douche risk to take. Mental note made.

But it seems to have the desired effect because with her next inhale, Abbey's nose widens like a dragon lady's. 'I don't care if you're some major league baseball player with a swanky penthouse apartment or just some... some dweeby jackass. If you don't stop banging and banging and goddamn banging every night, I'm going to take a baseball bat and shove it up your stupid, pigheaded ass.'

'Whoa, calm yourself, Fluffy Boots. What are you talking ab—'

Oh. The ball. Bouncing the ball off the wall.

Oh God, this is embarrassing. I've been banging a ball off a wall because I'm a loser from Loserville, whose international model girlfriend has screwed his best friend and now his business is at risk and he's hiding out in his brother's apartment, bouncing baseballs off a wall repeatedly because he has nothing better to do.

Except... Abbey thinks I'm Mike and Mike doesn't do relationships or break-ups. And hell, I can finally understand why.

'I'm just getting my practice in, babes.' I toss the ball in the air and catch it again – I must stop this; next time, I'll drop it.

'By doing what?' She throws her hands up in frustration.

Her two girls seem to have stepped closer, as if they're keen to know the answer to the question. As if they've been talking about it and— Wait, do they think I've been banging something or someone?

Ha, ha, ha, ha, ha. Classic.

Before I can answer the question, the elevator doors open to my floor and a group of five women, dressed like they're going to one of New York's hottest clubs, make high-heeled strides toward my – *Mike's* – apartment.

One very lavish woman seems to be leading the pack. Her legs go on for days, she smells like she's bathed in expensive perfume, and she might have been sewn into the dress she's wearing.

'Hi, honey,' she says, striding right by Abbey and leaning into me, holding my cheeks and pressing her painted red lips to mine. 'We're your Friday night, courtesy of your brother.'

She walks right by me, into the apartment, and the four equally made-up women follow her lead. *What the—?*

One of Fluffy Boots' friends moves closer to the door. 'I'm Dee, by the way,' she says. 'Abbey's sister.'

I lift my chin like a guy out of *90210* might do and say, 'Hey.' I keep my tone low. Masculine.

'Looks like you're having a party tonight,' Dee says.

'Looks like it.' *Am I?*

The elevator doors ping again and seven, no eight, more people get out. All dressed to party. This time a mix of guys and girls. The guys are pretty stacked, which is equivalent to a secret password into my brother's pad. I think I recognize one of them from a night out with my brother but I can't be sure. The way he thumps me on my shoulder as he heads by, though, tells me he recognizes me, too.

'Where's the free booze?' another guy says as he makes his way inside.

Of course, my brother has bribed people to come and keep me company with free booze.

'Hit up the refrigerator,' I call. I've zero idea whether that sounded cool. It was supposed to.

Music starts blaring through the apartment speakers and the next person to walk past me is Dee, Abbey's sister.

'Thanks for the invitation,' she says, patting my chest on her way inside.

Abbey and the other girl exchange looks, before the other girl follows Dee's lead and tells me her name is Shernette, passing by with a smile. That's more manners than my brother's cronies have shown.

One more elevator's worth of people arrive.

What is my brother thinking?

I really want to get the gigantic goof on the phone but right now, I'm trying to play the role of a chillaxed guy who totally knows how to host a party. I'm down with it. I'm... *street*? Whatever, I do this all the time, *obvs*.

'You coming in, Fluffy Boots?'

Abbey glances inside, to the loud mass of people, then looks me in the eye. Her anger seems to subside into something else, something less — resignation, maybe. She doesn't want to be here. She might be a goodtime girl usually, but tonight, she clearly wanted a quiet night in with her sister, her friend and her fluffy boots.

That makes two of us. I was perfectly content to sit and wallow alone with my thoughts. Now I have hours of drunken partygoers to listen to.

I incline my head, gesturing for Abbey to come inside.

'I'm wearing lounge pants,' she shouts above the music.

'I can see that. Come on.'

It's not like my shorts and hoodie combo are screaming 'party' either. I reach out to place a hand on her shoulder. I don't know why, for moral support perhaps. But she moves and my hand winds up on the bare skin of the nape of her neck.

Her eyes dart to mine and I expect to be yelled at for touching her. But her mouth opens without sound, exquisite, gold-flecked eyes wide. She has a smattering of freckles across her nose that spills onto her cheeks.

And she's really close to me. So near I can smell coconut in her hair. Without conscious thought, I inhale and am greeted with the scent of holidays. The calm of the ocean. The warmth of the sun. A mind devoid of stress. I almost forget there's a party kicking off right behind us.

A party. People. Mike's house. Mike who is me but isn't. Abbey who thinks I am Mike. And for some reason, I really don't want her to find out that I'm Ted, the tech guy, the non-athlete. That I'm Peter Parker, not Spiderman.

I could really use one of those free beers.

'Let's get a beer, Fluffy Boots.'

That breaks the peace we held for a fleeting moment. Her glower returns and her hands are back on her hips.

'Don't call me Fluffy Boots!'

'It beats Big Panties,' I tell her, laughing as her mouth forms a really big O.

I take two beers from the refrigerator and flip off the tops with an opener someone has helpfully found and left lying on the benchtop.

As I hand a bottle to Abbey, my cellphone rings.

About time, big brother.

13

ABBEY

'How do you know Mike?'

The woman who asks the question seems to come out of nowhere. As soon as Mike has gone, her proximity to me increases until she's practically on top of me.

I'm chastising myself but can't help thinking: *she smells expensive but looks cheap*. First, that's nasty and judgy and unnecessary. Secondly, she looks cheap in a way that probably cost a small fortune. She's wearing a black leather mini-dress and what I can only describe as hooker sandals, strapped from her ankles to her thighs.

How long must it take to put those things on? Wouldn't it be easier to just buy a pair of fishnet stockings?

I also can't help noticing the way her extremely pert breasts appear to defy gravity, as if she's managed to fit bones in the dress, as well as her body.

Would it be weird to ask her to give me a twirl so I can understand this feat of engineering?

She looks hot. Smoking hot. And the way she looks fits perfectly well with Mike's boastful attitude. His supercilious smirk. The way he speaks as if everything he has to say is important.

Yes, this woman's get-up could be described as Female Mike.

She leans her head to one side, letting me know that she's waiting for my answer.

'Ah I don't, not really. We're neighbors. I've recently moved in.'

'Ohhhhh.' With a wine glass in her hand, she gestures up and down the length of my body. 'This makes sense now. Do you need to borrow sugar or something?'

She laughs, as if her insult was the best joke ever.

I'll have her know these are my new capsule wardrobe lounge pants.

Any ounce of guilt I felt for stereotyping or objectifying her appearance has dissolved into my well of *what the hell am I doing here?* thoughts.

'Excuse me,' I say, spotting Dee and Shernette in a group of people by the lounge windows. I'm momentarily struck again by how much more impressive the view is from just one floor up.

I smile at the men and women in the group and wait for a break in the conversation, then I ask Dee, 'Are you ready?' And to Shernette, 'Can we leave? Please?'

'Why? We've not even been here fifteen minutes,' Shernette asks, surprising me. I was sure she'd be on my side in this. But I notice the subtle glance she throws to one of the guys she's been chatting with and I understand why she wants to stay.

'Dee?' I ask, pleading.

My sister places her hands on my shoulders. 'Abbey, I love you. I also fully understand why you hate men right now. But I saw the way Mike checked you out at the door and I think he's under your skin a little bit.'

'He is. Absolutely. Because he's one bang on my ceiling away from a 911 nuisance call.'

Dee rolls her eyes. 'We think...' She takes one of her hands off my shoulder and puts it on Shernette's. 'That the best way to get over Andrew is to spend time with another guy. I'm not saying you have to have sex with Mike – even though I think you should – but you are trying to find a date and there's a room full of guys here, be it a very hot pro-athlete or some other guy.'

'You're Miss In The Right Place At The Right Time,' Shernette adds.

I glance across my shoulder to see Mike heading back into the kitchen. He shoves his cell phone into the back pocket of his shorts and drags a hand through his messy hair. He wasn't expecting guests, I think. In fact, he looks like he wants to be at a party as much as I do.

Why would his brother send guests to his house?

He looks up and catches my eye.

'He is handsome,' I say aloud, not meaning to do so.

'Atta girl,' Shernette says.

My legs seem to be carrying me to the kitchen without my brain's instruction.

'Is your brother big on surprises?' I ask Mike.

He considers me. Unreadable. Then opens the refrigerator and flips the top off two more bottles of beer.

'Another beer, 7B?'

I take the full bottle and tap mine to his with a *ting*.

'In answer to your question.' He casually leans back against the countertop. 'My brother likes to think he knows what's best for me.'

'Partying?'

He shrugs. 'Looks like it, doesn't it?'

There's another knock on the door and the woman who was questioning me earlier goes to answer, as if this is her place. I wonder how many of these women feel like they have a stake in this apartment.

Another wave of people comes inside and they start navigating around Mike and me, helping themselves to drinks.

'You strike me as someone who can throw his own parties.' I look around and see Dee and Shernette still happily in conversations. Some people have started to dance on the balcony. The lights have been dimmed and there's a random disco ball rotating on a side table. It's like college but with older faces and more expensive alcohol.

'Where is your brother?'

'San Francisco.'

'Is that where you're based, when you're not here?'

'What makes you say that?'

Oops. Confession time.

'I've been told you play for the San Francisco Giants.'

He raises an eyebrow. 'You've been told or you've been doing internet research on me?'

Embarrassing. 'I've been doing due diligence on my nuisance neighbor. I'd like to know who I'm going to have to call the cops on.'

He laughs and I get a mini buzz from his finding me amusing. I can be funny. I *am* funny. People just don't often find me as funny as I find myself. Their problem.

Wow, three proseccos and a beer are going to my head.

'I am based in San Francisco, as it happens. I'm here temporarily.'

'How temporary is temporarily? I mean, when will I be relieved of the relentless banging above my apartment?'

He smiles into his beer bottle, then says, 'My banging balls will be going home soon.'

Banging balls? Urgh. Crass. I turn to gesture around the

room of increasingly rowdy people. 'Your fans will be devastated.' As I look around, I'm reminded of the shelved, signed baseballs around the lounge and the proverbial penny drops – he throws the balls off the floor, or the wall, or somewhere. Banging balls.

His eyes narrow on me as I silently draw this conclusion. 'You should be careful typecasting, Fluffy Boots. You might find your assumptions lead you down some wrong rabbit holes.'

'Hmm, well, my days of trusting have been curtailed recently.'

He nods, and seems sincere when he tells me, 'I can understand that.'

Shifting so that he's leaning forward on the bench top and watching the room of people alongside me, he asks, 'How about you? Is New York home? I think I can hear a Canadian accent?'

'New York has been home for more than four years. I'm originally from a small town on the edge of Banff National Park.'

'Do you ski?'

'Yes. And I board. But I prefer hiking to both.'

'Same.'

'Really? You seem like a guy who likes fast sports to me.'

'Again with the typecasting. I enjoy the adrenaline rush but you can't take in your surroundings when you're concentrating on flying down a mountain. I like bouldering, hiking, being outdoors.'

'Being one with nature? Finding yourself?' I tease. But the truth is, that's my favorite thing about hiking. Rolling mountains, drifting clouds, fluttering butterflies, breathing in clean air. Forgetting life below for a few hours.

I expect him to retort playfully but he doesn't. Instead, he continues to stare at the room in front of us and then says, 'Life can be noisy sometimes. It's nice to escape. To do something with no competition. No winners and losers.'

Of course, his job is all about winning and losing. Who's the best, the fastest, the strongest. I nod.

'Speaking of which,' he says, patting his hands down on the counter as if he's had an epiphany. 'I think my brother has a VR game box. Fancy it?'

I finish my beer, which seems to have made me brave or stupid, deciding to take on a Major League Baseball player.

'No baseball,' I say. 'And if I win, you have to quit banging balls every night.'

That smirk is back. He's clearly a fan of a crude innuendo. 'And if I win?'

'What do you want?'

He tuts as he ponders. 'You have to help me with the clean up tomorrow morning.'

I shrug. 'Fine. You're on because I won't lose.'

In truth, I might lose. I've never played a virtual reality game – I wore a VR headset once in a museum but that's my lot.

Nevertheless, the possibility of stopping that incessant noise every day is worth the risk of clearing up a few beer bottles. After all, it's the reason I got roped into being at this party in my lounge pants and slippers, so it's worth a shot.

'You're on.' He holds out his fist and I bump mine against it. 'Give me five minutes to set us up.'

It's only when I'm in the bathroom, staring into the mirror above the five-star, hotel-sized his and hers sinks, that I realize I'm smiling. For an obnoxious guy, he's a decent distraction.

After washing my hands, I rub some life into my make-up free cheeks and lips, then head into the lounge, where Mike is waiting with two VR headsets.

This was a mistake. He's tall and broad, and muscly and obviously good at sport. Fingers crossed the universe will shine down on this underdog.

'Did you give yourself a little pep talk?' Mike asks, holding up a headset and two hand pieces.

'Like I need one,' I tell him with confidence I do not feel. I've always been a loner when it comes to sports and working out. Coordination isn't my forte.

The large-screen television nestled into the lounge wall unit is displaying a snowboarding game.

Mike holds out the hand pieces, then steps to me and places the headset over my eyes, adjusting the strap beneath my hair tie.

I can't see him but I feel the size and heat of his body, his proximity overwhelming in a way that's more welcome than claustrophobic. His scent is subtle but manly. Like he's wearing a cologne he's had on all day and it's mixed with outdoors. It's distinctive, and it's all around me.

With my eyes covered and a handsome man pressed against me, I feel disoriented in the best way. I have momentarily expended with reality.

Suddenly unsteady on my feet, I reach out on reflex for the stability of his body. His torso is firm; it fills the sensitive skin of my bare hands, makes my fingertips fold into him.

'You're good to go.' His voice seems to break, or do I imagine that because there's a tightness in my own throat? 'Let me set myself up.'

His heat is gone and I'm left looking into the depths of a snowy mountain range. I can see the hands of my virtual persona, covered in purple ski gloves. I look down and find virtual me peering down what looks like a slalom run. Poles and flags highlight a path to a distant finish line, dotted between protruding rocks and pine, spruce, aspen and fir trees.

Something happens on the screen and we're switched into dual player mode, though it looks like we'll be racing one at a time – only my player looks set to snowboard, with Mike's an onlooker.

'Is now a good time to tell you I've never done this?' I ask.

'You said you can board. There'll be no novice or gender handicaps, Fluffy Boots.'

Grrrrr. I want to beat him so bad.

'You need to move the cursor with your hand to start.'

I do as my instructor tells me and I'm counted down on screen – three, two, one. I'm off!

Leaning my body to the right, I narrowly miss a slalom pole. I shift left, right, left. Sugar, this is fast!

A rock. Where did that come from?

Oh no, oh no!

Virtual me flies straight over the rock. I'm in the air and I shouldn't be. I reach down with my hand, as if to grab the front of my snowboard, but—

'Sugar and pies and berries!' I hit smack into a pine tree.

The screen changes so that I can see real me, in my VR goggles, and real Mike, in his goggles. He's folded forward, guffawing at my collision.

'You say you've snowboarded before?' He can barely draw breath.

'Every winter and spring!' I say, accidentally stomping my foot.

My words or my actions or the combination make Mike laugh harder.

'Well, you show me how it's done, ass-wipe!'

He's still laughing but can at least now stand up straight. 'Okay, let me see here. It's been a long time since I've boarded and I've never done it through VR.'

'Is this a hustle to get me to clean tomorrow?'

'Let's see, shall we?'

I can't see his face because the screen has now been taken over by the slalom hill and virtual Mike.

Three, two, one, the screen flashes. And he's off!

He leans right but runs straight into the first slalom pole. He leans left and makes it around the next one, then the next. He crashes into the fourth. He misses the rock I flew over. This *is* a hustle. Then he wallops right into the next slalom pole and falls into the snow, rolling like a sausage through the next pole until he comes to a stop.

Now it's my turn to laugh.

'Definitely not a hustle.'

'I made it further than you,' he says petulantly. Words which match the look on his face as he appears on screen, the real him, wearing his VR eye mask.

'Not this time,' I tell him as I reset for the next run.

I've got it this time. I know how fast the game is and I'm just going to treat it like January on the slopes in Banff. I clear my head of everything except the digital course and my posture on my imaginary board.

Three. Two. One.

I lean right. *Yes!*

Left. *Yes!*

Right. *Swish.* Left. *Swish.* Round the rock. *Come on!*

One, three, four quick succession, slalom poles. There's a ramp. I take a deep breath (needless, since the game is supposed to be fun and all), then bend my knees, looking down to the board and watching my character pick up speed on the screen.

I take flight, I'm in the air and I momentarily see myself on the slopes at home. The sun in the sky, wind in my face. I'm flying, free.

Leaning forward, I take hold of the front of my board. I'm going in for a 1080.

Using the virtual hand pieces, I rotate to the side and virtual me turns 360. Keep going, VR me! Imaginary Abbey turns through another 360. That's 720! I keep my hands twisting to the side, and I clear another 270 degrees.

It's not quite 1080, so I land facing the side, but with a quick correction, I'm heading back down the hill, avoiding a tree, missing pop-up rocks and making my way through another three slalom poles. Down the slope, the finish line appears. Real me leans forward and virtual me picks up speed, smashing through the finish line.

Both me and virtual Abbey are holding up our arms, squealing with delight.

The screen view through my headset changes so that I can see Mike, who I think is looking ever so slightly impressed, but it's hard to tell with his headset on, and for sure his expression is laced with stubborn huffiness too, as he quickly moves the cursor to instigate his next turn at the game.

'Who's hustling who now?' he asks.

Three, two, one. He makes the first pole, the second pole. He avoids the rocks.

He's going well.

Clearly he isn't going to take the side route and avoid the jump, not when I took the ski ramp.

I see virtual Mike, leaning into his board, picking up speed on the down slope. Then he's on the ramp and he's in flight.

Imaginary Mike grips the front of his board. He's going to try a 1080. His desperation to beat me is hilarious and, unexpectedly, since I would usually shy away from competition and conflict, real Abbey is desperate to see real Mike and his arrogance fail.

He turns through 360. Through 720.

But oh! He's lost speed.

He lands after a 900 degree turn and he's facing backward down the slope.

Oh boy! He faceplants and crashes ass first into a fir tree.

'Ouch!' I squeal, both at digital Mike's epic fall and the ache in my ribs from my torso-wrecking laughter. I'm crouched forward over my knees, trying badly not to pee my panties.

I lift off my VR headset and look up to see a stone-faced Mike, waving his headset at me. 'You said you haven't played VR before,' he gripes.

The severity of his expression has me belly laughing to the extent I have to tell him to hold that thought so I can run to the toilet to wee.

When I return to the lounge, he's set up a climbing game and is holding out my VR headset and hand pieces for me to take.

'I hope you didn't wet your big panties, Abbey. That would be embarrassing.'

I grab the gaming pieces from him. 'More embarrassing than face planting and ass crashing into a tree?'

Though he glowers, there's a definite joviality about his features. 'Put your headset on and put your betting terms where your mouth is, Fluffy Boots.'

'You get fussy when you're losing, Mr Pro Athlete.' My playful pout is perceived, as intended, as good-natured banter, but it's me who ends up put in my place when Mike flashes me a smile. Not a smirk, not a grin, just a smile. A smile that draws on his lips, lifts his cheeks, flashes his teeth and dances in his eyes. It's the kind of smile that lights sparklers in my tummy and forces an almost reflexive smile from me.

The girls are right; he's really rather beautiful.

It feels like we're caught in a moment. That moment in a cheesy romcom movie, when the characters fall for each other but don't know it. Cue slow motion shots and romantic music, the world around the characters fading into a background blur, as if the only two people in the fictional world who exist are Him and Her.

But that's not us. Mike is obnoxious, has a different woman on his arm at every red-carpet event (as demonstrated by Google), and he's a gargantuan noise pollutant.

'It's on,' I tell him, remembering what I stand to gain by beating him – blissful quiet in my short-term expensive let.

'Let's climb,' he says, roughly pulling on his headset. 'This apartment won't clean itself.'

14

TED

The sound of hammering on the front door infiltrates my dreams, the contents of which escape me as soon as I open my eyes to the sun beaming in through the windows, where I forgot to close the blackout blinds last night. I wasn't drunk when I came to bed but I was whacked, after hours of competing with Abbey on the VR gamer.

The last of Mike's party guests – the party at which he did not make an appearance and I was apparently host – left in the early hours of the morning.

I check my smart watch and see it's after nine. I'm an early riser, so this is a rare occurrence.

The thumping on the door is back, as I slowly bring my legs around to the edge of the bed, wearing my boxer briefs. *Who is knocking on the door and how did they get here?*

I yawn, stretch and rise from the bed, realizing I've had a solid night's sleep. The best sleep I've had since my fiancée ripped out my heart and set it alight in a trash can...

Padding through the apartment, I hear another round of pounding.

Who is this feisty in the morning?

My hands are already opening the door when it dawns on me...

'Abbey.' That's right, I won last night. It was a narrow victory but a victory nonetheless.

'Don't you look dreamy?' she says sarcastically, telling me exactly how sleepy and untidy my face and hair must look. And my—

'Sorry, I'll go get some clothes.' I look her up and down. Her short shorts, her string vest and... 'Rubber gloves?'

She holds up her yellow-covered hands. 'We might not be in a pandemic anymore but I don't need to fondle the beer bottles of your Friday-night crew.'

'You don't have a spare pair of those, do you? If my brother sent them round, those guys could be carrying all sorts of infestations.'

She puffs out a short laugh. Then her eyes very fleetingly run the length of my body.

'Did you just check me out?' I ask, channeling my brother, except he'd turn it into some sort of cheesy pick-up line and I just don't have enough pizazz for that.

She quickly drags her eyes back to mine, and her cheeks pinken. 'Only to note that you're in my way. Can we get on with this, please? I have places to go, people to see and all that.'

I step aside and let her in, now realizing just how much of a mess the apartment looks. Whilst Abbey and I were being antisocial last night, only engaging in the virtual world, beer bottles and pizza boxes were being scattered around almost every surface. It's a shame the cleaners don't come on Saturdays.

'I'll go grab a top,' I say.

'Erm, yes, please. We don't need any distractions. We've got our work cut out for us here.'

I'm walking away when her words land. 'Are you calling me a distraction?'

Mike would be proud. If this wasn't Abbey from 7B, annoying and kind of angry, I'd sound like I'm flirting. Something Mike and Roman have confirmed I am appalling at.

She rolls her eyes and shoos me with a wave of her fingers, making me chuckle. I head upstairs for a shirt.

'I'm sad to see you didn't turn up in your big panties and fluffy boots, 7B,' I shout down from the mezzanine level.

'They're for one week of every month, joker.'

I chortle all the way to my temporary wardrobe.

When I come back into the lounge, Abbey has made two coffees and is scrolling through her phone. Her hair is contained in a disorderly yet pretty bundle at the nape of her neck, exposing pale, flawless skin all the way down to beneath her shoulders.

Fleur was always tanned, be it from the sun or from a bottle. Her skin was punctuated with defined bones. Chiseled, she called herself. I guess that got her a lot of work as a model. She's beautiful. Photographed, she is truly a work of art. Unreal. Untouchable.

She proverbially knocked me off my feet the first time she showed an interest in me at Mike's celebrity birthday bash in San Francisco. It was star-studded and showy, the kind of thing I really dislike. I would have much preferred taking my brother for a celebratory beer. Fleur loosely knew a woman Mike is friends with and the two of them came along. Her friend got flirty with Mike. Roman found someone he knew to talk to. Then Fleur and I were kissing.

In the lounge, 'Fireflies' by Owl City is playing through Abbey's phone. I like this song. And I also like how Abbey's hips are wiggling and her shoulders are bopping to the beat. She's happy and somehow, that rubs off on me, too. I feel light-hearted as I head over to the coffee and the woman pulling back on her yellow gloves.

'You can play music through the apartment's surround,' I tell her, making her jump, as if she forgot I was in the building.

'Finally, you're decent,' she says, gesturing to my shorts and T-shirt. 'It's loud enough through my phone. As you're well aware, I don't like loud noises disturbing the peace.'

I roll my eyes. I may have ultimately won the game-off last night, impressing even myself with my virtual bouldering, but I have taken on board her complaints and will try to stop the absentminded banging of Mike's baseballs on the walls.

'Is one of those for me?' I ask, nodding in the direction of the two steaming cups of coffee.

'Yep. I wasn't sure how you like it, so you'll have to take it as it comes.'

'Which is?'

She shakes a black trash bag, opening it out, followed by three more. 'Something akin to a white americano. Unless you have an allergy or intolerance?'

There's panic in her voice, like she's terrified of having done something wrong.

I pick up the cup and take a gulp. 'It's perfect. Thank you.'

'Phew. I don't have an EpiPen and I definitely don't want to wind up cleaning alone.'

'My anaphylaxis is your secondary concern, then.'

'Anaphylactic shock probably would have stopped your ignorant banging sooner than me being forced to clean up your stinking apartment from your dirty friends.' Ah, she's back, the crabby as hell, stuck-up Abbey. She crouches down to pick up three of the trash bags, holding out two for me to take. 'Two each. Keep the recycling separate. We can save the planet one glass bottle at a time.'

'If we were being very eco-friendly, there'd have been a beer keg and reusable cups.'

She shrugs. 'I didn't throw the party, I just got sucked into it.'

As soon as I relieve her of two bags, she starts picking up mess from the kitchen floor. 'Your guests were animals.'

I had better start helping because she's right, it's as if my brother rounded up the filthiest of his New York friends and sent them here last night. I can also sense the genuine anger in her voice – she's clearly here to stay true to her word and nothing more.

I have all good intentions but... my phone starts to ring.

'Yo yo, little bro. How was the party?' My phone has defaulted to the surround speakers in the apartment. I make to switch the sound to come through the phone but not before Mike continues. 'A nice distraction? I hear I have a new neighbor and given who told me and the tone of her telling, I'm assuming she's a looker—'

'Shit.' I thumb the screen of my phone, switching my brother to my ear. 'Sorry, I'll be back in a minute,' I tell Abbey. If looks could kill, I'd be a very, very dead man right now.

'Whoa, not alone. Yes, little bro! I like your style,' Mike says into my ear.

Glancing back, horrified and trying to determine how much of that Abbey heard, I move into the downstairs bathroom, where I find a half drank glass of wine – at least I hope it's wine – and, more disturbingly, a pair of boxer briefs that aren't mine hanging on the toilet-roll holder.

'Jesus. You should know your friends are disgusting. Like, really grim, dude.'

'They can be,' he says, without a care in his voice. 'I hope the one you still have in my apartment this morning wasn't one of the *really* dirty ones.'

'God, Mike, come on. I literally broke up with Fleur just over a week ago.'

'Good riddance.'

'She wasn't just some girl, Mike; she was the woman I was going to marry.'

'A narrow escape, if you ask me.'

His tone is so astonishingly flippant, I've half a mind to hang up. Catching sight of myself in the over-sink mirror, I see my irritation. I also see how exhausted I look. Understandable really. And how utterly shambolic my bed-hair looks. Less acceptable.

'So, who is she?'

'Who's who?' I ask, dampening my hands and trying to dampen the cowlick that's worse than even Alfalfa's from *The Little Rascals*.

'Duh, the woman in my apartment?' Mike says, with mock-stupidity that suits him for real.

'That's just Abbey from downstairs. She's helping me clean up.'

'She wants a piece of you.'

'What?'

'Who in their right mind helps a guy clean up after a party?'

'Abbey. She lost a bet. And believe me, if she wants a piece of me, it's my head. She wants to murder me this morning. Most times, come to think of it.'

'Hold up. Do I know an Abbey from downstairs? Holy crap, is it the new hot neighbor?'

'She's not... Well, she is attractive actually... but not like the girls you know. More stuck up and uppity.' Big panties, fluffy boots and the fact she's cleaning the apartment aside.

'Ah-ha. Well, I'm looking at her Tinder profile right now and I'd say she's tickling my taste buds.'

'Mike, that's invasive, man, come on. Don't—' My phone gives me a notification.

'I've sent you a screenshot. She's an actress; of course she's good looking.'

An actress? She doesn't seem gregarious, like other actors I've come across – admittedly few of them and always loosely known by my brother or Fleur – but she is into designer labels and fake lashes.

She must be good, too. That I can surmise from her being able to afford to live in this apartment block. I wonder what else she makes up. Probably the parts of her I do like – the version of her who felt a bit nerdy last night. The part who doesn't seem interested in a big party and working a room. Then again, why would anyone want to appear nerdy and introvert? Maybe someone who didn't feel herself being at a party in her slippers. Someone who had charged upstairs to confront me without giving thought to what might be going on in my apartment.

People who aren't truthful are pretty much top of my list of dislikes.

The irony is, I'm playing a part with her, too. This confident guy, a Mike type, a Roman type. It's not me at all.

So maybe she does play a role and maybe I'll keep playing mine. After all, don't a pro ball player and an actress make a good match? Better than a computer coder.

In any event, she's helping to clean up the mess this morning and, when she's not being headstrong, she's a distraction I could do with whilst I'm here in New York. Bickering with her takes my mind off real life. And she's completely safe female company because she is so far beyond what would be good for me right now.

At some point, I have to make a decision on my next move and get out of my brother's apartment anyway. Out of Abbey's apartment block. Away from New York.

15

ABBEY

Is this man for real?

Most people would have reneged on last night's bet. He narrowly beat me at bouldering and frankly, I kicked his butt when it came to snowboarding.

But I let a competitive streak I didn't know I have until last night get the better of me.

New Abbey is a menace! I went all or nothing on one final game and Mike won.

Now, he's in the loo on the phone to his brother, and I am solo cleaning the apartment.

Moving over to the large dining table, a focal point in the open space, with the cityscape the focal point of would-be diners, I get increasingly slammy with the pizza crusts, pizza boxes, Coca-Cola cans and beer bottles as I thrust them into my trash bag.

Jarring amongst the chaos, neatly positioned at one head of the table, is a closed Mac and, on top of it, a bundle of papers.

I'm not looking *per se*, I just can't help noticing that the top document is a printed email thread.

Ted,

Thanks for your time on the phone earlier.

I have been through the partnership documents for Vanguard RED Technologies and I have broken down in the attached document the ways in which either you or Roman could instigate an exit from the business.

I'm genuinely sorry to hear things have gone sour. Hopefully I can help make this next step a seamless transition for you.

Let me know when would be a good time to discuss.

Hugh

Hugh Atkins

Head of Corporate Law

Atkins, Turner and Heath

Hearing the bathroom door open startles me and I jump, knocking a used plate from the table, wincing when it breaks into two pieces.

'Gosh, sorry, it slipped,' I tell Mike, fumbling to pick up the pieces from the floor, hoping he didn't catch me reading personal documents.

Although, clearly not personal to him, personal to Ted. Who is Ted and why was Mike looking at his documents?

Never mind, really none of my business. Plus, sports guys must make investments, right? Then, who knows what a pro baseball player gets paid. I could probably retire on as much money.

'Don't worry, I can afford a replacement.' The way he says it is so arrogant, it plays right into the thoughts I was just having – rich and carefree. 'That was my brother on the phone,' he says, as if it wasn't obvious. An apology for leaving me to clean up *his* mess would have been a better use of words.

Exasperated, I end up slapping my hands to my hips and snapping. 'Can we just get on with this? A bet is a bet but I have things to do today.'

He rolls his eyes as he turns his back on me to start picking up trash, but I catch it and there's no mistaking his sarcasm as he asks, 'Like shopping and doing your hair?'

I really want to take the half-eaten slice of pizza I pick up next and wipe the passata all over his smug face. 'Yes, actually. I have a date.' So screw you. I'm desirable and I can be funny and, oh crap, why am I going on a date? I have no idea what dating etiquette is in 2024. In fact, I don't have any idea what the dating etiquette is in any year and I'm absolutely nervous as hell.

'You have a day date?' he asks, turning to face me and dropping a beer bottle into his recycling bag.

'No,' I say, wounded because I know he's thinking a day date is a safe, probably not interested kind of date. 'It's an evening date but I— I've never actually been on a date and I want to be prepared.'

'What, ever?' He's mocking me.

'Is that so shocking?'

'I just— How is that possible?'

'Are you joking right now? I'm here to help you. You don't even know me and you're practically calling me undatable?'

'No, that's not what I—'

'Just because I'm not some kind of man whore.'

'Man whore? Me?'

'Gargh, can we *just* get this over and done with so we can go our separate ways and I don't have to see you anymore?'

'Abbey, look—'

'Ever. Period. Stop. Talking.'

16

ABBEY

I'm almost dressed for my first ever date tonight. I'm meeting the guy, Adam, in a small cocktail hang out in Williamsburg. Apparently it serves great cocktails but not in a pretentious way and it's perfect for a first or early date.

I literally googled the best spots in Brooklyn for a first date. I don't want to be too far from home in case the evening is an absolute car crash.

I have no idea what to expect. For all I know, my date could be fake as heck. A catfish. An axe murderer. I wouldn't have a clue.

Though I do recognize the irony here; *I* am being fake. He thinks I'm an actress. The last time I acted in anything, I was playing the role of a star in a school nativity play. A *star*. I didn't even have a line; I just had to hold out my arms and twinkle my fingers above a stable.

And I'm a truly awful liar.

Oh God, this is going to be horrendous.

Grabbing my phone from my bedside table, I call Dee.

'Hey, it's me again,' I say, bending to buckle the strap of my stiletto shoe. 'Two things: first, are you sure about this outfit? I feel like Lily Collins could probably pull off a miniskirt and T-shirt but I look kind of mismatched, like dressy on the bottom and going to a gym class on the top.'

'It's called trendy, Abbey. The bottom half says date and the top half says you're playing it cool. The perfect match.'

Shoes strapped, I stand and look into my mirrored wardrobes, checking the time on my watch as I do. *I've got to go!* I consider the outfit again and it doesn't really matter what I think of it now because I'm out of time.

Grabbing my keys and throwing them into my purse, I leave the apartment, Dee still on the phone between my ear and shoulder.

'You didn't tell me how your clean-up went with 8B this morning,' she says.

'Awful. Worse than awful. The place was a state. His friends are gross. And *he* spent most of his time on the phone to his brother and drinking coffee.'

'Awful? You hang out one-on-one with the hottest guy you've ever lived beneath and it was *awful*?'

That's hardly a ringing endorsement since I've only lived beneath an old man with too many cats and before that, tequila-obsessed students.

'It's such a shame that his personality doesn't match his face in that case.'

I've made my way down to the foyer and I wiggle my fingers in greeting at the concierge as I leave the building.

'Never mind that. The second and most important reason I called is to make a bit of a strange request. Are there any jobs going on the set of your new series?'

'Do you want to start acting now?' The shock in Dee's voice feels far from a vote of confidence.

'Not exactly.' I hail a cab and watch it swerve to the sidewalk to collect me. I do normally call an Uber but this is a short distance and I only need a cab because these new shoes are so awfully excruciating that just the thought of walking even two kilometers is painful.

'You know how bad of a liar I am, and if I'm going to be going on Tinder dates and having to make out like I'm an actress – thanks to you and Shernette for that, by the way – I just think I need to have at least a clue about what happens on the set of a production. Then I won't be lying, technically.'

I pause our conversation to tell the driver where I'm headed.

'We always need extras,' Dee says. 'Or there's a chance we'll need an extra runner, especially if you're willing to be cheap.'

'Less of the cheap, I'm already wearing a belt in place of a miniskirt.'

'I'm sure I can get you something. Leave it with me.'

Shortly after we end the call, I step out of the cab at the cocktail bar and see a guy who I think is Adam sitting at a table for two, outside on the sidewalk. He most certainly is not the six feet and four inches tall that he felt the need to share on his profile. Which makes me question whether he really does speak five languages, is an art professor, a self-confessed coffee snob, and a gym bunny.

Of course, I am an actress if you believe Tinder, so Adam could in fact be anyone.

He holds up one hand. Despite the peculiar outfit I'm wearing, he seems to recognize me, which is a good start. I enter the restaurant through the front door because there's a fence around the tables outside. It gives me an extra second to calm my nerves.

I shouldn't be this nervous. It's ridiculous. Shernette does this kind of thing all the time, but it's my first date. Admittedly, it's not like I'm losing my virginity, but surely it is a rite of passage, an occasion in a person's romantic life?

The maître d' tells me that my friend is waiting outside. Hearing the word *friend*, I feel my nose scrunch like a bunny rabbit's. This all feels a little bit weird. I don't even know this guy.

Adam is looking my way as I head outside toward our table. His profile pictures certainly displayed him as more angular than he is IRL. He's wearing dark jeans and a white shirt. Appropriate first-date attire, I think, particularly by comparison to my outfit.

He stands when I reach the table and we have an uncomfortable greeting, whereby I think he leans in for a kiss that I don't want. Reflexively, I pull back a little too vehemently and he ends up stroking my arm, as I pat him on the shoulder like a dog.

I'm not entirely sure what to do or say next, until he asks, 'Shall we sit?'

There's a tone of, *Are you for real?* about his words. Hopefully that's in my mind.

'I took the liberty of ordering us a bottle of wine, is that okay?' He sounds like he might genuinely be an art professor. A little... snooty?

I might have preferred a cocktail in a cocktail bar but I suppose it's a sweet gesture, if not a tad gaslighty (a term I learned from reading *Online Dating for Dummies*). 'That's great, thanks.'

We take a seat and I mess around with my purse, not knowing whether I should put it on the table or behind me on the seat. This wouldn't even be a thing if I were out with Dee or Shernette.

Glancing across the sidewalk, I see other people going about their Saturday night food and drinks in the surrounding bars and restaurants. This is a normal thing to be doing on a Saturday evening and as awkward as it is, this is a short-term solution to Andrew turning up to a party with a date and making me look like even more of a fool than I already feel.

'You're a professor of art,' I say, smiling at my date and thinking: *if you weren't wearing shades, I might be able to better judge your character.* 'Do you have a specialism?'

'Dante,' he says.

Internally, I roll my eyes and he begins a cliché monologue about Dante and the passion of his love for Beatrice.

I don't have a drink yet and I already know I would prefer to clean Mike's apartment than be on this date. It's *that* bad.

Our bottle of wine arrives and a waiter pours two glasses. I swear he also gives me a look that says, *I know what you two are going to do later*. But there are two things I know resolutely from having been in this bar for less than ten minutes. The first, I will not put out on a first date. The second, I will never put out to the Dante specialist.

'You're an actress,' Adam says. 'Are you famous?'

Oh boy. How quickly can I drink two glasses of wine and leave?

The conversation continues in the same painstaking manner. Snippets of information, both lies and truth, drip like a broken tap between us. I can almost hear the rhythmic *dink, dink, dink* in my mind.

After very quickly finishing my first glass of wine, I excuse myself to the ladies' room to message my sister and best friend three words:

No, no, no.

This date is up there with the top three most awful experiences of my life, including my final dinner with Andrew and a nasty bout of shingles when I was sitting my finals at college.

Which is why I'm both horrified and aghast when I return to the table to find that my wine glass has been topped off, and

Adam, now with slightly glazed eyes, is giving me a look like a vampire might give to his human prey.

Reluctantly, I take my seat, purely because it would be impolite to leave before at least finishing our drinks, but as I raise my freshly topped off wine glass to my lips, Adam looks at me in a way I think he believes is sultry. He leans across the table, speaking more quietly than he has been up to now.

'What do you say to just skipping straight to the good bit?'

'Excuse me?' I ask, fairly sure I know what he's insinuating.

He presses his hand to mine on the tabletop. 'We both know why we are here and it isn't small talk, is it?'

Ick. All sorts of ick. I slide my hand out from under his and rise from my seat.

What I want to say is: *Adam, I apologize if I've given you the wrong impression of the kind of woman I am. I don't know how, frankly, because the last hour has been truly awful for me, and it must've been something close to painstaking for you, too. I didn't come here with the ambition of taking you to bed, nor will I ever take you to bed. I'll pay for my share of the wine on the way out.*

What I actually say is: exactly what I want to say! Go me!

I tap my card for half the bottle of wine on the way out and would really like to flag a cab but more pressingly, I would really like to get out of those predatory eyes of my horrendous date.

So, I start walking two kilometers home in my toe-breaking shoes.

17

TED

'I know where you are and if you don't start answering my calls, I'm coming to Mike's place to make you speak to me.'

I keep replaying Fleur's voice message in my mind as I pound the streets of Brooklyn, music plugged into my ears, my feet impacting the hard surface with each beat, running as fast as I ever have after already pushing through six miles.

Running is not my favorite pastime, far from it, but hearing Fleur's ultimatum ranks even lower on things I'd like to be doing, and at least running is curbing my anger, rather than creating it.

Would she really come? Would she really fly across the USA to hunt me down? And say what? Sorry, Ted, I didn't mean to have sex with Roman, his dick just kind of fell in?

Who am I kidding? Of the multiple times Fleur has broken up with me for hours or days at a time, she has never said sorry. Not once. She's always turned it on me.

And I've accepted it. Sucked it up. Taken her back. Like an idiot, falling for her time and time again.

My heartrate is skyrocketing again, my watch tells me as much, and I know it's not just from cardio. I can't get the image of the two of them out of my head. I hate it, yet it won't go away. I'm not sure I'll ever be able to erase their betrayal.

I'm so lost in my reverie, I come to an abrupt halt, almost crashing into a very pert bottom sticking up in the air on the sidewalk in front of me, its owner bent forward, unbuckling her shoes.

'Hey, you need to watch where you stop, I almost ran right into—'

The woman turns her head to look at me, hands still on her shoes and wrestling with her buckle. 'Abbey?'

She stands and I can't help but appreciate how she looks in her short skirt and T-shirt, which was casual but has been twisted and knotted at the back to make it fit snug to her waist. She looks nice. She's wearing make-up. Her hair is styled to fall across one shoulder. I'm drawn to her glossed lips – pink, natural, which surprisingly, I'm not used to. Fleur's lips are filled to an unnatural size. Abbey's lips look soft, some people might think inviting.

'Mike.'

That's right, I'm Mike. Mike isn't running because his ex has cheated on him and is threatening to arrive in New York. Mike is just out for a run, casually bumping into a woman who Mike would probably be chatting up already.

Except in my head and heart, I'm not Mike Mike, I'm Ted Mike.

This is getting confusing. What started out as passive acquiescence to a misunderstanding is rapidly becoming an outright farcical lie.

I don't think I want to be lying to Abbey, or anyone for that matter. But, Christ, the real me is an absolute car crash right now and I don't really want to be him either.

I stop my watch from recording my workout, I guess subconsciously resigned to talking to Abbey for a while. Wait, wasn't she supposed to be...?

'What happened to your date?'

She scratches her head and scrunches her nose.

'That good, was it?' I ask, amused by her reaction.

'The guy ordered for me without asking what I might like and one glass of wine in, do you know what he said to me?'

I twist my lip as I think, and I have a feeling I know where this is going.

'Abbey,' she says, in a woman putting on a deep male voice. 'What do you say to just skipping straight to the good bit?'

She laughs the way I heard her laughing in Bloomingdale's, like she means it. It's a good laugh. Surprising, since she's so crabby most of the time. 'By good bit he meant to the sex bit, I presume?'

'Precisely.' She bends back down to her shoes, finally releasing the buckles and taking them off, standing on the dirty sidewalk in bare feet. 'I couldn't stand being in his seedy eyeline long enough to call a cab, so now I'm walking home and these ridiculous shoes my sister convinced me to buy are absolutely tearing shreds off my feet.'

Pah. She says it as if she needs any persuasion to throw a load of money at impractical shoes. Nevertheless, I beg her, 'Please don't put naked feet on this grubby sidewalk. This isn't a west coast beach, this is Brooklyn.'

'I hear you,' she says whilst picking up her sandals and dangling them in one hand. 'But there's no way in hell I'm putting my feet back in these shoes tonight. I'd rather walk across burning coals than put those devils anywhere near my delicate tootsies again.'

'We're still a good way from home. Let's get you a cab.'

She starts walking away from me in the direction of home. 'No one is going to take me this short distance. I'll get a tetanus jab tomorrow.'

She catches me off-guard and I laugh. She'll need one. Then I jog to catch her up. 'Okay, either we can do a newlywed marital threshold-style carry, or you can hop on my back, but there's no way my constitution can stand watching you walk home barefoot.'

She plants her hands on her hips in that way I'm becoming familiar with. But she has stopped, so she must be considering the offer. 'I'm not a child.'

'I wasn't calling you a child, I was calling you a kind of disgusting human being.'

She scowls but looks along the road, considering the distance to our apartment block, then back to me. 'I'll take a piggyback, but you don't have to take me all the way home. I need to make a pitstop for food because my gentlemanly date didn't factor that in, or else he thought I would be the meal.'

Unwittingly humored, I crouch down and she pops up onto my back.

I've already taken a few steps before I realize that my hands are on her bare thighs, which are wrapped around my waist, her skin smooth under my touch. In hindsight, this might have been a bad idea.

'I can't believe you would call me disgusting when your back is completely saturated with sweat and you've just made me squash into it.'

'Yeah well, at least you only need a shower and not antibiotics this way.'

'Definitely the lesser of two great evils,' she says.

On the way home, she's lost in bizarre ramblings about Dante and Beatrice, whilst I am lost in the feel of her arms around my shoulders, her legs gripping my hips, the sound of her voice, all of which is much more pleasant than anything I was thinking about whilst I was running.

We're both so lost in thought that we make it all the way back to our block before remembering we meant to stop for food.

'For your troubles, can I tempt you with an Uber Eats order?' Abbey asks, hopping down to the tiled floor of the foyer of Blake House.

'Can it be a feast? I just went for a run and feel deserving.'

'Deal,' she says, right as her ex walks into the building, stilling her.

'Oh, hey.' He seems to check us both out and maybe realizes her fancy outfit is an odd match for my sweaty sports attire. But actually, she's an actress and I'm a ball player, so...

I sense Abbey's mood shift. Her muscles stiffen. I notice she tugs on the hem of her skirt, despite the move being very subtle.

I don't like it. I can't stand this guy or what he's done to Abbey. I hate the way his presence alone is sparking this reaction in her, making her question whether she's good enough. It's a reaction that thrusts me right back to my own circumstances and Fleur's threat to turn up here, regardless of whether I'm ready for her.

Empathizing completely with Abbey, I drape an arm around her shoulder – playing the part of a protective boyfriend, like I did that night she first met her ex's new woman. I press a kiss to her temple.

'Shall we go order dinner?' I ask.

She glances up to me and there's so much warmth in her look. It's not like the scathing looks she usually gives me. It's the kind of look another man, who isn't mentally all over the place, would kill for.

Then she smiles, and that other man would melt under the sincerity of it.

'Let's go,' she says.

As we turn to walk to the elevator, she slips her hand into mine, our fingers becoming entwined, and she squeezes, as if to thank me. Andrew is still looking at us when we step inside and as we start to ascend, Abbey and I both whisper, 'Dick.'

18

ABBEY

I offer to host our takeout in my apartment, but on the grounds that Mike needs to shower more than I do, we end up in his penthouse.

'Any preferences?' he asks, tapping away on his phone, his elbows resting on the kitchen island as I get us two bottles of beer from the refrigerator and locate the bottle opener.

'Sushi would be good. Do you like sushi?'

'Love it. Any allergies?'

'None.'

'Dislikes?'

'Eel.'

'Same. Mixed nigiri platter, salmon hand roll and chili edamame suit you?'

'Perfect.' I hand him a beer. 'How much do I owe you? I'll transfer.'

He submits our order and sets his phone face down on the countertop, as if he doesn't want to be disturbed. Then he clinks his bottle against mine as I come to sit next to him on a stool. 'My treat.'

'No, I owe you the going rate for eight hundred yards of piggy backing and being my fake boyfriend, again.'

His lips curve up behind his beer bottle. 'What kind of man would I be if I charged a damsel in distress?'

I gasp. 'I was not! I was independently striding toward home. You imposed your white knight-ness on me.'

He raises one brow. 'Are you complaining?'

I raise a leg and bend then flex my red and sore toes. 'I guess not. But you also just pretended to be my boyfriend again downstairs and spared me being tongue-tied and undignified in front of my ex. Just because you're...' I gesture around the luxury pad, beer bottle in hand. '...rich, you don't need to always buy.'

'How about you just say thank you and we call it quits?'

'Thank you. Despite your frosty demeanor and *filthy* house guests, you're kind... sometimes.'

In truth, he doesn't know how helpful him paying is. It's a stark reminder that I need to start bringing money in and not send it exclusively in the other direction.

'A qualified thanks if ever I heard one.' Despite his words, his eyes are shining with good humor. 'Speaking of frosty demeanors, I'm struggling to put you and your ex together. You don't seem alike.'

Maybe that's because you don't know me well enough to know that I'm just a numbers geek and Andrew is in finance, too. I don't say that part.

What I do say is: 'We're both from small town Canada. Our families still live there and they're very close; we were marked for each other from a young age. He ticked boxes on the pre-thirties goals checklist.' When Mike gives me a look of confusion, I explain, 'Career, marriage, babies.'

'You want all that stuff?' Mike asks, his gaze intense, as if I'm being interviewed for a job.

'I did. I do. I don't know anymore. Andrew cheating on me has sent me into unknown territory.' I take a drink of beer, thinking. 'He's forced me to change and I want change, I think. I'm starting to see things differently. I just don't know how yet. Some might say I'm a hot mess.'

I try to smile but the truth in my words means it's tight and forced.

Mike holds up his bottle. 'To being a work in progress.'

We tap bottle heads. 'Not you, you've clearly got it all together.'

He gives me one of those expressions I'm getting used to, as if he's holding back, saying, *if only you knew*.

When he's not being obnoxious, maybe I would like to know.

'Not nearly but that's a story for another day,' he says, putting a fence around that potential thread of conversation. 'I'll tell you something, though: your ex is very jealous of this.' He gestures between us. 'You and me. Us. Our fake relationship.' He pushes off the island, standing up to his full height. 'I'm going to take a shower before the food arrives. Help yourself to whatever.'

'Thank the heavens for that. I could hardly breathe over here from the stench of you.'

He shakes his head but he's taking my joke as it was intended. One side of his mouth curves up, a lopsided grin, a lazy smile. 'The shoe does fit, Cinderella. I can see how you'd be good at your job. You certainly have a bent for theatrics.'

'Theatrics?' *Oh.* 'My job as an actress, you mean.'

I think his skin flushes. 'Ah, yeah. That's what you are, isn't it?'

Well, not really, no. Which means… 'You've read my Tinder profile.' I point to him, my finger near touching his nose.

'My brother sent it to me; it's not like I went searching for it. I'm showering.'

He can't leave quickly enough. He's walking away from me

like Road Runner from dynamite. *Now who's funny?*

I could tell him it isn't true. I probably should. But I didn't write the profile, nor did I invite him and his brother to nit-pick over it and, frankly, if I told him I'm actually a numbers nerd, he might start banging balls again.

I'm not lying; I'm just failing to correct his assumption. He's pretending, too. He's pretending to be my boyfriend in front of Andrew.

I watch him walk upstairs, appreciating two things. One, I am bizarrely pleased that Andrew is jealous. It's his turn. Two, my stomach is still leaping at the sound of *Us*. At the idea of us faking it together.

If only he was serious when he joked about being my superfly date to my parents' vow renewal. Ha, imagine people's faces if I turned up with a pro-baseball player.

Imagine *Andrew's* face.

And I'd be able to stop searching for someone else. An added bonus!

But there's no *actual* chance Mike would agree to something like that. So dating apps it is.

Sighing, I slip down from the chair and visit the baseballs on the shelves in the lounge area, looking at the names of the players who've signed them. I don't know the game but even I recognize some of these names. They bring with them the reality that Mike is famous. Of course he's arrogant; he's adored by thousands of fans. Crazy.

From this new vantage point, I look around the open space and wonder who dressed the home. An interior designer? A woman? I wonder if Mike has ever lived with a woman?

Then I notice the laptop that was on the table this morning. The pages of print out that had been in a neat pile hours ago are now scattered around the table. Remembering the name of the company, and after a cursory glance to the mezzanine level to make sure Mike isn't watching me – I don't know why I feel guilty, it's not like I'm plotting his murder here, I'm just searching a company name – I type Vanguard RED Technologies into a search engine.

Just as my thumb moves toward 'go', there's a knock on the door. *Food!*

The concierge has, as instructed, allowed the delivery guy up to the eighth floor. I set my phone down on the sofa and I'm about to make for the door when Mike appears on the mezzanine level, behind the glass balcony wall.

And *boy* does he appear.

Wet from the shower, his hair just washed and messed, wearing a white towel around his waist. Wearing *only* a white towel. He's leaner than I'd have expected, water shines on toned muscles of his torso, but his firmness is not unapproachable; it's welcoming. Inviting.

'Could you get that?' he asks. 'It'll be the delivery guy.'

Oh God, I'm staring, open mouthed. I've been doing it long enough to become conscious of it.

'Sure,' I croak, my mouth dry.

Reluctantly, I drag my eyes from his body but they meet his gaze and it would take a very dumb man to misunderstand the lust that just washed over me.

What do you know, it turns out weedy *used to be* my thing. Or at least I convinced myself of that because Andrew's physique is exactly that. *Now*, I'm pretty sure ball-player physique is my thing.

'Abbey?'

'The door! On it.' I need to stop drinking around this man. My inhibitions have been lowered, my ogling has been upped and my memory of his self-importance has failed me.

Finally, my feet move in the direction of the door and I drag my focus away from the semi-naked man on the balcony toward the reason I am here – food. After tipping the Uber Eats guy in cash, I go about finding plates and opening the chopsticks that came with the delivery.

'This looks so good,' I say to myself as I remove the lids from the cartons.

'Precisely what the doctor ordered,' Mike says, his hand gently grazing my back as he leans across the island and picks up a piece of salmon nigiri.

What doctor? I think. *Because there is nothing wrong with your body.*

When I turn around, Mike is taking a seat on a stool, thankfully now clothed in shorts and a T-shirt, and my sugar levels are about to return to normal. Ergo, our normal fractious relationship can resume.

I've just put a piece of California roll in my mouth when Mike asks, 'I was thinking in the shower, if your family is still in Canada, then is your parents' party going to be there, too?'

His question is out of the blue and I have a mouth full of food, but I nod.

'And you need a date for it?'

'Mmmhmm,' I manage, still chewing.

'How long would you be out of New York?'

I shrug, finally taking a drink and clearing my mouth. 'A few days. A week, maybe.' Where is he going with this?

'Well, Andrew already thinks that you and I are dating, so wouldn't it be strange for you to turn up with some guy from a dating app?'

My eyes narrow. He's surely not offering? Is he?

'I guess,' I say, tentatively. Hopeful.

'So why don't I do it? No strings. No emotions. No funny business. Just a guy helping a girl out.'

Riiiiiiight. The way pro ball players help out random girls they don't really know or get along with. 'What would be in it for you?'

His eyes narrow and I have the distinct impression I'm missing something. As if there's something he wants to tell me. But all he offers is, 'I've never been to Alberta.'

* * *

Oh. My. Gosh. Are we really going to do this? Are we really going to go to Canada? Michael Thomas of the San Francisco Giants and little old me, in a fake relationship?

He's bound to change his mind. Rethink. Realize how crazy this is.

But what if he doesn't? What if this is the answer to me saving face and keeping all my family and family friends off my case, questioning me about the split from Andrew, trying to get us back together? Mike's right, Andrew hates that I have someone new. And he deserves to hate it, too.

I'm now lying in my bed, sinking into my mattress, my feet no longer throbbing from ill-fitting shoes, full of scrumptious sushi. My disastrous date with Adam is already forgotten.

Even though he has possibly provided the solution to all my problems, Mike agreeing to be my fake date wasn't the only *okay* thing about our impromptu dinner date – or fake date. The evening actually went really well, with Mike telling me about beach life in California – sleeping to the sound of waves, waking up to the smell of salt air. I really must visit San Francisco. The Bay Area sounds wonderful, not to mention I want to take a tram, like every couple in every movie ever set in San Francisco, and I'd like to take a boat out to Alcatraz, maybe snap a shot of the Golden Gate on the way, possibly head on up to the wine country.

We also played a couple of games on the VR and we were overall tied this time, so no forfeits required.

And I guess we're going to have to be able to get along because we have *a lot* to learn about each other in a very short space of time if we're going to pull off being a couple.

Which reminds me... I pick up my phone to message Dee but see a WhatsApp notification from her.

Got you a job as an extra if you want it? On set Monday at 8 a.m. $75 for the day x

An extra. Like, acting. Great. Perfect. Invaluable insight to help make my white lies stick and some much-needed income.

Except, I can't act. Then again, don't extras just sort of mill around the place, filling spaces?

I reply to tell her I'll do it because for one thing, beggars can't be choosers and, for another, at least I'll technically be an actress, therefore I won't need to lie to Mike and he'll think he's going to Canada with someone a bit more like him and a lot less like me.

When my family meet Mike, they need to believe he's my new boyfriend. To pull that off, Mike and I need to be great at bluffing and genuinely speedy at learning all the things a couple need to know about each other. But Mike thinks I'm an actress, so I not only need to know a few things about being an actress, but I also need for my family to believe I'm an actress if Mike brings it up.

Because one, he won't be able to lie to my family about me. And two, he's a professional athlete; there's no way I can confess to being an auditor.

Whoever heard the story about the MLB player and the auditor who fell in love?

No one. Ever.

19

TED

'I'm just giving you a heads up that Roman asked Kimberley this morning to book two flights to New York,' Mel tells me. It's Monday and another working week has begun. 'I've only just found out – Kimberley was gossiping by the water cooler.'

I can tell from her face, displayed on the screen of my laptop, that Mel told Roman's PA exactly where she could shove her water cooler chat. The pair don't get along in any event, not since Kimberley spread a rumor about Mel flirting with a gay guy in a bar and getting knocked back. I don't know whether it was true or not but Mel didn't take kindly to her personal life being discussed in the office. Something I can entirely empathize with.

Suddenly, my hasty suggestion on Saturday night that I be Abbey's fake date to her parents' vow renewal doesn't seem so absurd. What are the chances her parents want to move up the renewal of their vows, to like, today? Or at least that Abbey wants to arrive two and a half weeks early?

I take a tactical drink of coffee, both to process the fact my ex-best friend and ex-fiancée, now a couple, are imminently winging their way from the west coast in my direction, and to hide my humiliation.

I'm Mel's boss. I'm a grown man. I'm a successful businessman. Yet I've been taken for an idiot. Played by two of the people in the world I'm supposed to be able to trust implicitly. Whom I *did* trust implicitly.

'Can you book me on a flight home asap?' I ask the question tongue in cheek. I know I can't play cat and mouse forever; I need to tackle this eventually. 'Joking.' Kind of.

'You don't have to put a front on things for me, Ted. They're total shitheads. Both of them. Sorry, you know I'm Team Ted.'

I smile my gratitude yet, incongruously, I feel protective of Roman and Fleur, as if I don't want anyone to hate on them except me.

'Alright, let's get down to business. How is my Monday looking?' I ask, abruptly bringing talk of my personal turmoil to a close.

We speak for another quarter of an hour about my calendar, my tasks for today and where I need Mel's support. It's all standard stuff, a regular Monday.

At least I can rely on the constant of work, I think as our video call ends. Just as quickly, I remember I can't, because Roman wants to sell out and whilst I want to stay in our partnership, or I did before recent catastrophic events, our working together has become, in the words of my lawyer, untenable.

Unfortunately, it seems our partnership documents don't legislate for one of the partners having an affair with the other's wife-to-be, and so my options are to sell the partnership or disband it. Neither appeals to me and the only alternative, if Roman agreed, would be for me to buy his share but realistically, I can't run the business alone, nor can I afford to buy him out.

So, in a nutshell, my lawyer has used many words, many

pages and many of my dollars to tell me I'm fucked. Personally and commercially between a rock and a hard place. Having salt rubbed into my wounds. Sitting on a powder keg between two fires.

I have been totally and utterly shafted by Roman.

20

ABBEY

After a second consecutive day of arriving on the set of my sister's TV show at 5.45 a.m. (I never thought I'd consider the sun a late riser), I was made to look like a vampire (fangs, cape, the works) and spent five hours jumping off a wall onto a pavement over and over until the scene had been through twenty-odd takes and two re-writes.

Following a short break for water and a freebie protein bar, I was whisked off to a dressing trailer again, where white paint was scrubbed from my face and I was made to look like someone out of *Bridgerton* dressed for a stroll through Central Park.

It was hot, relentless, tiring work.

The perks were: getting to see my sister in action (she's as fabulous as I've ever seen her on screen), getting paid seventy-five bucks for the second day in a row, agreeing to act as a paid runner-cum-flexible extra for the next week, and toning my butt with all the vampy jumping.

Given my early rise, I'd finished my day's work early enough to come home, change, stroll the promenade with a coffee in hand, update my resume and search for jobs. The coffee and walk were wonderful. The search, however, proved fruitless. I found nothing that I would be qualified for or confident enough to apply for.

Perhaps that's karma telling me, *Be careful what you wish for*. I am now employed as an actress, in a bizarre twist of fate, and it's only a matter of time until I'm found out and booted off set, embarrassing my sister horribly in the process.

I'm at home, making pasta for one, when my mom calls. I slip a garlic flatbread in to cook and bring my cell phone to the sofa.

'Hi Mom.'

'Hello, Abigail. How are you?'

Her tone tells me instantly that she's still, more than four weeks on from that fateful day, angry, or worse, disappointed, that I lost both my suitor and my stable job.

'Good, actually, thanks, Mom. A little tired—'

'This party has done what my parties tend to do.' She titters and I can visualize her holding a hand to her chest as if she's going to explode because the joke's so funny. 'It's grown much bigger than I ever intended.'

Than *Dad* ever intended, she means. Mom loves a huge bash.

'And, well, since you're unemployed and single, I thought you might be able to come home and give a helping hand.'

Help Mom throw a party? She's never once asked me if I can—

'Is this some kind of plot to get me near Andrew's family and friends? Is Andrew going to be home? Because, Mom, if you're trying to lure us back together, it's not—'

'Oh, darling.' She chuckles again, high-pitched, like she's been caught in the act. 'Do you always have to be so severe? I thought it would be nice to spend some mother and daughter time together. I'm sure, as a consequence, you could catch up with family friends but that isn't a motivating factor.'

I hear a voice call out in the background, then Mom say, 'The groceries have arrived, darling, I have to go. Will you come?'

I sigh. We both know I always give in to Mom, whether I have obligations or not, because... she's my mom and I love her, despite the absolute pain in the ass she can be at times. 'When?'

'As soon as possible, darling.' I can tell she's shoved the phone between her ear and cheek, her voice sort of muffled. Then I hear her whisper-talk, presumably to the delivery driver.

'I can't come for another week because I'm working,' I tell her.

I genuinely wouldn't want to let down the crew my sister is working with but more than that, I'm bringing my new pro-athlete boyfriend. I'm fairly certain he won't extend his generosity as far as two weeks in my home town and, even if he would, we have far too much homework to do on each other before we go.

'You *are* working? Oh sweetheart, that's fantastic news.'

Hmm. 'Yeah, it's great fun. I'm working as an extra on Dee's new gig.'

'Acting?' Her tone shifts to hysterical in a nano-second. 'Acting?'

'Err, yeah.'

'But you can't act!' Her words are shrill. I imagine her thumping a hand onto her hip.

I chuckle, perhaps nervously, maybe because I know she's right. Or it could be because this is a trial, the first person other than Andrew whom I've lied to, and it isn't going well.

'I don't make a bad vampire, actually,' I tell her.

'Abigail Mitchell, do not antagonize me. I've seen you play the roles of a donkey's ass and a star in your school plays. A donkey's ass!'

I have to cover my mouth with my hand to stop my laughter from bellowing out.

'Never mind the party, you need to come home where I can

screw your head back on, young lady. All the money we've spent on your education!'

'Oh Mom, stop being so dramatic.' I'm silently sniggering. Dee and I do enjoy winding Mom up from time to time. 'Dee is an actress and you don't tell her she has to come home.'

'That's because she can act!' Mom shrieks.

Oh gosh, I have to hang up before I die from split sides. But not before I say very quickly, 'That's true. Also, I have to run but I'll check with my date and see how soon we can come out, okay? Love you. Byeeeeee.'

'Date? What *date*?'

I hang up and laugh all the way back to my boiling pasta.

Jokes aside, once I've had some dinner and soaked my tired feet, I'll head upstairs and ask Mike how flexible he is on travel dates.

And hope that he hasn't changed his mind entirely since Saturday.

21

TED

It is nearly 7 p.m. when the noise I've been dreading since my call with Mel yesterday occurs. I've been hoping all day that I was wrong, that it wouldn't really happen, that I could somehow escape to Canada with Abbey before...

The building concierge buzzes my intercom for a second time and when I eventually answer, he tells me, 'I have a Miss Fleur Dumont for you. Shall I send her up, sir?'

I feel like I'm having an outer-body experience, as if my spirit is levitating above me and only my physical body says, 'Yes.'

As I move the few steps to the door, I tell myself that I'll open it, pin it back into the magnetic holster and walk away, let Fleur come into this new space alone, without welcome.

Yet, I find myself in the open doorway, staring at the elevator doors, watching the digital counter above rise from the ground level through to the eighth floor, my spirit finally rejoining my body as I take two big involuntary breaths.

I suppose I want to see her face, read her initial reaction to seeing me. I guess I want to know whether she feels any ounce of remorse.

Does it matter? Probably not. What's done is done.

I'm sick with anticipation. It's no wonder Abbey wanted to bury herself in a chocolate calzone after her first meeting with her ex.

When the elevator doors open, the way I feel is how I imagine a person feels when they're staring into the headlights of an oncoming truck, right before it ploughs into them. A thousand emotions wash over me. I see the future I thought I'd have with Fleur, the past I had with her, and this absurd current reality.

Fleur is out-of-this-world attractive. The kind that takes hours to perfect. Immaculate. Flawless. Undeniably intimidating, like a higher power. Untouchable, unreal, like staring at the front page of the world's finest and most overpriced magazines.

Her good looks catch me unprepared, the way they do when she returns from a trip to one of the fashion capitals, like Milan or Paris. Over time, with proximity, I've become acclimatized to it, but when I first see her after a while, it blows me away to the land of dumbstruck.

She looks as if she's going to go hell for leather at me and if I could form a coherent thought, I'd think she has a nerve.

But then she softens, leans her head to one side and gives me the kind of look she might give a puppy who had an accident on the rug. It's pity and annoyance all at once.

'Teddy Bear,' she says, almost sighing the words as she makes her way across the hallway.

She lifts her arms, blind to my current overriding sense, which is to run. In a fight or flight situation, I always choose flight.

But the boldness of her. This isn't a social occasion. This isn't a meal out. This is our entire lives together she's ruined. It's my closest friendship she's crushed.

Has she always been this person? Is this on me? Did I choose to propose to the devil?

I hold my next blink and in the fleeting darkness, I hear Mike telling me to grow a pair. That's exactly what I need to do: listen to my big brother.

'What are you doing?' I bite at her. 'Fleur, when I look at you, all I can see is you sleeping with Rome. You seriously want me to give you a hug?'

I walk away, leaving her standing on the threshold. If she wants to come in, it's up to her, but I'm not wilting or bending to her like I normally do.

I head to the refrigerator for a beer but at the last second take a can of soda because I know I'll regret not having a clear head for this. I'll for sure regret it if my inhibitions are lowered. I've just displayed a scrap of backbone, probably for the first time since we met.

I hear the front door close, so I know Fleur has come inside the apartment. I can sense her nearness.

'Ted, don't be like this,' she says, startling me as I chug down cold soda, the fizz catching in my throat.

I notice now that she's wearing her Burberry raincoat – one she was gifted as part of a magazine shoot, one I used to think looked sexy on her. Every time she wore it, I'd wonder what the heck she was doing with just some guy like me.

Now, I think she'd be better suited to a brothel in that coat and those red-soled high heels.

Is just some guy like me so bad? I guess it is, otherwise I might not be leading Abbey to believe that I'm someone else.

I plant my can down on the countertop. It lands with a thud that's unintentional and draws Fleur's gaze from me to the can.

'This isn't like you, Teddy Bear. It doesn't suit you.' She takes a step closer, so close her usual perfume is nauseating – at least I think that's what has my stomach feeling like a spinning pinwheel of death.

'How exactly do you want me to behave, Fleur? You act like this is just one of life's little happenings, as if it's normal or okay to do to people what you've done to me.'

'I'm sorry. I am. I'm sorry that we hurt you. Is that what you want to hear? Is that what you're waiting for to stop running away?' She slaps her hands against her thighs, as if she's the one who should be incensed.

Has she always been this cold? This... narcissistic?

I think my predominant emotion is anger and so I'm going with the fact that feeling so enraged is making my eyes sting but honestly, I'm all over the place here; it could be any of a colossal dump of emotions going on in my head.

I can't believe my vision is clouding. It makes me madder. Mad at myself, at how pathetic I'm being. I think of Abbey, her red eyes and tear-stained cheeks after meeting Andrew's new girlfriend. Was she sad or angry?

Shaking my head, I walk away because I won't show her. Here I am thinking I'm about to melt down and she's being as facetious as I've ever known her.

'No,' I manage, I hope hiding the weakness I feel from my voice. 'What I want to hear is why? When? For how long? Where?'

Please don't let where be our bed.

'Does it matter?'

'I think it does,' I say, maybe more to myself than Fleur, moving to stare at the East River from the lounge window. 'I don't want to hear it but I need to know how deep the deceit runs.'

'Don't use words like that,' she says, close behind me. 'You make it sound—'

'Clandestine? Illicit? Adulterous? Faithless? Sordid?' The

words leave me calmly, I guess passive aggressively, which is not the kind of person I want to be; it's someone Fleur and Roman are making me be. I didn't ask for any of this. But I know there are two sides to every story... 'What did I do, Fleur? What was so bad that you wanted to get out?'

I turn to face her and I'm caught off-guard by her glazed eyes. Crying? *She's* crying?

Now the biggest betrayal in the room is coming from my own heart. I can't bear to see her cry. That's how I know, beneath all the animosity, I still have feelings for her.

Instinctively, I want to hold her, to kiss her hair and tell her everything is going to be okay.

But it isn't. It can't be.

I rub my hands roughly across my face and through my hair in frustration. Fleur comes to sit on the sofa and I take tissues from a box on the coffee table and hand them to her.

She looks up to me as she takes the tissues, wearing an expression I've seen every time I've comforted her because she hasn't been cast for a job, or something negative has been said about her on social media.

Are these just the same tears? Is the end of our relationship the same as being trolled to her?

Argh, none of this makes sense. I don't know what I was expecting, whenever I saw her again; maybe I knew it would be a big mess of conflicted emotions and that's why I was still hiding here, in Mike's apartment, the entire country between us. That's why I'm desperate to pose as someone else and run to Canada with Abbey.

My thoughts feel heavy and my body weak as I come to sit on the coffee table, facing Fleur, our knees grazing until I shuffle my legs back. I can't touch her.

Two weeks ago, I was able to touch her, I wanted to touch her, our world was fine. Then...

'Can we try again?' Fleur sniffs, looking me in the eyes and stilling my heart.

Yes. No. Of course not. Because as I blink, I see her and Roman in his office, limbs naked, wrapped around each other, bound to each other. *No.*

I shake my head, perhaps saying no, maybe just trying to make sense of everything whizzing around up there, shaking away the image of Fleur and my best friend, willing the vivid memory to disappear.

With our contact broken, Fleur lets out another sob. 'It's over between Rome and me, I promise.'

I scoff, standing, needing to be away from her.

'Is that so? It's over and now you want me to be here, waiting, happy to accept anything you send my way?'

'No. It's not like that. I made a mistake and now it's over.'

I'm pacing the floor, needing to move. 'Last week, you told me you love him. *Him*, not me.'

She sobs harder. 'It was a mistake. I was confused.'

Sinister laughter comes from a place of darkness I didn't know I had. 'Were you confused when you thought you loved me? Were you confused when you agreed to marry me? Or are you confused now about being in love with my best friend?'

As Fleur blows her nose, a thought occurs to me. 'Who ended it?'

'Pardon?' she says, in a way that tells me she is playing for time, orchestrating a response, weaving another lie.

'He ended it, didn't he? Roman ended it between you two.'

She rubs a knuckle under her wet eyes. 'Yes. Officially. But we both knew it was wrong.'

Pressing my fingers to my temples, I continue to pace. 'Fleur, you need to leave.'

She stands from the sofa. 'I just got here.'

I walk to the front door and pull it open. 'And you've already been here too long.'

God, am I kicking her out? Where will she go? She's familiar with New York but I don't know that she has any real connections here, any friends. Ha, for all I know, she could be screwing someone in this building.

'You are not serious?' she says, her eyes pleading from where she remains in the lounge, unmoving. 'Where will I go? Can we just talk about this?'

I can't look at her or I'll cave. Until... her tone changes from desperation to anger.

'We both have things we need to work on,' she says, hands on hips.

Unbelievable.

'Fleur, I know I am far from perfect but—'

I'm interrupted by the pinging of the elevator as it arrives at my floor.

Who now?

My stomach sinks. Tell me Roman hasn't followed her. Is he here for her or me?

But the doors open and when I see Abbey's beaming smile, a moment of calm washes over me.

Abbey. It feels like she walks toward me in slow motion, bringing down the pace of the last half hour, turning hate to peace with the curve of her lips.

'So, I think I have another favor to ask of you,' she says, and God knows I'd rather hear about Abbey's favor than spend another second arguing with Fleur.

'Who is it?' Fleur's voice cuts through the peace as both women approach me from opposite sides of the door.

Abbey's sunny demeanor switches to surprise and Fleur scrutinizes Abbey in a way that irks me, the way Fleur considers every woman who isn't her own reflection, in fact, like she's superior to them.

'Oh sorry, I didn't realize you had company,' Abbey says, flush with unnecessary discomfort. 'I don't know why I didn't think you would.'

She starts to back away toward the elevator.

Fleur pouts.

'Who is she?' she snaps. 'It looks like there are two of us keeping secrets in this relationship.'

I know she'll be wearing a condescending look, a possessive offensive, but my eyes are on Abbey, who looks pretty in jeans and a buttoned vest with stylish sneakers, her hair loosely tied up, understated.

'She's just...' I'm thinking on my feet and doing a bad job of it.

Fleur leans closer to me, her hands on my shoulder, claiming ownership of me.

Abbey and I are locked in a moment, as if we're holding an unspoken conversation. *I can explain*, I want to say. Except I can't, not right now. Even if I could, Abbey has turned her back on me and she's making for the fire-escape staircase. 'Don't worry about it.' She shakes her head. 'You're clearly busy. I'll ask someone else.'

'Well, she seems crazy.' Fleur hoots, taking the door from my hand and encouraging it shut. 'Now, where were we.' She raises her palm to my cheek. What used to be warming feels like fire on my skin.

'She isn't crazy, Fleur, she's the woman I'm seeing.' I can't believe I've said it. Our fake relationship came much easier to me when it was me helping Abbey out.

'Come again?' Fleur gripes, her hands on her hips, her head cocked to one side.

I'm in shock myself, so I stare at her, not wanting to undermine what I've said with my next move.

Then Fleur cackles like something out of *Hocus Pocus*. 'A girlfriend? No, honey, she's your payback and it ends tonight.' She scoffs. 'Why would you want a princess when you can have a queen?'

I rub my chin roughly in frustration. 'Right, Fleur. And why would anyone choose a prince when they could have a king?' I make for the staircase to pack myself an overnight bag. Her words strike me on so many levels. I don't see Abbey as a princess to Fleur's queen but I do see myself as the prince to men like my brother, even Roman. Which is exactly why I'm pretending to be just like Mike.

'Where are you going?' Fleur demands.

'To a hotel.' I start climbing the stairs. 'For the record, my girlfriend isn't a princess; she's an incredible actress.'

22

ABBEY

I'm sitting on my sofa with a mug of green tea and a ramekin filled with mixed nuts, my feet pulled up beneath me, hearing occasional shouts from the apartment above, wondering who the outstandingly pretty woman is in Mike's apartment. Hoping he doesn't have a girlfriend I don't know about and worried my fake date might be no longer.

Unable to resist temptation, I type *Michael Thomas baseball girlfriend* into my phone's search engine. There are an incomprehensible amount of photographs of Mike with women, nearly always with a different woman, and every single time, the woman is very attractive. Though none quite as striking as the woman upstairs.

It takes a lot of scrolling before I find a picture of Mike and the woman the internet tells me is Fleur Dumont, a model. Of course she is! The model and the pro ball player. Like Adam and Eve, pepper and salt, pen and paper. A natural pairing. Utterly glamorous – him in black tie, her in a floor-grazing black lace Chanel gown.

She looks every bit the example of a model as she poses and

smiles, a truly exquisite smile, with wide lips and perfect teeth. So very, very slight, her body looks the way I expect every fashion designer wants a woman to look in their clothes. Her stance looks as though it's been perfected throughout her career, or perhaps it comes naturally, but the shot captures her in an undeniably flawless light.

Only when I manage to tear my attention from the most attractive woman I have ever seen in the flesh do I focus on Mike's image. He looks different in real life. His skin is softer and less tanned. Though he's smiling in the image, the creases at the sides of his mouth and around his eyes aren't quite the same.

Then again, I guess it's red-carpet lighting, maybe even photoshopping. It's close enough to the real him and that's certainly the woman he is upstairs with.

Currently, raised voices are coming through the ceiling as a muffled sound and I wonder what's going on up there.

I pop a cashew nut into my mouth and click into Mike's Wikipedia page. Naturally, he has a Wikipedia page.

His profile image looks like a swap card sports picture – he's running in full San Francisco Giants kit. The page is full of stats and the teams he has played for. Though I do notice his date of birth – he's older than I thought. I had guessed at him being in his early thirties but by this calculation, Mike is thirty-six. Maybe I don't know the man upstairs at all.

I scroll down to what I'm really interested in: Personal Life. No spouse. So whoever Fleur Dumont is, she *isn't* his wife. Son of Ed and Elsie Thomas. Brother of Theodore Thomas.

Why, if Mike is in a relationship with Fleur, would his brother have thrown him a party full of sexily dressed women?

I click on a link to Theodore Thomas. His picture is in profile and his gaze cast down but the brothers definitely share a likeness. He goes by Ted and he's one of two partners behind

Vanguard RED Technologies – the email I saw in Mike's apartment was about his brother!

According to his Wikipedia page, Ted has made numerous headlines of national finance and economic publications, like the *Financial Times* and *Bloomberg*. He's a very wealthy entrepreneur, less famous, but wealthier than his brother, in fact. Probably just as arrogant, in that case.

I type the name *Vanguard RED Technologies* into the internet and click through to a website that looks very Matrix-esque – the focal point an image of what I believe is computer code.

Apparently, Vanguard is one of the fastest growing technology innovation businesses in the USA. I scroll to the bottom of the page and find the section *About Us*.

As I dig, I find that Vanguard software is amongst some of the key software packages used in the finance world. Software I have used and loved – logical, solutions-driven technology. It's seriously impressive. I can't believe the business is still run as a partnership and not a huge company.

Whilst my head is still very much in my new research project, now back to digging about Mike, there's a knock on my door, which can only be one of three people – Dee, Shernette or Mike, because they're the only people that I know who have access to this floor.

I take my mug of tea with me to the door, where my suspicions are confirmed.

'Please don't close the door in my face,' Mike says, not at all his usual, overconfident self. His hair looks disheveled, his eyes look exhausted and he has a backpack slung across one shoulder.

The thought actually hadn't occurred to me, but now that he mentions it, he was rude earlier and he's clearly been lying, or at least withholding the truth from me, about Fleur Dumont. Not that we've known each other for a long time but I might have thought if he was seeing someone, he'd have told me.

'I ought to,' I tell him. 'You made me feel like a prize clown.'

He just nods, accepting, as if there's no fight left in him, and despite whatever truths he hasn't shared with me, despite the fact I don't really know the man on my doorstep, I feel for him.

'So, Mike, are you in a relationship?'

He drags a hand through his hair and puffs out air, then his eyes fix on me and I think he's about to tell me yes, that he is, or something of that magnitude.

Then he shakes his head. 'Not anymore.'

He's drained and I know that feeling. When I was at rock bottom, he was there to put an arm around my shoulder and be whoever I needed him to be.

So I scowl in a way he knows is good-humored. 'Are you a psychopath?'

One side of his mouth quirks up ever so slightly. 'No.'

'Then would you like to come inside for a mug of green tea?'

His eyes drift to the laptop resting on my coffee table, on which is a photograph of him playing ball. *Oops, caught red-handed.* 'It looks like you've been doing some digging on me,' he says.

I don't dare look at him in case my rapidly heating ears actually spark into flames, so I head over to my kitchen to prepare him a green tea.

He follows me inside, depositing his backpack by the door.

'Are you going somewhere?'

'A hotel, when I find one with availability.'

I turn to lean back against my kitchen benchtop and he steps into the area, resting his hands on the bench. 'I'm sorry for how I treated you upstairs, Abbey. In my defense, I was blindsided by my ex turning up and the doorstep wasn't the place to explain who each of you are to the other. But I swear, she and I aren't together anymore.'

'I suppose I can understand that. Was it a recent break-up?'

'Recent. Messy. She cheated on me with a colleague.'

'Another player?'

He hesitates, then says, 'He's a player all right. My best friend, too, incidentally.'

I finish making his tea and hand him the mug, honestly in shock. Mike just doesn't seem like the type of guy who gets cheated on. 'I'm sorry, Mike. It's a really shitty thing they've done to you. I thought being cheated on by my long-term boyfriend and being told about it on the night that I thought he was going to propose to me was bad, but being cheated on by two people you love is double the pain, I imagine.'

He stares off into the distance for a moment, as if gathering himself. 'Is that why you're actually going easy on me here? I half expected you to slam your door in my face.'

'Maybe. That, and I guess for a man quite as obnoxious and arrogant as you, it must hurt even more to be cheated on.' I finish with a smile, because whilst there is truth in my words, I'm largely teasing. Thankfully, his expression says he gets it.

'Not that I expect you to believe me but the arrogance can be a front sometimes.'

'Said like every arrogant man who ever got called out on his arrogance.'

He chortles and it's nice to know I can break his gloominess, if only briefly.

I think, actually, I do sort of know the man standing next to me. I think this man might be the man I've seen between the arrogance, between the repetitive tossing of a baseball off the wall above my head. I think he might be the bits I've seen and liked.

'It makes sense now, why you helped me out with Andrew and why you agreed to be my date to my parents' party.'

He nods, seeming lost in contemplation. 'Abbey, actually... the truth is... the truth is, I just want— I just stopped by to find out why you were really coming to see me? I should also probably tell you that Fleur thinks we're seeing each other.'

'Oh! Why would she think that?'

He winces. 'Because I told her as much. She thinks you're my very successful actress girlfriend, actually.'

I fleetingly forgot my own misrepresentation about acting. Though, I am technically an actress now. This is precisely *why* I am making good on my pretend career. For moments like these, when Mike needs to hold me out as something extraordinary to his ex.

'Oh. I guess that'll do it.' I want to ask why and if he's crazy but I know why. For exactly the same reasons as I lied about Mike being my boyfriend. To save face and maybe, in his case, to make Fleur jealous. 'Did she believe us?'

'Yes. Not that you helped me out much, running back off downstairs the way you did. I guess all that money spent on drama school was wasted, huh? I'm going to have to drag you through this on my coattails.'

I gasp, offended on behalf of the sham version of me. 'I'm going to let that slide, Michael Thomas, but consider that strike one.'

'Ah, so you do know baseball?'

'Actually, I know zip about baseball. And to answer your question, I was coming to see you because my mom called and asked if I, well, *we*, I guess, can go to Canada earlier, like, maybe Tuesday next week?'

'Oh.'

'Don't worry. It's a silly idea. You probably don't want to go through with it at all now, what with everything you have going on. And a week of faking it is a very different proposition than a couple of nights. Forget I ask—'

'Sounds good. Let's do it.'

'For real?'

He gives me a mockingly questioning side-eye. 'Exactly the opposite of reality. Expending with it as soon as possible would be good.'

Ha, true.

'But I have one condition.'

'Go on.'

'No more googling. If you want to know something about me, just ask. Deal?'

'Deal.'

He finishes his tea and places his cup down on the coffee table, then looks at me and asks, 'Are we good? Because I don't really know many people in New York and you've been a somewhat difficult and smartass distraction, but a distraction nonetheless and I'd kind of like to keep you around, if that's okay?'

'Oddly, that's one of the most critical yet sweet things anyone has ever said to me.' I smile gently and he returns the expression as he pushes off from the countertop.

'I better be off. Before hotel reservations close for the night.'

'Why are you staying in a hotel?' I ask as we walk toward the door.

He shrugs and picks up his backpack from the floor where he left it. 'My ex is staying upstairs and whilst I really can't stand to be around her right now, I'm not going to send her out into the city looking for another place to stay.'

That's really very civilized of him, particularly in the circumstances. I open the door and he steps out into the hallway. 'Why don't you just stay here?'

'Wow, you're really forward. We haven't even had our first official fake date, yet.'

Is he flirting? No. Surely not. Of course not. But I can't help the feeling like I have jumping Jelly Beans in my tummy. He's a pretty hot guy to have flirting with any woman, particularly one who is prone to disaster with men of late.

'I knew the egotism wasn't fake,' I say, though in reality, thinking how decent it was of him to come here and apologize. How truly unexpected. Yes, he misled me but I've been fabricating things too, and he actually cares about my opinion of him. 'Clearly not like that. I have a sofabed in my spare room and you'll be closer to home in the morning.'

He looks up, as if remembering his ex-girlfriend is above us. Then he glances along my hallway to the bedrooms and back to me. I have no idea what he's thinking because I'm too busy enjoying the way he's looking at me. 'If you're sure it's okay.'

Oh boy. That silly fluttering is back in my stomach and it had better disappear because I am *not* in the market for a real relationship; I don't even know who or what *I* am right now.

Mike *certainly* isn't in the market for a relationship, given his most recent one was shambolic.

Nevertheless, it's nice to have him look at me the way he just did.

23

TED

I guess I'm staying over with Abbey tonight whilst Fleur sleeps upstairs. If I overthink it, it's weird, and if I don't, it's logical. She's my girlfriend to anyone who'll believe us and I need a place to sleep. So I'm not overthinking it.

My mind is sufficiently depleted by Fleur for it to sit in this thoughtless void.

Though I knew Roman had asked for two airplane tickets to New York – what happened to him is one of the questions I have for Fleur – I was still shocked to see Fleur standing at my door. Then with her words, seeing her, I went through every feeling from betrayal and fury to longing for my life as it used to be.

I still have feelings for my ex-fiancée. I wish I still had my best friend to talk to about all of this stuff. But what residual feelings I have after their deceit is the part I haven't worked out yet and what I don't want to consider anymore tonight.

Seeing Abbey has calmed my mind, even made me laugh, miraculously, and I'm not going to get riled up again.

I can't replace years of friendship with Rome but I do like

hanging with Abbey. I like her influence on my mood. Her quietude.

She has shut down her laptop and agreed not to search the web for information about me – well, Mike. I want to tell her the truth. I almost did. I hate liars and the very last person I want to lie to is Abbey. She flips between spoilt rich girl and the girl next door with ease but I'm starting to think she isn't like Fleur. I typecast her and I was wary of her, I still am to an extent, but she's helped me out tonight. She helped me out cleaning Mike's apartment. And I think I've seen a lot more of the girl next door than the uptown girl.

We're sitting on her sofa, each with a bowl of mixed nuts and a second mug of green tea, both sharing the same side of her U-shaped sofa, facing her wall-mounted television.

'Sadly, I don't own a VR machine but I do have Netflix,' she says, switching on her TV. 'I'm due a re-watch of *Ozark*, otherwise it's true crime?'

'Either works.' I feel like I'll be staring absentmindedly at the screen either way, depleted of mental energy.

'Helpful input.' She rolls her eyes. 'Let's go with true crime. I'll try to find a homicide. We might pick up some tips on how to kill a cheating ex.'

I scoff. 'And you asked if *I'm* a psychopath?'

'Lol.' She drops an almond into her mouth.

'Abbey, don't take this the wrong way but you can be a bit weird.'

She laughs so hard, she chokes on her nut. For a very attractive woman with a cool job, she's a bit of a geek. I should know because it takes one to know one.

Whilst we're waiting for a documentary about a New York serial killer to start, Abbey pulls her legs beneath her, tells me I am welcome to put mine up on her coffee table, then asks, 'How often are you in New York?'

It feels like the question comes from nowhere and it catches me sleeping. The real me is rarely in New York. I come for business every once in a while and sometimes come over for a weekend when my brother is here but, of course, I'm not me. 'I spend the season in San Francisco, but in the off-season I spend time here. Whilst I'm injured, I can be here more.'

'Do you prefer New York?'

'God, no.' Oops, too severe. 'I just mean, I love San Francisco. Though I will say, the more time I spend here, the more I realize there's a laidback aspect to the city. Not just the party life my brother tries to show me.'

She focusses on me intently. 'You're a bit of an onion, aren't you? You seem to revel in your success and not to labor the point but my brief internet search showed you enjoy the sports guy lifestyle. Yet, you weren't really into the party on Friday night and sometimes, *sometimes* you have moments where you actually seem... considered.'

Now I choke on my laughter. Without knowing it, Abbey just summed up this ridiculous double-identity I'm running. If I'm an onion, I have two layers. The first is Mike. The second is me. Even I'm starting to get muddled and trip myself up.

Maybe I should just come clean. But tonight, I don't have the energy, so I change the topic to something safer. 'So, you're an actress. What kind of things do you work on?'

It's an abrupt segue and it feels like the question hangs awkwardly between us for a beat longer than it ought to. Maybe she's suspicious?

Then she smiles and tells me, 'Actually, I started filming for a new series on Monday. It's a sort of family drama but with vampires. I, erm, don't have a starring role but the production has a really good cast. I also get to work with my sister, and it's being filmed in Central Park for the next week or so, which is great because it means I don't have to go away. I'm kind of a home bird. I like my own space and my own things.'

'But you're from Canada. If you love home so much, how come you're in New York?'

She does it again, takes a pause before she answers. And just when I think she's about to, she shifts her attention to the TV. 'Ooh, here we go. I love this detective. He's done loads of these documentaries.'

At some point, I get lost in the documentary and forget the need to make conversation. Abbey and I just watch the show in companionable silence. It's... nice. Really nice. I can't remember the last time I hung out with someone like this. Easy. Relaxed.

Between episodes one and two, Abbey refills our snacks and when she returns to the sofa, she sits much closer to me, tugging a blanket from the back of the sofa and laying it over our legs.

* * *

I never did make the end of episode two. I fell into a remarkably peaceful slumber.

Until I awoke under a blanket on the sofa, still wearing yesterday's clothes. By my watch, it wasn't even 2 a.m. and my mind started wandering, spiraling.

I don't want to spend another day with Fleur. Speaking to me as if this is the same as every other time she's broken us off then changed her mind and come crawling back. And I've taken it, every time.

Not this time.

But insomnia has also proved to me that I am an emotional train wreck. I'm vulnerable to her.

On top of that, I have no idea what's going on with Roman and I'm for sure not ready to take him on, too.

I've laid still as long as I can but I absolutely have to go to the toilet. It's around 6 a.m. The sun is up. Abbey isn't.

In the bathroom, the sight of the man I catch in the mirror is ghastly. There's no denying that I look and feel like crap – pale skin everywhere except the darkness under my eyes.

Where I was wound up a few hours ago, awake with conflicting thoughts, now I feel sluggish and confused about what comes next with Fleur, Roman and Vanguard.

After splashing my face with cold water, I step into the corridor, only to be near bowled off my feet. 'Whoa.'

Abbey presses two hands to my chest. She has one sneaker on and would be stumbling toward the ground but for me blocking her fall as she tries to move and put the other shoe on at the same time.

'Yikes, sorry.' She straightens herself and the canvas bag that has fallen from her shoulder. 'I should be on set by now.' She starts walking backward in the direction of the apartment door as she speaks, a little disheveled-looking, like she's literally just jumped out of bed and grabbed the first clothes she could lay her hands on. Not in the way I look like hell but sort of sweetly dopey. 'I'm blaming you, by the way. I'm never late. Never. You kept me up way past my bedtime.'

'I fell asleep! And I'm not accepting blame for your failure to set an alarm, Fluffy Boots.'

She points at me, I think mock cross, but keeps walking backward. 'Gotta run. No time to put you back in your box.'

Ha. I hold up a hand. 'It's been real,' I call to her.

She stills and I realize I'm smiling at her – remarkable this morning.

'Wait. How are you doing? Are you okay?'

Despite her clearly calamitous start to the day, she still asks if I'm okay.

I shrug. Rather than give my usual token response, along the lines of *I'm well thanks, and you?* I tell her, 'Spent the night asking myself what I did so wrong, amongst a million other questions, like am I doing the right thing not taking her back, knowing I can't.'

Abbey sighs, her shoulders sagging, and I remember why I usually go with a standard response. Then she runs back to me, places her hands on my shoulders, bounces up to her tip toes and kisses my cheek. 'You've got this. Some people are just shitty humans. You are not one of them.'

I'm too startled to reply. The feel of her lips was light and soft, and it lingers on my skin.

'If the world is too much, you can stay and hide in my apartment. Or you're welcome any time to come and watch my sister in action; she's awesome.'

'Or you.'

'Right. Yep. Or me. Ha.' Then she's gone, running forward until she's out of sight.

Watching her go, it strikes me how rare it is for anyone to stop and ask me if I'm okay. I spend the staircase climb to the eighth floor – a delay tactic – trying to recall Fleur or Roman ever asking me about me, ever caring about the answer if they did.

Part of me would really like if Fleur had taken her stuff and left for a flight back to San Francisco already. Another part of me, I think small but very much present, wants to see her. God knows why. I haven't worked out yet if I'm holding onto something and what that is. The good parts of us, maybe?

What were they? That's another question I was asking through my insomnia last night. What is it that I love about Fleur? What made me want to spend the rest of my life with her?

There's music playing inside Mike's apartment, which I can hear from the hallway as I approach the door. It's happy music, something Fleur would sing in the car, though I couldn't tell you the artist's name. It's not the choice of artist that disturbs me, however, so much as the fact Fleur feels in the mood for bright, cheerful tunes. I'm more in the mood for something haunting myself.

Pausing before I open the door, I accept I have to go inside. If I wasn't ready for the music, I certainly wasn't ready to see Fleur floating around the kitchen wearing a brightly colored summer dress, making coffee and plating what looks like bought-in breakfast.

'You're still here then,' I say, animosity oozing from me, yet my words not quite as venomous as I intended them to sound.

'Oh, you're home. You've not eloped with the actress downstairs, then?' She stops mid-action and gasps. 'You didn't stay with her, did you? Not whilst I was sleeping up here? Not after I told you to end your little rebound fling?'

'What?' I snap.

'Just checking, no need to be so tetchy.' Clearly, she's still holding onto her crown, dismissing Abbey as lesser, nothing. 'Let's start again. I was hoping you would be back to see that I'm being the perfect wifey.'

The sight of Fleur in the kitchen is perplexing enough, never mind her trying to play *wifey*. She always tells me a woman's place is out in the world, as far away from the kitchen as she can afford to be.

'I've made us breakfast and coffee,' she adds.

'Fleur, what's going on? Why are you even here? And where's Roman? I know he booked two flights, presumably one for himself and the other for you, so, where is he?'

She pauses in her task, putting fruit onto a plate. 'I'm here because I did a lot of thinking last night, Ted, and this...' She gestures between the two of us. 'It's not done; we just had a blip, that's all. We can move on from this.'

A blip? Is she for real? I scratch my head until it hurts, frustration driving me insane.

'Fleur, you slept with my best friend. One of the things I keep asking myself is how many more times would you have slept with him? How long would it have gone on behind my back if I hadn't walked in on you two by chance?'

'I just don't see the use in going over the details, Ted. The fact is, the silly little thing between Roman and me is over. And you've had your payback now anyway.' Not even close. Even if Abbey and I were really together. 'You were so busy with work and I need attention sometimes, too.'

I shake my head. 'No, don't put this on me.'

She's out of the country more often than she's in it and all I do is respond to her demands for attention. Every night out I don't want to go on, every photograph I don't want to have taken, every cancellation of the things I'm doing to please her. Ironically, in a bid to keep her.

She brings a plate closer to my side of the kitchen island and puts it down in front of me. 'Coffee?'

She doesn't listen to my answer – standard – then sets about preparing coffee. With her back to me, she says, 'I'm saying we both need to be better, that's all.'

I'm standing in stunned silence. She hands me a mug of coffee then reaches up to kiss me on the lips – a gesture I don't want and that makes my stomach turn in all the wrong ways. She finishes by tapping my cheek with the palm of her hand.

I think back to Abbey's kiss this morning. The kindness of it. The sincerity behind it.

If that was medicinal, Fleur's touch is the root of the condition.

'Now, I know you like to work things out on your own and hide away from the world, so I'm going to give you the space you need to think this through.' She moves into the lounge area, where she picks up a large handbag and hangs it on her wrist.

She grins, as if there's nothing wrong in the world, as if the entire future I saw before me just two weeks ago hasn't been thwarted.

Turning on her high heels, she heads for the door, leaving me staring after her and holding two mugs of coffee.

* * *

When my senses come back to me, I call Mel.

'Do you know where Roman is?' I ask after our usual greetings.

'He's here, in the office. Apparently only one of his tickets to New York was used, so I'm guessing Fleur is with you?'

'I must have sinned so bad in a past life.' I scoff. 'So Roman never caught the flight?'

Mel starts to whisper. 'From what I hear, he did go to the airport, so I don't know what went down there but he came back alone, and obviously Fleur has come your way.'

My best guess is they weren't over until right before Fleur got on the plane to see me. During her six-hour flight, she must have decided our relationship was back on. I'm the best, or only, available option right now, it would seem.

'Okay, thanks. Could you please book a one-way ticket from JFK to San Francisco this evening or as soon as possible tomorrow morning?'

'In your name, or hers?'

'Hers. I'm not ready to return until I've worked out my next business move.'

'You've got it. Are you going ahead with your meetings today?'

'It's a normal working day for me. Thanks, Mel.'

I consider the plate of fruit Fleur made and dismiss it, heading upstairs to my makeshift office. I want nothing more from her.

24

ABBEY

Television production is a tough business. After being rushed through make-up (on account of being late) and spending the morning acting (in the very loosest sense), I've run around after people all day. I've barely had time to eat or drink, which was helpful really because I had zero time to go to the bathroom.

All of this for significantly less money than I was earning as an auditor, which largely required sitting at a desk all day.

The last person I have the energy for is my mom. Not because I don't love her; I do. But she's hard work and especially at the moment, when every time I speak or message with her, I'm increasingly aware of the secrets I'm hiding.

I'm listening to the extravagant plans for Mom and Dad's vow renewal, my AirPods in my ears, a brown paper bag full of takeout Indian food in my arms, as I try to find and tap my access fob against the door of my apartment.

'Are you listening to me, Abigail?'

'Yes, Mom, one hundred percent,' I say. She was moaning about how she's cross with Dad for not engaging in the details.

'I'm also trying to juggle some heavy bags and navigate my way into my apartment.'

'Oh, I see,' she titters, as if she knew I *must* be enthralled by the talk of florists and live bands.

I am lucky and so happy that my parents have made it together for forty years but this party feels very much like something my mom wants and nothing like the kind of thing my dad would enjoy. He's quiet, reserved. Business-confident and strong-willed but far from flamboyant.

'Anyway, the other reason I called is to say I've spoken with Victoria and she says Andrew has nothing but nice things to say about you, still, despite whatever has the two of you upset with each other.'

My fob unlocks the door but I'm too stunned to step inside. 'Upset? Mom, we broke up, for good.' I also doubt that Andrew does have anything good to say about me, whether to his mom or anyone else. Actions speak louder than words.

'A love like yours doesn't disappear overnight, darling. You and Andrew are perfect for each other, always have been. Everyone agrees. I was at lunch with Victoria, Caroline and Marta just yesterday and we were—'

'Mom, Andrew is dating someone else.'

She gasps in a way that would be comical if she hadn't put me in a bad mood.

'He is? Well, Victoria never men—'

'And I've already told you, I'm bringing a date, too,' I snap.

'Oh. I thought that was just an emotional overreaction. This date is real, then?'

'Yes, he's real!' I say, utterly affronted that she'd think I'd make up a date to save face… Oh wait!

'He's as real as Andrew.' Who couldn't be more of a bullshitter.

'Now, don't play tit for tat, Abigail, it doesn't become you.'

I roll my eyes.

'And don't roll your eyes at me, young lady.'

'I didn't!' She can't even see me.

'Well I won't pretend I'm happy about these games the two of you are playing—'

'It's not a game, Mom. I... I really like this guy.'

She sighs down the line.

'Plus, your vows aren't some kind of match-making event; it's all about you and Dad. I'll be there for *you*, no one else.'

I can hear her smile in her voice.

'I'm very happy you think so, darling. So you will come home early, won't you? The timeline is tight and both your brother and sister are too busy. You also need to try on your vow-maid dress.'

'Vow-maid?'

'Yes, I want you and your sister to walk down the aisle with me.'

Wow, this is going to be *big*.

What I'd like to say is: *Mom, the thought of people staring at me and wearing a big puffy dress literally gives me the heebie-jeebies. Please don't make me do it.*

What I actually say is: 'I'd be honored, Mom. So will Dee. Also, I've spoken to Mike. We can come on Tuesday. Is that okay?' I don't want to drop Dee in it on the set but more importantly, Mike and I need time to learn the things about each other that other people will expect us to know.

'I'll have Dad's new secretary book you a flight. That will give us a few days. I suppose I'll need to arrange a ticket for this date you're bringing?'

'Yes, please, though I can pay you back for both tickets.'

She sighs again, like I'm ruining her plans for a rekindling between Andrew and me. 'There'll be no need for that. Does he have a full name, this new person of yours?'

I place my bags down in the lounge and look up to the ceiling. 'Michael Thomas.' *Please don't ask about middle names because I have no clue whether he has one or not.* 'I'll get his passport details for you. Mom, I've got to go.'

'All right, darling. I'll send flight details through. Let me know if *Mike* decides not to come, won't you?'

'Love you, Mom. Speak soon.'

'I love you. Even if I don't always approve of—'

I end the call, then kick off my sneakers and swap them for my fluffy slippers. I'm about to dish up the food from my takeout cartons when I hear the familiar, grating sound of *bang, bang, bang*.

Oh dear.

I think I know a guy in apartment 8B who might need a poppadum pick-me-up.

25

TED

'Things with Fleur went *that* well, huh?' Abbey says when I open the door. She's holding what look like takeout food cartons and smell like Indian food and she nods to the baseball in my hand that I've been tossing against the lounge wall.

I shrug. 'She left for the airport an hour or so ago, laden with a full day's worth of shopping from Fifth Avenue.'

'So do you want to tell me why you're bashing that godforsaken ball off the walls again?'

'Not really. I just want whatever smells so good in those boxes.' I pad into the kitchen and start fixing us drinks whilst Abbey pulls up a stool.

'You get a bite for every feeling shared,' she says, shoving a piece of poppadum dipped in mango chutney into her mouth.

'You didn't share a feeling and you got a bite.'

'Buyer's prerogative.'

My lips betray my battered mind. 'I booked her a flight, told her it's over, that you and I are together, and she needs to take her things out of my place and back to hers. In response, she told me we aren't over, that you and I are over, and that I can have two more weeks in New York before I have to go back and tell her to her face that I don't love her anymore.'

'Wow, that's a lot,' Abbey says, covering her mouthful of food with her hand. 'What did you say?'

I snap off a piece of poppadum and dunk it in lime pickle. I chew through the bite-full enough to be able to speak, then tell her, 'I looked her in the eye and said, "I don't love you anymore."'

'Burn. Then she said?'

'"You need time, so I'll give you time. Two weeks." Then she left, wheel-on case, bags full of shopping and all.'

Abbey stops eating and rests her hands on the island top. 'Do you still love her?'

I pause, too. That's the question I've been asking myself for the last hour since Fleur left. But this time, I'm also questioning the tone of Abbey's voice, the way she's looking at me, and wondering if she cares in more than a platonic way. 'I can't, can I? Not after what she's done.'

Abbey neither agrees nor disagrees, not giving me a hint as to the answer to my silent question. The way her attention is fixed on me, it's like she's trying to read my source code. I hope she can find my next instruction in there and tell me what it is because I'm clueless.

But I do know I'm glad she's here. I also wonder whether I was tossing a baseball to numb my mind or because, on some level, I wanted Abbey to hear. I wanted her to come.

She moves and opens another carton of food, tandoori spices assaulting my senses. She slides the box closer to me. 'You deserve a piece of fish for that disclosure.'

I take the fork Abbey holds out to me because I really do need that delightful-smelling food. 'So, now I need to wait two weeks before Fleur will officially leave my place in San Francisco and I'm basically on the countdown to having to go home and front up to my team mate. That's if he doesn't try to find me here first, now that he knows from his mistress where I am.' I take another forkful of fish. It's outstandingly good. 'Which means,' I begin, my mouth still full but the fish too fantastic to stop eating, 'the sooner we get to Canada, the better.'

A smile breaks on her lips, like she's genuinely happy to be going. Fleetingly, I forget everything else, including the fact I'm going across the border as her fake boyfriend, not her real one. For reasons that are nothing to do with Fleur or Roman, reasons that are as yet unfathomable to me, I might be a little disappointed by reality.

'We do need to start probing each other to pull this thing off,' Abbey says, wagging a fork at me. 'But first, are you sure you're okay?'

'I'm not even sure I know how to answer that question. Honestly, I'm a bit all over the place. I need space from Fleur but we need to sort a lot of stuff out. I don't ever want to see Roman again but he's my— my team mate, and that's a whole load of sorting out I can't get my head around. I'm squatting here on the east coast, living a make believe life with this crazy but sort of great lady who, by her own admission, is a bit of a hot mess, too.'

She frowns, making me chuckle. 'Hmm, I think I preferred you when you were just straight arrogant.'

I literally bellow a laugh – the sound so loud, it feels like a release.

'For what it's worth, it does get easier. But admittedly, I didn't have to train and play baseball with Andrew's new girlfriend.'

I close my eyes and drag a hand through my hair, exhausted. 'I've no idea what I'm going to do about that.'

Abbey holds out the last poppadum for me and as our fingers touch, our eyes meet.

'Abbey, I'm telling you this because I trust you and, honestly, you're pretty much the only person who has seemed to care how I'm dealing with all of this. But the whole reason I'm in New York is because I have no idea how to unpick all of this and if I'm in San Francisco when word gets out, there'll be a media circus. Fleur is a model and influencer.'

'And you're a MLB player.'

'Right.'

'Your secrets are safe with me, Mike.' Though her words are finished, she doesn't take her gaze from mine, contemplating, I think, what comes next. 'Mike, I— You've been really honest with me and, especially since we're really going to do this fake relationship thing, I need to tell you something because I'd rather you found out from me than my family.' I see her swallow deeply.

Oh Jesus. What's coming? Does she know who I actually am?

'My family don't know the reason Andrew and I split. No one except my sister, my best friend and now you know the truth.'

Not what I was expecting.

'See, my mom has always drummed into me that I need to have everything figured out by the time I'm thirty – the husband, the career path, the child even. So when they find out that I'm definitely not going to rekindle the romance with Andrew, that we are never getting married, that I won't have a child by the time I'm thirty-two, they're going to be disappointed at best. At worst, they're going to try their damnedest to get us back together.'

'Then why not tell them the truth?'

'Because Andrew's family and mine go way back. Why risk their friendship and have everyone hate Andrew? Why make me feel like even more of a fool than I already do?'

I'd like to challenge her but I also need to remember that I don't know much about Abbey, not really. Instead, I tell her, 'You're almost as much of a mess as me.'

Somehow, in our joint misery, we end up laughing together, and the fact that we are both laughing at each other seems to make us laugh even harder.

26

ABBEY

This whole impromptu dinner feels like good homework. Despite his super rough last twenty-four hours, Mike's been... sensitive and thoughtful. Melancholy yet completely charismatic. And through all of it, his kind of mischievous, playful streak has still been here.

Not that I'd say it to him but I'm starting to wonder whether some of what I perceived to be arrogance isn't just his cheeky personality. He's arrogant, for sure, but tonight he's been open and honest.

That's why I don't want to keep my lies from him anymore. I almost confessed to everything, being an auditor, not being an actress, lying to my family about Andrew and me.

But at the last moment, I decided, I *am* an actress, I've made good on the lie and I'm really pleased I have because being an actress is more fun, way cooler than being an auditor and Mike might have run a mile rather than agreeing to be my fake boyfriend if he knew that, on top of lying to my family, I'm also just a very plain and ordinary numbers girl, who is closer to being unemployed than employed. Far from a match for a sports star.

I'm certain I'll be discovered in Canada in any event but for now... I kind of like him.

In fact, I *really li*— Whoa! Hold up, Abigail. Hold up.

Fake relationship. One hundred percent *not* real.

I can't deal with a relationship right now and Mike sure as hell can't.

Even if there was a fleeting moment when I asked if he was in love with Fleur and I think, maybe, maybe not, probably not... but it's possible that he cared what I made of his answer?

Stop. Stop. Stop.

Dangerous. And. Unnecessary. Thoughts.

Focus on something else, anything else, like... his laptop and the swarm of papers around it again, this time on the coffee table in the lounge.

'What does a baseball player need with a laptop and a stack of important-looking papers?' I remember the names I saw – Ted and Vanguard RED Technologies.

Mike points in the direction of the coffee table. 'Those? Ah...' He scratches his head, as if he's playing dumb in a sitcom. 'Ah... My brother is in a spot with his business and he asked me to take a look at some stuff for him.'

I can feel my brow creasing without intent. I don't mean to be rude, it's just... 'Why would he ask you? Sorry. I just mean—'

Thankfully, he smirks. 'Are you typecasting me again?'

I bite my lip. 'Sorry.'

He shrugs but doesn't verbalize that I'm off the hook. 'Actually, I'm a silent investor in his business and I'll probably up my stake when I retire. Not that I have the first clue about business.' He moves toward the papers in the lounge.

Finally, something I'm comfortable with. I take the last forkful of curry from my plate, pick up a garlic and coriander naan and head toward him.

We both come to sit on the sofa and Mike tells me, 'My brother, Ted, has ah, fallen out with his business partner and he needs to come up with some kind of solution to getting his partner out of the business, whilst leaving him in control, and knowing he can't afford to buy his partner out.'

'That, I might be able to help you with.' Forgetting myself entirely, I tell him, 'I have a degree in forensic accounting. I used to be an auditor.'

'You did?'

Sugar. I. Am. The. Worst. Actress. In. The. World.

'Ah, yeah, but don't worry, I saw my senses and I'm much more fun these days.' *Urgh, I wish*. 'Anyway, that's the kind of thing my boyfriend would know about me, right?'

'For sure. And, ah, for the record, it's... impressive.'

I snort. 'Yeah, right. Impressive slash extremely dull.' I feel myself grinning, baring teeth like the grimacing-face emoji.

'Well, thanks for exposing your darkest secrets, Abbey.' He chuckles.

'Hey, don't laugh. I'm cool now. Though my family are still livid about the career switch, especially Mom. So it's another thing that might come up whilst we're in Canada.'

Oh God, I need to move this on before he decides to fake dump me. Playfully, I nudge into his shoulder and ask, 'What is it with you Thomas boys and pissing off your best friends?'

'They piss us off because they're lying, faithless, narcissistic dickheads.'

'Ha. Got it.'

'Can you really help with this stuff? My judgment and ability to process anything to do with Roman and I— My brother separating is barely existent. I've known Roman for years, since he and my brother were in college, but ultimately, I'm on my brother's side in this, obviously. I just can't decipher legal jargon or frankly, see the wood through the trees.'

'Sure. I mean, I might be a little rusty,' I say, tearing off a piece of naan because I don't dare look at him as I tell another fib. 'Come on then, you'll need to give me some background. Beyond your brother's business partner being a lying, faithless, narcissistic dickhead, what's going on?'

Mike chortles. 'I think I like you more every time we meet, Abs.'

His words cut his amusement short. Mine, too. I'm taken aback, I think. With the exception of my sister and Shernette, no one calls me Abs. Though I'm less surprised by Mike's familiarity and more by the effect his words have on me. I... liked him giving me a nickname. It was kind of cute. Short of intimate.

I'd chastise my mind for wandering to dangerous places, but the fact that Mike has stilled at his own words makes me wonder, for a nanosecond, if he felt the same.

Stop. It. Abbey.

Stop. It. Now.

As. If.

He opens his mouth, as if he's going to speak again, then closes it silently. Are his cheeks flushed? Is Mr Bigshot embarrassed?

There's some sort of fission going on between us. To take the sting out of it, I joke, 'Consider yourself amongst very highly regarded acquaintances, Big and Burly. Only my sister and Shernette call me Abs and get away with it.'

'Sorry, I—'

'I don't mind at all.' *You probably wouldn't have said it if I wasn't playing the part of the new me but I liked it.* 'Now...' I pull my legs up beneath me on the sofa, getting settled for the long haul.

'Wait. Big and Burly?'

Now it's my turn to blush. 'Shhh. Tell me everything I need to know about your brother and Vanguard.'

That supercilious smirk he often wears pulls on his lips. Damn him. Big, burly and flipping sexy.

Moving on to safer ground, I hold up a hand to stop him as he reaches toward the pile of documents on the table. 'Before we start, Mike, I just need to tell you, I'm looking at this as a friend, not a professional adviser. I mean, I'm an actress. If you share any of this with your brother, he should know that.'

'Got it,' he says with a nod, bringing the documents between us on the sofa.

'And you should think about confidentiality,' I tell him. 'I mean, I assure you I'm not going to share anything outside of this apartment but before you tell me anything I can't find out from the public domain, you should be comfortable with that. Your brother needs to be comfortable with that.'

'Abbey, I trust you.'

'You do?'

He doesn't flinch at my surprise, only looks me in the eye and says, 'I do. And Ted will be immensely grateful. I know him better than anyone, believe me.'

Okay. I nod but don't speak because suddenly, with Mike confirming his faith in me, I am doubting myself. I was going to be fired as an auditor, never mind a business analyst. Anxiety makes me chew my lip. *Can I do this?*

'Abbey, let's just eat food and hang out; forget this. You don't have to—'

'It's not that I don't want to help. I love this kind of business analysis and troubleshooting, or used to. I've helped my dad out with this kind of thing multiple times, but you need to know I'm not qualified. I mean, I'm just an auditor. *Was* an auditor.'

I laugh but it's nerves rather than amusement driving it. Then I'm silenced by Mike's hand on my knee. As soon as his skin contacts mine, I feel something change in my body. My pulse quickens, my heartrate rises, my skin heats, and I want more contact.

Am I crushing on Mike? No, that is literally the last thing on my mind.

He snatches his hand back, as if in horror. Hardly surprising, given his ex-girlfriend may not even have left the state yet.

Business is a safer space to be than whatever else might or might not be going on here. My mind is busy enough with fake dating, fake acting and generally being fake, never mind real crushes, and Mike's mind is surely full enough of the last twenty-four hours alone.

I take hold of the pile of papers, set my self-doubt aside, and start reading. Mike says he doesn't understand all of this at all, so I have to be an improvement on that position. 'Okay, on the basis you should take away anything I say and get an actual employed adviser to bless it, let's get into it.'

I listen to everything Mike knows about his brother's business and his business relationship with his friend Roman. He also lets me read a detailed note Ted's lawyer provided about the partnership. Mike is way smarter than I've previously given him credit for. He's also incredibly close to his brother, that much I can decipher.

We finish the Indian meal I brought and Mike makes us two rounds of coffee, which we drink whilst eating nuts that I send him to retrieve from my place as I work on his laptop.

I get lost in it, remembering how much I love this stuff. I try to relay my thoughts and suggestions as my fingers speed type each pertinent point into a business analysis document I'm creating. Somehow, time turns into the early hours of the morning, and despite the fact I have to be on set by 8 a.m. this morning, I am still going.

27

TED

It's peculiar to see someone so into what I consider an absolute nightmare of business restructuring and financial speak.

It's even more bizarre to see someone who quit this stuff to become an actress be so into it. It makes me wonder why she ever did quit.

Then again, she said it herself: being an actress is much more happening than being a numbers girl.

I guess my tech nerd is sort of equivalent to her previous career and I have to confess, though I might like numbers and code, people like us don't get to keep the girl.

I also know for sure now how uncool she thinks people like me are. But Mike, cocksure sports guy, he'd keep the girl.

After nearly four hours, Abbey has compiled a document I would have expected to pay my accountants and lawyers tens of thousands of dollars for. More than that, she has explained everything to me as she's worked, in a way I understand. And she's given me something my lawyer didn't – a way of getting what *I* want, rather than what Roman wants.

In a nutshell, Roman goes, I can keep doing what I love and I won't lose control.

'Abbey, I don't even know how you've come up with this but if it works, you've come up with something that Ted and I couldn't in more than two weeks of thinking about it and it's taken you four hours. I don't even know how to thank you.'

Her cheeks flush at the praise and I know before she speaks that she's going to qualify my statement. I know because I saw how riddled with anxiety she was just about helping me out. But she overcame it and ploughed on. She's resilient, whether she knows it or not. But in her bashfulness, I'm reminded how different she can be to her fancy-pants persona sometimes.

'Remember, you need to get someone proper to take a look at this and sanction it. They'll probably come up with something better. The document I've put together is in really rough form, so—'

I place my index finger across her lips, feeling her soft pink skin under my touch. 'Stop putting yourself down. Take the compliment.'

Her lips curve beneath my finger, then she takes my hand away. 'You're welcome. For what it's worth, though, I'm sorry your brother is having to go through this. You're both in the relationship wars at the moment, huh?'

Right now, in this moment, I'm not sorry. My gaze falls to Abbey's lips, where my finger has just been... *Heyyy, steady*. She's getting me through a massive mess, regardless of who she thinks she's helping, and I'm grateful. I don't need to read too much into it.

What I need to do is just *stop*. Squash those crazy thoughts.

'I should go,' Abbey says, yawning as she sets my laptop down on the coffee table. She checks her watch. 'I have to be up in a few hours for work.'

Good idea. 'I'll show you out,' I tell her, walking her to the door, where I tell her, 'Thanks, again.'

She shrugs, dismissing her hours of brain power. 'Any time.'

I open the door. 'Can I ask you something? If you love this stuff so much, which you clearly do because I've watched you grin as you type for hours, then why don't you do it as a job? Why acting?'

'I did briefly. I did a rotation in the department at my firm but when it came to applying for jobs on qualification, there was a guy who was great at it and I knew he'd get the job. I liked numbers and there were a handful of jobs in the auditing team, so that's where I went.'

I lean my head to one side, trying to get a better view of her downcast look. 'You avoided competition.'

'I don't like conflict.'

'I can understand that.' I avoid it at all costs in my personal life, despite the fact I'm smack in the middle of the worst personal conflict I've known. Maybe that's part of the reason I can't bring myself to confess who I really am to Abbey. I want to, desperately, especially after tonight. But I don't want to fall out with the one person I know in New York. Particularly when that one person is... pretty great, it turns out. 'But sometimes competition in business is a good thing.'

She scoffs. 'May I remind you that I'm a very successful actress these days. I've lucked in.'

'Still, I'd happily pay you for everything you've done tonight. I mean, my brother would.'

She pats my chest and starts to leave the apartment. 'And this was a friendly chat, remember. He needs to get everything blessed by a professional.'

She's in the corridor and heading for the stairs. 'Then how can I repay you, as a friend?'

She opens the door to the stairwell then turns back to me. I expect her to be dismissive again but she surprises me. 'You're already repaying me by agreeing to be my fake date in Canada for a week.'

'I guess.' She's helping me by getting me off the grid.

'Now, get some sleep. Sweet dreams. Don't let the bed bugs bite but if they do, use dynamite.'

Her voice echoes in the stairwell as she goes, leaving me to watch the fire door start to close behind her.

Before she disappears from view, I shout out, 'Hey Abs, for the record, some people might like the big panties, fluffy slippers numbers girl better than the impractical-shoe-wearing actress.'

I think maybe I started bouncing balls again tonight in the hope she would come.

'Said no one ever,' she calls back.

She's right. No one ever preferred the tech developer to the MLB player either.

28

ABBEY

It's my last day of filming today. Mike and I will be taking our show on the road and performing our relationship for my family in Canada tomorrow. I don't know if I'm an appropriate level of anxious about it or over-the-top anxious but we've both been so busy in the last few days that we haven't done as much preparation as I would have liked.

New York is muggy today and filming is taking place on location in Central Park, which means I'm running around following orders and my clothes are sticking to me like the humid air. A hefty thunderstorm is what this day needs.

'Abbey, we're taking a break in ten, can you get iced water ready for the actors and crew?' One of the production assistants addresses me, holding a hand over the microphone attached to the headset she's wearing as she does. It's not even 3 p.m. and this is something like my millionth instruction of the day (not including my early morning stint acting as a young maid walking a dog).

I hand her the spare microphone pack I was sent to find as my latest task and tell her, 'Will do.'

Gosh, I used to hate being stuck inside at my desk as an auditor – mostly in summer, the aircon on full power, while the sun beamed down on tourists and outdoor workers in the parks below. Now, I realize I had it easy. Not that I'm ungrateful, just appreciating that the world of television and film production is much less glamorous than people might expect.

I feel for my sister, still not out of her yucky first trimester, dressed in full period-drama costume in this sticky heat.

I head out of the park, where our production vans are parked on the street near the closest entrance. I prepare jugs of filtered water with ice and a stack of recycled card cups.

We can't stop passers-by using the sidewalk. Naturally, tourists who aren't used to something being filmed in New York every day are gathering around to catch a glimpse of the cast and crew at work.

'Excuse me, coming through,' I call as politely as I can, navigating the spectators as I head back to the set. When I get to the camera crew, who are all sitting on the highly sought after fold-out chairs, I recognize a handsome face approaching one of our temporary barriers.

Setting down the water, I make my way over to Mike and wave him inside, telling security, 'He's with me,' and feeling more important than I am in the process. 'He's my boyfriend,' I say, entirely smugly because, let's face it, Mike's a catch (no pun intended).

'Hey, you came to see my sister in action,' I say, placing a hand on his elbow to guide his big frame under the fence tape.

'I came to see you, actually, but I did notice your sister, she looks great. Very... Tolstoy.'

Only now do I remember I'm supposed to be an actress, not fetching water. I think on my feet. 'Well, my shots were filmed this morning. Clean takes. Smooth as a... smooth thing.' *Stop. Talking.*

Abbey. 'I'm just helping out with refreshments because the, ah, runner got sick. Dodgy seafood.'

Is he buying any of this?

He's wearing his usual shorts and T-shirt, casual, but his hair looks different, maybe he has product in it, and he hasn't shaved. His usual clean-cut look is gruff. A bit rough and ready. Totally not what I would call my type. I'm more clean, suited, shoes. Yet, I can't take my eyes off him and I'm hoping between my shades and his own, he can't tell that I'm having a moment of indulgence.

Noooooooo. Thou shalt not crush on the famous, ball-playing, wall-banging mess of a man from apartment 8B.

Abigail, this is your conscious intervention. Your life is off course sufficiently enough without falling like a teenager at prom for the hottest guy in school.

Don't. Even. Fantasize. About. It.

No. Just... no.

'I feel for Dee being pregnant in this heat,' I say, changing the subject.

'She's pregnant?'

Oops. 'Very early days and my parents don't know yet.'

'Let's add that to the list of Canada secrets then, shall we?' He looks bemused. Like we didn't have enough to think about.

'Come on over, I can set you up with a headset if you'd like to listen?'

He declines, but still follows me, moving closer to the action. 'I came to tell you that I— My brother sent your report to his accountancy firm this morning and asked them to bless it. He sent it to his lawyer, too, for visibility.'

My stomach sinks. They'll find all my errors. Not meaning to, I worry my lip, only becoming aware when Mike is staring at my display of nervousness.

'It's going to be great. You've saved Ted a lot of time and

money. More than that, you've done something his advisers never do, which is explain in plain English what he needs to be thinking about.'

I look away. 'It was nothing. Like I said, I've done it for my dad's businesses a few times. But your brother shouldn't take it for red.'

Mike goes to speak but time is called on set and I'm instantly shouted into action on drinks.

'I'll be right back,' I tell him, placing a hand on his chest, which is as firm as I remember it looking when he was dressed in nothing but a towel. And now my mind is in the gutter as I'm pouring drinks and I'm busy wondering where this sudden desirous minx has come from because she didn't exist for most of the years I was with Andrew.

Age and hormones is what I decide it's down to, right as Dee whispers into my ear, '8B is looking sharp today. Can't keep away, can he?'

'Oh, ha ha!' My reply is almost reflexive. Protective even, sparing myself later rejection, a hangover from years of similar comments from Dee about the cute, untouchable guys in school, I suppose. 'Remember there's nothing but a ruse between us. He came to see the set, and you.'

She gulps her iced water as I take a sip from my own glass. 'It's such a shame I'm up the duff.'

My water never makes it to my stomach, as it sprays from my mouth with my amusement. 'You're shocking, Dee.'

'And he is a delight. Recently dumped or not.'

Mike helps me clear away after the drinks session and hangs around on set, us sharing an occasional joke or comment about the onscreen drama, until I'm dismissed around five when there's a sudden downpour of rain.

* * *

After reluctantly taking the subway back to Brooklyn on account of the rain, Mike and I decide to have our homework session learning about each other – or, in my case, Mike and baseball – walking Brooklyn Bridge Park, opting to walk the path around the piers, instead of the shorter route along the greenway. I definitely don't feel like I need the exercise after running around all day on set, but walking north from the Pier 6 entrance, we'll get the view of Brooklyn Bridge for most of the way.

Since the weather broke, the evening is beautiful. There's a light, warm breeze and the humidity level is pleasant.

'I love evenings like this,' I tell him. 'The air smells like summer, especially here, on the waterfront. The grime and smog of the city seems so far away.'

I hold my next blink as I breathe in. It isn't like the air at home – untainted, mountain freshness – but I feel more content tonight than I have for months. Since Andrew and I split. Before then, I'm coming to realize. Before even my work trip to Texas.

I need a proper job and a long-term plan but tonight, I have company on my sun-down stroll, and I have a date for my parents' party. Life is okay.

'New York is growing on me,' Mike says, slipping his hands into the pockets of his shorts and looking up to the cityscape across the water. A small boat zooms along the river, a groom driving his bride. 'It's still not San Francisco but there's another side to life here that I haven't seen much of before.'

'I'd have thought you'd decided that before you splurged on a penthouse apartment.'

Then I remember *GQ* magazine and Mike's suit, all the women and red-carpet events, the sports-guy lifestyle *and* salary. He can afford to be throwaway with cash. But it's as if I know two versions of the same man sometimes. On the one hand, self-assured and flippant with cash, on the other, considered, smart, kind.

'There are some perks to being rich,' he says. His words are crass but the way mischief dances in his eyes tells me he knows it.

'Welcome back, Mike. I was worried I'd lost you to sincerity but you've reminded me that your lack of modesty knows no bounds.'

'That's right, baby,' he says. Then he winks and with it makes me chuckle.

'Please don't call me baby or anything equally as misogynistic in front of my dad next week.'

'Why, does he think you're a virgin?'

'Ha, I doubt that but he is traditional.'

Mike nods and I think he's made a mental note, which I appreciate.

The irony is, my dad liked Andrew because he was well-spoken, well-mannered, respectful and emotionally balanced. There was never any spontaneity or crazy outbursts. We were always just steady.

Until we weren't. I wonder what Dad would make of Andrew sleeping around behind my back.

Andrew.

Andrew and his girlfriend.

At my parents' wedding vows.

My imminent humiliation.

'So, Michael Thomas,' I begin in my most serious voice, usually reserved for my clients. 'Tell me everything I need to know about my new beau, the professional baseball player.'

Mike's playfulness seems to disappear, which is reassuring. He's taking this seriously, as if my dignity depends on it.

He clears his throat. 'First, try to not believe everything you read on the internet. Like I said, please just ask me.'

'Okay.'

'Well, I've been good at sport all my life. Dad bought me my first bat and glove for my third birthday. I hated academia – that's my brother's bag, not mine. I was drafted right out of high school and moved around a few teams but I've been with the Giants for the last four years.'

'Three years old, wow. How come your brother wasn't the same?' I'm not sure why I ask that, except I find his brother sort of fascinating. Even more so after Mike and I got under the skin of Ted's business last night. I guess the insanely successful tech guy is more of an endearing prospect to me than the arrogant athlete guy. Or would have been, before Mike started to make me rethink my biases.

Undoubtedly, Mike would be sexier to most women and would be hated by Andrew. It will also be totally unexpected for little old me to be dating a professional athlete.

'Ted had a glove and a ball. Older brother's prerogative meant he always let me play whatever role I wanted, but yeah, he was pretty good. Good enough to help me train, that's for sure. He didn't love it the way I did. He liked lots of things and I just loved ball. But I've told Ted a thousand times, I would never have made it pro without those games with my brother in the local park.'

I nod. 'Well-rounded is good. I'd like my kids to be well-rounded. Studious. Sporty. Good at life skills. Smart without being a smart ass. Talented without being boastful. Not afraid to roll up their sleeves and clean a floor or cook a meal.'

Mike snorts. 'You want an imaginary kid.'

'That child exists,' I say, shoving his arm playfully.

'No, it doesn't.'

I scowl at him. 'Only because I haven't had it yet.'

Mike laughs, then his eyes catch mine and he stills momentarily. Is this a look? Is he giving me a look? I think I'd like him to be giving me a look.

Nope, that would be all kinds of messy. The very worst timing, for both of us. Like discovering the world is round right before it gets struck by a ginormous asteroid and flattened.

'Would you like a family?' Mike asks, looking away from me and recommencing our stroll.

'It's on my checklist to do by the time I'm thirty-two.' My checklist which has always seemed to add stability and structure to my life but which lately is feeling like a leash that I'd like to be free of. 'Just to be sure we don't get caught out next week, you're still injured, right? I'm not sure any of my family are hugely into baseball but Dad likes most sports and some of my cousins are the same, so they might recognize you and know about your injury.'

Mike's next breath seems unsteady, which I put down to him not being comfortable talking about his injury. 'I'm still a few weeks of rehabilitation away from playing. It was a pretty bad rotator-cuff tear and I'm getting on now for a pro player; my recovery time is longer than it would have been a decade ago.'

'I guess when the game is your life, it's tough to watch from the sidelines, huh?'

'The worst. Honestly, though, I'm generally a silver-linings kind of guy. I bounce through life. Nothing really drags me down.'

Hmm. 'If you don't mind me saying, it hasn't seemed that way in the last couple of days.'

'Fleur. I guess we'll call that a red herring. Unchartered territory, since I've never really had a serious relationship.'

'You two were a longer-term thing, then? You haven't actually mentioned how long you were together.'

He clears his throat again. 'Would you mind if we stick to other things? I just feel all Fleured out at the moment.'

'Yes, sure. I get it. After Andrew did what he did, I got so fed up of thinking about it and asking why. Wondering what is so bad about me he had to do that to me.'

Mike takes me by surprise, stopping in his stride and turning to me. 'Hey. *He's* a coward, Abbey. The world is full of shitty humans and you, Abigail Mitchell, are not one of them.'

I recognize my words he speaks back to me and smile. And in a total moment of madness, want to stand on my tiptoes and kiss him for being so sweet.

This. This is what I struggle to remedy with his arrogance. These moments of true tenderness. Mike is a man with many layers, it would seem.

Perhaps that's why I protect myself by ignoring my instinct and continuing on our walk.

We reach the end of Pier 1 and without either one of us suggesting it, we both come to rest on the metal railing overlooking East River. We watch as the DUMBO ferry comes toward the dock.

'I find it hard to believe you don't care about anything except baseball, Mike. I think you care about your brother enormously. You care about his business.' I'm speaking my thoughts more than asking him a question as I watch two kayakers slowly glide through the water, ripples spanning out across the surface from the fronts of the vessels, like swimming ducks.

'I care where it matters. I'm loyal; that's a family trait. I'd move heaven and earth for Mom, Dad or my brother. At the end of it all, when I'm old and grey, I won't be worried about how much money I have or how successful I was; I'll care about the hours I spent with the people I love.' His eyes are still on the activity on the river as he interlocks his fingers and speaks his next words more to himself than me, I think. 'That's why it's like a fist to the gut when they throw it back in your face.'

His break-up with Fleur – if their relationship really is done – is still so fresh, his pain is visceral.

'I know the feeling,' I tell him. 'I still wake up some days and think *surely* Andrew didn't mean to hurt me. Surely there's been a big misunderstanding because the alternative means I wasted years of my life on one giant hoax and the only person who fell for it was me.'

'I hear that,' Mike says.

Then we watch in companionable silence as the DUMBO ferry's lines are tied to the dock and its passengers – an eclectic mix of suits, tourists and many other categories of people New York's melting pot contains – walk onto our side of the river.

When the full ferry departs again, a loud crash of metal hitting metal makes us both dart our heads to the lawn behind us, where fencing is being moved around an open-air cinema area and a poster for *E.T.* is being displayed.

Mike looks my way, smiling now. 'What do you say, are you up for it?'

'Do you have a pack of tissues? Because I've never gotten through *E.T.* dry-eyed.'

'Hmm...' He pats the side and back pockets of his shorts. 'I don't but I can offer the sleeve of my T-shirt and a large helping of chips and dips?'

'I'm more of a sausage kind of girl.'

He chuckles. 'Not something I'd recommend for your Tinder profile.'

'Hey!' I flick his arm. 'For your information, I no longer need Tinder because I only needed a date for my parents' party and now I have you. Come on, then!'

We stand in a queue for Mike's chips, my hot dog, two large

soft drinks and a bag of sweet and salty popcorn. For an athlete, he gives zero credence to nutritional value. I like that in people. Especially in fake boyfriends.

We pay five dollars to hire a picnic blanket and find ourselves a spot on the lawn, waiting for the movie to begin as the space around us fills with fellow moviegoers.

Mike leans back on his side, resting on one arm as he uses the other to scoff his snacks.

'This is so trashy, it's delicious,' I tell him, wiping a dollop of mustard from the side of my mouth with a napkin.

'You look like you're enjoying that, Sausage Girl.'

Rolling my eyes, I take another moreish bite of my food and once I've swallowed it, I ask, 'What is it I love about Michael Thomas, then? Why have I fallen for you enough to bring you home to meet my family?'

Mike licks his thumb then his finger and leans back on both elbows. 'Besides fame and fortune, you mean?'

I grimace, leaning my head to one side, but actually, I imagine there are a lot of women keen on catching themselves a sports star, if they actually knew anything about the sport, that is. 'For real.'

'Ah, okay, for real. The fact I'm great at something. My confidence and bravado.'

'Which knows no limits.'

He snorts. Genuinely snorts. 'You asked. Honestly, I think his, *my* most admirable quality is that I know who I am and I don't care about what I'm not. Bad things that happen and just wash over him, me, but when something bad happens to people I care about, I'm there for them, in a heartbeat.'

'You do make yourself sound like a pretty good guy.' I finish my hot dog and lean back next to him so we're both facing the big screen, behind which the sun is setting and casting an orange hue across Manhattan.

'And you're surprisingly smart,' I say, only teasing in part because I really *do* think he's a very intelligent man. To me, that's worth more than his fame and fortune.

'Ouch, that sounded like pigeon-holing the jock, right there.' In response to my flicking his ear, he flinches and says, 'I'm kidding.' He eats another chip. Then he tells me, 'I guess I am smart,' and chuckles. 'I can recite the sporting averages of just about every sports player, across every sport played in the States. That's something, right?'

'Oh, so you're a numbers guy! Now we're talking.'

Mike twists his face, as if he's confused by numbers being a standout characteristic for me. Of course, I'm an actress to Mike. Not some ordinary girl who likes simple things, especially logic and math.

'We also both like being outdoors,' I tell him, quickly skimming over my faux pas, licking mustard from my thumb.

'We might be the most compatible fake boyfriend and girlfriend known to man.'

Lol.

As we talk, the sun falls lower behind downtown Manhattan, until there are burnt-orange and red wispy clouds in the sky and it's dark enough for the movie to begin.

Despite the ancient graphics, I'm just as enthralled by the opening scene – creepy music, spaceship, adorable alien and all – as I have been every time I've seen this movie. It's one of Dad's all-time favorites. I remember how we used to watch it on the sofa together, Dee and I each tucked under one of Dad's arms, Nate usually lounging somewhere like the floor or on a beanbag. We watched it every Christmas holiday season.

Mike and I whisper our childhood memories to each other,

eyes fixed on the screen. The sky grows darker and we end up pulling the bottom of our blanket over our legs as we lie side by side.

When we get to the death scene, despite willing myself not to, I blub. True to his word, Mike offers me the sleeve of his T-shirt. I find my dirty hot dog napkin and use that instead but I'm grateful for the offer and even more grateful that he doesn't laugh at how utterly pathetic I am. I blame Spielberg's movie-making prowess.

It's nice just being with someone, watching something we both enjoy, doing something I've never done before. Stopping, for once in my life, not rushing to or from the office, not running to the grocery store, not attending another one of my or Andrew's client functions or watching him practice his work presentations, not feeling guilty about not having the time to do any of these things as well as I ought to.

When the movie ends and my tears have been wiped away, Mike returns the blanket and I trash our rubbish. Then we head across Squibb Park Bridge, back to Brooklyn Heights and home. It's late and I've had a busy day, yet I don't feel tired.

Mike and I are too busy talking about aliens, spaceships, which planet we'd like to live on when Earth combusts and how a flying basket bike would be pretty cool, for me to want to sleep.

We're almost back at our block when suddenly Mike wraps an arm around my waist and leans into my ear. The move takes me by surprise. We've joked around for most of the night but we haven't been in close contact, not really, not like this.

His hold is heavy, yet warm and welcome. His cheek grazes mine and the scent of him forces my eyes to close as I inhale, stilled by our connection, his familiarity. Lost in a sudden rush of desire for him.

I open my eyes to his, noticing we've stopped on the sidewalk and people are having to maneuver around us. Extraordinarily for me, I don't care one iota what anyone else thinks because I'm consumed by my own feelings.

Our eyes meet and I tense, wondering what's coming next, maybe hoping he'll—

'Your ex is across the street,' Mike whispers, his breath hot against my lips.

'Andrew?'

'Don't look now.' Then he nudges the tip of his nose against mine, playfully, and I could even be fooled into thinking lovingly, if it wasn't all an act for Andrew.

I rest a hand on his cheek, improvising, all the while my disappointment like a weight falling through my insides, crushing my stomach.

This isn't real, I remind myself. *You can't miss what you don't have.*

I glance across the street to Andrew, who's walking hand in hand with his girlfriend but his focus is most certainly on Mike and me. Andrew holds up a hand in hello and for some obscure reason, I return his wave. Mike's jaw clenches, in response to my reaction, I think, and who could blame him; I'm mad at myself for being polite.

'Looks like your plan to make him jealous is working,' Mike says, tugging me closer to him.

I guess he's hating on cheaters as much as I am of late. I want to tell him that I'm not simply trying to make Andrew jealous, I'm just trying to not look like a girl who thought she had everything one day then had nothing the next.

But neither of these sentiments leave my mouth because I'm still dumbfounded by my body's reaction to his touch. By my irrational and momentary lapse in judgment, because I really did want him to be making a move.

Neither of us are in the market for that.

29

TED

Last night was... What was last night? Not how I thought it would be? Spontaneous. Unexpected. Head messing.

It started out as a learning meet up – I've been so busy with meetings, trying to learn all the things about Vanguard that I've previously left to Roman, and Abbey has been pulling long hours filming, so we haven't had much time for Abbey to learn about Mike. Me, as Mike, learning about Abbey.

It was intended to be a homework session. Friendly. An arrangement. A favor in return for a favor.

Only at some point, it felt like I was getting to know Abbey. Me, not Mike. And I liked it. I like her. Increasingly. I just don't know in what way.

I tried to give her as much insight into me as possible. I suppose I was testing the water at times, seeing what kind of guy she's really into. Even though sensibility tells me the actress wants the ball player. The king to her queen.

So why am I curious? I don't know. I kept asking myself that too – what game am I playing?

Because I know I can't fall for her and it wouldn't be fair to let her fall for me.

She doesn't know who I really am. And though I wanted so many times to expose my true identity last night, I couldn't. I can't. I'm too deep in the lie.

We fly to Canada *tomorrow*.

But there's a very real part of me that's... confused. That needs to be reined in.

I was desperate to touch her all night. Lying next to her on our movie blanket made me feel like a teenager with his first infatuation. It was torture.

Then Andrew appeared and it was bittersweet. A reminder that she isn't looking for a new guy and I am so far from being datable or wanting to dip my toe in that ice water again. I'm not even sure that Fleur considers me unequivocally out of a relationship right now.

But finally getting to touch Abbey, to feel the shape of her against me, to nuzzle into her neck and breathe in her heady mix of subtle perfume and outdoors, that was sweet. Too sweet.

For one thing, anything I might be feeling, even if I will admit to anything, is not reciprocated. For all I know, I might just be having some kind of existential crisis, or rebound lust or whatever.

It really doesn't feel like it. It feels... No, I won't let myself make more of this.

In any event, if Abbey did give any sign that she might have more than companionable feelings toward me, I need to remember that they aren't actually for me, they're for Mike. I'm Mike to her. That's who she thinks I am and who she wants me to be, even if it is all fake.

It's just... I don't think I've ever met a girl who is so like me in so many ways. When she isn't in stuck-up actress mode, she's a bit nerdy, she likes space and numbers, exercises mostly because she needs to in order to stay healthy, comfort eats, which goes back to the needing to stay healthy thing, would rather be outdoors than anywhere else, finds arrogance off-putting, hates showiness.

I may have put words into her mouth with some of those descriptors, but the point is there are times when I feel like we get each other. And that's without mentioning the biggest thing we have in common of late, which is that we both just ended serious relationships because our other halves did the dirty on us.

I'll add one more thing about Abbey, then I'm putting these thoughts to bed for the day, with zero innuendo intended.

I can't help wondering what would have happened if we had met under different circumstances. If we had met first. Before Andrew. Before Fleur. Before I became Mike. Because I think possibly, maybe, we'd have been a good fit.

It's Tuesday morning and I should be ecstatic because I am finally getting out of New York, bound for Canada with Abbey, but in my latest moment of self-doubt, I've turned to one person I know, without a shadow of doubt, I can truly rely on.

My brother is literally guffawing down the line. Despite the wind blowing around him, loud through his cell phone as he jogs along Ocean Beach, I can hear the depth of his amusement.

Back home, Mike lives further north than me, closer to Oracle Park, the Giants' stadium. Though also coastal, I'm based nearer to Santa Clara. I love heading up to him on the weekends and us getting out for a beach run or trail run. The smell of the salty air, the feel of the wind whipping off the Pacific, the sound of crashing waves.

If I ignore the man laughing at me, I might be homesick for the first time since arriving in New York. Not longing for the life I had a few weeks ago but missing San Francisco, missing home. That yearning brings with it a stark reminder that at some point I need to return, give Fleur yet another but absolutely final terminal diagnosis for our relationship and fess up to my family and friends how much I've been played by my best friend and fiancée.

'Let me get this straight,' Mike says breathlessly, I hope more because of exercise than because he's laughing so hard. 'The hot new actress from downstairs, who you keep telling me you aren't fooling around with, wants you to go with her to Canada for a week, to pretend that you're me? Ah, man, I'm dying.'

'Are you done already?' I snap. 'I was being serious when I said I want your advice.'

'What do you want me to tell you, little bro? It's awesome being me. Enjoy it while it lasts.'

'Could you just— You know what, forget I called.'

'Whoa, whoa, whoa. Hold up.' The wind calms and I think my brother has stopped jogging, maybe put a hand around the speaker to shield our conversation from the wind. 'Jokes aside, what I really think is that you should come home and give Roman exactly what he's got coming to him. As for Fleur, she needs to get the hell out of your place. Never did think she was good enough for you and now she's proved it. But if you're adamant you're not ready, why not stay in NY for longer?'

'Because Rome is going to come here and I want to get things in order from a business perspective before I see him. That's going to take at least a few more days.'

'And you have to fly to Canada today?' Mike asks.

I do because Abbey's mom has booked us flights for today and if I'm going as Abbey's boyfriend, I need to go with her. Not to mention it lowers my risk of seeing Roman before I'm ready.

Even without any of this, I want to help Abbey. I want to support her when she deals with her troubles in Canada. I owe her at least this much for all the truths I'm keeping from her. Every lie I feel increasingly guilty about.

'Yes,' I tell him simply.

He whistles as he exhales and I imagine him scratching his chin as he considers his next words.

'Can't you go as you? I mean, I know I'm way more dope and all...' He pauses and I know he's waiting for me to react to his teasing. If I wasn't feeling so anxious, maybe I'd find him entertaining. Maybe not. Probably not. 'Look, Ted, don't let this go to your head or anything but I think you're a pretty great guy. This Abbey chick would be lucky to have you, as you, not me.'

'You have to say that; you're my brother.' Though it's true, I still fight back a small smile because it's rare my brother is genuinely affectionate, despite the fact I know he loves me. 'But honestly, there's nothing between Abbey and me, just friends. She's been burned, I've been burned. She helped me out, I'm returning the favor.'

Even if I've felt lines blur in my mind at times, they've been lapses in judgment, that's all. Neither one of us is in a position to get into a new relationship. It would be relationship suicide, in fact, to start something now.

I'm not even contemplating it.

Mostly.

Ever.

'A favor she needs because she doesn't want her ex to think she's single—'

'He already thinks she's seeing me, or should I say, you. *She* thinks I'm you.'

'And she hasn't fessed up to her folks that her childhood sweetheart was a jerk and went behind her back, so instead of her folks trying to get the pair of them back together, she's turning up with you, me, to put them off the scent?'

'Broadly right.'

He blows a raspberry down the line, then whispers, 'So fucked up. Do you like her, Ted? Tell me you haven't fallen for her because the identity crisis aside, she's clearly still into her ex.'

'She is?'

'She doesn't want to fess up to her ex being a dick in case she gets back with him. Isn't that plain as day?'

'Maybe. I really don't think she wants him back.'

Does she? I hope not.

But as I stand here in Mike's spare bedroom, I stare at my half-packed luggage, questioning this trip for the zillionth time since I started packing my bag for tomorrow's flight.

I doubted whether I was over Fleur and I guess I'm not over what I've lost and how things panned out. But I do know, after seeing her here last week, after listening to more of her lies and bended truths, that I could never get back with her.

I know I'm not in love with her.

Has Abbey had that epiphany yet? God, I hope so. She's better than that. *Him.*

'You didn't answer whether you like her,' Mike says, his tone demanding.

'Not in the way you mean. She's just... I don't know, calm, relaxed, unassuming and funny without being obviously out for a laugh from her audience. When she's not being the actress version of herself, she's... the kind of person I can handle being around right now.'

I wait but there's no reply, yet I can still hear the sound of the outdoors down the line. 'Mike? You there?'

'Just thinking if she's playing a role for all her family. Ted, what makes you think the parts of her you like aren't an act?'

I suppose he could be right but the more I'm around her, the less of the crabby, showy Abbey I see. In fact, she might even be changing my opinions on designer-clothes-wearing TV stars. It also sounds like delving into that, applying my usually analytical mind to the game of *if*, would be a rabbit hole I don't want to fall down.

'I just don't want to see you get hurt again, little bro. But if you tell me you've got this and this fake relationship works for you right now too, then I guess you have my blessing to be me.'

'That was uncommonly heartfelt,' I tease, not wanting to focus on his warning too much. Am I risking getting hurt in all of this? Am I so numb to everything right now that I can't see what would be bad for me?

If my head is messed up and my heart broken, all I have to go with is instinct and my instinct is telling me to go to Canada, that Abbey isn't out to get me in all of this.

I zip my luggage shut and set it down on the ground. 'Good talk, big bro.'

'Catch you later, mini me.'

30

ABBEY

'You are still coming, aren't you?' I ask Shernette, my cell phone tucked between my cheek and shoulder as I put the last of my toiletries into my wheel-on cabin luggage.

She's heading into the office. I can hear chatter as she passes people on the sidewalk and her heels, or someone's heels, clicking the ground as she moves.

'Absolutely. I have a half day and I'm heading to the airport right after work on Friday afternoon, so I'll be with you in time for dinner.'

'Amazing. I'm going to need all the moral support I can get, especially since Dee now won't be coming until Friday evening either. My morale will be battered and bruised by then.'

'No! How come Dee won't be there sooner?'

I zip closed my luggage and lift it down from my bed to the bedroom floor. 'She has an afternoon shoot on Friday. They're front loading all of the scenes where she'd be expected to have a full body shot or where she's doing something particularly active before she starts to get a real baby bump.'

'Makes sense but that sucks for you. Still...' The surrounding noise falls away and I suspect Shernette has walked through the revolving doors into our— *her* office block. 'You'll have your new beau to keep you smiling and to keep your mom's matchmaking at bay.'

'Ha, yes. Well, assuming he's not going to get cold feet and ditch me.'

'Do you think he won't show?'

'He's already on the run from his best friend and fiancée. I'm just some girl he met not even three weeks ago.' I wheel my suitcases to my apartment door then take hold of the phone in my hand. 'Oh God, this is a terrible idea, isn't it? We hardly know anything about each other, except the crash lessons Mike has given me in the last few days. He thinks I'm actually a decent actress! Someone is going to find out the truth – maybe they know baseball, follow the Giants, know about Mike's model girlfriend, maybe they even know Mike and—'

'Abbey, take a breath. You and Mike might have had a crash course in getting to know each other but you do know each other and he wouldn't have said yes to coming along with you if he didn't like you. Not to mention the fact he wants to expend with his own reality for a few days.'

'Yes.' I nod, trying to reassure myself. 'You're right. Plus, he says he's doing it as a favor for my help and he's just not the kind of guy to let someone down. I know that much about him. He's loyal. He's kind. Funny. Sometimes even unintentionally, you know, in a sort of geeky way.'

'Erm, do you *like* Mike? Not that I can't see the obvious attraction – he's hot – but up till now you've maintained you don't like him.'

'I don't! And neither of us is in a place to want to be anything more than friends anyway.'

'Riiiight, but Abs, this whole thing is based on you getting back to New York and not seeing Mike anymore.'

'It is? It is. Because this isn't real and Mike lives in San Francisco and dates models. He's a freaking Major League Baseball player.' And I need to get a real job, the boring kind that an MLB player wouldn't crush over at all.

'Exactly.'

We both fall silent, for my part silenced by the realization that by this time next week, Mike and I will be no longer. He'll go back to California. Back to his exquisitely beautiful girlfriend, who seems to be having trouble accepting that their relationship is over. Or any one of a hundred different gorgeous women – the type professional athletes date.

That was always the plan.

Which is great; it makes this whole arrangement cleaner. Like a business transaction. I did work for him and his brother and, in return, he's fulfilling this agreement for me, then we'll go our separate ways. I'll get a new job, find a sensible apartment that I can afford and embark on my *real* new life, post-Andrew and pre-the rest of my actual life.

'Abbey?'

Shernette's voice pulls me out of my own headspace. 'I'm here.'

'Just be careful, okay? I don't want to see you get hurt, again.'

I draw back my shoulders and straighten my spine. 'It's just business, Shernette, I promise. Can't wait to see you on Friday.'

'You too, lady.'

We each blow a kiss down the line and hang up.

I wheel my luggage the rest of the way into the lounge, glance around the plug sockets to make sure I switched everything off, then I leave my apartment.

What if he has changed his mind?

The elevator arrives and I wrestle my stuffed over-shoulder bag and cabin case inside. I have no idea what we'll be doing for the week, so I hope I have enough luggage to cover the eventualities. Maybe I should have brought hold luggage?

Chewing my lip, I only realize I've reached the ground floor when the concierge waves and calls, 'Morning, going somewhere?'

'Just a few days at home,' I tell him.

Then I see him. Mike is standing outside, waiting by a black car that looks much fancier than an Uber. Next to him, on the sidewalk, is one small weekend bag and a suit carrier. His usually messed up hair has been styled, like he wore it when *GQ* came to interview him, and he's wearing a blue button-down shirt tucked into smart pants, though his signature sneakers are on his feet.

He looks every inch the man for the task.

'You came,' I say, both happy and relieved.

'We had a deal,' he says simply.

His tone feels cooler than usual and it makes me wonder whether he's having doubts. I wouldn't blame him, though, and he's here, so I decide to go with it.

'Nice ride,' I say, gesturing to the car.

'I don't like being late so I pre-booked.'

So he never had any intention of backing out? Wow, he has more conviction than I do about this. He must really want to leave New York.

The driver gets out of the car and takes my luggage to the trunk. Mike adds his own bag and we both get into the backseat, a full seat between us, which is good. We'll be spending a lot of time together on this break and if he looks and smells as good as he does right now, then—

'You look nice,' he tells me, and as I blush, the devil on my shoulder tells me I wore this blouse and pants combo for all the wrong reasons.

'Thanks, you too. I did wonder if you'd be in full Giant's kit.'

He scoffs, right before the driver asks, 'Have you got your passports? You don't want to have to make a trip back in rush-hour traffic.'

* * *

The flight time from JFK to Calgary is around five hours. Though my mom offered to book us tickets, which would have been coach, Mike refused to let her, so I'm currently sitting in business, courtesy of my fake boyfriend. Another reminder that our lifestyles are completely incompatible.

Not that I'm complaining about the breakfast we're served and the mimosa I decide to have on the side.

Mike and I are sitting next to each other with a table between us and on it, he's using salt, pepper, butter and jelly sachets to demonstrate the positions of baseball players during a game. He's using a fork as a pitcher and I'm holding a knife where the batsman would stand but we've been at this for a while and frankly, 'I'd like to hit a home run now, please,' I tell him.

'You already think you're a star, huh? You've been at this for...' He checks his wristwatch. 'Twenty-three minutes.'

'Feels like an eternity,' I say, sighing dramatically, receiving an amused shake of the head in response.

'Alright, a home run it is. Are your bases loaded?'

'Oh yes, maximum adoration is coming my way.'

'Look at you craving the limelight, actress girl.'

'Ha! More that I recognize the need to boost my confidence before my mom starts criticizing everything about me and my life choices.'

Mike looks at me like I have ten heads. 'She's really that big on your having everything figured out by the time you're thirty?'

'Really. She's already furious about the actress thing.'

'You mean your career change? Is it a very recent thing?' His eyes narrow, contemplatively.

I. Am. Such. A. Bad. Liar.

'Ah, yeah, quite recent.'

'I guess I assumed you'd been at it for a while, what with the apartment and...' He gestures to my outfit. 'Swanky wardrobe.'

'Be careful, Mike, assumptions kill.' Kill the idea of new Abbey, the one you have agreed to date. Though, I have to admit, being in front of a camera, however brief my acting career has been, and maybe flaunting an MLB player around the set, have, I think, given old me the tiniest confidence boost. 'So, can I have loaded bases, please?'

'Go for it.'

I hold my knife as Mike twirls his fork as if he's pitching the ball. I'm about to cheer and declare my home run when Mike interjects. 'Strike one.'

He didn't!

He braces to pitch a second ball. I flick my knife as if I'm swinging my bat. I set off on my run around the bases, bopping the knife off the tray table, but Mike calls, 'Strike two.'

'Hey!' I don't mean to do it but my foot stomps the floor. 'Stop it. Let me have this. I need this.'

Mike can barely contain himself.

'Nobody likes a comic who laughs at his own jokes.'

I'm really quite cross. Yet my words only make him laugh harder.

But when we reset, Mike pitches with his fork and I knock that ball right out of the park, yelling, 'It's a home run. The crowd goes wild. All the bases are home!'

He doesn't have a chance to call a strikeout. *Ha!*

I only realize I'm being way over-the-top with my celebrations when Mike's eyes widen and he looks around our otherwise tranquil cabin area. I slowly bring my hands down from the air and pinch my lips together. *Oops!*

Mike leans across the table and whispers, 'Now who's a freak?'

Placing my fingers across my lips, I mutter, 'Me.'

I scan the nearby passengers and see an elderly lady, wearing a chic silver-grey crop of hair and a boldly patterned two-piece suit. She smiles at me and I hold up a hand apologetically, to which she flicks her fingers – *not a problem*.

Then she says, 'Young love is a beautiful thing.'

I'm about to tell her that Mike and I aren't a couple, but we are. We're in public, therefore we are acting the part. So, I drop a hand to Mike's lap, drawing his gaze to mine.

31

TED

If I thought my life was confusing before this trip, it just got a whole lot worse.

These looks and touches, the way we talk so easily, the way she makes me laugh, like no girlfriend or fiancée has before her, are they real? Am I just Mike and her playing a role when she does these things? Because I can't keep up a pretense all day, and the way she stirs something inside me I don't think is a lie. The timing is truly awful, atrocious even, and though it's one-sided and ill-judged, I can't help but think that I might be falling for Abbey.

I don't have the best track record with women, putting it lightly. I was late to the girlfriend party in my teens, and in my twenties I so often had my head in a tech project or in starting my own company that relationships were few and far between.

My longest relationship to date was Fleur and look how that turned out. But despite my lack of knowledge and dubious history with the opposite sex, I'm fairly certain Abbey and I have a connection. I think I'm developing a sense of what people mean when they talk about chemistry, as if we're two molecules that aren't supposed to be put together, but we have been and the resultant product is exciting, bubbling away in a test tube.

But this test tube is narrow and fragile because this whole trip, this arrangement, is just a convenience for both of us. Abbey doesn't even know who I am and if she finds out now, after all the time we've spent together, she'll hate me.

There's no point hurting her more than her ex already has. At the end of the week, she can get back on with her life and her online dating. As for me, I need to go and unravel the web of lies and mess awaiting me in San Francisco.

Though my mind is racing with an infinite number of thoughts, I've been locked on Abbey's eyes for just seconds. The amount of time it's taken us to process that the lady sitting nearby believes we are a couple.

That lady has no idea how with one innocuous sentence she sent my mind into a spiral.

'Hello again from the flight deck, this is your captain speaking. In a little over ten minutes, we will begin our descent into Calgary. Please take this time to pack away your belongings and to use the facilities if you need to. The seatbelt sign will be switched on in ten minutes. The weather in Calgary is seventy-two degrees and sunny with a light south-westerly breeze. We should have a smooth journey in.'

Abbey has the window seat, and the captain's words seem to turn her attention to the view outside. As I follow her focus, I see the arresting mountainous terrain of the Rockies. I've seen the Rockies from stateside, but never from across the border and never in their sheer enormity from the air.

Despite the time of year, the tallest of the peaks are still capped with snow. There's a serenity amongst the view, amongst the sense I have that something new and exciting, an adventure that has me full of adrenaline, lies ahead.

And if the mountains are beautiful, the sense of calm that descends around Abbey, like an aura, an energy, is completely mesmerizing. As she observes her home, I watch her, the way her breaths are slow and peaceful, the way her entire body seems to breathe with her. It's a slow and subtle shift but I think I might be getting a moment of insight into what Abbey looks like when she's completely relaxed.

Between the two images I have in my sights, I feel more inspired. My worries about whether this trip is a good idea or a disastrous one seem to fall away, out of me, into my seat, out of the plane and across the surreal landscape, until they're nothing.

* * *

As Abbey and I head out of arrivals with our luggage, amongst cab drivers and shuttle drivers, I see a guy trying to flag us down. He's wearing hiking boots, shorts, and a T-shirt, with winter-sports-type shades resting in his short hair. He's holding out his arms as if to say, *Give me some love*, and calling Abbey's name.

'It's my cousin,' she says, before picking up her pace and allowing herself to be welcomed by the guy. I hang back to allow them time together, then when he looks my way, I move closer and offer my hand, which he shakes, telling me, 'I'm Nick. And you are *not* Andrew.'

'Happily, I'm not. Hey, I'm Mike.' My brother's name leaves my lips awkwardly.

It's my first lie of the trip and it's to a member of Abbey's family. It's a reminder that what started out as a bluff to fool our exes is about to get significantly bigger.

It makes me feel uncomfortable, though not nearly as uncomfortable as I feel every minute I don't tell Abbey the truth.

'Well, I never did care much for that douche. Nice to meet you, Mike.'

He throws Abbey a look that I think he intends to be subtle and suggestive of him having questions for her later, when I'm out of earshot. A look that makes me appreciate that not everyone in Banff is going to know that Abbey and Andrew are over, let alone the reason why, and they certainly aren't going to know that I'm a fake boyfriend.

This is going to be interesting.

Though I'm much taller and could use the extra leg room, I'm happy to let Abbey take the front passenger seat of the SUV and catch up with Nick. I'm content to take in the view of the national park with its imposing peaks, the quaint stores and residences of Banff town we pass through. Occasionally, Abbey and Nick bring me into a conversation, but given it's mostly about baseball and why it isn't as good a sport to watch as ice hockey, I try not to overly engage, limiting the lies.

It's safe to say though that having a professional sports player in a car is a talking point, and it's clear that talking baseball is going to be one of my major pastimes whenever we're in company over the coming days.

Nick seems nice, if a little edgy and buoyant.

It transpires he's employed by Abbey's father in his leisure and tourism empire, working the winters as a ski and snowboard instructor, and as a guide leading group hikes and adventures in the summer months, otherwise being a 'jack of all trades' when called upon. Through the conversation, I'm getting a sense that Abbey has underplayed the size of her dad's business.

The drive takes us up hills and down valleys. When Abbey tells me we're five minutes from home, we're ascending the foothills of a mountain and I see nothing but trees. When we round a bend and turn off the main road, I'm surprised that the trees open up, and a driveway emerges through the pines. It's a driveway that just keeps going. Space like I've never known where I grew up, and it's not as if I grew up in a city like New York; I grew up in suburbia, within a short walk of sand and sea. I wind down my window to be assaulted by the smell of fresh trees, clean air and newly chopped wood.

'Soak it all in, dude. This is home,' Nick says as he and Abbey exchange a look that says, *How lucky are we?* And they are. If this is home, if this is where they grew up, they're extremely lucky. It's magnificent.

Hearing a rhythmic *chop, chop, chop* and searching for the source of the sound, I see a man in khaki shorts and big boots swinging an axe in a way I'm not sure I would ever dare at a felled tree trunk. Beside him, a substantial stack of firewood shows the fruits of his labor.

Eventually, branches disperse and into view comes what I would describe as a ski resort – but I think it's Abbey's parents' house.

It makes more sense now that the Abbey I first met was so comfortable amongst flashy shoes and designer handbags, and that she so easily slipped into enjoying her business class seats on the airplane. But I was wrong when I prejudged her. Abbey is one of the most genuine people I've ever met... The whole con of this visit aside, of course.

The home is three stories of a magazine-perfect ski lodge, with balconies all around the second and third floor, looking down across the valley behind us. If this is my digs for the next six nights, count me in.

We pull up to the front where there are two large wood doors and overhanging them is a huge wood carving of the head of a moose.

Nick tells us he'll bring our bags in so Abbey can get inside to see her mom, but after a back-and-forth exchange, we agree that I'll carry my own.

'Your mom is out back,' Nick tells Abbey, then quieter, but not so quiet that I miss it, he says, 'Fair warning, the new guy is for sure going to get the backlash from your fall out with the ex-guy.'

Abbey gives me what I think is an apologetic smile. It looks like Mike is going to have to bring his A game, which is fine. But if Abbey's family doesn't like an ego, they won't like *actual* Mike's personality. There's going to be a fine line to be walked here. I may have to be a chameleon.

But carrying two bags in my hands and following Nick into the house, I'm left wondering, not for the first time, why Abbey hasn't told her family the truth of her break-up with Andrew – she doesn't surely want to protect him, and if she does, why? In case they might get back together?

She deserves so much more than his lies.

More than mine, too.

The inside of the house is a mix of old-chalet charm – wooden beams and carvings – with elegant, modern upholstery. I slip off my sneakers at the door then look up, startled by a life-size statue of a brown bear. *Jesus*.

Nick catches my reaction and chuckles. Then he continues toward a central staircase. 'That's nothing by comparison to her mom,' he says.

The staircase turns back on itself and onto the first floor, where a wall of windows gives a panoramic view of the stunning surrounds. I'm drawn to it so much that I forget to follow Nick, until I hear him call, 'This way, bud.'

We pass three closed doors as we move along a corridor and finally Nick opens one at the end. 'This is you guys,' he says. 'Abbey's room.'

He pushes open the door and lets me walk in of my own

accord, and I see why. It's like he's inviting me into a shrine of Abbey and her ex – there are photographs of the two of them everywhere.

'Sorry, Mike. You might run into his face a few more times whilst you're here and I doubt her mom has done anything to make you feel more at ease. This was almost a predestined marriage, whether Abbey liked it or not.' Nick sets Abbey's luggage just inside the door. 'But I won't bullshit you, she did buy into it.' He pats me on the back. 'Still, I reckon being an MLB player gets you a few extra man points.'

Right. For sure it does, otherwise I might not still be misleading a woman I've come to respect. I might have found the confidence to be myself in spirit and name.

Nick says he'll take me outside to Abbey but when I confirm I'm happy to make my own way, he leaves and closes the bedroom door behind him.

The walls are a subtle green color, the bed is fittingly resting on a wood frame – the logistics of the one double will be something I'm sure Abbey will have a view on already. The bedspread is white and teal checks and the soft cushions around the pillows are the same color as the walls.

It has an ensuite and the open door allows me to see a bathtub with a shower hanging over it, a small sink toilet and vanity unit. It's like a hotel ensuite in size and finish. Patio doors lead on to a balcony and they're open, white curtains hanging either side and framing the stunning view that I saw at the top of the staircase.

Abbey used to wake up to this every morning. I turn my back on the landscape and look to the bed, imagining her lounging and happy in amongst nature. This whole place tells me so much more about her than her warm but minimalist apartment in Blake House.

This room feels more Abbey. Her want to be outdoors, close to nature. Where she doesn't need to wear painful shoes or feel forced to go online dating. Though how I remedy that with acting, I'm not sure.

Thinking about her dating makes me realize that she and Andrew will have lain in this bed together, waking up to this view in the mornings *together*, and my attention is brought to things that make this room feel like it might be exactly how Abbey left it when she moved to New York. An entire wall of pictures above a white desk with a lamp on it and neatly arranged stationery that gives me the sense that Abbey used to get very giddy about going back to school.

I don't want to pry without her permission but she does know that I'm up here. So I don't think she can be mad at me seeing all the pictures of her: she and her sister, heads together and smiling, sitting on a wall at what looks like an après-ski café, both wearing matching pants and jackets with ski boots.

There are numerous variations of the same two smiling faces, as well as multiple pictures of Abbey and Shernette.

The likeness between Abbey and her mom is uncanny. I recognize Abbey in pictures with her parents and her older brother. There's a family picture that looks like it has aunts and uncles, maybe cousins – I recognize Nick's face.

But in amongst all of these pictures, there are a multitude of pictures of Abbey and Andrew, arms around each other, lips pressed to each other's, even phonebooth pictures of them wearing moustaches and top hats with their black-tie outfits. There are group pictures with Abbey and Andrew standing next to each other amongst family and friends.

The pictures of the couple span years of Abbey's life. There's even one of two toddler-aged children, whom I might have mistaken as Abbey and her brother, but for the fact that at some point, Abbey drew a love heart around the two tots.

Staring at this wall, I'm wondering if this whole trip is founded on a giant fallacy. Maybe Abbey doesn't want to save face; she wants to make Andrew jealous, to make him want her back. And I'm the bait.

I head out to the balcony, lean my forearms on the rail, and breathe in the scent of the pine trees, tuning in to a woodpecker somewhere in the distance.

What am I doing? And why do I have a distinct feeling of jealousy after looking at that wall?

Mike was right; there's every chance I'm going to end up hurt, again.

I need to protect myself. Forget Nick's dislike of egos; I need to bring Mike into play in a big way. Do what he does – love 'em and leave 'em with just an air of arrogance in my wake.

32

ABBEY

I find Mom outside, sitting on the patio furniture with Gail, who I know to be a florist because she has decorated many of Mom's parties. They're sitting on opposite sofas, with books on the glass-top table in front of them and alongside is tea, served just as Mom likes it – poured from a fine China pot into matching teacups and accompanied by a tray of cakes that I know she's unlikely to eat herself, but which she likes to have out whenever we have guests.

'Mom,' I say gently, so as to not startle them when I step onto the patio. The expanse of our lawn rolls into forest around us.

'Abbey, darling!' Mom rises from the sofa, her wide beaming smile that I love drawn on her painted lips, arms outstretched.

She folds me into her chest, where I smell jasmine and lily of the valley – nostalgia.

My mom has embraced aging and wears her grey hair with just a few platinum highlights. It's loosely gripped by a butterfly clip with a few wisps of hair intentionally left dangling either side of thick bangs. Though she's in her own home, she always looks immaculate – her cream blouse is tucked neatly into duck-egg blue tailored pants, both items fitting her perfectly and matched with a cute kitten-heeled sling back.

I breathe her in, tightening my hold and feeling her do the same. I never realize quite how much I've missed her until I'm home. She drives me crazy and I think I probably do the same in return, but I love her beyond measure.

I also know I'm going to need to remind myself of that over the coming days.

'Look at you,' she says, taking one step back from me and turning the ends of my hair in her fingers, scrutinizing me from head to toe, reminding me of my recent makeover. 'Your hair. Your clothes. Shame about the footwear but I can't remember the last time you dressed to complement your figure. Maybe this acting business, as absurd and temporary as it had better be, has done you some good.' I roll my eyes but Mom misses it, as she's too busy telling Gail, 'She might like wearing a vow-maid dress after all.'

I can feel my frown crease my face.

Mom makes her way back to the sofas, beckoning me to follow. 'I've picked out the most wonderful dress for you. You'll look magical, darling.' Now sitting, she turns over a clean third cup and starts to pour what I know will be Lady Grey tea for me, then pats the sofa next to her with her free hand. 'Just wait until Andrew sees you.'

He has seen me since the wardrobe transformation – and it hasn't made a difference. No U-turn.

Not that I want one, not anymore.

'Mom, Andrew and I aren't together. I'm here with someone else. Andrew has met Mike multiple times.' After all, isn't that where this whole make-believe me began? I take my tea cup and saucer, avoiding making eye contact with her. I don't want to see the look of disapproval I know she'll be wearing. 'Let's just make this weekend what it should be.' Finally, I glance up from my drink. 'All about you and Dad.'

She smiles sweetly. Things being all about her generally makes her happy. But as she shifts her attention back to Gail's sketch pad on the table, she adds, 'Though you should know that Andrew isn't bringing a plus one anymore. Apparently, he doesn't want to hurt you.'

Grrrrrrrrgh!

What I want to say is: *He ripped my heart out. He broke us. He cheated on me.*

But what's the point in having everyone hate him? It doesn't change anything. Our families still have to be friends long after this is all swept under the rug – why make things awkward for everyone?

So, what I actually say is: nothing.

Whilst my mom starts telling me that there's a last-minute change to the table decorations as the forecast is showing a light breeze, making shorter flower arrangements a more sensible option, my mind starts to process the fact that Andrew isn't bringing a date.

Why? Does he really want to spare me? Does he want me back? Or is this all a big ploy to have everyone on his side? He knows I haven't told people our truth.

Thankfully, my insanely handsome fake date appears from inside the house, interrupting my thoughts, not least because he's changed into a tailored shirt and Bermuda shorts with suede slip-on shoes.

I've never seen him dressed like this. Where are his sneakers? Is this part of his performance? Or is this what he's really like, at home in San Francisco? Whatever the reason for the new look, it reminds me of the suave version of him I saw on the day of his *GQ* interview. Similar to that day, his shirt displays his physique in a way I'm ashamed to admit I am ogling. I seem to have softened to my new boyfriend wearing suits.

'Mrs Mitchell, it's a pleasure to meet you,' Mike says, extending a hand to my mom. There's something about his manner that's slicker than the man I've gotten used to, more like the version of him I first met.

My mom rises from her seat, full of elegance and etiquette, and it's comical how disarmed she looks. Did she expect him to be dressed in sports kit and wearing a baseball cap? I can tell that on appearances alone, she approves of my sportsman beau. I can also tell that it's absolutely killing her to approve, and that is what's making my insides jiggle with amusement.

That and maybe the fact that I'm taken back by Mike's presentation, too.

Mom sits and offers Mike tea, noticeably not telling him to call her Anna in place of Mrs Mitchell.

Surprisingly, he takes back control, picking up the teapot and saying, 'I'd love tea. Can I repour for you, ladies?'

Sitting opposite him on the sofas, I give him a questioning look – *now who's the actor?*

He's suave and completely at ease. Not that he isn't normally comfortable with me, but this is smoother than the usual Mike in a way I can't quite put my finger on. It actually makes me think that if his brother loses his business partner and front man at Vanguard, Mike should offer to replace him. This afternoon, Mike could sell snow to a ski slope.

'These flower designs are divine,' he says, pondering the images on the table, paying attention to both my mom and Gail as he speaks. 'The white selection is classic, chic; you have a good eye, Mrs Mitchell.'

Oh my God, I could vomit in my mouth, but my mom is lapping this up, clearly having forgotten the son-in-law she so desperately wants in Andrew. It gives me a chance to just enjoy a cup of tea without the pressure of ruining all my mom's dreams for my future, without wondering how long it will be before she starts reeling off all the things from my checklist that I'm failing to achieve.

But I should've known the peace would be short-lived because once Gail has finished going over the new, shorter flower arrangements for Saturday, and just Mom, Mike and I are left sitting on the sofas, it begins.

'So, you're a sportsman, Michael?' She speaks with an edge of contempt now – *my daughter was never supposed to be with the school jock.*

I know before her next words that she won't talk about Mike's successes as a professional baseball player, that her focus will be elsewhere. But I don't expect her to be so rude and direct as to say, 'And what is it that you plan to do after baseball, Michael? You must be, what, thirty-two or three already?'

'Mom!' I try to protest but Mike simply leans back into the sofa, his cup and saucer in his hands, and says, 'I'll coach or do commentary, hopefully. Probably some public speaking. I'm not short of a business investment or two either, Mrs Mitchell.'

He plays the role of a disgustingly self-assured man just as well as my mom plays the role of Monster-in-Law. Though arguably, neither of them is having to try hard.

My pretend boyfriend and my mom are at loggerheads already. I check my watch – it took all of thirty-seven minutes to get to this point. Though, that's thirty-seven minutes longer than I expected.

In Mike's defense, it's a rather impressive show. Maybe some of this Mike-ness should rub off on me, help me grow a backbone, but watching him also makes me appreciate the humble side of his personality more. A side I think not many people get to see. One I feel lucky to know.

My mom can be a very headstrong woman but it seems even she's losing the battle of wills as Mike provides an answer to each one of her demeaning questions. I know this because she turns her attention back to me.

'We have a dress fitting tomorrow morning and your dad will be back from business in Vancouver for dinner. Then you and I have a luncheon on Thursday, so I'm afraid you'll have to entertain yourself for a few hours each day, Michael. For a dedicated athlete like you, I'm sure you can find something to appease yourself in our home gym. Or you can take a hike.' She smiles sweetly, as if the words didn't have an alternative meaning. I don't like this manner on her at all.

'You see, I had planned a luncheon for our closest friends, since Abbey and Andrew were expected to be home, but I can hardly present Abbey and her new boyfriend to Victoria, can I? That's Andrew's mom. Consequently, I've had to make arrangements for it to be a female-only event.'

As if to emphasize her point and really drive home the level of inconvenience I've caused by bringing Mike here, Mom does what every actress in a scripted-TV series does at a similar juncture. She rises from her seat, needlessly brushing down her pants before she walks away, stomping her kitten-heels on the decking, her chin held high. 'Dinner will be at eight p.m. Your dad will be back from business in Vancouver and he's just *dying* to meet you, Michael.'

In her wake, I take off my shades and roll my eyes for Mike's benefit. 'Now you've met my mom.'

Mike sips his tea, casually bringing one ankle up to rest on his opposite knee. 'I think she likes me,' he says, and all of my nerves from the morning spill over into a gargantuan laugh.

33

TED

After a bumpy ride from Abbey's home, in a little powder blue Fiat 500, which gives me another flash of high-school Abbey, we're waiting in line for a gondola to take a ride to the top of Sulphur Mountain.

'I've got to admit, whilst I'm looking forward to this, I'm shocked you didn't make us hike up the mountain, or are you all talk?'

She scowls playfully. 'I'm not all talk; just you wait until Friday, then I'll show you how I hike. But we don't have time today, since the dress fitting took half the damn day, so you'll have to make do with the view from inside a gondola.'

Timely, the next carriage in line comes to a stop and Abbey and I climb inside, together with another two people, each wearing impressively large cameras around their necks.

I must admit, after my nervousness this morning, my doubts on the phone to Mike about coming here at all, then the interesting family meets since we've been here, I'm pleased to be taking it easy for a couple of hours. So much so, I exchange pleasantries with the other tourists in the gondola but make a point of looking away quickly to avoid getting drawn in to further conversation.

With Abbey, though, I've got all the time in the world to listen to her telling me tales of growing up in Canada. From dog sleigh rides and black slopes, to kayaking and zip lining, her life here sounds almost dreamlike – the fresh air and open spaces. Completely at odds with a move to New York.

'Tell me, then, if Canada is so amazing, why leave?'

We're both sitting on the bench seat, angled toward Abbey's window, immersed in the kind of backdrop an artist might sketch for a Disney animation – the kind that would make a child gasp with surprise. The view coming in to land in the airplane wasn't a patch on this close-up of the Rockies. Yet, I'm able to take my attention away from the majesty of the view to see Abbey's contemplation.

After moments of silence, she eventually shrugs, and says, 'It is amazing and I've always liked being at home. Even though my mom drives me crazy at times, and my dad is often so busy that I could go days and weeks barely speaking to him, as a girl I still preferred being in my own home to being anywhere else.

'But I thought I was in love with a guy and supposed to marry him. I thought I was supposed to move to be with Andrew, like we couldn't have worked if I didn't put in enough effort. It was on me to keep him. It sounds pathetic, doesn't it? Particularly now, in light of what happened between us?'

'I'm starting to think that some of the things we lead ourselves to believe, or that get ground into us, about who or what we should be and who we should want to be with, make no sense. I guess I'm trying to say, I don't think you're pathetic. Not at all.'

She's staring at me silently, probably trying to determine

some meaning in my nonsense, and I'm only just beginning to decipher it myself.

'From the moment Fleur paid me any attention, even though we were so wrong for each other, I think I felt obliged to be with her. Like I should be so wowed by the fact that a girl like her showed a guy like me any attention. As if I'd be letting down men all over the world if I didn't make her mine. Now who's pathetic?'

The way Abbey is looking at me makes me feel naked, exposed and vulnerable. It reminds me that I just said those words aloud, in a gondola with two strangers. Worse than that, I spoke those words as me, as Ted, the tech geek who could never get the girl.

I don't dare look anywhere other than at the mountains. Damn mountains making me emotional, making me forget who I'm here to be.

Surprisingly, Abbey doesn't pick up on it, or chooses not to question it. It's as if she knows who I am, like she can see through the façade, see *me*.

Instead, she asks, 'But you love her?' As if it's the only answer she cares about.

Her question drags me from my spiral of self-analysis.

Do I? Did I? I wouldn't have asked her to marry me if I didn't. I have to at least have some faith and conviction in myself. I surely must have been in love with her on some level. Even if just the idea of her and us.

But if Abbey had asked me if I've ever sat next to Fleur having a deep and meaningful conversation, feeling like there's nowhere else in the world I'd rather be, no one else in the world I'd rather be sitting next to, I'd have to say no. I'm not convinced I had that with Fleur. Not now. Not now that I've felt the connection that can exist between two people, not now that I've felt an overwhelming urge like the one I feel now to touch another person, to kiss another person, to hold another person.

No, I'm not convinced I was truly, unequivocally in love with Fleur.

For the whole time those questions have been dancing around my mind, I've been watching Abbey and she's been staring at me. And suddenly it occurs to me that she's waiting for an answer. Do I love Fleur?

No. But am I willing to say that and take down one of the walls between Abbey and me? Risk finding out that she *is* still in love with Andrew. That I'm here as a prop.

I can't do that. It's self-preservation.

So I answer, 'I don't know.'

Her expression is unreadable, even as her eyes never leave mine, despite the fact I'm desperate to read her thoughts.

Her opinion of me matters. I don't know why or since when exactly but it does.

I care what she thinks of me because I care about her. Only, I have to keep reminding myself that she doesn't know who I am. And that's the biggest shield I have against the risk of getting hurt again.

I know I need it because sitting here, I don't want our conversation to end. I could spend every minute of the rest of my life talking with Abbey.

Which is a very dangerous place to be.

So I change the subject. 'Where would you live, for you, no one else, if you could live anywhere in the world?'

'Anywhere?'

'Anywhere.'

'Other people aside?'

'Yep.'

She inhales as she thinks, then a smile creeps on her lips and she looks out of the window to the mountainous peaks. 'Well, you made San Francisco sound very appealing. But, ultimately, eventually, right here.' Then she turns sharply to face me. 'I'm not sure I could handle living with my mom again, though. Not unless Dee or Nate were here to deflect some of the maternal attention.'

Our gondola is drawing close to its highest point and we both shift to the edge of the bench, ready to alight.

'I've always hoped I'd work for my dad, so maybe that's one justification for being in New York that is about me. You know, getting experience to work for him – I'd want to earn my place.' We both stand, waiting for the doors to open. She suddenly darts her attention to me, eyes wide, and says, 'But that was the old me, boring me. Dad definitely doesn't need a footloose and fancy-free actress.'

It's a bizarre reaction, one that throws us both, and I don't know why but it makes me say, 'What about as a business analyst?' We step off our ride onto the platform. 'You were great with me the other day.'

She shrugs. 'If I were good enough, my firm would have asked me to apply for qualification in that department.'

I'm about to protest but Abbey is heading off along a purpose-carved walk cut into the side of Sulphur Mountain. 'Plus, like I say, life can be much more fun than being stuck in an office, right?'

Right. Like working on a TV-production set, or a baseball field.

We explore the breathtaking area, a lightness back in us both. Everything else that's going on is so far beneath us here – out of sight and out of our minds as we laugh and joke through the walk, pausing at the viewpoints where we both take pictures of the scenery and a couple of selfies together.

Refreshingly, we don't have to take a thousand pictures like I had to do with Fleur, each exploring an ever so slightly different angle, a hair fix in between and a reapplication of lip gloss, knowing one of the bunch at least must be Instagram worthy.

It's just a picture, capturing a moment between two friends. Easy and not forced.

34

TED

At seven thirty, Abbey and I are in her bedroom getting ready for dinner with her parents. I haven't met her dad yet and I'm not sure whether I should be excited or nervous – if he's anything like her mom, he'll be a force to be reckoned with, a little hostile and very anti my fake relationship with his daughter.

Abbey steps out of the ensuite wearing a dress I haven't seen on her before. It shows off her figure in a way that's sophisticated. It's understated but quite fancy for a dinner with parents, and I wonder if this is always how she dresses at home, or if this is supposed to be the first meeting with a new boyfriend, an occasion.

'You look... nice,' I tell her. It's a huge understatement, but in a nanosecond of consciousness, I decide 'nice' would be better than something like stunning, mesmerizing, beautiful, in the circumstances. We are, after all, friends helping each other out.

Nevertheless, on seeing her, I do make a mental decision to wear smart pants and a shirt, rather than jeans and a T-shirt for dinner. I climb off Abbey's bed, where I've been lying chilling out whilst she's been getting ready. I locate the pants I hung up in her wardrobe earlier, slip out of my shorts and T-shirt, and fold them into a drawer.

As I'm standing in my underwear, I catch a glimpse of her reflection in the dresser mirror and realize she's scrutinizing me. It's nothing she hasn't seen already, but I wonder what she makes of me. Does she find me lacking in some way? Or would she be happy to have me if this was a real relationship?

I've heard from Fleur so many times that I need to do this exercise or that exercise, how I shouldn't eat this or that, and ridiculously, I've often taken her advice on board. It's not that I don't want to feel good and fit my clothes well but the constant nagging to be an Instagram fiancé is tiresome.

Abbey catches my eye in the mirror and starts.

'Sorry, I didn't mean to stare,' she says.

'As my girlfriend, I think you get a free look.' I'm smiling, though I don't feel the sureness my words suggest, and I slip into my shirt.

'Well, if you will look like that, and as this is a short-term arrangement, I might as well get my fix.'

She laughs but I see her skin change color. She's embarrassed, or nervous, I'm not sure. Either way, it's kind of cute.

She's this incredible, extroverted, sassy woman one minute and vulnerable the next. She's like a city of secret passageways and I wonder how many other people get to see her hidden places, or if I'm the lucky one.

It's seventy forty-five when we make our way downstairs to the dining room, somehow deep in discussion about the increasing prevalence of artificial intelligence and its use in the finance industry, joking about robots and space. It's sort of crazy, as if it's Abbey and me, rather than my brother. I've forgotten the lion's den we're about to walk into because we're finding ourselves highly amusing as we happen upon Abbey's parents, standing by a large, set dining table, each holding a glass of fizz.

I'm pleased I decided to go with smart pants. I'm also bracing myself for an evening of interrogation. All the calmness I've been feeling this afternoon and this evening with Abbey fades away and I tune in to the psyche of Michael Thomas.

Abbey's dad is a tall man, heavy set and with a shock of grey hair. He's wearing a suit jacket and separate smart pants in a way that reminds me of Richard Branson. I make this assessment whilst Abbey bounds into his chest and is folded into his arms. I avert my attention as they speak quietly to each other, Abbey's dad kissing her hair.

Then, as Abbey steps aside, her dad does what every successful businessman is able to do in a matter of seconds – he weighs me up in one glance, so subtle another person might miss it, but I've seen it many times before; I do it myself.

My initial thoughts are that Abbey's dad seems like a decent guy. He holds out a hand and when I take it, we shake firmly, but he doesn't try a power hold, or to twist his hand so it's on top of mine. He seems open, earnest, as if he's treating me as an equal. A contrasting approach to Abbey's mom.

'You must be Michael, or is it Mike? I'm Terrance, call me Terry. You've already met my wife, Anna. I hope she didn't give you too hard a time?'

He makes an expression that causes Abbey's mom to roll her eyes, but surprisingly, it's in a way that demonstrates years of alliance and love between them, which I recognize from the way my own parents behave after forty years of marriage.

Abbey and I must've had a similar upbringing in that respect. I already know she's a family person, despite her grumbles about her mom at times, and I like that about her. I do miss having more time with my own family. It's something that got eaten away slowly but steadily, not so much by work as Fleur. I want to take that time back with them. And one day, should I have my own family, I'd like to think they would look upon me and my wife with similarly fond reflection.

'No more than I'd expect from a loving mother,' I reply, being kinder toward Anna than she was to me.

There's a chance Anna's smile is genuine, though the thought is fleeting because she quickly throws me to the wolf, or more appropriately, the grizzly bear.

'Come and help me, Abbey, darling; we'll finish the starters. Terry, you can pour the wine.'

When Abbey and Anna have left the dining room, Terry moves to two wingback chairs by the window, looking out over the land at the side of the house. Fir and pine trees dominate the view but there's an area near the house with lying tree trunks surrounding a fire pit that looks very inviting. I can imagine the family sitting out there together, the fire burning, sharing a drink or two.

'Let's take a seat; the girls will be a while,' Terry says, grabbing a bottle of red wine and two glasses from the table before we sit side by side, a short glass-top table between us. It feels more by design than accident that Abbey and her mom might be missing for a while.

'Anna's a formidable woman but she keeps this family together.' Terry leans forward, filling my glass. 'Always has. And with all our children in New York these days, her protective instincts are constantly working overdrive.'

I nod. 'I can understand that.' I've known Abbey for three weeks and I don't like when she's out alone in the city at night. I don't like that she dates men from Tinder – for more reasons than one. And I really hate that she moved to the city for her ex and he screwed her over.

I really hate her ex.

Terry lifts his half-full measure of wine to his lips and I drink from my glass in response. Then he rests back in his seat and exhales, as if that one mouthful has gone some way toward removing the stresses of the day from his body.

'You know you're fighting an uphill battle here this weekend, don't you, son? Ball player or not, Anna and Victoria – that's Andrew's mother – they've been planning for Abbey and Andrew to be together since they were in diapers.'

I nod, holding my drink between my hands. What can I say? Andrew's an idiot and a liar but Abbey has chosen not to tell her family why they ended. She's chosen to hide from them or shield Andrew. I'd love to know which is her main driver but I don't and the reality is, I'm just some guy to her. I could have been anyone. I could have been my brother. A man to fill a gap and make her ex jealous.

My wandering mind makes me take another, longer drink.

'I don't follow baseball closely but I do know that to be at the top of your game in any sport or business, it takes guts and commitment. I commend you for that.'

I clear my throat. 'Thank you.'

I want to be grateful as Mike, to accept the praise as my brother would, but it doesn't feel right that I'm misleading Terry.

I decide he mentioned business and I am doing well in business. I take the endorsement on those grounds but recognize the missed opportunity – Terry and I could have more in common than I'm at liberty to explore. Exactly as I could with Abbey.

He sets his wine glass on the table and suddenly he's regarding me in a way that makes me want to leave the situation. 'But I'm no stranger to hard work and I know that success comes at a price. Sacrifices have to be made.'

Here we go...

'Sir, are you asking about my intentions with your daughter?'

He stares as if he's boring holes into me, eventually saying, 'I should imagine it's still too early days to know your full intentions. That's for the pair of you to work out. But she cares enough to bring you up here, so I would be interested to know your plans for the future.'

'Business, sir. I come from a family of entrepreneurs and hard workers. Contrary to what the media might have people believe, I don't blow every dollar I earn on women and champagne; I have investments.' I don't know what possesses me to say my next words but they come. 'My brother has a tech company in Silicon Valley and I'd like to get in on that.'

'He does? What is it your brother does?'

'He develops software. Right now, he's working on a big AI product, which might just be the biggest development he's ever created, once it's finished.'

Terry's eyes narrow on me, then he continues to ask more questions about my business and I lose myself in my passion for what I do. I'm animated as I speak, more than a little nerdy. And I almost blow everything when I tell him, 'Abbey's been giving me – my brother, I mean – advice on business strategy, actually. She's pretty incredible.'

Though Terry has been listening to me intently, watching me closely, he smiles now and gently chuckles, his pride evident. 'She's always had a natural flare for business analysis. Not that she'd say as much herself.'

I scoff. 'Tell me about it. She's lacking self-belief but certainly not business knowledge. She knows her stuff.' I hear my own pride in my voice, too. 'Though she's obviously acting now, so I don't suppose it matters.'

Terry lets out a short laugh. 'Ah the carefree switch. My darling wife is thrilled about this rebellion.' He considers me before adding, 'Perhaps she's finally sewing her wild oats or whatever. Personally, I think it's good for her. It will be good for her self-esteem, but don't let Anna catch me saying that.'

I'm starting to get the sense no one really believes in Abbey being an actress, though I know she is because I've been to her set. Plus, the Abbey I met three weeks ago fits that typecast.

Yet, the Abbey I'm increasingly coming to know, less so.

'I've got to tell you, son, you seem to have your head screwed on more than I would have given you credit for. Don't judge a book by its cover, isn't that right?'

Right. I'm Mike. But I agree, my brother might prefer sports banter to any other kind of conversation but he isn't stupid.

'People aren't always who they seem, that much is true. I've learned that lesson the hard way recently.'

'It's a hard but necessary lesson in life and business.' He sips his drink, his focus never leaving me. 'People can always surprise you.'

He knows. I think he knows I'm not who I'm pretending to be. Does he? How could he? But I need to stop the business chat, get back to baseball and channeling the persona of a top sportsman.

'What did you say the name of your brother's business is?' Terry asks.

I panic. I'm like a moose caught in headlights. Do I tell him the truth? What if he looks it up? What if he connects me to the business? But if I make something up, I could undermine everything for Abbey.

Fueled by anxiety, I tell him, 'Vanguard RED Technologies.'

'Food's up,' Abbey says, bumping open the door to the dining room with her hip and carrying two bowls of soup.

Please don't leave me again.

35

ABBEY

Dinner was a bit weird. Mike was odd and in a way I can't quite put my finger on. He was outwardly happy and composed but at the risk of sounding too Gen Z, he was vibing some strangely nervous energy as he sat next to me at the dinner table.

Or maybe there was some peculiar energy between *us*.

'Is everything okay?' I ask once we have tidied up from dinner and are heading upstairs to my bedroom.

My bedroom, from which I haphazardly removed all easily removable traces of Andrew and high-school weird earlier.

'Yeah, I'm good, just cooked. Are you okay?'

We reach the landing. Standing outside my bedroom door, I can see his face, the way his jaw seems taut; his hands are resting in the pockets of his pants, and his shoulders are placed higher than usual.

'Is it awful? Is it too bizarre, being here, meeting my parents, us pretending we're... you know... in love?'

My throat tightens around that last word and I realize my mouth is dry. I need to swallow but it's hard to swallow and I'm staring at him, and he's staring at me.

And now he's looking at my mouth and I'm looking at his.

He's reaching a hand and he's going to touch my face, maybe tuck my hair behind my ear, maybe touch my lips and—

I reach for the door handle and hastily push open my bedroom door with too much force. It bangs against the wall.

'Crap,' I say, making a futile attempt to catch it.

Then Mike is inside my bedroom, where there's one bed, my bed, and we're both going to be lying in there soon, and—

'I'll just grab some things and sleep on the sofa,' he says, reaching for a T-shirt and his wash bag. 'Do you have a spare blanket or sheet?'

Oh.

'The sofa? Why? You can stay with me. We're two adults and, in any case, my parents actually think that we're having... you know...'

'Sex.'

It's out there. He said it. And it's hanging in the air between us like fragile glass – hovering, waiting to drop and shatter.

It's ridiculous how one word has made my blood pump faster, my palms heat, my breath hitch. But it has.

We're standing in the room, the only things between us Mike's toiletries and spare T-shirt. All I can think about is how he'll undress before bed.

He's so close to me, I can feel the warmth of his body, smell wine on his breath.

His tongue wets his lips as his eyes penetrate mine.

There aren't words to describe how much I want him.

Not the version of himself he's playing for other people.

Him.

My feet inch forward and my hands leave my sides, aching to touch him as I remember his body the night he stood in just a towel on the mezzanine level of his apartment. Unexpectedly lean. Firm. Extremely desirable.

I think he shifts toward me, or maybe I imagine he does because I want him to. More than that, I want him to want me. I'm suddenly very aware of the fit of my clothes on my body and what's beneath them.

But he was just in a relationship with a model. Might still be. And what she had to offer beneath her clothes would have been ten times anything I ever could. Men like Mike don't go for girls like me and even if he might, he thinks I'm an actress, which might not strictly be a lie, but it sure feels increasingly uncomfortable.

I blink, my eyelids closing for longer than usual.

'I can't stay in here with you, Abbey,' Mike croaks.

I get it. I do. Everything I just thought, he already knows – career path aside.

'Not because I don't want to but because I'm not sure I trust myself around you, and the timing, us, this, everything, it's just all...'

I open my eyes. 'A lot?'

He inhales deeply and nods. 'A lot.'

I think I manage to smile; I'm not convinced but I want him to know it's okay, I agree, he's making the right move for both of us. 'At least stay in the guest room. We'll tell Mom you're traditional. She'll love you for it.'

'You mean she'd actually like something about me?'

I do smile now. 'I'm sure she likes you... just not as much as Andrew.'

Mike shakes his head. 'You should tell them the truth about him.'

'And explode a can of worms? I'm here for a week, then this will all be over – no need to create a drama.'

'Are you sure that's the only reason?' he asks. He doesn't wait for my answer, leaning in to kiss me on the cheek, holding his lips to my skin longer than necessary and inhaling as he does.

I lean my cheek against his as I breathe in his scent. 'Go,' I whisper.

Go before I add another mistake to my ever-growing list.

36

TED

That was a near miss. *A lot* definitely describes what's going on here in Canada and what's happening in my head.

I'm in turmoil, pacing the floor of the guest bedroom in my boxer briefs and T-shirt, desperately wanting to find out what would happen if I did spend the night in Abbey's bed. Knowing I can't.

It wouldn't be right. Or fair. She thinks I'm someone I'm not.

But *God*, I'm being pulled in her direction by some kind of invisible force. And I—

Stuff it.

I leave the bedroom and head back along the corridor to Abbey's room. There's soft lighting shining through the crack under the door. She's still awake.

I raise my fist to knock on the door.

This is it.

The moment of truth.

What happens when I tell her? Does she hate me, send me away, never to see me again, disappointed that I'm not Mike, furious that I lied?

I lower my arm, bracing my hands on either side of her door, staring at the ground as if the answer to my question is written on it.

Or… is there some other alternative? Like she actually forgives me for the lies and we finally have that kiss, and that kiss turns into what I want. *Her.*

I raise my fist again.

It's now or never.

But maybe never is for the best. I've thrown myself into a relationship once before and look how that turned out.

This feels different. Very different. I think I want Abbey for all the right reasons, some of them I can't even explain, except to know that I can't stop thinking about her. This isn't as it was with Fleur. I don't want Abbey because I think I'm supposed to want her.

I want her despite knowing I ought not to, not right now.

She's just out of a long-term relationship and I can't say for sure that she doesn't still have feelings for her ex.

Feck.

I start walking back along the corridor to my bedroom.

But the one person I want to talk to about all of this is behind that door.

And I can't talk to Abbey.

Not until I'm willing to tell her the truth. Take the risk.

She deserves as much.

I turn back toward her room. It's time.

I raise my fist to knock on her door and—

'Michael? What are you doing?'

I near jump out of my skin. 'Mrs Mitchell.'

I don't know what to do first: explain why I'm standing in the corridor outside of Abbey's room wearing my boxer briefs and a T-shirt, or hold my hands over my crotch.

'I was just—'

She smiles at me knowingly, or so she thinks. With a mischievous twinkle in her eye, she says, 'Goodnight, Michael.'

She really has no idea. 'Goodnight, Mrs Mitchell.'

Once she is safely behind her own bedroom door, I head back to mine.

Tomorrow. I'm telling Abbey tomorrow.

37

ABBEY

We come to a stop on the forecourt, to one of Banff's finest hotels – a castle amongst mountains – and Mike turns off the engine of my Fiat 500, which he has once again managed to squish his long legs and big frame into.

My nerves have been building during the drive, but now that we're here, they're in overdrive. I don't feel like the new me, the fake me, or even the New York version of me. Perhaps in part because I didn't pack clothes from my new wardrobe expecting this lunch today – Mom typically sprang it on me, knowing it's not my thing.

So what I am wearing is an old dress that I've probably had for a decade. It's pale blue with daisies all over it. It has long sleeves and a high, square neck and it floats down over what would have been my flat chest at the time I bought it. Compared to my new wardrobe, it's baggy and shapeless, which I might not have minded even a month ago, but today I'm acutely aware that this is not a flattering dress.

Last night, I went to bed feeling desired. It was surprising and strange and pretty incredible. But this morning, I'm just the same old Abbey, who isn't being looked at the way Mike looked at me last night. In fact, we've barely spoken to each other so far today and when we have, there's been an odd tension. As if he regrets our almost-nearly kiss.

Hardly surprising. Why would he want shapeless daisies when he could have Chanel?

I hate to admit that my mom has been right all these years; I've hidden my body and I don't know why. In hiding my body, what am I trying to conceal about myself? I'm sure there's a podcast that could help me answer that question but right now, I just need to accept that this lunch is happening. That last night was nothing more than a blip to Mike. That today, I'm going to be scrutinized and analyzed and picked apart by my mom's old friends, including Andrew's mom, and I need to haul my ass.

Mike has opened Mom's door – nice touch, charming, she'll like that – and as she gets out, he comes around to my side of the car and opens the door. I watch our hands as I place mine in his, and I see that my fingers have a tremor.

I try to get out and find that I haven't undone my seatbelt. Mike watches me as I release myself from the seat and step onto the ground in front of him – at least my shoes are sexy, though extremely painful. And in these shoes, I don't have to strain my neck to look up to Mike; he's only a couple of inches taller than me.

Anxiety has stolen my words and seemingly my ability to close the car door behind me. Mike leans around me, nudging me back against the side of the car, and closes the door for me. He's close, tantalizingly close, leaning into me, and I'm leaning further back into the car.

Unexpectedly, he brings his fingertips to my cheek, tucks my hair behind my ear and whispers, 'I think that your mom would expect me to kiss you goodbye. Would that be okay, if I kiss you?'

He's going to kiss me? I spent most of last night wondering what it would have felt like if we had kissed. This morning, I've thought I'll never find out.

I really, *really* want to know.

I think I nod my head; I mean to.

Then his lips are pressed against my cheek where his fingers were just seconds ago. He feels safe and whatever else has been filling my head this morning is gone with his touch. Closing my eyes, I imagine that I'm really his for the first time. That he can kiss me any time he wants.

This crush is like a spaceship. It's prepared and loaded, the burners have been switched on, and it's being propelled out of the atmosphere to a place beyond the ordinary world.

I know, despite everything Andrew put me through, that this crush I have on Mike is going to come crashing down and when it does, it will be the crash to end all other crashes. I want to stay here just a little while longer before coming back down to earth and eating lunch with the bitchy doctors waiting to give me an all-over check.

'Alright, Michael, that's enough,' Mom says.

At her words, I finally feel my eyes open. I don't know if I expect to see him smiling but he isn't; he's just looking back at me.

'I've watched you through the rearview mirror fidgeting and chewing your lip through the whole drive here,' he says. 'You are beautiful, Abbey. You're clever and witty, and you're worth a thousand of any person who wants to try to tear you down. Where's the stubborn and vivacious actress I've seen plenty of, huh? You walk in there with your head held high, okay? Fuck Andrew and what he did to you. And screw whoever in there thinks you don't deserve better than that dirt-bag.'

Angry Mike. I find him kind of... staggering and... hot. *Sheesh*, I find *everything* he does hot at the moment.

He's right; what would gregarious, artiste Abbey do?

'Good pep talk, buddy,' I say, patting him on the upper arm as if he didn't just rock my entire world with one kiss on my cheek.

I move out of his space and around the car toward my mom.

Before we head inside, I cast one last glance across my shoulder, and see that Mike is facing forward, his forearms resting on the roof of the car, his head bent as he blows out heavily. Maybe, just maybe, he has even the tiniest sense of what I'm feeling, what is stirring up my insides every time I'm near him.

Mom and I are shown through the grand hotel, abuzz with meandering guests, and out back to an alfresco dining space on the lawn. I take a beat to appreciate my native scenery. Towering mountains, tall trees and birds tweeting all around us.

The area is shaded by a canvas canopy and I spot a long table, already half full with familiar faces sitting on seven of the fourteen chairs. One such familiar face is the woman I thought would become my mother-in-law.

Victoria, Andrew's mom, appears to be smiling at me through gritted teeth.

'If it isn't the lady of the hour,' one of Mom's friends says. She is up from her seat as we approach the table and engulfs first Mom, then me, in her copious bosom. 'Little Abigail, let me see you. It must have been three, maybe four years since I've seen you. You haven't changed a jot.'

She holds me at arm's length and considers the dress I may well have been wearing the last time she saw me. I cringe inside, my momentary conviction stirred by Mike's touch disappearing rapidly. All the while, I sense the gaze of Victoria on my back.

I'm embraced and petted like a child by another five of the women around the table and, somewhat unsurprisingly, the last woman to stand to greet me is Victoria. I have sought her approval, her love even, for most of my life. Now, the look on her face tells me unequivocally that I have neither and I hate to admit even to myself that I'm disappointed.

Another guest arrives as Victoria and I come face-to-face, meaning happily the watchful eyes of everyone else at the lunch are diverted when Victoria simply stands before me and says, 'Abigail.'

I feel chastised. I'm the child outside of the principal's office after a fallout.

I've never been the child outside the principal's office and this agitated encounter is literally my worst nightmare.

'Hi Victoria.' My smile is meek but at least I try. 'How are you?'

She leans her head to one side as if I've asked the dumbest question in the world. 'Disappointed, Abbey. Very disappointed. I thought you and Andrew would be together forever.'

I shrug. What I want to say is: *Me too, Victoria. And on the day I expected your son to propose to me, he told me he'd been screwing someone else behind my back. But don't worry, he seems very happy now to be bedding half of the women on Tinder in New York.*

What I actually say is: 'Me too.' And I say it annoyingly apologetically.

'Now I find out that you're dating some sportsman and you've brought him *here*, to Andrew's home, where all of his friends and family are going to see him ridiculed by you.'

What I want to do is: laugh, so hard. And tell her how ridiculed *I* have felt by *him*.

What I actually do is say: 'I'm sorry you feel that way, Victoria. But it has been weeks since we broke up and—'

'And he hasn't brought anyone with him, Abbey. Surely that tells you he's still invested in what the two of you had. How could he not be? You've been together as long as anyone can remember.'

Actually, not true. We were together for a long time but I still remember when he would date anyone in school except me. I still remember how he took Maisie Daisy to prom instead of me. What did Victoria say about that back then? I'd bet Andrew didn't get this treatment.

'I guess sometimes people grow apart and not together,' I tell her, hoping to put an end to the conversation.

'Pfft. My Andrew clearly doesn't see it that way.' She leans closer to me and lowers her voice even further. 'I had better not find out that this sportsman turned your head before you and Andrew were separated.'

I gasp. My mouth literally falls open. How *dare* she?

My mouth is still open as Victoria leaves my side, rounds the table and welcomes the latest guests to arrive. As if someone in the clouds is messing with me. As if this lunch couldn't get any worse. The next people to arrive are Mom's friend Francesca and her daughter, who happens to be responsible for my first ever heartbreak in junior high. The very same prom date I was just thinking about.

Maisie freaking Daisy.

I would rather stick pins in my eyes than be at this lunch.

38

ABBEY

I gave lunch my best effort. Mostly, for my mom's sake. Also to put on a brave front because it was truly awful. The prodding and poking of me, the 'ooh's and 'ahh's and 'that's a shame's about Andrew' and I continued after the initial greetings and all through the meal.

Now, I'm heading outside ten minutes earlier than the time I asked Mike to collect Mom and I, under the guise of checking he isn't early, because I can't stand being amongst those women, especially Victoria and Maisie, for one second longer.

I feel proverbially beaten up.

But as the saying goes, when you think things can't get any worse, they always can.

After firing an SOS message to my sister and Shernette on my way out of the hotel, I look up from my phone and run right smack into...

'Andrew!'

His hair is slicked the way he wears it for work and he has one of his favorite Italian shirts tucked into cream chinos.

'Abbey.' He holds my arms to steady me but lets them linger

longer than necessary, as if he has a right to touch me. 'I'm here to pick up my mom but I was hoping we'd bump into each other.'

'You were? Why?'

He titters, as if it's a stupid question. Then he beams at me, the way he used to. As if nothing has changed between us. 'I thought maybe we could grab a drink at the bar, like old times. I can't remember the last time I was in this hotel without you.'

A drink? After the last two hours I just endured because of him? After everything he's put me through?

I jerk my shoulders, forcing him to finally let go of me. He's right, this hotel has always been special for us. We've celebrated graduations, anniversaries, even births here. And one lunch was all it took to obliterate those good memories.

'Andrew, I can categorically say, I do not want to get a drink with you. Thanks to you, I've been picked over and interrogated, and even accused of cheating on *you*. The whole reason I'm here and playing stupid games is because of you.'

'Abbey.' His hands are back on my shoulders. 'I've done a lot of thinking about us and I know we can move past this. I think maybe I just needed to get it out of my system, you know? We've been together since we were so young and you can't blame me for wondering what else might be out there.'

What. The. Actual.

'But I'm over it now, Abbey. Seeing you with that other guy, I've realized that there's only one woman for me, and it's you.'

Huh?

I'm silent. Speechless. And blinking over and over, wondering if I'm seeing and hearing things.

Andrew is pleading with me, asking me to take him back. For years, I've felt like it's been me doing the chasing and now, it seems, the boot is on the other foot.

I'm waiting for my adrenaline to hit. That giddiness in my

stomach because Andrew wants me. The feeling of warmth, contentedness, safety, knowing I can say yes and we'd head back in that lunch room and everyone would be ecstatic for us. Then we'd fly back to New York together and I'd get a job as an auditor and move back into our old apartment. And eventually, we'd get married and have the grandchildren our mothers so desperately want from us.

I wait for those feelings but they don't come.

What do come are three thoughts simultaneously.

Firstly, I guess my fake relationship with Mike worked if the objective had been to make Andrew jealous.

Secondly, if I said yes now, I'd spend every moment of the rest of my life looking across my shoulder, waiting for the next transgression.

Thirdly, I really don't love Andrew anymore.

What I'd like to say is: *Go fuck yourself, Andrew.*

But I've had all the confrontation I can handle for one day.

So what I actually say is: 'Maybe next time, Andrew. I'm waiting for Mike to pick me up.'

And I just want to get the hell out of here.

39

TED

During Abbey's lunch, whilst I was taking pictures, drinking coffee and intermittently dealing with work emails on my phone, my accountants called me. They've read the paper Abbey put together, the proposal for the new business structure and my plan to break my partnership with Roman, whilst not exactly giving him what he wants.

'We're onboard with the plan, Ted. Everything checks out. We'll confirm by email and you can give us the formal go ahead when you're ready.'

It's happening. Thanks to Abbey, I have a way out. I feel relieved, as if a burden was lifted by the call.

Then my accountant said, 'The woman who put this together for you, she's clearly astute and commercial in her approach. Why don't you give her my number and ask her to call me. I'd like to take her for lunch and chat about what we could offer her at the firm.'

'Funnily enough, I had a similar thought about her working for me.' But I think she's set on being an actress, even if everyone else is questioning that shift. Regardless, after this week, I think

I'd like her to be more than my colleague. Otherwise, and more likely, she's going to hate me for doing exactly what her ex did and lying to her. 'I'm at her home in Canada with her at the moment; I'll chat to her. The thing is...' Acting aside. 'She lives in New York and I don't know how she'd feel about a move to San Francisco.'

'We have offices in New York, San Francisco, Toronto and Vancouver, Ted. She could take her pick.'

I ended the call ignoring the devil on my shoulder that was reminded that Abbey and I live an entire continent apart.

When I pull up at the hotel to collect her from lunch, I find her sitting on a wood swing by the entrance, alone.

All I want to do when I see her – head down, arms wrapped around her waist – is head inside the hotel and give every person at that lunch a piece of my mind. For a peaceful guy, the thought of someone hurting Abbey can sure get me riled.

Anna chats through the car ride – buoyed by wine – but Abbey is near silent in the back seat for the entire drive.

She thanks me for the ride when we get home but quickly heads inside, kicks off her heeled shoes, and practically runs upstairs to her bedroom.

Afraid of what I might say to her mom if I hang around downstairs, and wanting to make sure Abbey is okay, I follow her upstairs and find her face down on her bed, her head in her pillows, shouting into the soft stuffing to muffle the sound.

I quietly pad into the room, closing the door behind me, and sit on the edge of the bed next to her.

'Was it that bad?' I ask.

I reach out and rub her back, which she seems to accept. She wants someone to comfort her but I know her well enough to know she won't ask.

'Imagine the worst day of your life, multiply it by infinity, and you'll come close to half as bad as that lunch was,' she says, mumbling, but audible, into her bedding.

I chuckle. Not at the situation but at the ridiculousness of her statement. It's not like Abbey to be dramatic... 'Worse than the day Trump was elected?'

She rolls onto her back, bringing a pillow with her and holding it to her chest for comfort. 'At least when Trump was elected I always had the option of bailing to Canada.'

I scoff. 'True enough. Why didn't you just tell them to stick lunch and leave?'

She sighs. 'I couldn't just leave. Plus, the thing I hate most about what Andrew did to me was his cowardliness. If I just left, ran away, wouldn't I be just the same?'

Her words strike an immediate chord. 'Like me, you mean?'

She springs up to sit. 'Gosh, no, I didn't mean that. It's not the same. You would have had media attention to contend with and—'

'It's okay. You're right. I've been thinking it myself. It's time to go and face the music at home.'

Her silence speaks volumes. She agrees.

'So, do you want to dissect the lunch and tell me the finer details of your demise, or would you like me to tell you something interesting, maybe even quite cool?'

She pulls a face like an actress might pull for a theatre to show she's weighing up the options. 'Cool like the first man on the moon? Or like my own peanut-butter-making machine with an endless supply of nuts in my bedroom?'

I shake my head. 'You're such a freak.'

She smiles. Finally. 'Pot calling the kettle black, my friend. Go on then, tell me something really cool.'

I tell her about my call with my accountants and Matt's offer to speak with her about a job.

I'm met by a blank expression. Maybe I've got this all wrong. Maybe she's more into acting than I've appreciated and possibly I let myself think she might not be because that would make her more accessible, more like someone I wouldn't be as afraid to start a relationship with.

'Mike... I need to tell you something.'

I still at the severity of her tone. What this time?

'I'm not really an actress. I mean, I am. Kind of.' She shakes her head, eyes to the ceiling, though I'm not following why she seems so exasperated. 'When I needed a date for my parents' party, Shernette and Dee set me up a Tinder profile and, given I was actually unemployed and, let's face it, had a fairly dull job by most people's standards, they set me up as an actress.'

Huh. 'That's not what I was expecting.'

She exhales heavily, like a weight has been lifted from her. 'Then you made the assumption, understandably, that I was an actress and, well, I figured you wouldn't want to even fake date an auditor. Not when you're...' She gestures from my head to my toes. 'You. So I let you believe it.'

She lied.

'But I also didn't want to lie. So I asked Dee to get me a job on her set and she did. I was acting, just as an extra.'

So much slots into place with her words. So much doesn't. 'What about your apartment? How can you...?'

'Afford it as an unemployed auditor?' She sighs. 'I blew my entire wedding fund on six months' rent in a bid to fake it until I could make it. Except, I'm not sure what I'm trying to fake anymore. Then you've just told me something the old me would have been ecstatic and nervous about in equal measure and... I don't want to mislead you anymore, Mike. I'm really sorry, and if you don't want to go through with this whole façade anymore, I... I get it. But I'm really hoping you'll stay.'

She's been lying to me.

But she just shared the truth and it would be the perfect opportunity for me to do the same.

'Abbey…' I have to tell her now.

Except, my reveal would be much bigger, much worse. She thinks her white lies are despicable, when actually, I'm pleased she's not an actress. I'm happy she's normal. Normal is a great thing.

Her reveal only highlights how big and deep my deceit runs.

Or is now selfish? Is now about me and how much I'd like to lie her back on that bed? She's had a shitty day and finally some good news. Better news than I even thought it would be earlier today.

I'm not going to ruin it for her.

God, I need some space. This is all too much and too weird and my head is an absolute car crash as it is.

Coward, coward, coward, coward, coward.

40

TED

I'm sitting at a table out on the back deck, a mug of coffee and a cinnamon bagel next to my laptop. Even though it's my R&D Friday, I wade through work emails that I should have been dealing with yesterday.

Abbey heads outside from the kitchen, biting into a slice of toast smothered in peanut butter and holding a mug. 'Are you ready to put on those hiking boots, Mr Athleticism?'

'I'll happily put on my hiking boots, but if we find a good spot for bouldering, I'm going to give you a piece of your own medicine, how does that sound?'

'I'd expect nothing less, Mr Thomas.'

She seems so much lighter today as she leads me out to a garage which has more adventure kit inside than I have ever seen. What has the appearance of a triple garage from the outside is in fact car free and looks more like an extreme sports store than an outbuilding.

The walls are lined with shelves and on them are boxes full of hiking boots, ski helmets, snow boots, ropes and carabiners. There are road bikes, mountain bikes and electric bikes standing in racks. There are five surfboards, two SUP boards and two bright-orange kayaks attached to the walls with their paddles. A clothes rail is loaded with different colored ski jackets, what look like climbing jackets and others that look like they've been worn by hunters.

'Here, these will fit you and I'll get you a pair of hiking socks.' Abbey hands me worn but clean but Gore-Tex boots, then she throws me a pair of socks from a box on another shelf and finally, hands me a cap.

'I did bring a cap,' I tell her, 'but I'll take the boots and socks, thanks. Do you have enough kit for the whole of the province in here?'

Abbey smiles. 'Just the town.' She grabs herself a pair of walking boots, socks, and a backpack. 'Mom loves nothing more than playing host.'

'Could have fooled me.' It's like the words fall out of me without my brain engaging first. 'Sorry, I didn't mean that—'

'Yes, you did,' Abbey says straight-faced. She picks up a can of something from another shelf and puts it inside her backpack. 'Bear spray,' she explains, so casually I don't know whether she's pulling my leg. If she isn't, I'm even more intimidated by her than I was walking into this trove.

My trepidation must be showing on my face because she steps close to me and pats my chest, with the ghost of a smirk about her mouth. 'Don't worry, big guy, I'll protect you.' Then she winks and sort of knocks me dead with it. The look, the sureness, the playfulness, her touch. I much prefer this version of her than seeing her cry into a pillow. Maybe her becoming an actress just to make good on a Tinder profile has had a silver lining.

'And I probably should have said Mom loves entertaining people she wants to be here.'

I laugh, part in relief, part because of the honesty in that statement.

Around twenty-five minutes later and with little strategic input from me, Abbey and I have strapped two kayaks to a roof rack on an SUV that she assures me she can drive, despite never driving in New York. Abbey seems to have a full backpack, which she filled whilst I was changing into hiking-appropriate gear. She wedges it into the footwell behind her seat and we set off to a destination she has chosen.

About a half hour later, she pulls into a well-marked car park and after untying the kayaks, we lug them along a fenced pathway through some trees, which eventually make way to an incredible view of a vast lake. There are actually a couple of other people paddling kayaks in the distance, who look like they set off from the same spot we're standing.

It's been a while since I've squished myself into a kayak and all I remember from my last flirt with the sport is how much of a back breaker it is.

'Where are we headed?' I ask.

Abbey tucks her T-shirt into her shorts, then ties back her hair. 'To the start of the hike.'

I really need to pull my attention away from her lips. From the urge I have to press mine to hers.

It took everything I had not to kiss her lips by the car before her lunch yesterday and only the thought that she might not have wanted it made me kiss her cheek instead.

I know all of the reasons that me kissing her would be a bad idea. A pointless idea.

But right this second, watching the breeze blow the fallen wisps of her hair away from her face, seeing the sun dance on her skin, her cheeks rosy with heat, I'm struggling to focus on them.

'You're really making me work for this walk,' I croak, my

throat hoarse. 'I'm expecting big things from the view. Postcard perfection.' Honestly, I couldn't ask for more than I'm already witnessing. It seems like every time we step outside in Alberta, I'm gripped by some of the finest views on Earth, transposed into tranquility with one sniff of the wildest, freshest air.

'Ready?' Abbey says once we've hauled our kayaks to the lake's edge, ready for us to nudge off the shore when we're in position.

'Let's do it.'

This. This is the version of Abbey who has me utterly captivated. Her sense of adventure, her inner wild, her ease in her own skin. This is the Abbey I lo—

Whoa, hold up there, Theodore.

Like the most. That's what my next thought would have been. And with my jumble of thoughts comes the stark reality that today is the day. I'm going to tell Abbey who I really am. I have to do it because I care. I care a lot now about how this is all going to end. At some point, this trip has stopped being about escaping New York and started being about Abbey and me.

Maybe it always was and I just didn't know it. Or maybe there has been a shift and that's why she revealed her story to me last night.

'I'll hold it steady for you,' she says, crouching down and putting a hand on my kayak.

I'm actually grateful, given I know this will be more of an inelegant, grunting struggle into the seat for me and my big frame, but there's no way I'm looking like a wimp who can't help himself.

'I'll be fine, you do you,' I tell her, knowing that I shouldn't bother offering my help in the reverse. There's a fine line between manly and anti-feminist.

It feels like Abbey clicks her fingers and lands perfectly into her seat, as if a wind has pushed her off the shore and gently set her sailing. She's already gliding her paddle through the calm waters of the lake, sending picturesque ripples that sparkle under the sun's light in my direction.

Then she stops moving forward, turns in her kayak and catches me watching her – gormlessly, practically drooling over this impressive woman.

Yes, I definitely care too much to continue the lie.

With one foot onshore and one in the boat, I lower myself toward the seat.

Maybe if she can see how much I genuinely feel for her, she'll see past the lies.

I lift my standing leg off the shore and come to sit in the kayak but... '*Holy shi—*'

I crash into the lake. Waves bow around me as I'm fully submerged in the cold water and thrusting my arms and legs against the stone-covered bottom to come to stand. Chest high and completely saturated, the only sound I hear above my own heavy breathing is Abbey's laughter bellowing out around the lake.

She paddles toward me, her amusement making her breathless as she says, 'So much for being an athlete.'

She's dead right. I'm not. And now seems as good a time as any to confess.

Her kayak comes close to me and I reach out for her paddle to gently bring her my way, except she raises it to paddle and we're in an unintentional tussle until—

'Arghhh...' She's in the lake with me, gasping and splashing around until she's standing in front of me, shoulder-high in the water. 'I can't believe you just did that.'

'I genuinely didn't do anything, all I did was grab your paddle. You—'

She cuts me off by resting her hands on my chest and through my wet T-shirt, I feel her gentle warmth, a contrast to the cold bite of the lake.

Silencing me with the way she looks so deeply into my eyes, she says, 'Shut up and kiss me, Mike.'

So I do. Without any doubt or apprehension. I kiss her because I'm desperate to. Because not kissing her these past days has been agony.

41

ABBEY

Finally, his lips crash against mine and I match his ferocity, entirely consumed by him, by lust, by want and need. A desire I've never felt in my life.

My stomach knots, my pelvis nudges forward toward him and my hands seem to move without instruction from my brain to the hem of his wet T-shirt, the feel of his hips. My fingertips slide onto the skin of his lower back.

His breath hitches with my touch and he breaks our contact briefly, his gaze still on my lips, his chest rising and falling as quickly as mine.

Then he reaches out to my cheek and with his other hand, he pulls my back until I'm fully pressed up against him.

I don't think I've ever been described as a sexual person. I don't think I would have considered myself to be a sexual person.

Before now.

Mike drops his forehead to mine and groans. 'God, I've wanted to do that for days.'

Never have I ever been looked at the way he's looking at me

right now. Not in all the years I was with Andrew did he look at me like he wanted to tear my clothes off, like he'd stop at nothing to get what he wanted, and that what he wanted was me.

It isn't someone looking at me out of jealousy and wanting me purely because he thinks I'll come crawling back, the way Andrew looked at me in the hotel yesterday.

This is what it feels like, what it looks like, to be yearned for.

I feel like more of a woman standing in this shockingly cold lake, wearing sports clothes, with messy tied-up hair and make-up free, than I have ever felt.

Perhaps it's less about the clothes and more about the way people, *someone*, can make you feel.

If we were anywhere more practical than submerged in near freezing water, I don't think I'd let this end.

Solely because voices of other hikers reach my ears do I lessen my grip on Mike's body. With his loss of contact, in the space between us, I can feel the imposter in my subconscious coming back, telling me to be wary. Either those thoughts, or the water, turn the heat I just felt between Mike and me into a shiver.

He drapes an arm around my shoulder. 'Let's get you out of here. There's something I need to tell you.'

I feel his body sigh against mine, then we're dragging our kayaks back to shore and I'm afraid. I don't want to burst the bubble we're in. I don't know if I want to hear what he has to share.

So as we stand on the pebbled waterline, I tell him, 'Let me go first, please.'

He takes a deep breath in, as if he's also feeling the enormity of what just happened in the lake. Okay, here goes...

'I'm nervous, Mike. Nervous and terrified because I think I'm falling for you. I've *fallen* for you.'

Finally, he exhales.

'But you're a sports star. You date models and live in San Francisco.'

'Abbey—'

'No, wait. Please let me say this. I've changed my life for someone before. I moved across the continent for him. And I was burned by his lies.'

Mike's eyes narrow now, as if he's truly processing my reservations, listening to me.

'I'm also afraid I'm just a rebound fling to you and you have the potential to be so much more than that to me. I guess I'm saying I'm afraid because I just don't want to get hurt again.' I puff out my next exhale, my shoulders dropping from where I didn't realize I was holding them, by my ears. 'But just for now, for the rest of today, I'd really like to put everything and everyone else out of our minds and pretend, for real, that we're free to enjoy each other and be whoever we are and want to be whilst we're in the refuge of the Rockies.' I reach for his hand and lock my fingers through his. 'Can we do that? Can we just have one day?'

He stares at me for so long that I think he's going to say no. Then he brings my hand to his mouth, where he presses his lips to my skin. Then he kisses my temple and tugs me into his side, so that we're both looking out in the same direction, across the lake, up to the mountains, where fellow hikers have moved on and the only sound is the chirping of grey jays.

'Abbey, I can be whoever you want me to be for another day. But just promise me something. When this week is through, please remember that not everything is a lie.'

It's not a confession of love. It's not even an admission of like. It certainly isn't confirmation that at the end of this week, we might be left with something real.

But for today, I rest my head onto his shoulder, content enough, for now.

'Abbey?'

'Mmm?'

'What the hell are we going to do about these wet clothes?'

42

TED

We've done exactly what Abbey wanted us to do. We've lived the day like it was just us, as if none of the reasons Abbey and I can't work exist. We've kayaked, hiked and bouldered, laughed and joked, touched each other and got lost in each other, given fellow hikers something to talk about once or twice.

It's so unlike me, *us*, I think, to cut loose, to be truly liberated from all the noise down below. Chatting like two old friends who have a thousand things in common and so much to catch up on. It's better now that she's a numbers girl; I like that about her. The multiple colors of her personality seem to fit, not that my instinctive mistrust of her has vanished. When we have fallen into silence, it hasn't been awkward. I've not searched for the next words to fill the void; we've been content in each other's company.

I just like being around her. Almost as much as I like the sensation of her lips on mine, the feel of her in my arms.

The way she kisses me takes me to another world, one where I've never been kissed.

Because I haven't, not the way she kisses me.

It's urgent yet gentle. Hot, yet tender. And I believe, when we're locked in these moments, that she wants to be with me every bit as much as I need to be with her. Both frustrated that we're on a rock in one of the most beautiful places in the world and so many other people seem to know it and want to walk here, too.

Abbey checks her watch and sighs – a sound I don't want to hear because I know it's the ticking bomb on today, on the time we have left before I have no option than to tell her who I really am.

'I think we're going to have to head down; we've still got a way to go to get back to the car and Shernette and Dee are flying in.'

Leaning back on my elbows, I raise my head to the sun that is telling me it's late afternoon. 'What if I say no?'

She reaches for her backpack and looks inside. 'Well, I could leave you with the bear spray and one last nut protein bar but I doubt you'd make it until morning.'

Reluctantly, I share the joke. 'I'll take my chances with the bears but I can't face another snack of nuts.'

Abbey chuckles but it's short lived and I know she's feeling what I am: the dawning inevitability of this day coming to a close on us. Except she's afraid that at the end of it all, I'm going back to San Francisco and a life of sport, models and booze.

She has no idea that the truth is worse.

43

ABBEY

The phrase 'you could cut the tension with a knife' is absolutely apt to the feeling of being in this vehicle with Mike. Before we set off for home, we shared one more kiss and it was passionate, fiery, chaotic and expectant. If it hadn't been for other people in the car park...

We've been making small talk on the drive but I know all I've been thinking about is getting home and getting into the shower in my ensuite. Then...

I've never had shower sex. I've never had sex out of a bed, actually. I'm not even sure I've had great sex, especially after today. After feeling more lust from a kiss than I've ever felt from sex.

Sex. Sex. Sex.

It's all I can think about. But not just sex. Sex with Mike. The body that I've been feeling against mine all day. That body naked, on me, over me, in me.

Garghhh, I'm a mess. I can't think straight. It's a wonder I've even made it to the driveway of home.

The sun set on our drive back – a legitimate distraction I

could pretend to be admiring whilst my mind was completely absorbed by images of Mike semi-naked in a towel, his skin wet from showering, Mike in a see-through shirt in the lake. Now, as we get out of the car, we're surrounded by dusk and quiet. Though the lights are on in the house, I'm beyond thankful that there's no sign of my family.

I get out of the car, already having decided the kayaks can be untied tomorrow, and knock my door shut. I make for the rear door to pick up my backpack from the footwell – I don't know why – but I don't make it as far as opening the door before I feel Mike behind me, his breath, then his lips, on my neck.

Thank God he wants this, too.

He turns me, nudging me back against the car, and I'm so pleased we're getting a second chance at this kiss-up-against-the-car thing because today, without lies standing between us, a gentle caress of my cheek is not going to cut it. He knows I'm not really an actress to match his sports player, yet he still wants me.

His face is close to mine and I want to look at him, just for a moment, enjoy him, take him in, willing my mind to stay present and not overthink what tomorrow could bring. He steps closer to me, so I can feel his pelvis against my stomach. My hands find his hair and I pull him closer to me, tilting my chin, parting my lips.

But something shifts in his expression and I physically see his retreat from me.

'Abbey, before this goes any further, I have to be honest with you—'

'You're back, then.' My mom swans out of the garage holding a bottle of wine in each of her hands and heading for the front door.

His words are quiet but I'm pretty sure when Mike buries his head against my ear, he mutters, 'You've got to be kidding me.'

I could cry. I could literally cry with frustration. Sexual frustration and terror, because what does he mean by 'honest'? Was he about to tell me we've had the most amazing day and I've fallen even deeper for him than I was this morning but he's still in love with Fleur and his big-shot lifestyle in San Francisco?

'Hi Mom,' I manage through gritted teeth.

'You'll need to get washed up; dinner is about ready and your sister and Shernette are starving after their travels.' She heads inside, seemingly oblivious to, or not caring about, what she interrupted, calling back, 'Airplane food has no sustenance.'

I can feel my eyes clouding over. This is ridiculous but I'm so wound up, and seeing my mom is bringing all the noise of reality back into my mind.

Mike will think I'm crazy if I cry over this. It is crazy. So, with a heavy sigh, I slip out from under him and start walking to the house.

For the first time today, it feels like there are hundreds of unspoken words hanging in the air.

44

ABBEY

In the lounge, Dad is laughing at something Dee has said, telling her she's nuts.

Shernette leaps to her feet from the sofa and hugs me. Dee is next in line and whilst maybe not obvious to everyone, I can see that her tiny little baby is starting to grow beneath her clothes.

Somewhere in amongst it all, Mike has shifted from my side. 'I'm going to grab a quick shower before dinner,' he tells me.

I watch him go. So happy to see my sister and friend. Unnerved by what is to come between Mike and me. Bereft at the loss of and wishing we could go back to our day in the mountains.

Maybe this whole day was another of my awful ideas because if I was afraid before it, I'm terrified now.

'Erm, we're going to need to catch up about *that*,' Shernette teases, inclining her head in the direction Mike just went.

'Yeah we are!' Dee adds.

I can't stop my skin from flushing pink, my fingertips caressing where Mike has kissed so often today, my lips stretching into a smile so wide it aches my cheeks.

I glance Dad's way to find him rolling his eyes and shaking his head.

'Terry, come and open the wine, would you?' Mom calls from the dining room.

Dad pushes up out of his chair, his shirt unbuttoned by two, no jacket or tie, but his pants smart – his off-duty look. As he passes by Dee, Shernette and me, he leans in to my ear and tells me, 'Any man who can put a smile like that on my daughter's face is okay with me.'

Huh?

He likes him. Not that that's astonishing. I know Mike's great. But isn't he Team Andrew with Mom?

This day is full of surprises.

'So what have we missed?' Dee asks.

'Urgh, a seriously awful luncheon, attended by Victoria, who now vocally hates me, and Maisie!'

'Ew, Maisie Daisy, spring shines out of her ass?'

'The very same.'

'What am I missing?' Shernette asks, as she and Dee retake their seats.

'Maisie Daisy snogged Andrew behind the bike sheds in high school. Then asked him to prom,' Dee says.

'I thought Andrew and I were starting to get together, become more than the girl and guy next door. But Maisie, with her big boobs and false eyelashes, made herself too available to resist.' I'm still mad about it now. 'I actually tried to switch my home room because of it but I had no luck.'

'Then she and Andrew got it on after a house party on prom night and it was all anyone wanted to talk about for a week,' Dee adds.

Even now, I could curl up and hide at the memory.

'I thought you and Andrew were always a thing. I thought you were each other's firsts?' Shernette asks.

'He was mine. Maisie was his.' Before this conversation, I don't think I'd put my mind to the similarities of then and what he did to me six weeks ago. Was I an idiot for much longer than I'm giving myself credit for?

'Speaking of the lying jerk. Guess who I ran smack into right after lunch with his mom?' I come to sit on the sofa between my sister and best friend, both of whom have a glass of wine on coffee tables placed at either side of the sofa. 'Should you be drinking that?' I ask of Dee.

Her eyes go wide and she raises her arms from her sides. 'What could I say? Mom brought out the good stuff and she knows I'd never turn it down. I'm not actually drinking it.'

'Isn't now a good time to tell her about the baby?'

'Are you kidding? The night before her vows? She's going to hate me when she finds out – the fact I'm not a virgin will be the biggest shock.'

'I think she knows you're not a virgin, Dee.' I think about my dad's reaction just now – still baffling and unexpected. 'Or maybe she'll be happy? It will be her grandchild, after all. Speaking of which, is Nate home, yet?'

'Meh.' Dee flicks her hand. 'They were on our flight, sitting in fancy class, naturally. Didn't even bother bringing us a dessert back each. They're meeting some of Nate's friends for dinner tonight, apparently. Absolute lead balloon with Mom.'

'Erm, sidetracked,' Shernette says. 'What happened with Andrew?'

I pick up Dee's wine and take a sip. 'He told me he made a mistake and that he wants me back.'

'What? Is he serious?' Dee asks, furious on my behalf, I think.

It's a conversation we'll continue later because Mom calls to us from the kitchen. 'Girls, come and take your seats, please.'

There are things about my mom that drive me potty – like her drilling into me a checklist of life choices that I've never been able to fully attain – but the way she looks after us all and welcomes my friends into our fold as if they're her own isn't one of them.

We take our seats at the table. Though Mom has removed the extension piece from the middle of the large oval, we adopt our usual positions. Dad is sitting at the head of the table and Mom will sit opposite him at the other head when she takes a seat. I'm next to Dad on one side and Dee is next to him on the other. Shernette sits between Mom and Dee, where Nate would usually sit, and there's a space for Mike between Mom and me, where my sister-in-law would be when we all get together.

There've been times, of course, when Andrew has been here and Nate's kids, too, and we've added the extension for them to squish into the middle spots. But not tonight and, so far as Andrew goes, never again.

Six weeks ago, that thought would have made my eyes sting and brought a lonely pang to my chest, but not tonight. No more. I am *so over* Andrew and his bullshit.

There's music playing lowly in the background – Dad's old country tunes. I can smell Mom's famous lasagna cooking and I'm not at all surprised when she walks into the room carrying plates of bruschetta topped with sliced mozzarella to start. Her classics never get old.

But I am surprised when she's followed into the room by Mike, who's also carrying three plates. 'You can pop those three on your side, Michael,' Mom tells him, with not a hint of resentment or ill-will.

He's freshly showered, his hair still wet, and he's wearing a shirt tucked into smart pants, similarly open at the neck and casual like my dad.

I'm pretty sure my heart just skipped a beat. Then he reaches into the wine bucket Mom generally rolls out when we have guests, dabs water off the bottle of white with a napkin, and tops off the glasses around the table, kindly not making a deal of it but missing out Dee.

All the while, the scent of him – clean and spritzed with flirt potion – infiltrates my senses. I'm putty for the millionth time today.

He replaces the bottle in the wine bucket, receiving thanks and smiles from Mom, then sits into the seat next to mine.

Just when I think I can't take any more, his fingers find mine beneath the table and he locks our hands together, then brings them to his mouth, pressing his lips to my skin.

God. Help. Me.

Putty is way more solid than the way I am feeling right now. One hundred percent liquefied might just cover it.

I'm still in my sportswear, disheveled from our day and very much underdressed at the table. Yet the way he looks at me, his eyes hooded and gentle, it's like he hasn't even noticed.

Is he a fantastic bluffer or does he really feel the connection between us that I can feel with every part of me?

Will it matter in a few days' time?

As my sister asks about his injury and when he'll be back playing for the Giants, I remember that none of this is real and it can't be real. He has a complete mess going on with his girlfriend or ex-girlfriend and his team mate that he hasn't fully resolved.

I try to push all of this from my mind and remember how great today has been – one of the best days of my life – and it's not so hard to do as the wine and conversation flow around the table.

My sister and Shernette are on top form. My fake boyfriend is being as funny as I've known him. My dad is full of joy. And Mom seems genuinely happy.

Time flies as we work through Mom's lasagna and, much to Mike's amusement, the peanut butter and chocolate fudge cake she has made especially for me.

Without the pressure of letting people down, I could really miss home.

Everything is going swimmingly until Dee asks, 'So what do you think about Andrew telling Abbey he's still in love with her yesterday, Mike?'

If my eyes could leap from my head, they would have.

Mike lets go of my hand he was holding beneath the table. 'You saw Andrew?'

I clear my throat and feel all eyes around the table on me. 'I bumped into him. He was coming to pick up his mom.'

Mike's eyes narrow but he doesn't speak; he only looks at me, reading me, searching for truth, I think. I've lied to him again.

I remember my reaction when I got home from lunch yesterday. My tears, screaming into my pillow. I'd be willing to bet he thinks that was all down to Andrew.

What does he make of it? I don't find out because he twists on a smile – he has gotten so good at faking it. Picking up his dirty plate, he says, 'I'll help you clean up, Mrs Mitchell.'

We all pitch in with the clean-up and retire to the lounge for coffees – Mike joining Dad with an Irish coffee and talking business, whilst the rest of us drink decaf and look at the old photographs Mom has dug out.

I keep trying to get Mike on his own and explain that I told Andrew there was no chance of us getting back together but he's avoiding me, I'm sure of it.

I wonder what he's thinking. How he's feeling.

I wonder if the only person who has fallen for our hoax is me.

'I'm pooped,' Dee says, yawning.

'Yes, and we've got an early start tomorrow, girls. Shernette, you'll get ready with us in the morning, won't you?' Mom asks.

'I wouldn't miss it, Mrs M.'

'Right then, gents,' Mom says, rising from the sofa, putting the last of the photographs back in the box they came from and tucking them away in an ottoman footstool. 'We'll let you talk business and sport whilst we ladies get some beauty sleep.'

She heads over to Dad and gives him a quick kiss. 'Goodnight, my darling. Don't jilt me at the altar, will you?'

'I never did first time,' Dad says, which is typically him. A closet romantic.

Then Mom turns to Mike, places a gentle hand on his shoulder and says, 'Sleep well, Michael. I'll look forward to seeing you tomorrow.'

It's far from an expression of love but it's also a near 180 on their first meeting.

'I'm looking forward to it, Mrs Mitchell.'

'Would you call me Anna?'

Mike smiles outwardly but his eyes don't dazzle the way I know they do when he's genuinely happy. 'Anna.'

I'm disappointed today is done. I'm even more disappointed by the way it has ended, and that I'm sharing a bed with Dee tonight.

But I can't resist one last opportunity to kiss Mike before the day closes out. To try to figure out from his touch where his head is at.

He's touched me whilst we've been here in Canada because he's my fake boyfriend, but it hasn't felt anything like it has been between us today. Today felt real, at least to me.

Whilst the others wish each other sweet dreams, Mike stands.

On tiptoes, I hold his cheeks in my palms and lean in to kiss him again.

His lips meet mine briefly. Chastely.

Our day is done and I'm... devastated.

But as I walk away, he grabs my hand, tugs me back to him and kisses me in a way that turns my devastation into elation.

Maybe. Just maybe.

45

TED

'You were right, I'm in so much trouble here,' I tell Mike through my phone.

I'm sitting on a bench on the lawn out back of Abbey's parents' house. Over the course of the morning, the lawn has been transformed into an aisle and guest seating for the vow renewals. Anna has gone all out with flower arrangements and bows tied around chairs. It looks like a first, big white wedding, rather than a renewal of vows. But hats off to her, a marriage as long as hers and Terry's deserves to be celebrated.

There's also a giant gazebo, with round tables underneath that are decorated with flowers that match the ceremony area.

A stage has been erected on which a swing quartet is currently setting up. Two men are almost through hanging lights from every tree and hedge around the lawn for this evening.

I'm already in my suit, having spent the morning filling time, making hot drinks and taking breakfast on trays to leave outside the room where Anna, Abbey, Dee and Shernette are getting ready. I took the kayaks from yesterday off the roof rack of the SUV and put them back in the garage. Then I took a walk nearby in a bid to clear my head and stop thinking about the voice inside me that's saying...

'I haven't felt like this about someone since... I've never felt like this about *anyone*, Mike.'

It's like there's been a cosmic shift and the relationship Abbey and I thought we were here to perform has turned into something fundamentally different. Bigger. Real.

Yet all day long, people have been calling me Mike. And I've tried to tell her the truth, I have. I intend to. But every time, I get cut off or caught out.

'But now her ex wants her back and she said there was nothing in it, but she also never told me she'd seen him and I can't stop myself wondering, what if she wants him back, too? Or am I overthinking it? I can hardly call her out for withholding the truth.'

'Oh man, you really are in trouble. I told you this trip was a bad idea.'

He's right. In the main, it's an absolute disaster. I'm a mess. Though...

'It's done some good. I'm sitting here looking at essentially a wedding being set up and I'm thinking I had a narrow escape. I can see how wrong Fleur and I are for each other. This could have been me getting married to the very wrong woman. So if there's a silver lining to what she and Roman have done, it's that she's saved me a divorce.'

'Well, that is good. Great that you're finally seeing what everyone else could see,' Mike says. He's also outside, walking his dog, a Staffie called Ruth, after the infamous Babe.

'How about you drop the whole "I told you so" routine and help me out here?'

'I don't know what you want me to tell you, little bro. The

timing is godawful. Equally, I've never heard you talk about anyone the way you talk about this chick.'

'Please don't call her a chick.'

'See? That's what I'm saying.'

'You're useless. Be more big brother.'

He sighs. 'Man, I've never been in love, what would I know? But are you sure this isn't just a rebound thing? Or getting your own back on Fleur?'

'Love? I'm not in love with her.' *Am I?* I stand from the seat, unable to sit any longer, and drag a hand through my hair, staring up at the window of the room I know Abbey is getting dressed in.

Maybe, if I could just see her, everything would make more sense. 'I'm pretty sure this isn't a rebound thing. I literally felt like... I don't know, like the earth shifted or something yesterday. When I kiss her, it's like—'

'Jesus, you are in deep shit, kid. Listen, why don't you just— Ruuuuuuth! Ruth, get your ass back here!'

'Mike? Mike! Why don't I just what?'

He's panting when he speaks next. 'Tell her, Ted. There's no point hypothesizing. You have to tell her your truth. Maybe she slaps you across the face and tells you to go screw yourself. Maybe she slaps you then tells you she's still in love with her ex. Or maybe—'

'Or maybe?'

'She recognizes that you've both been lying to people up there and she agrees there's something real amongst the pretend.'

I sigh, not knowing which of these options is most likely but worried it's not the last one. 'She's right, you know, you can be pretty smart, Mike.'

'Right back at you, Mini Mike. Oh shit— Ruuuuuuuuth! Gotta go.'

Bleep, bleep, bleep. The call ends.

No one comes to the window where Abbey is, so I look back to where a pianist is now sitting at a white baby grand piano in front of the rows of guest seating. He starts to play a wistful melody, practicing. I suspect guests will be arriving soon, filling the seats either side of the aisle.

It's funny how the stars align sometimes. Months from now, if Fleur hadn't cheated on me, I'd have been standing at the front of an aisle like that, waiting for the wrong bride to walk toward me. I know I never would have chosen to end things with her.

If Fleur and Roman hadn't gone behind my back, I never would have wound up in New York, living above Abbey. Without them breaking my heart, I wouldn't have pounded a baseball off the wall over and over, until Abbey came upstairs to give me what for.

And if Andrew hadn't cheated on Abbey, she might have walked down the aisle toward him one day.

Both alternate scenarios terrify me.

But when I imagine me standing at the front of an aisle like that waiting for Abbey to walk toward me, I'm not afraid at all.

She's the mirror image of the real me – a bit of a nerd, a bit of an introvert, outwardly a pacifist, a lover of nature and the outdoors, someone who laughs at the same silly things I do.

But am I in love with her? I can't be, surely. It's only been weeks since I first met her and her big panties and fluffy slippers.

One thing I do know is that the very last thing in the world I want to do is hurt her.

So I'm going all in. I need to know how she'll respond and it can't wait.

I turn to head in the direction of Abbey and smack right into Terry.

'I'd like a word in my office,' he says.

At first, I miss the severity of his tone because my mind is still whirring. 'Ah, now? I was just going to speak to Abbey.'

'Now,' he tells me sternly, already setting off in the direction of the house.

I glance up to Abbey's room one more time. I'd like to see her and I'd kind of like her moral support right now. What does Terry want?

As I walk into his office, he takes a seat behind his large wood desk, framed by a floor-to-ceiling window.

'Close the door, Theodore.'

I do as he asks, then—

Wait... *Theodore*?

Oh shit.

Terry opens a drawer beneath his antique style desk and takes out a magazine. Only when he places it on the desk between us do I realize it's the latest edition of *GQ*. He flips it open as if the relevant page has been marked for his attention, and when he does, I see a picture of me, sitting in a chair by the window in Mike's lounge. The opposite side of the page shows Roman standing in his office in San Francisco.

'You look very alike, you and your brother, but not so alike I could mistake which one of you is the businessman and which is the sportsman.' He leans back in his chair and brings his hands to rest on his stomach. 'What I can't work out is why you're lying to everyone and why in hell you're doing it in my home.'

I swallow the ginormous knot in my throat. He knows.

How the heck do I explain this? Where do I even begin?

'Does Abbey know who you really are? Does she know that you're engaged to be married?'

Fuck.

My voice finds me. 'That isn't right. I swear to you. The engagement is off; it's just that publicly, that's not knowledge yet and when I gave that interview, I'd just found out my fiancée and best friend, my business partner, were having an affair. It was so recent that I— I just got caught out and didn't know what to say. I swear to you I would never do anything to intentionally hurt Abbey. You have my word on that, sir.'

Though aren't I? Haven't I been by letting her believe my lies?

He rubs his chin, softening, I hope, ever so slightly. 'That's something at least. Now I don't have to feed you to the bears after I've killed you.'

I genuinely don't know if he's joking or not but I fear it's the latter. He picks up the magazine and rolls it into a tube. I wonder if he's tempted to beat me with it but he taps the end on the edge of his desk instead. 'That still doesn't explain why you're pretending to be your brother. Nor does it tell me why you're lying to my daughter. So I suggest you start talking, Theodore.'

I'm sweating. My throat feels like it's constricting. But Terry deserves an explanation. I only wish I was giving it to Abbey first. 'The affair is how all of this started. I never expected that what started as a case of mistaken identity would go this far.'

I tell him everything. From Abbey moving into Blake House and me winding up there after running from San Francisco. From me banging a baseball against the wall to my brother throwing me a party and Abbey turning up in her fluffy slippers.

Then I tell him about Andrew seeing another woman in the apartment block and how I pretended to be Abbey's boyfriend the night Andrew took a date to dinner with Abbey's siblings. I miss out the ensuing Tinder date Abbey went on and I don't mention that Andrew is a deceitful, lying jerk and Abbey deserves better. Those are her stories to share.

When I'm finished, Terry stands from his chair and moves around the room to a bar table, where he pours himself a glass of something I suspect is whisky from a decanter and offers the same to me, which I decline.

I shift in my seat to face him, not knowing what's coming next but feeling like I have to tell him... 'Abbey is an incredible woman, sir; I'm sure I don't need to tell you that. She doesn't deserve my lies and for what it's worth, I've been beating myself up about not telling her. When I bumped into you just now, I was on my way to tell her everything. I just... got so deep into this that I didn't know how.'

I'm terrified of finding out her response.

'And for her part, Terry, she didn't set out to hurt anyone; she did this to protect herself, I think. She knew she would come up here, where everyone loves Andrew and the idea of them as a couple, and she thought Andrew would bring a date.'

His eyes narrow. 'She doesn't want him back, does she?'

'I— I hope not. I don't think so. I think she thinks you and Anna would like her to get back with him.'

He nods, thoughtfully. 'Then that's my failing.'

'Terry, please don't let this be something that comes between you and Abbey. She loves you so much; I see that every time she looks your way, every time she talks about your business and how she loves helping out with your work.'

He sips his drink, stoic. 'There are some holes in your story, son. I don't know what they are but I understand you've got an allegiance to my daughter and I'm grateful for that. I'm also grateful to you for looking out for her these past weeks.'

'She's very easy to care for, s—'

'I don't appreciate being lied to by either of you. I won't tell Abbey who you are because you're going to do your own dirty work. But this will upset my wife immensely when it comes out.' He moves to the window, turning his back on me, but I see in his reflection that he takes another drink. 'Given where we are with our occasion and the efforts Anna has gone to, I'd like us to keep this between ourselves. Whether you tell her today or tomorrow, you and Abbey can keep up your façade for one more day, I'm sure?'

I nod. 'Yes, sir.'

I wait for a response, his approval, I think, but it doesn't come and I'm left staring at his back, not knowing what to do or say next. Knowing that even if, in some universe, Abbey managed to forgive my lies, her family might never. It's another hurdle we might not be able to leap.

Eventually, Terry speaks, dismissing me. 'Go.' But before I reach the door, he says, 'Andrew was unfaithful, wasn't he?'

I turn back into the room and find Terry looking my way.

'I don't feel like that's my story to share,' I say.

I don't deny it. He should know. One day, everyone will know and maybe their knowing would be the only hope I have of Abbey and I being able to see each other after this trip. The alternative being something I really don't want to have to think about.

So for now, I'd at least like to have another person on Abbey's side, another person who loves her and can shield her from the venom of others.

Terry makes a noise somewhere between a grunt and a snarl. 'I never did like that boy and I should have made my feelings known. Now I want to tear his head off.'

'Join the queue,' I say. I'm not a violent man but it's true. For what he did to Abbey, for everything he's still putting her through here in Canada, and for the confidence he zapped from her recently and never helped her find in herself for all the years they were together, I hate that man.

'And the apartment she's living in – should I be worried about where she's found the money to rent an apartment in a building expensive enough for a professional baseball player to want to live? God knows she's no actress, despite her ruse of the last few days.'

'Not worried. I have a feeling Abbey will work things out just fine in the end.'

I run a thumb along my chin, pondering my next words, but I am fully aware of how astute Terry is, so I tell him, 'It's been a better way for her to spend her wedding fund than getting hitched to that jackass.'

Terry's eyes widen, then he gives me one curt nod and I take it as my cue to leave him alone with his drink.

I open the door, then think I best check: 'Are you happy for me to stay here for the weekend? It's your home and I'd understand, what with everything I've told you, if you don't want me here.'

'I trust my daughter, Theodore, therefore I trust that she knows what she's doing. The only part I don't follow is why you think she'd be better off with a sportsman than a very successful and level-headed businessman who seems much more her type.'

I fight the smile that threatens to play on my face at the compliment. Now that I know she isn't an actress, maybe... But Terry is definitely not on my side here.

'So I can stay?'

'You can stay. On the condition that my daughter finds out the truth in the next twenty-four hours, and I'll be here for her when she does.'

46

ABBEY

I've caught glimpses of Mike from my mom's bedroom window, wearing a three-piece suit and looking hot as heck.

He glanced my way once when I opened the window an inch to let the sound of the pianist sift into the room. I don't know why but I darted away, as if it's *our* wedding day and I'm not supposed to see him until I get down there.

If my nerves today are anything to go by, if we ever did get married, I'd be a wreck. I shake my head, shaking away the thought of him being my groom. It's not a healthy place to be because after today, Mike will fly off into the sunset, back to his high-flying life in California. That was the plan. It still is.

But God, I'll miss him. I miss him now and we still have days together. It's like a countdown to the end of a vacation you wish could continue forever.

'It doesn't fit. *Damnit.*' Dee's panicked voice brings me out of my reverie. I dash over to where she's struggling to pull her silk dress down over her swollen tummy.

Thankfully, Mom is in the ensuite and out of earshot because Dee, Shernette and I know exactly why the dress doesn't fit.

'Here, let me see,' I say, encouraging her to hold up her arms and breathe in so Shernette and I can try to tease the dress down her waist. 'Dee, I don't think it's going to work.'

'I don't want to squish the baby,' Shernette says. 'There's no give in this material.'

'It's too tiny to squish yet. *Feck, feck, feck,*' Dee says, bouncing on the spot like she used to as a child when she took a tantrum. 'What am I going to do?'

We all look at each other, then Dee's eyes narrow on me and she considers the dress I'm wearing. The floaty, stretchy and kind of frumpy number chosen for me, which is only a match for Dee's in color. 'We'll have to swap,' she says.

As she speaks, there's a tap on the door. 'Who is it?' I call.

'It's me, Abbey. Mike. Can we talk?'

'Mike, I'd like to but now just isn't the time. We're having a wardrobe crisis. I'll see you down there, okay?' I will, won't I? Today is what this whole performance has been about.

'Yeah. You will.'

Phew.

'What crisis?' Mom shouts from the bathroom.

* * *

Shernette has gone to take a seat next to Mike, somewhere near the front of the guests, as instructed by Mom. Mom, Dee and I are standing in the summer room, behind glass-paned French doors. I can't see them and I can't see Dad and Nate, who should be standing at the front, because all of the sixty or so guests have been told to be upstanding.

I'll admit, a month ago, this ceremony seemed needless and one of Mom's over-the-top ideas, but today, it feels like the perfect way to celebrate Mom and Dad's anniversary.

Our mom looks exquisite in her two piece with her hair salon-styled and her make-up done by Dee, which is equivalent to professional. Dee and I are each wearing the other's dress and Mom must be running on adrenaline because she hasn't even seemed to notice.

The pianist starts to play something beautiful that makes my eyes well momentarily. Then Dee and I hug Mom, each under one arm and tell her, 'We love you.'

'I'm so pleased I get to do this again with my girls beside me,' Mom says. 'Now, hurry along, I don't want to keep your dad waiting.'

Chuckling, Dee and I stand side by side and as the doors are opened for us by Mom's party planner, we head down the aisle.

Near the back of the guests, I spot Andrew, standing next to his parents and Maisie Daisy and her parents. Seeing him startles me. It makes me feel sickly nervous. I guess because I've built up today and seeing him into something huge. That's why Mike is here, after all. But right now, looking his way, I have no idea why.

I'm pleased I saw him at the hotel on Thursday. I'm pleased I got to see how manipulative he is because I know, without a shadow of doubt, that I don't want to be with him anymore and I don't care whether he's with someone else. I don't care about making him jealous anymore.

All I do care about is my family, my best friend, and—

Mike is standing at the end of the row, right near the front. I'm suddenly very aware that my hair has been styled and I'm wearing Dee's much sexier dress than my own. And I'm extremely sensitive to the way his lips curve into a soft smile when he sees me, the way his chest visibly rises with his next breath, and the way his eyes are focused only on me.

My own breaths feel like they've stopped, like I'll never be able to breathe again. My heart hammers in my chest and...

'Oh, God, Dee, I feel sick.'

'Urgh, me too. So sick… Wait, why do you feel sick?'

'I can't feel my legs either.' And I can't take my eyes off the man in front of me. 'I think either my body is malfunctioning or, maybe, this is what it feels like to fall in love.'

Dee links her arm through mine, pulling me into our next slow step, and through a smile, she tells me, 'This may be the best mistake you've ever made.'

I glance her way now because of all of the random, rash decisions I've made in the last few weeks, Dee is yet to tell me that any of them is a mistake, which means she must really mean it.

'I know,' I confess.

But this mistake has been the best time of my life.

We reach the end of the aisle and tuck into the row of seats in front of Shernette and Mike, turning to watch Mom coming down the aisle.

But I can't look at Mom because the man standing next to me looks incredible, he smells so good, and when he whispers to me, 'You're beautiful,' every single cell in my body wants to kiss his face until my lips are numb, to feel his fingers in my hair, to feel his body under my touch.

Oh my God, I am in love with Mike.

This really has been the worst idea ever.

47

TED

I've been placed on a table with Shernette and Nate and his wife and kids. Nate's okay, a bit brash and self-centered but he seems like a good guy at heart. His wife and kids are a *lot* but not bad people on first meeting, just a little noisy and frantic. I don't know, maybe that's just life for parents with young kids. I've got to admit, if my kids were as cute as Abbey's niece and nephew, I'd probably let them have ice cream for main course, too.

It's a decent table. Shernette is a great laugh and doing a stellar job for the most part of keeping my mind at the table and not drifting off into wondering what tomorrow will bring for Abbey and me. How this will all end.

I can't bring myself to meet Terry's eyes. I congratulated him and Anna after they renewed their vows but it felt tense, fraught. He wants me to tell Abbey the truth. I need to.

Because the best thing about sitting on this table is that I'm right in front of the top table and the most incredible and attractive woman in the room is in my direct eye line. I love Abbey in her fluffy slippers, her big pants and loungewear. Watching her move in her form-fitting sportswear yesterday did all kinds of things to my hormones that shouldn't happen just from seeing her in Lycra.

But today, she truly is mesmerizing. From the dress and shoes to the way her hair has been curled and tucked behind one ear; even the light touch of her make-up and the smell of her perfume. Despite those things, I've mostly watched the bedazzling smile she's worn nearly non-stop. The way she loves her family is immeasurable and wonderful.

I'll be sad to have to leave all of this but that will be nothing compared to the way it would kill me to walk away from Abbey. So I have no choice. I have to tell her and give us the minutest chance of getting through this.

I already know I'm fighting a losing battle.

I saw the way she sought out Andrew in the crowd of guests as she walked down the aisle earlier.

She didn't look at him the way she looked at me. I know that. But she still searched for him. She still cares that he's here.

I may have been a fool when it comes to Fleur and I might not have the most extensive experience of relationships with women, but I'm not fool enough to think that the three weeks we've known each other can compare to the years Abbey and Andrew were together. Their shared experiences. The way they must know and understand each other.

And I'm Mike. *Fecking Mike.*

I've made an absolute disaster of this.

***

The heat of the day is cooling off and some of the trees are providing shade as Abbey's dad makes a speech, followed by Nate. There's no cake cutting but there is going to be a first dance and it's the string quartet who announce the song and ask the newly re-vowed couple to head on up to the dance floor.

Terry doesn't strike me as someone who naturally wants to dance in front of others, but he lets Anna lead him onto the purpose-laid floor and as the quartet begin to play, he twirls his wife under his arm.

I can empathize. I'm not a very public person and I have two left feet in any event. But Mike would dance at a party. He'd be the first person on the dance floor, even at a vow renewal. That's my job today; it's my return favor to Abbey.

And for the part of me that isn't a lie here, I can't miss an opportunity to hold Abbey in my arms and do what I've been wanting to do all day: kiss her.

As other guests begin to move onto the dance floor, I make for my fake girlfriend and the girl I'm fairly certain I'm falling in love with.

She looks up to me and beams when I hold out my hand, making me feel like I'm finally enough for someone, more than enough. 'I'm not much of a mover but I'm not going to miss an opportunity to dance with the most beautiful woman here.'

Her lips grow wider and my heart skips at the thought that I made that happen. She slips her hand into mine – finally, I can touch her – and we head onto the dance floor, where other couples have started to dance alongside Abbey's parents.

I pull her into me and, at last, my lips are on hers. She's still Abbey from yesterday, even if we are one day closer to this being over. The woman I fell for in the mountains is still here now and kissing me back like she feels as much for me as I do her.

I don't question it or overthink it, I just lean in.

We dance through two or three more slow songs, kissing, touching, twirling, until the quartet declare they're done for the day and will be replaced by a DJ for the evening.

* * *

I've pulled my seat up to the top table now to sit with Abbey and share a glass of champagne. Her mom declares she's going to change out of her outfit into something she can 'boogie' in and Terry stands to pull out her chair – nice touch.

None of us are expecting to see Andrew, with some woman following behind him, charging toward the top table.

And he's making a beeline for Abbey. *What the actual?*

I'm not worried for her safety but I don't like the look of fire in his eyes, so when Abbey stands, I rise with her, noticing as I do the magazine in Andrew's hand. *Fuck.*

'Have you seen this?' he snarls at Abbey, shaking the rolled-up magazine angrily, his steps faltering. He's drunk.

'Seen what?' Abbey asks calmly, though I hear a tremor in her voice. She'll hate this scene, the conflict, but more than that, she's going to hate what Andrew is about to expose.

'Him,' Andrew snaps, pointing now at me.

'Andrew, don't do this,' I beg him. 'Not here. Let's go somewhere—'

'He's no baseball player, Abbey,' he yells. 'The only thing he's playing is you. Look at this.' He casts the copy of *GQ* down on the tabletop.

Terry steps to Abbey's side. 'Calm yourself down, Andrew. This isn't the time or the place.'

'Oh it is, Terry. She needs to know right now. His name isn't even Mike. It's Theodore. Theodore Thomas and he's a tech developer, not a sports star.'

Andrew steps right up to us now and I've never wanted to smack another guy in the face as much as I do this jerk. I've never hit a man or anyone in my life. But the rage that slams into me like a bullet train is indescribable. I understand what people mean when they say a red mist descends. It feels like a fire has engulfed me. For the first time in thirty odd years, I want to hit something, some*one*.

'He's been playing you, Abbey, and you're so trusting and unsuspecting that you've been a doormat to him.' He leans his head to one side. 'Abbey, he's making a fool of you.'

Fuck, fuck, fuck. 'Abbey, I can explain.' Can I? Right here? Now? I'm not sure I can.

In all my calculations of how and when this whole thing could implode, I did not envisage it happening like this.

Andrew is shouting at us from the other side of the table and every person in the room is looking our way. Abbey's dad tries to weigh in. I want to tell him not to. I don't want to get him tied up in this, too.

But I've lost my voice entirely. My legs feel weak and I'm cold. So cold.

'What have you got to say for yourself, hotshot?' Andrew yells at me.

I'm mute.

'Andrew, that's enough,' Terry says, shifting closer to Abbey.

'Terry, he's engaged to be married.' Andrew picks up the magazine and slams it back down on the table. 'Read it. He talks about how much he and his fiancée can't wait for their wedding. Can you hear me, Abbey? Can you understand what I'm saying?' He repeatedly pokes his fingers against his head, like she's stupid.

With his actions, I find my backbone. 'Your problem is with me, Andrew. And I swear to everything mighty, if you speak to her like that again, I'm going to give you a real problem.'

48

ABBEY

Mike's voice is low, ominous. I haven't heard him like this before.

But to me, he says quietly, 'Abbey, that interview was done when—'

'When you were already in New York, I remember.' Finally, my words come as I speak only to... Who am I speaking to? 'Theodore? Ted? Your brother?'

'Yes. And yes, but I couldn't say anything else. The world doesn't know I'm not with Fleur yet. You know all this; you just think she was engaged to Mike, not me.' He's pleading with me and I understand the logic but right now, it's making me look like even more of an idiot than I already do. He's not Michael Thomas. He isn't a baseball player. The only thing he's played is... *me*.

'You're a piece of shit,' Andrew gripes at Ted.

'Andrew—' My dad goes to speak again but I find some strength from somewhere I've never explored and put a hand to his chest, silencing him, in order that I can have my voice heard.

'This is my mom and dad's day, Andrew. This is the moment you've chosen to get your revenge. Like this? Will you stop at nothing to humiliate me? Ruin their day in the process?' I slam my napkin down on the table. 'Anything you have to say to me can be said outside. But I want everyone to hear this... I know what Mike isn't. He isn't the only person being fake here and it's about time I owned the truth, too.'

I look to my mom and dad apologetically, then to my sister, who looks genuinely sad. And I tell everyone, 'Ted isn't my boyfriend.' I look his way. He's nothing to me, in fact. I don't even know him. 'I asked him to come here with me and pretend to be my boyfriend.'

Andrew's face contorts, first with confusion, then hilarity. He's mocking me.

'You don't have to do this, Abbey,' Ted tells me gently.

'Yes, I do. This part is on me. Do you know what the irony is, Andrew? I did all this to save face with you. After your throwing other women in my face in New York, I couldn't bear to come here and see you with someone else. I couldn't stand the thought of our families and friends trying to get us back together and you rejecting me.'

In my peripheral vision, I see Ted sit into his seat and hang his head.

'So you brought a fake date to your mom and dad's vow renewals and pretended he's a professional ball player? Abbey, you're crazy.'

I feel my nostrils flare with anger. 'If I'm crazy, Andrew, it's because of you. Everyone thinks you're this great guy and God knows why but you had me fooled for long enough, too.'

'Now you wait a minute, young lady,' Andrew's mom says, rising to her feet. 'It's you who's making a fool of my son, bringing someone up here to make him jealous. Faking a relationship. It's vicious.'

What I want to say to this woman is: *Oh shut up, Victoria.*

What I actually say to her is: 'Oh shut up, Victoria.'

God knows I should have said that a long time ago.

'Don't you speak to me like that, you little vixen,' she jibes back. 'My son hasn't done a thing wrong except call you out on your lies.'

Shernette springs up from her seat. 'Oh no, I'm not listening to this crap. Abbey, I love you and I respect why you've kept it secret but it's time, babe. It's time to tell everyone what a dirty, rotten liar this fool is.'

'Shernette, don't I look ridiculous enough? Please.'

Ted is shaking his head, his hands locked together, his knuckles white.

'Abbey, you're right,' Andrew says, softening now and reaching his hand to my elbow, still from across the table. 'Let's go somewhere and talk this out.'

Ted rises to his feet again. 'Don't touch her.'

'I'm not an object, Ted. Please don't make me into one.'

Meanwhile, Dad has picked up the edition of *GQ* and cuts across us all as he asks, 'Where did you get this? This is my copy. You've been in my office.'

Huh?

Andrew drops his hand away from me, caught in the act, and only now do I see who came charging into the room, hot on his shirt tails.

Maisie freaking Daisy. And the reality is, she could have been anyone. Just another woman.

I scoff. 'Really, Andrew? You and Maisie? It's like we're back in junior high.' I push back my chair. 'I should have realized then that leopards don't change their spots. You cheated on me then and who knows how many times you've done it before you finally confessed.

'I really hope you two will be happy together and *thank you* for giving me the strength to tell you that you're a lying piece of shit. The only thing I regret about us is how much of my life I wasted on you.' I look him in the eyes, seeing his shock, knowing it reflects everyone else's shock in this room because, for once, I'm not walking away from the fight. 'Go fuck yourself, Andrew. Or Maisie. But you can definitely *stop* fucking me over.'

With that proverbial mic drop, I step out from the table and storm through the silence of the room, making it past everyone and almost to the door before my rage turns to tears.

'I have an announcement to make.' I stop in my tracks and turn, seeing through blurred eyes as my sister steps onto a tabletop. 'I'm pregnant. Yep. And I'm not even dating the guy who knocked me up.'

God, I love her.

49

TED

Goddamnit, she was *not* supposed to find out this way.

None of this was supposed to unfold the way it just did. I could scream in frustration with myself, my idiocy. And I want to wrap her up and tell her she's okay, hold her together.

Because if I had just been stripped naked in front of my friends and family like Abbey was, I'd sure as hell need putting back together.

I follow her away from the party, eventually catching up to her at the edge of the lawn, where the sound of music at the party can still be heard but we're out of the eyes and ears of the prying guests.

'Abbey, please stop. Let me explain.'

'Explain?' She swings around to face me and the sight of her cuts me like a knife to my heart. Mascara-stained tears are rolling down her cheeks. 'How can you explain what just happened, *Ted*? I didn't even know your real name!'

'I know that. And I'm more sorry than you'll ever believe, Abbey. I swear I've tried to tell you so many times bu—'

'How hard can it be?' She throws her arms up. 'Hey, Abbey,

you know how you think I'm Mike the MLB player with the model girlfriend? Well, actually, that's my brother. I'm Theodore, tech guy, and that model, she's my *fiancée*.'

'Was. She *was*.' I step toward her and make to touch her arm but she snatches her body away from me. I hold up my hands in apology. 'Fleur and I are done, I promise you that. And the guy she slept with was my best friend. He just isn't a ball player; he's my business partner.'

'Your business partner?' She scoffs. 'That's why I was giving you advice about getting out of the partnership. That's why you fell out?'

'Yes.'

She rubs her temples angrily, as if she can't process everything that's going on. I don't blame her.

'I'm mortified, Ted. Humiliated.' She sniffs, wiping her nose with the back of her hand. 'When I lived here, I was never the girl who got the guy. I was never popular. People couldn't really believe that I even had a boyfriend, let alone a clever one, who went to an Ivy-League college and could still hold court in a room.

'So when Andrew cheated, I figured every one of those people, if they knew the truth, would think, *Yeah, that fits, she could never have kept him happy*.' She shakes her head, worrying her lip as she does. 'I thought, if I brought another guy here with me, I'd show people I can be the girl who gets the guy, just a different guy. And that happened to be you.

'But I fell for it, Ted. I fell for this incredible guy. Funny, smart and self-assured. Only to find out that he was faking all of it, not just our relationship.

'Now I'm more humiliated than ever. Because somewhere along the line, I stopped caring about replacing Andrew. I believed the lie.

'I'm more hurt than I think Andrew ever could have hurt me and everyone at that party probably hates me.'

She's right. I fell for it too and I'm in agony, all of my own doing. She's staring at me expectantly and I don't know if I have the words to put any of this back together.

'For what it's worth, Abbey, no one who knows you could hate you. And I promise, if you can believe anything I say, that I'm hurting, too. I fell for it too. I've fallen for you.'

She scoffs, shakes her head and turns her back on me, walking away.

No. I always walk away from the fight. Not this time. This is the biggest fight of my life and she's worth every second of it.

I run to get in front of her. 'Abbey, please, just hear me out, and if you never want to speak to me again afterward, I'll respect that. I'll hate it but I'll respect it.'

She closes her eyes and sighs but she doesn't walk away, which I take to mean I can at least try.

'At first, it was a case of mistaken identity. You made an assumption that I was my brother.

'Then I saw you in Bloomingdales, laughing and joking with your friends. You bought all this designer stuff and I— I guess I thought you were someone like Fleur. So I couldn't be bothered to correct you. I was messed up and tired. I was hiding in Mike's apartment. Running.

'Then I had that interview with GQ. The timing was awful. Nobody knew about what had happened with Fleur and Roman, so I couldn't say anything different to what was printed in the magazine. I was hurt and embarrassed and would have given anything for it all to just go away.

'The only thing I did in that apartment was bang those stupid baseballs off the wall until I felt numb. So when you called me out on it, I could hardly admit to the real reason behind it. That I was mentally all over the place.

'Somewhere in amongst all of that, I decided life would be easier if I was more like my brother, even Roman. They always get the girl. I never did. So, I put on a front for you. Cocky, arrogant.'

She throws up her arms. 'Those were the worst parts of you.'

I feel my lips rise slightly in a sad smile at the irony.

'But that was all when we first met, Ted. You could have come clean so many times since then.'

I nod. 'I should have. I can't defend myself. You were just the only person I knew in New York and I liked hanging out with you. I didn't want to risk losing you. Then when I thought you were an actress and you kept saying it was a much cooler job than numbers, I didn't think a computer coder would be cool enough for you either.'

I drag a hand roughly through my hair at my own stupidity. 'Then I was too deep into it, Abbey. I fell so hard for you that I've been tormenting myself for days, knowing I should tell you the truth but not daring to find out which way you'd land.'

'Which way I'd land?' She sniffs.

'Whether you'd tell me to go screw myself or—' I shrug because I know now, in this moment, there was never another option, only my own hope.

'Or what?'

Here goes. The words that have been flying around in my head since we came here. The words I should have been saying under very different circumstances. 'For so many reasons, what's happening between us doesn't make sense. But every instinct I have in me is telling me to lean into it. Into us. I can't promise that one or both of us won't wind up getting hurt. But I can tell you honestly that I'm a better version of myself when I'm with you. And I really don't want to give you up.'

She bites her lip, that way she does when she's contemplating, and glances back across her shoulder, where the party seems to be back underway. But when she meets my eyes again, I know which side she's come down on.

'Ted, I just got out of a relationship where I was lied to. Maybe some of the lies we've told and the time we've shared has been good for us both. But I can't walk willingly into that again.'

I exhale heavily. I get it. In her shoes, I'd be saying the same thing. 'I know.' I look at her one last time. Her eyes, her lips, the dimples in her cheeks. Just as beautiful on the outside as she is on the inside. 'For what it's worth, you do know me, Abbey. It wasn't all a lie. In name and job title maybe but the bits in between, they were me. I just got swept up in the lie. Swept up in us. In *you*. And I think... I think in another time and place, we could be pretty perfect for each other.'

I don't know what I expect from her but what I get is nothing. Only an unreadable look into the depths of me.

So I turn and walk away from the one person I really never want to walk away from, up the lawn, back toward the house to get my things.

'Stay tonight,' Abbey says into the dusk. 'You won't get a flight out until morning, so stay.'

That's not what I hoped for. Not even close. I nod and keep walking.

'And Ted, for the record, some people might actually prefer the tech designer over the ball player. A little less cocksure, a heap more honest, and a self-confessed geek, like someone else I know.'

I can feel pressure behind my eyes, so I don't look back. I keep walking as I say, 'But not the one that matters.'

50

TED

I lay on the guest bed all night fully clothed. I heard the DJ play music, I heard Abbey's parents, then Dee and Shernette, come to bed.

Now, as the dawn breaks, I quietly grab my things to leave.

I head downstairs in yesterday's clothes and make for the kitchen to call a cab to the airport, hoping I'll pick up a flight to San Francisco today.

Only when I reach the kitchen, Anna is sitting at the table, her hands wrapped around a china cup and next to it is a teapot.

'Sorry, I didn't think anyone would be up.'

'I'm an early riser. I have been since my children were small. I'd get up and have a cup of tea in the quiet before the madness of the day. And it appears that I'll have a grandchild here before long, waking me up to play at five a.m.'

She gets up from the table to retrieve another cup from a display cupboard, then brings it back to the seat opposite her.

'Is it appropriate to say congratulations?' I ask tentatively.

'Despite the circumstances of my coming to know I'm going to be a grandmother again, I'll never be sad to welcome another little person into the family.' She fills the teacup from the teapot then gives me a look that I assume means I'm expected to sit.

'I don't know what you think of me, Mike—' She stops herself and corrects. 'Theodore.'

'It's just Ted, Mrs Mitchell.'

She nods. 'Ted, then. I'm not sure what my daughter must have told you about me that made her want to lie to us all, but you ought to know how fiercely I love my family.'

'I can already see that,' I say, reluctantly lowering myself onto a chair.

'If I had any inkling that Andrew had cheated on my daughter, there's no way I would have encouraged them to get back together. I'm not the big bad wolf my daughters seem to think I am. All that I've ever wanted for both of them is a good life, strong morals and the right kind of people around them.'

'I'm sure you and Abbey have things to talk about today but I can tell you that this wasn't about you. With the benefit of hindsight, Abbey and I got caught up in something that spiraled and grew but at the heart of it, I was running from things I need to deal with and Abbey was trying to save face.'

I sip my tea under her watchful eye. 'You might not believe this but I'm truly sorry for deceiving her, everyone. I want all of the things you want for Abbey, Mrs Mitchell. You have a beautiful family and I hope that Abbey eventually has a marriage that's as long and happy as your own. Just not with Andrew. She deserves someone who'll treasure her and remind her every day how amazing she is. Someone who knows what they've found in her and who'll shift heaven and earth to never lose it. That's not him.'

'Is it you, Ted? Are you in love with my daughter?'

Finally, words I don't need to think about before answering. 'Yes. Whether I'm the right man for her, we might never get to find out after everything that's happened. But am I in love with her? Absolutely. Completely. Insanely.'

Anna sips from her teacup, watching me the entire time across the rim. I'm not sure if I'd actually like to know what she's thinking or not but I am intrigued.

'Despite my initial, perhaps ill-judged, reluctance, I like you, Ted. Ironically, I respect your honesty. I like who my daughter is around you – her deception aside, which perhaps I'll come to understand, as you seem to think I will.

'You make her happier than I've seen her, even despite the circumstances she's been suffering recently. Her sister and Shernette tell me you're a good man, and you're right, Abbey does deserve to have someone who'll adore her.'

She sets her cup down on her saucer with a clink. 'Give me a minute to get dressed into something other than my pajamas and I'll take you to the airport. Presumably that's where you're headed.'

'It is.' Last night, Abbey stood her ground, defended herself, and showed me what kind of person I want to be. She showed me that I need to stop running, too. 'But you don't have to take me. I can call a cab.'

She's already out of her seat and walking for the door. 'You've made sure you're up early enough to escape before anyone sees you and you're in the middle of nowhere. How do you think you're going to get a cab at this hour?'

She has a very good point and I really don't want to have to say goodbye to Abbey again. I can't. So I concede, and whilst Anna gets dressed, I manage to book onto a flight home, to confront my idea of hell the way Abbey did yesterday.

51

ABBEY

I've been awake for a while when my mom brings a cup of steaming coffee and two slices of peanut butter toast into my bedroom. I've changed out of yesterday's dress, which I was too exhausted to change out of last night, and into an old dressing gown. But I'm still wearing yesterday's make-up and I can only imagine how red and puffy my eyes look because they feel horrendously sore.

Mom comes to sit on the bed next to me, fluffing my pillows behind her back first.

'I'm so sorry I ruined your day yesterday,' I say, my tears coming back to my throat and burning my eyes. 'I'm so ashamed of it all. Lying to you, the way it all unfolded. Generally messing up everything so badly.'

'Don't be silly; the added drama will mean our party is talked about for years to come.'

We laugh together because we both know it's true.

'You know, that's exactly why I lied about Ted in the first place. I mean, him being Mike wasn't my doing but bringing him here as my boyfriend was supposed to stop any drama about Andrew and I getting back together and stop the truth from coming out and embarrassing me. I just wasn't enough for him and I think everyone has thought as much since the day we got together.'

Mom turns to face me. 'Now you listen to me, young lady. What he did to you is despicable and it's entirely a reflection of his bad character. I'm only sorry that I didn't see this a long time ago. I would never have wanted you to settle for someone so unworthy of you. *You* are enough. And I spent an entire ride to the airport this morning with a charming man who thinks that you're more than enough for him.'

I blow out hard. 'Another thing I've messed up. We can't go back from here. He lied to me about who he is and he's only just broken up with a woman he was engaged to. I mean, it's not even public knowledge yet. Not to mention the fact he lives in San Francisco and I live— That's probably another thing I should own up to...'

I tell her everything. From my dinner with Andrew when I came back from Texas to his admission of sleeping with someone else. From quitting my job and blowing my wedding savings on a swanky apartment. Getting the acting job on Dee's TV series out of necessity and keeping the superficiality of it from Ted. From meeting Ted and how obnoxious I thought he was at first to somehow ending up in a fake relationship.

'Ironically, the only person who fell for the lie was me, Mom.'

'Oh, darling.'

'It's true. If there's something good to come of it, I know definitively that I was in love with the idea of being with Andrew, someone from home, who my family loved and wanted me to be with. Someone who ticked that box on the checklist of things you've always wanted for me – husband, career, marriage, grandchildren. But I didn't love *him*. I know that now because I've felt what it's like to truly fall for someone, the way I fell in love with Ted.'

'Abigail.' Mom shakes her head and I realize her eyes are full of unshed tears. 'I hate that you thought I wanted you to fulfill a checklist more than I want you to be happy. If that's the case, then I've failed you as a mother.' She wipes a thumb under her eye and sniffs.

'Mom, no you haven't. You've been the best mom I could have ever asked for, just maybe… very vocal about your intentions and hopes for me, that's all. I only ever wanted you to be proud of me.'

'Abbey, I am immensely proud of you.' She reaches for a slice of my toast and takes a bite. 'You know, I had a career before we had you children. I had the career, the handsome, rich man. I always put my all into everything I did and when we had Nate, then you and Dee, your dad and I decided that I should be mother and housekeeper, life administrator and supporter of his growing business. I'll never regret that decision, but maybe that's why I wanted you all to be… perfect.' She takes another bit of toast, shaking her head. 'I suppose you were my projects and I could only demonstrate my worth through each of you being a success.'

'You're worth so much more than just being a mom.'

She smiles but it's with sadness. 'I'd like to think so because now it seems I've been failing as a mom. So, I'm the one who's sorry, Abbey, for pushing you to be who *I* want you to be, instead of listening to who *you* want to be.'

I exhale. 'If only I knew who or what that was.'

'You're a young woman. There's plenty of time for figuring it all out.' She stands up. 'Evidently, I'm still working on it. Now, there's an awful lot of fancy food left from the buffet last night and now that your sister has come clean as to the real reason she couldn't fit into her dress yesterday, if you don't smarten up and get downstairs, there'll be nothing left for you. Dee is exampling eating for two down there.'

I give a short laugh. 'Don't give her too hard a time, Mom.'

'Oh, I will. But I'll also start picking out things for the baby's nursery. And I'd like you to help me persuade your sister to come home and have the baby here, where I can take care of them both. For now, though, I'd like to find out more about this Brett character she's been unchristianly with.'

Now I really laugh. 'Mom, it's 2024.'

'And your boyfriend just spent four nights sleeping in the spare room.'

'Well, as you know, he wasn't real.'

Mom walks into the ensuite and turns on my shower to preheat, then makes to leave the bedroom. 'Wasn't he? I saw the way he looked at you when he didn't think anyone else was looking. I also believed every word he told me this morning when I drove him to the airport. Including the part where he told me he is absolutely, completely and insanely in love with you.'

The door closes behind her and I trudge miserably to the shower.

I step inside and close my eyes as the jets stream water across my face.

Absolutely, completely and insanely in love with you.

'What on earth am I doing?'

Practically falling out of the shower, I grab a towel and run into my bedroom, pulling on the first clothes I can lay my hands on. Then I run downstairs.

'I need to get to the airport,' I announce to my family.

'Hell, yes!' Shernette says.

'I'm coming!' Dee adds.

'I'll drive you,' Mom says.

'Over my dead body – you'll kill them all,' Dad says, grabbing his keys. 'I'll drive.'

52

TED

It's already been a long day, since waking up in Abbey's guest bed to finally heading toward security for the flight I managed to book on as a standby.

I've done nothing but think. About Abbey, about how I got it so wrong. About Fleur and Roman and moving on.

But I get nowhere because all I truly want is Abbey and she doesn't want me.

I set my luggage on the belt for security and stand in line to be called through the scanner.

Good came of all this, I'm sure of it. If only Mike's confidence rubbing off on me and Abbey's heart last night as she stood up for herself. I need a little more Mike and a lot more Abbey in me.

I'm going to stop running.

There are two more people ahead of me in the line, elderly and slow. They fuss each other like they've never been on a flight, each one encouraging the other to go through the scanner first. Each giving the other orders and directions.

I smile at their cuteness and hope I'll be catching flights, going on adventures and making memories with the woman I love when I'm gray and old.

And finally, the proverbial penny drops. 'What am I doing?'

I'm telling myself I'm a better person for this whole mess, telling myself I'm through with running, but that's exactly what I'm doing.

I dart out of line and grab my luggage right before it becomes irretrievable.

'Sir, what are you doing?' the security agent asks me as I hop around, pulling on my shoes.

'Can you bag those things up for me? I have to go. I'm in love with a girl and it's about time I started fighting for what I want. *Who* I want.'

The security guy smiles and starts shoving my liquids and electronics back into my bag. He's too slow.

'Don't worry, I've got it,' I tell him, calling my thanks as I run back through security and to Departures in search of a cab—

'Abbey?'

'Ted.'

She's wearing shorts and a T-shirt but her hair is wet like she's just gotten out of the shower. A little way behind her, Dee, Shernette and her mom are looking our way.

'What's going on?' I ask through panted breaths.

'Well... I couldn't let you leave before I told you a few things.'

She puts her hands on her hips and her sass reminds me of when we met in the elevator before my *GQ* interview, when she stormed to my apartment claiming noise pollution, and when she huffed over losing our bet and cleaning Mike's apartment. I can't help the smirk that draws on my lips.

'You messed up. I mean, big style messed up. And you have so much making up to do for it.'

I nod. Happily. I'll spend the rest of my life making up for it, if she'll have me.

'But it would be hypocritical of me to hate you for lying when I've been lying to everyone I know up here, and I think lying to myself for even longer. It's time I started doing what I want for me, not other people.'

God, I'm allowing myself to hope again and it's got my insides in knots. 'What do you want, Abbey?'

She meets my gaze now and sighs. 'I want the man who loves codes and would rather play VR games with me than party. The man who'll listen to me talk for hours about numbers, math and space. The guy who would rather be outdoors in the fresh air than crammed into a gym. The man who never seems to judge me and accepts me for exactly who I am.' She shrugs. 'Just a girl, an ordinary girl with sometimes questionable dress sense, who has confidence issues and truly knows nothing about baseball.'

My elation tips into a short chuckle. She's so incredibly unordinary. She's beautiful. 'Abbey, I rushed into an engagement once and I promise not to do it again. But I want to take you hiking, I want to teach you how to boulder. I want to kiss you on the top of the highest Rockies whenever I like, and go snowboarding with you on the fresh slopes of Colorado.

'Then, if you want, I'll happily marry you by the time you're thirty and make babies with you by the time you're thirty-two. Not because those things are on your checklist but because I want those things too, and I only want them with you.'

She laughs but her eyes have glazed over and damn it, I feel my own begin to sting. I reach out and stroke her soft cheek. She leans into my palm.

'Abbey, can we skip to the part where I kiss you now? Because it's all I've been able to think about since—'

She grabs the collar of my jacket and pulls me to her, her

mouth meeting mine, cutting me off with a kiss that's long, deep and tender.

When we break, I rest my forehead on hers and whisper, 'I love you, Abbey.'

Her smile is as wide as I've seen it. 'I love you, too.'

53

TED

That night

She loves me.

That thought has made heading home to San Francisco without her bearable.

I want her to come, to be with me, to stay in my bed every night and be wrapped around me when I wake every morning.

But this is for the best. I got the girl of my dreams, now I need to man up and take care of my business, clear a path for Abbey and I to have the best shot at being together and happy.

So, I sent Fleur a message before boarding my flight to tell her I'm coming home tonight and I want us to talk tomorrow.

I've been thinking about what I'll say to her, whenever I can keep my attention from drifting to Abbey. Now, all I want to do is get home, message Abbey sweet dreams, crawl into my own bed and sleep with the sound of the ocean's crashing waves coming through my window. Then wake up and make strides to get on with the rest of my life.

After paying the cab driver, I take the elevator up to the top floor of my apartment block. I'm faced with one of the last things I want to see, lights from inside my apartment glowing faintly under my door in the corridor, and the sound of something like oriental music – a bamboo flute? – playing inside.

With trepidation, I move inside and the nightmare becomes real. Fleur is lying on my dining room table, naked but for tens of pieces of sushi she has displayed around her body. I'm vaguely aware that this mirrors a scene from one of the sitcoms she likes. I'm acutely aware of how much I don't want this in my life.

'What are you doing, Fleur?'

'Darling...' She puts on some kind of low, breathy, flirty voice that doesn't even sound like her. 'I've been waiting for you.'

I turn up the lights at the dimmer switch and say, 'Alexa, stop playing music.'

I guess tomorrow has come too soon – adorned in fish.

Leaving my luggage by the door, I head to the master bedroom, see that Fleur hasn't moved out at all and find her silk robe still hanging off a hook in the ensuite.

'Get up, Fleur, and please put this on.'

Huffily, she stands, raw salmon and tuna falling to the floor around her.

'Why are you still here?'

'Because we agreed you had two weeks before you had to come back here and we can start moving forward, planning our wedding. I know you've been wanting me to plan for ages and I'm ready, Ted. I'm ready to commit to you.'

I laugh shortly, rubbing my hands over my face.

She pouts, fastening her robe around her. 'And, like I said, I've decided to forgive you for glancing in the direction of that actress girl in New York. We're even now and we can move on.'

Forgive me? I can't even.

'Fleur, I *am* sorry. I'm sorry that I let things get so deep with us. I actually want to thank you, even Roman too, because you've saved me from making a big mistake. I can never forgive you for being with someone else whilst we were together and I'll never forgive that the person you chose was Roman, but I can recognize that we were never right for each other. I was in love with the idea of us but I realize now that I'm not in love with you.'

Not at all and I doubt I ever was, truly, but that feels too cruel to say even to Cruella De Vil, so I say, 'Not the way you should be loved if you're going to spend the rest of your life with someone. So, I'm begging you, listen to me this time. Please take your things and go back to your apartment. No more sushi sitcom pranks or surprise visits. I'm here, I'm back, and we are over. Truly, definitively, forever, done.'

* * *

The next day

I'm up at 5 a.m., despite going to bed last night – after cleaning fish from the floor of my lounge – and feeling like I could sleep forever.

I message Abbey to see if she's okay and to give her the lowdown on my run-in with Fleur, then head out for a head-clearing run along the beach front. On the way back, I pick up a newspaper, a pastry and a coffee, purely to pass the time until 7 a.m.

Late last night, Roman and I agreed to meet early at the office today. I want to do this when the office should be empty. I've had enough of public showdowns for a lifetime.

Whilst I'm killing time, thinking I'd so much rather be hiking up a mountain with Abbey than settling old scores, Abbey sends me a screenshot of her smiling – that devastating smile – and pointing at an email on her laptop that makes me insanely happy in return. She's setting up a meeting with my accountant, Matt, about the business strategy role.

She'll crush it. I tell her as much in a reply.

And I'm so proud of her but I decide to keep that part under wraps. There's a real risk I could come on too strong with this, with us, because what I'm also thinking is, I really freaking hope she wants to take a job here, in San Francisco.

When I arrive at the office, Roman is already here, standing behind my desk and looking out of the window across Silicon Valley.

I pause in the hallway, watching him through the glass walls.

It's the first time I've seen him in the flesh since everything went down. Seeing his name in emails had me seething. His face being in that stupid *GQ* article and all the trouble it caused made me livid. I watched Abbey stand up for herself on Saturday and it's about time I started doing the same.

I'm waiting for the red mist to descend but all I feel is gutted. Hurt beyond measure. He looks like the guy I've been friends with for more than a decade. The guy I've spent nearly every day with for as many years. But now he's just the man responsible for the biggest betrayal of my life. Armed with the documents my accountants and lawyers have prepared based on Abbey's strategy, I step into my office and finally see the whites of Roman's eyes, in the flesh.

Give him his due, he looks drained. Exhausted and, I don't think I'm imagining it, remorseful.

No matter, we can never, ever come back from this.

'Ted,' he says, without his usual brightness, without animosity. I'm staring at him, still weighing him up, trying to get a hold of this situation and how we could possibly have gotten here but I finally conclude, face-to-face, that there's no reason that can make this okay. There's no universe in which a friend can do this to another friend and move forward amicably.

So I toss the business papers on the desk between us. Ted looks at the pile, then up to me.

'Don't you want to beat the shit out of me? Demand answers? Ask why?'

I realize I'm emotionally depleted on this now. I have no more energy to waste on this guy.

'I know why. You place more importance on money than friendship, or even being a decent guy.' I gesture to the pages between us. 'So you'll need to sign those. We can't work together, so we'll restructure. You'll get your equity but not the way you want it and you'll lose your voting rights, have no responsibility or say in how the business is run going forward. You can accept it or you can refuse and I'll take a demolition ball to the partnership and we'll both lose. Except I'll be able to start again and rebuild without you.'

His chest rises and expands slowly, his nostrils widening as he inhales. He didn't expect this and he didn't want this. Tough shit. I turn away from him and leave the office, slamming the door shut on him, on us, on our friendship and working relationship. I'm at the elevators, the doors already opening because no one else has called one since I arrived.

'I am sorry.' His words come from behind me and make the hurt I'm feeling cut deeper.

I'm not falling for it. I'm not going to let him charm me or manipulate me. Sorry isn't enough.

'I don't want to hear it, Rome. It's done. We're done.'

I step into the elevator, not glancing his way, but he stands between the doors, forcing me to look him in the eye and see that he's hurting, too. It's surprising but welcome. It makes me feel like less of an idiot for thinking we had an unbreakable bond all these years.

'It wasn't only about cashing in, no matter whether you believe that or not.'

'Then why, Rome? Go on, hit me with it. Why did you start sleeping with my fiancée?'

'Jealousy.' It's direct and definite, as if it ought to have been obvious, as if there could have been no other explanation.

'Why on earth would you be jealous of me?'

'Because you are and always have been everything I'd like to be. Intelligent and successful, sure, but decent and liked by everyone, loved by everyone. Your family, your friends, the people who work for us, even the goddamn tech world. I've always been the sidekick. The glorified salesman.'

'What? That's... absurd.'

'Be that as it may...' He steps back from the doors and holds his hands out from his sides. 'I'll sign the documents.'

The doors literally close on our friendship and on everything I thought I knew about the dynamics of our relationship.

54

ABBEY

Five days after Ted telling me he loves me

'Are you sure about this?' Dad asks from the driver's seat of his car. We're parked outside departures at Calgary airport. 'The offer stands for you to come into business with me.'

'I know, Dad. And I can't wait to work with you one day, when the time is right. But first, I need to prove to myself that I can get where I want to be on my own.'

'You sound like me when I was your age.'

'Well then, it's true that I'm the apple and you're the tree.' I lean over and kiss his cheek. 'Wish me luck.'

'You don't need it. They'd be mad not to hire you.'

'You have to say that, you're my dad.'

'And an astute businessman.'

Smiling at his biased vote of confidence, I head into the airport to catch my flight to meet with Ted's accountants about a potential job as a business strategist.

I use the flight time to run through my resumé, which isn't actually great for a business strategy role. Most of my experience has been informal. But like Ted says, they've seen an example of my work.

Ted. Garghhhhh. I'd get a lot more interview prep done if I could stop my mind wandering and my face breaking into Cheshire Cat-style grins every five minutes when I remember... he *loves* me. *Me.*

Five days has felt like forever. Completely the right thing to do, going our separate ways, him back to San Francisco to put his past to bed – which sounded awful to me, yet when he relayed the sushi scene and the showdown with Roman, he seemed... *fine*.

I did *not* like that Fleur had been naked in his apartment. Not one single bit. Yet, the way Ted spoke about her, there isn't a shred of doubt in my mind that they're done.

I also spoke to Shernette before I agreed to the interview today. It turns out Greg has been running his mouth drunk to some of my old colleagues about how I took the fall for his mistakes because *he* changed my numbers in that report. He should really learn to hold his beer.

Shernette and my dad had the same advice – they both encouraged me to speak with my old boss and set the record straight on why I quit and that report I thought I'd messed up.

It turns out my old boss never would have fired me and she wasn't surprised to hear the truth about the report.

In her words, I'd 'never made a mistake with numbers'. Apparently, I was her most diligent auditor. So she was only happy to give me a reference – and it's a great one, too.

My nerves build, as does my imposter syndrome, on the flight over but when I'm collected in arrivals by a driver holding up a board stating up my name, I try to remember all the people who are supporting me in this roll of the dice.

I'm wearing a tweed-style work dress that fits me perfectly and makes me feel kind of... work hot? *So* not what I used to wear to work and I... really like that? I may not have had my capsule wardrobe in Canada but I had something even better – girl time with Mom, Dee and Shernette, who helped me choose some clothes for today and who glared like guard dogs at anyone in our hometown who dared to stop and whisper as I passed by. My Lady Guard.

I'm whisked in a fancy executive car to the offices of WBO – big four accountancy firm – where I meet Ted's client relationship partner, Matt.

'Abbey, at last we meet,' he says, friendly and warm, settling my nerves in an instant when he shakes my hand.

I should have expected as much from someone Ted recommends.

***

The interview, it turned out, was more of a casual chat over coffee and less than an hour later, I'm stepping through the big glass revolving doors onto the sidewalk of San Francisco's Financial District with my small suitcase dragging behind me. Leaning my head back, I breathe in deeply and smile up at the Transamerica Pyramid.

I negotiated terms in a way that my dad and Ted would have been proud of – a way that took even me by surprise. So, I have the job of my dreams, the sun is shining, and WBO are paying the remainder of the rent on my apartment in Blake House.

I might not have a pot of wedding savings back but I'll have a pot I think I'll designate for outdoor adventures, for the time being.

And as I lower my gaze, I'm surprised to see the one person in particular I have to thank for pushing me to follow my dreams. For truly believing in me and making me want to believe in myself. Leaning back against a swish black car, his arms folded across what looks like a dorky slogan T-shirt, his sneakers poking out from under his jeans.

His lips turn up in that smile I'm starting to think is reserved especially for me. 'Get over here, Numbers Girl.'

I chuckle but don't close the distance between us because I want to take him in – this, us, all of it.

'What are you doing here?' I call across the space.

But my words are absorbed by suited people crossing the path between us.

'What did you say?' Ted asks.

I didn't think this through.

So, instead, I ditch my suitcase and run (in high heels!) toward the man I am fiercely in love with. Dodging bodies, I throw myself at Ted. In return, he scoops me up in his arms, laughing when I take his cheeks between my palms and tell him, 'You're still as sure of yourself as ever I see, Tech Guy.'

'Well, you did tell me you love me, so I assume that means newfound arrogance and all?'

I kiss my answer, forgetting everything else and getting lost in the feel of his lips on mine. Lips I get to kiss any time I want.

When Ted lowers me to the ground, I suddenly remember my luggage, but when I turn around, a man in a black suit, whom I can only assume is Ted's driver, already has my case and he's setting it in the trunk of the car we're standing against.

'You have a driver?' I ask, raising an eyebrow.

Ted shrugs, as if it's completely normal, and tells the man, 'Could you take it to my place, Jack? I'll make my own way from here.'

'Sure thing, Ted.' Jack turns to me. 'It's nice to meet you, Abbey.'

'Ah, yeah, and you, Jack. And, erm, thank you.'

'Don't look at me like that,' Ted says when we're alone again. 'It's not a pretentious as it seems. It's a good drive from my office and I had some loose ends to tie off. You look beautiful, by the way.'

'Thank you.' He slips his hand around mine effortlessly, like it's supposed to be there, as if there's no question. It's the tiniest move and it sends my insides into a spin. 'Do you want to know how my interview went?'

He smirks. 'I already know.'

'Matt told you he made me a job offer?'

Ted shakes his head. 'He doesn't need to. Anyone in their right mind would have offered you a job, Abbey. But I would like you to tell me the details, while we get on with the rest of my plan for the next few days.'

He starts to walk along the street, my hand still in his, and I follow next to him.

'Your plan?'

'Mmmhmm. Get you riding that tram like we talked about, take you to see the Golden Gate at sunset, taste clam chowder in a bread bowl by the sea.'

'Don't you have to work?' I ask.

'Probably. But I'm reevaluating how often I take breaks for what's important to me, and making you fall in love with San Francisco is currently top of that list.'

His words make me swoon. I mean, literally. If he wasn't holding me up, I'd probably wobble on my legs. Yet...

'Fall in love with San Francisco, or you?' I tease, leaning into his arm and receiving a kiss on the head in return. One that makes my heart leap.

'You've moved across the country for someone before and as much as I'd love for you to take a job here in San Francisco, I know you have options, and I won't ask you to rush into moving here for me.' When I shift my position to glance up to him, kind of amazed by him and the way he knows me, I find he's already looking at me. 'So, I'm going to sell you on San Francisco, instead.'

I tug on his hand, bringing us to a stop in the middle of the sidewalk. Facing him, I shake my head, making sure he's real, that *this* is real. And the answer is written in the depths of his eyes. I snake my arms around his neck and bring my face as close to his as I can without our lips making contact.

'Ted.' The word leaves me as breathlessly as I feel. 'I already told Matt that I want to work in San Francisco. So would you please kiss me and tell me that part of your plan is to take me home and *finally* make love to me?'

The tip of his nose brushes mine. 'I definitely built in time for that.'

He closes the gap between us and kisses me so deeply I see stars behind my eyelids.

When we part, I slip my leather backpack from my back, down to the ground.

'First things first,' I tell him, pulling out a pair of Chucks. 'I'm going nowhere until I swap out of these shoes.'

Ted chuckles. 'There's the girl I love. I was worried I'd have to piggyback you around town all day like a damsel in distress.'

I snort. 'You should be so lucky.'

And we start the rest of our day as seems to be our way, laughing together. Only now, we get to do it hand in hand, too.

ACKNOWLEDGEMENTS

I have dedicated this book to every person who thought they had to be someone else to be loved because haven't we all been there at some point? Tweaking ourselves or wholly reinventing ourselves to be cooler, wilder, smarter, prettier, slimmer... The list goes on. I have two things to tell you: first, stop doing it because you *are* enough and the good people around you already know that. The lucky people who are yet to meet you will find out, too. Secondly, thank you so much for taking Abbey and Ted and their fake relationship into your heart and mind.

This book was both magical and difficult to write – ask my incredible editor, Emily Yau. Thank you, Emily, for your patience and perseverance whilst we got this right. You've taught me lessons through this book that will stick with me for my career, so now every book going forward is sort of yours, too.

I write the books and Emily Y does some real heavy lifting but we are very much part of a team of special and hardworking people at Boldwood Books. Massive thanks to my copy editor, Emily Reader, and my proof reader, Jennifer Davies, and Hayley, who quietly arranges it all behind the scenes. Thank you enormous amounts to Amanda, Nia, Issy, Claire and Jenna for your continued efforts to market and sell my romcoms. You are all lionesses. To Ben for, amongst other things, getting me the very best narrators to bring these stories to life in audio. I don't mean to miss anyone by name, so know if I haven't listed you, you are very much appreciated (and this includes the interns).

As always, I need to give a huge shout out to my wonderful, enduring and supportive agent, Tanera Simons, who is frankly on top of *everything*! I wouldn't have any romcoms out in the world without you (and lovely Laura and the rest of the Darley Anderson team). More importantly, I just wouldn't be able to manage the life juggle and do something I am truly passionate about, so thank you, for helping to make me whole.

Lastly, importantly, with boundless love and affection, thank you to my husband and best friend, and our tiny tots. You all try to side-track me and test me, usually at the very worst of times, too, but my goodness I love you all with every single cell in my frazzled body. Forever.

ABOUT THE AUTHOR

Laura Carter is the bestselling author of several rom-coms including the series *Brits in Manhattan* which she is relaunching and expanding with Boldwood. She lives in Jersey.

Sign up to Laura Carter's mailing list for news, competitions and updates on future books.

Visit Laura's website: www.lauracarterauthor.com

Follow Laura on social media:

instagram.com/lauracarterauthor
x.com/LCarterAuthor
facebook.com/LauraCarterAuthor

ALSO BY LAURA CARTER

The Law of Attraction

Two to Tango

Friends With Benefits

Always the Bridesmaid

Fake It 'til You Make It

LOVE NOTES
LOVE IN EVERY CHAPTER

WHERE ALL YOUR ROMANCE
DREAMS COME TRUE!

THE HOME OF BESTSELLING
ROMANCE AND WOMEN'S
FICTION

WARNING:
MAY CONTAIN SPICE

SIGN UP TO OUR
NEWSLETTER

https://bit.ly/Lovenotesnews

Boldwood

Boldwood Books is an award-winning fiction publishing company seeking out the best stories from around the world.

Find out more at www.boldwoodbooks.com

Join our reader community for brilliant books, competitions and offers!

Follow us
@BoldwoodBooks
@TheBoldBookClub

Sign up to our weekly deals newsletter

https://bit.ly/BoldwoodBNewsletter

Milton Keynes UK
Ingram Content Group UK Ltd.
UKHW021705061124
450774UK00001B/2

9 781785 135705